The Bad Behavior of Belle Cantrell

"With a screenwriter's skill, Despres touches on all the pressure points of a Southern town in the grip of change. Readers who loved Despres' earlier work will see that a taste for adventure, not to mention doing the right thing, runs in the family. . . . Spunky Belle is a good companion, with her wit and wisdom."   —*New Orleans Times-Picayune*

"At first glance, this is an upbeat little romance novel set near New Orleans in 1920. Read a bit deeper, however, and you'll discover that author Loraine Despres uses heroine Belle Cantrell, a widow and mother of one, to tackle the issues of racism and the treatment of women in a setting dominated by good old boys who belong to the Ku Klux Klan and desperately don't want females to vote."   —*Chicago Tribune*

"In this prequel to *The Scandalous Summer of Sissy LeBlanc*, Despres, herself a native Southerner, introduces readers to Sissy's grandmother, the strong-willed Belle of Gentry, Louisiana. . . . Despres successfully spins her story against a turbulent political backdrop . . . [with] galloping prose and Belle's consistent liveliness."   —*Publishers Weekly*

"In this often funny prequel to *The Scandalous Summer of Sissy LeBlanc*, former screenwriter Despres demonstrates a fine ear for witty dialogue. . . . Breezy and enjoyable."
—*Kirkus Reviews*

"Reading the adventures of Belle is like listening to a friend recount a story. You know when the story starts the ending will be good. With wit and humor, [Despres] unfolds Belle's life. . . . This book is a hoot!"   —*Huntsville Times*

Jan Sanders

About the Author

LORAINE DESPRES is the author of the bestselling novel *The Scandalous Summer of Sissy LeBlanc* and its tie-in title, *The Southern Belle's Handbook*. Raised in Amite, Louisiana, Despres is a former television writer and international screenwriting consultant. She lives in Beverly Hills.

www.lorainedespres.com

The Bad Behavior of Belle Cantrell

Loraine Despres

HARPER

NEW YORK • LONDON • TORONTO • SYDNEY

HARPER

A hardcover edition of this book was published in 2005 by William Morrow, an imprint of HarperCollins Publishers.

THE BAD BEHAVIOR OF BELLE CANTRELL. Copyright © 2005 by Eastlake/Despres Company. All rights reserved. Printed in the United States of America.
No part of this book may be used or reproduced in any manner whatsoever without written permission except in the case of brief quotations embodied in critical articles and reviews. For information address HarperCollins Publishers, 10 East 53rd Street, New York, NY 10022.

HarperCollins books may be purchased for educational, business, or sales promotional use. For information please write: Special Markets Department, HarperCollins Publishers, 10 East 53rd Street, New York, NY 10022.

First Harper paperback published 2006.

The Library of Congress has catalogued the hardcover edition as follows:

Despres, Loraine.
    The bad behavior of Belle Cantrell: a novel / Loraine Despres.— 1st ed.
      p. cm.
    ISBN-13: 978-0-06-051524-9
    ISBN-10: 0-06-051524-4
    1. Women—Louisiana—Fiction. 2. Louisiana—Fiction. I. Title.

PS3604.E76B33 2005
813'.6—dc22   2005050617

ISBN-10: 0-06-051526-0 (pbk.)
ISBN-13: 978-0-06-051526-3 (pbk.)

06 07 08 09 10 ❖/RRD 10 9 8 7 6 5 4 3 2 1

To Carl and David,
who taught this Southern girl most of what she knows
about men and other perils of modern life

The Bad Behavior
of Belle Cantrell

Chapter 1

BELLE CANTRELL FELT guilty about killing her husband, and she hated that. Feeling guilty, that is. *A lady shouldn't do something she's going to feel guilty about later* was a rule Belle kept firmly in mind, along with its corollary: *No sense in feeling guilty about all the little pleasures life has in store for you.*

But Claude's death hadn't been a pleasure at all. She'd fallen in love with him at fifteen, galloping down clay roads with the leaves of autumn swirling around them. They'd discovered the nooks and crannies of passion in his mother's darkened parlor on a rolling sea of dark wine velvet, amid a flotilla of lacy white antimacassars, when his parents were away.

By sixteen she was pregnant. They married before the baby was born, and in spite of numerous and persistent offers, Belle had never had, nor wanted, another man in her sixteen years of married life. It wasn't as if she aspired to sainthood. She didn't even know if she'd have felt guilty about committing adultery, but she knew better than to take the risk. Now, after almost a year and a half of mourning, a peculiar, guilty longing had begun to float around in the back waters of her mind, swamping her at odd moments.

She decided to bob her hair.

SHE SQUARED HER shoulders as she approached Arnold's barbershop, housed in the Nix Hotel, where traveling men slept on dirty sheets, laundered only occasionally but always freshly ironed between guests. She'd never been inside a barbershop. She'd read about exotic places called beauty parlors opening up in big cities, where they applied youth-restoring creams to a lady's face and knew all the secrets of curling irons, but if you wanted a haircut, you had to go to a barbershop. And in Gentry, Louisiana, that meant Arnold's.

She paused on the street. Red and white paint was flaking off the barber pole, showing the wood beneath it. Why hadn't she noticed it before? She peered through the plate-glass window, streaked with grime. A balding man sat in the second chair, hidden under shaving cream, while Arnold scraped his face with a straight-edged razor. Belle took a deep breath, drew herself up, and, with head held high, opened the screen door. The odor of day-old ashtrays and cheap cigars assaulted her. Arnold looked up, his razor raised. His gaze was not welcoming.

At that moment, her stepfather, Calvin Nix, owner of the hotel, sauntered in from the lobby. Mr. Nix was only five feet two, but he was quick and clean. He sat down in the first chair for his morning shave and Arnold's all-important, stress-reducing, laying on of hot towels. A shoeshine boy crouched in obeisance at his feet. Through the brown-speckled mirror, he saw his stepdaughter standing in the doorway. His face lit up. "What you doing here, sugar?" His voice was a shade too welcoming.

The smell of sulfur impregnated the air.

At that moment, Belle's mother, Blanche, stepped out of the front door of the hotel and onto the brick sidewalk. With her fine posture and thick salt-and-pepper hair arranged in an old-fashioned upsweep, she'd become one of Gentry's leading Matrons for Morality in her latter years. "Belle! What in tarnation do you think you're doing?"

Belle swung around. "Hey, Mama."

Blanche Nix glared. There was enough impropriety lurking in the memories of the high-minded residents of Gentry without her daughter providing her with any extra sources of embarrassment. "You ought to be ashamed of yourself. You know a barbershop's no place for a decent woman."

A high-pitched whistle shrieked.

Belle turned and saw the nine-thirty train to New Orleans rumble into the depot across the street, belching out great clouds of sooty smoke. She had fifteen dollars in her purse. She let the screen door bounce behind her.

Blanche shook her head as she watched her daughter run for the train.

TWO HOURS LATER Belle was standing in the barbershop of the Monteleone Hotel in New Orleans, where gleaming plate-glass mirrors reflected brass chandeliers, and expensive after-shave lotions perfumed the air. A rotund barber turned. If he was surprised to see her, he didn't let on. Belle pulled herself up into her best imitation of a Southern aristocrat. "Does anyone here know how to bob a lady's hair?" Her voice was clear. It didn't break once.

"Yes, ma'am. I surely do. Now you just sit right down," the barber said, patting the first chair. What hair he had left was beautifully manicured.

A little boy shrilled, "Look, Papa, a lady—" He didn't get a chance to finish before his father shushed him.

A man under the razor in the second chair strained to look at her, causing the barber to nick his customer's cheek. Belle pretended not to notice, but a spot of blood spread over the virginal clouds of white shaving cream. It seemed like an omen.

A bad omen.

Belle swallowed hard and climbed into the first chair. The barber shook out a big white cape. "Wait," she said.

All activity stopped. The bootblack looked up from the shoes of the man being shaved. Scissors and razor were held in suspended animation. Everyone turned toward Belle.

She pulled a picture out of her purse. She'd cut it out of *Vogue* magazine two weeks before while she'd screwed up her courage. Underneath, the caption read: "Bobbed hair is the mark of the new woman. Young, easy to take care of, it's for a woman who wants to get on with her life."

"Do you think you can cut my hair like this?"

"Don't you worry none," the barber said.

Belle hated it when someone told her not to worry. How dare he tell me how to feel, she thought. She took one last look at her thick pompadour of deep brown hair that had never known scissors. The barber spun the chair around so her back was to the mirror. She felt him pull out her combs. Hairpins scattered in reckless abandon across the floor. Her rich mane dropped over her shoulders and spilled down her back. Her right hand caressed an innocent lock that slid over her chest.

She startled at the first click-click of the scissors, sneaking up behind her. The long blades penetrated her thick tresses. They fell in mounds over her shoulders. Then, one by one, piles of dark hair dropped around her onto the barbershop floor.

A trumpet wailed. Saxophones took up the dirge. Trombone and clarinet joined in. A bass drum boomed. Through the plate-glass windows Belle saw a horse-drawn hearse move slowly down Royal Street in somber procession to the graveyard. Behind the hearse and jazz band, mourners on foot filled the street.

IT HAD BEEN A YEAR and four months since she'd killed Claude.

It had happened the very night he came home safe from the Great War. She'd planned to take the Panama Limited to Chicago, to meet him there for the honeymoon they'd never had. She tried to imagine what it would be like to sleep overnight on that luxury train, to sit in the dining car eating steak and oysters while the world flew by the window. Her friend Rachel had told her about the museums, the concerts, and the theaters. She'd shown her pictures of skyscrapers and of a park with trees covered in snow. That's what Belle wanted to see most in the world. Snow. She tried to imagine what it would be like to stand in a snowstorm, to watch all those flakes fall down from the sky, to touch them, to taste them on her tongue.

She checked the Illinois Central timetable and bought a suitcase.

But all Claude wanted was to come home. So Belle put the suitcase and timetable away and decided she really wasn't disappointed. After all, her husband was coming home to her. They could take the Panama Limited to Chicago together, some other time. They had the rest of their lives.

She spent days getting ready for him. She'd never felt rich enough to spend cash money on store-bought underwear, especially since Claude was always so quick to take it off, but for his homecoming she bought some beautiful red silk and creamy lace. She made herself a diaphanous camisole and clingy bloomers, all the while imagining him unhooking the hooks, slipping the camisole up over her head with his rough, calloused hands, or pulling the bloomers down over her thighs. Sometimes she had to leave her sewing machine and lie on her chaise longue just to catch her breath.

Along with the silk, she bought some practical navy blue wool to make herself a sensible dress to wear over it. After all, the Primer of Propriety ruled: *A man likes his wife to look proper in public,* which worked just fine for her, because she added a short corollary: *as long as she's bawdy in the bedroom.*

That seemed to work just fine for Claude, too.

The night before he was expected, she covered her hair in sweet almond oil and washed it with lemon juice. As she pinned it up the next morning, she added a drop of jasmine scent, remembering how he loved to pull the pins out. She longed to lean over him in bed, swishing the tips of her fragrant hair across his naked chest until he grabbed her around the neck and pulled her down on top of him. *Nice girls aren't supposed to enjoy sex.* Now that was an example of a rule from the Primer of Propriety that Belle just couldn't work up any enthusiasm for at all. She figured she never would be what you call "nice."

THE AIR IN the depot reeked of steaming wool. She went outside in the morning drizzle, but she didn't want to ruin her new navy blue hat, so she came back and paced as the station filled up with people. "Sit down, honey," her mother-in-law said. "You're making me nervous." At sixty, Effie Cantrell was a model Victorian with steel gray hair mounted unshakably on top of her head and skirts that barely cleared her high-button shoes. Secure in the righteousness of her opinions, she resisted any and all change. Born on a plantation shortly before the outbreak of the War Between the States, the only curse word in her genteel vocabulary was "damn," which she figured was all right because she always attached it to "Yankee."

But Belle couldn't sit still, not this morning. Claude was coming back to her. She was going to have him today and every day afterward, for the rest of their lives. Finally she heard the train whistle and rushed outside to peer down the tracks as the train rumbled in.

Claude leaped off the iron steps in his dress uniform. Belle flew into his arms. He dropped his bags, lifted her up, and swung her around, pressing his buttons into her flesh. She even enjoyed the pain, because Claude was home! She could begin to live again. She had time to whisper, "Wait until you see what I've got on underneath this dress."

And he had time to whisper, "I know what you got underneath your dress, darlin'. I been thinking about it for almost two years."

Then the world crowded in on them. Fifteen-year-old Cady threw her arms around her daddy's neck. Miss Effie, wearing royal purple, kissed her son's cheek. Abe Rubinstein, his gray felt hat covering his bald head, hurried over from Rubinstein's department store to shake Claude's hand. The Methodist minister, Brother Frank Meadows, arrived a touch out of breath just as they were leaving. Brother Meadows was tall, with handsome features and a full head of flowing white hair. He had that professionally caring manner that lets you know right away he's some kind of preacher, even if you were to meet him on a train. Miss Effie was one of his most faithful parishioners, unlike her son, who didn't have anything against church except getting up for it on Sunday mornings.

Brother Meadows gave Claude a manly handshake and said, "Glad you got back safe, son. Your mama's been worried." Then he added, with a note of humorous chiding, "I expect we'll see you in church this week."

He would, but not in the way he expected.

As they left the platform, Floyd Taggert from the *Gentry Post* stopped by with his photographer to shoot some pictures of the returning hero. They would run on the front page the next day. And the day after. And the day after that.

Mike O'Malley, who'd lost an arm and part of one leg during the war, Titus Pruett, who owned a bicycle shop, and the mayor's son, Pruett Walker, intercepted Claude as he helped his mother into their buggy. They invited him to a poker game that evening in the back room of the Nix Saloon.

"Thanks all the same, boys, but I got plans for tonight," Claude said, slipping his arm around Belle. "Big plans."

"That's what we figured," Pruett Walker said with a smirk.

Titus sniggered.

"We just didn't want you to feel left out," said Mike O'Malley.

Back home, Cady showed her father all the prizes she'd won in her home economics class. He told her he was proud of her. She was going to make some lucky man a wonderful wife. Miss Effie smiled. Cady beamed.

Belle didn't say a word. She wanted her only daughter to go to college and take up a profession, not mend some man's socks. But Belle knew, *Only a fool burdens the unwilling with the unnecessary.* She decided to make that sentiment a rule in her Southern Girls' Guide to Men and Other Perils of Modern Life, a humorous counterpoint to the Primer of Propriety, which was what Belle called the rules of ladylike behavior Miss Effie had tried so hard to instill in her over the years and that Belle had set herself to learn. The Primer of Propriety floated around the rivulets of her mind, splashing up against another primer, the Down-Home Primer of Right Behavior, a tangle of regulations her mother, stepfather, and all the other Meddlers in Morality had tried to beat into her when she was a little girl, before she went to live with the Cantrells.

She knew the rules were for her own good. They were there to help her navigate the shoals of society. But sometimes, okay, most of the time, she found she had to twist them a little or break them or at least give them a permanent kink, because no matter whether the words were highfalutin or homey, they all pretty much said the same thing: "Don't."

And a girl has got to live.

AFTER CADY HAD shown her father all her excellent report cards and sung him a song she'd been practicing for his homecoming, with Miss Effie accompanying her on the piano, Stella, their cook, called them in to dinner. She'd spent most of the week collecting ingredients for Claude's favorite dishes and had been cooking since early morning.

As they spooned up the crawfish bisque, Miss Effie urged her son to tell them about the war, but he didn't say much. Over their main course of baked ham with pineapple rings and cloves, fresh butter beans, and mashed sweet potatoes, Belle asked about Paris. But Claude never had been one for talking. However, when Stella brought out her special double-chocolate cake, he did manage to tell a couple of cleaned-up army jokes. Belle was amazed. Claude didn't go in for jokes. She'd never heard him tell one before.

After he'd had a cup of Creole coffee with fresh cream straight from their cows and given Stella the genuine, silver-plated teaspoon he'd brought back all the way from Europe with the words "Paris, France 1918" on the handle, he announced what he wanted was a hot bath. He said he'd been dreaming about their big, claw-footed bathtub for two years. Belle turned to him and smiled. He reached for her under the table and slid his hand up her thigh with an urgency that made her jump. Cady ran upstairs to the big bathroom they all shared. She turned on the taps and brought her daddy a pile of fresh towels.

While her husband bathed, Belle unpacked his bag and threw all his clothes into the hamper. Something crinkled in the pocket of his dress shirt. She pulled out a letter. It was in French. His father's parents spoke Creole French and Claude had learned it as a child. Belle couldn't read what it said, but she understood "*chéri*" and "*mon amour*" and "*je t'embrasse.*" And she knew he didn't have any cousins named Lisette.

She sat down on the bed and fought to inhale. So that's what he was doing while she was raising their daughter, taking care of the farm, and listening to Miss Effie prattle on. He was catting around with Lisette!

She tried to tell herself it didn't mean anything. The words were out of context. There was probably a perfectly good explanation. Besides, men have their needs. At least that's what men tell you.

Wonder what they'd say if we told them women have needs, too? She knew what they'd say. She even knew the word they'd use. It rhymed with "floor."

Belle walked around the room swishing the letter in the air. The malodor of dead violets invaded her nostrils. She told herself, He's been away a year and a half and not just away, he's been in a war. He was afraid he was going to die over there, so he might as well . . . She couldn't finish that one.

She went over to the window, blew onto the cool glass, and then wiped away the little round cloud she'd made. One little fling in a foreign country didn't mean anything, not in a real marriage. She assured herself, it didn't mean a thing. Of course, she didn't know anyone who wrote letters after a fling.

She looked at the letter again. It was written on purplish blue stationery to match those stinky violets. He'd worn it in his shirt pocket, right over his heart. She searched his pants. No letters there.

She emptied his bag. There were no more letters, not even one of the hundreds she'd written. He'd kept only one. This one.

She felt tears well up. She willed them not to spill out. She wasn't going to be sentimental. She got up and put the letter in the bottom of his bag, as if it had fallen out, as if she hadn't discovered it. She heard the bedroom door open. She dropped the bag and turned around. Had he seen her? Claude, wearing only a towel, filled the doorway. He closed the door behind him.

And dropped the towel.

Bathwater glistened on his naked body, flushed from the heat, smelling of soap. For a sliver of a moment, the voice of Brother Reginald Scaggs, minister of the Church of Everlasting Redemption, returned from the deep recesses of her childhood Sundays. *It's up to decent women to denounce all sin and bring the reluctant sinner to the Lord, so he can repent.*

I guess I'm not all that decent, Belle thought, especially at a time like this, when she saw how the muscles of her husband's arms bulged and how his abdomen had hardened. He scooped her up. To heck with decency. He tossed her onto the bed. The bedsprings sang, as they had sung to them on so many nights of their young marriage. They crooned and trilled that all her needs were about to be satisfied.

She wouldn't even think about the letter. He bent over her. She wouldn't even think. He was too excited for mere kisses. She felt his right hand rush and fumble with the hooks on the side of her navy blue dress and give up as his left hand slipped under her skirt, crawled up her leg, inside her bloomers, and went on a reconnaissance mission into no-man's-land. Belle had to bite her lips and remember not to make a sound, but it had been so long, so very long.

Suddenly another hand, a very unwelcome hand, rapped on the door.

"Claude! George is here to see you." Sheriff George Goode was Miss Effie's second cousin once removed.

Claude groaned. "Tell him to come back later." His hasty hands pulled her bloomers down around her knees.

"Claude Cantrell, you get downstairs this minute." The door flew open and Miss Effie caught sight of something she hadn't seen for over three decades: her son's naked bottom, and it had sprouted black hairs!

Belle saw her mother-in-law's temples pulsate, saw her whip around and face the hallway. Claude Sr. had never gone to war or been away for more than a week. Belle doubted that the old woman had ever even considered having what she called "relations" with him during daylight hours. The dowager's voice wavered. "George is a busy man. Whatever you're doing can wait until tonight."

And because we are all children in our mother's home, Claude got up and pulled on his pants, while Belle shimmied back into her bloomers. "Tonight," he whispered with a raunchy wink that promised satisfaction. Then he grabbed her and pressed her to him, until Miss Effie turned back and frowned. Turning her gaze on Belle, she didn't need to speak the words "You ought to be ashamed of yourself." Her look said it all.

"You go on and see George. I'll finish putting your things away," Belle said, trying to breathe normally.

He kissed her on the forehead and left the room. She heard his heavy boots shaking the house as he clumped downstairs, leaving her with his dirty clothes, his bag, and the purplish letter that she was never going to think about again.

WHEN BELLE WENT DOWNSTAIRS, he was surrounded by relatives and neighbors on the glassed-in sunporch next to the dining room. Her mother and stepfather had shown up to bask in the reflected glory of the hero returned from the war. Although the Nixes never visited with the Cantrells except on major holidays, and even then they hadn't ever had much to say to Belle's big, taciturn husband, Mr. Nix made a point of telling everyone how proud he was of his son-in-law's service to their country, and Blanche Nix declared to anyone who'd listen that they thought of him as their own dear son. Mr. Nix agreed, "Couldn't have a better son than Claude."

Cady was delighted to see her grandmother. She sat down next to her and asked if she'd teach her how to crochet. Blanche said she'd be happy to, Cady had only to stop by the hotel after school. Belle, who'd been keeping an eye on her daughter, got a sour look on her face. She wasn't about to let her daughter spend time at the hotel, but she refrained from saying anything just then. However, when Blanche got up to inspect Miss Effie's camellias and Mr. Nix slid over next to Cady, asking her about school, Belle was quick to intervene. "Cady, honey, why don't you pass around that plate of Stella's butter cookies?" Belle smiled innocently at her stepfather. He didn't smile back.

The rest of the day Claude stood tall in his blue-and-gold sergeant's uniform. All the while, Belle smiled. She brought out lemonade and smiled. She passed around slices of the angel food cake that Darvin and Debbie Lou Rutledge of Rutledge Ford and Livery had brought to the hero returned from the wars, and smiled some more. Once, when she was sitting on the wicker lounge, Claude sat down next to her and put his big arm around her shoulders, but almost immediately new visitors arrived, demanding manly handshakes and more chairs for the ladies. Belle began to feel the muscles at the sides of her mouth ache from so much smiling.

Finally, when the last visitor had gone home to supper, Belle and her husband were able to slip out of his mother's house,

Claude riding Jack, his black stallion, and Belle on her roan, with Claude's hunting dog, Dawg, running ecstatically at their side. Belle had named her horse Susan B. for Susan B. Anthony. Claude had raised a most gratifying fuss about it and Miss Effie had shaken her head, but Belle was firm. It was either her horse to name or it wasn't.

Cady, who'd been told she was named after Elizabeth Cady Stanton only after she started school, was not amused. "That's swell, Mama. What'll you think of next? Maybe you'll want to chain me and your horse to a fence post out in front of the state capitol until women get the vote."

It serves me right, Belle thought. I never should have brought her up to have spunk.

What Cady didn't know was that when Belle chose the name, she'd never actually met a real, live suffragette, she'd only read about them in magazines. But after having been surprised out of the freedom of childhood by such an early pregnancy, Belle had wanted to assert herself. And she knew when she explained the genesis of the name, once the birth certificate had been signed and witnessed, she'd get a most satisfactory rise out of her ever more taciturn husband.

Claude and Belle galloped down the clay drive and through the winter forest. It was that magical hour after the sun sets, when the sky has turned to gold. They walked their horses through fields of dried-up stalks from last year's cotton harvest. Claude slid off Jack and ran the dirt and stubble through his big hand. "I've missed this."

Then he slapped off the dirt, put his big hands around her waist, and lifted her off Susan B. The sweet smell of the earth and country air enveloped them, but they'd become edgy with each other after the interminable afternoon of socializing. They led their horses through the fields.

The air had turned cold. Belle saw clouds of steam floating

on her husband's breath. She wondered, Who is this man in Claude's big body, sneaking glances at me and then quickly facing forward as if he were studying something serious on the horizon? The evening stretched out before them in anticipation and silence. Before they got to the creek, the cotton stopped and a field of strawberry vines spread out in front of them, lush and green and starting to flower.

"What in God's name!"

"This is what I wanted to show you," Belle said, pleased to be able to give him such a surprise.

"What did you do with my cotton, woman?"

Belle explained how she'd plowed it up and planted strawberries. "It was Abe Rubinstein's idea. He has a buyer for them in Chicago. Now, I know we need a lot of extra help to raise strawberries, but—"

She never got a chance to tell him how crates of berries shipped on the Crimson Flyer at six in the evening would arrive in Chicago before noon the next day, or what Yankees paid for fresh strawberries, or that their soil was perfect for the crop, or that the berries weren't susceptible to the boll weevil, because Claude, so taciturn before he left for the war, began to rage.

Maybe it was the way Sergeant Cantrell yelled at his troops, or maybe it was because he couldn't yell back when the officers chewed him out, or maybe, just maybe, she didn't measure up to Lisette.

She knew *a real lady never raises her voice.* That was one of the premier rules Miss Effie, the Queen of Propriety, had tried to teach her. But Belle was afraid she'd never get the knack of being a real lady, because after the first couple of volleys, she returned fire.

They screamed at each other in the fading light.

They fought not over Lisette, not even over her aborted trip to Chicago. They fought over strawberries.

Claude jumped back on Jack and headed out across the fields, kicking up soil, trampling the plants. Belle watched him as the skies darkened. She rode back to the house on that starless night cursing her temper.

But she couldn't help smiling to herself when she thought about how she was going to make up with him when she got back. She didn't care what her mother-in-law said, she was going to get Claude to herself sooner rather than later. There's nothing like a night of love to cheer a man up, Belle thought, and a good fight always got Claude's juices flowing.

She was rehearsing the teasing words she planned to say to him, when she put Susan B. in her stall and saw Claude's stallion was still gone. She ran up to the house. Claude wasn't there. They waited supper until it got dry and cold. Still Claude did not return. Stella set Claude's plate in the icebox and went home.

"What did you do to him, Mama?" Cady asked. Belle shook her head. Miss Effie said nothing, but she watched her daughter-in-law as her knitting needles went click, click, click. The clock ticked and chimed.

Belle went upstairs. She undressed and slipped between the sheets naked, even though the house was chilling down. Claude loved to find her like that. She picked up one of the books her friend Rachel had lent her, but although she could read the words, by the time she'd reached the end of a paragraph, she couldn't make sense of them. She got up and put on one of Claude's old shirts. She'd worn them as nightgowns every night since he'd gone to war. They made her feel closer to him.

What kind of woman was she, anyway? She couldn't even hold on to her man the night he came home from the war?

Where was he?

Who was he spending that night with?

After Cady and Miss Effie were asleep, Belle slipped on her

Chinese silk wrapper with the yellow and red chrysanthemums and sneaked into Cady's room where she rummaged around until she found her daughter's French textbook. She thought she might try to translate the letter. But once she got back into her room, she changed her mind. To heck with it. To heck with him. Besides, suppose he came home and caught her at it?

She tried to sleep, as she had all during the war, in their big, empty bed. She rolled over and listened to the bedsprings whine. Dawn caught her sitting up, staring out the window. An hour later she was in the kitchen hunched over a cup of bitter coffee, her hair streaming down her back, when Sheriff Goode knocked on the front door.

She answered it in her wrapper. "Claude's not here."

"I know, Belle," the sheriff said. "You better let me in."

She led him into the parlor, perpetually darkened against the Louisiana sun. In this crepuscule, the flotilla of lacy antimacassars seemed to founder. Belle asked him, "What did you say?" So the sheriff had to repeat himself, but she'd heard him right the first time.

Instead of spending his first evening with his wife, Claude had played poker with Pruett Walker, the mayor's son; his cousin Titus Pruett; poor, crippled Mike O'Malley; and some other men in a private room in the back of the Nix Saloon. Apparently a fight had broken out. Pruett Walker claimed Claude was upset about something and attacked him with a busted beer bottle. Pruett had pulled a knife and stuck the blade in Claude's ribs in self-defense. The witnesses, mostly Pruetts or Walkers, were backing up his story. No arrests were planned.

Throughout the horror of the wake and the funeral and the reception after the funeral, Belle went over their fight in her mind. Strawberries! If she hadn't raised her voice, if she'd been more understanding, Claude would have stayed home. He would have been much more cheerful in the morning. He wouldn't have wanted to fight with anyone.

But dammit, Pruett Walker didn't have to kill him.

The day after the funeral, Belle marched into Sheriff George Goode's office. She demanded he arrest Pruett Walker, even if his father, Lloyd Walker, was the mayor and the owner of Gentry's biggest sawmill. Pruett was in politics, too, some kind of fixer and power behind the state throne. It had kept him out of the army, but it shouldn't let him get away with murder.

The sheriff was a tall man, with auburn hair and a winning smile. He called all the men "pal" and the ladies "ma'am." He had fine posture and was particular about his clothes. You just naturally trusted him. There had never been a scandal about Sheriff George Goode.

He sat Belle down and closed his door.

"You can't let Pruett Walker go scot-free."

"Belle, your husband was a sergeant in the United States Army. He was trained in hand-to-hand combat. Pruett was a civilian judged unfit for military service. He was afraid Claude would kill him."

"That's no excuse!"

"But that's the way the jury is gonna see it. You know it as well as I do."

"Then let's put it to a jury."

Sheriff Goode sighed. He hated being the repository of society's unwashed secrets. He unlocked a drawer and pulled out a manila envelope. "I didn't want Effie to know."

He handed Belle a police photograph of herself in a bathing costume, her legs splayed, as a fat officer hauled her into a paddy wagon. "How did you get this?"

"Pruett Walker got hold of it. You know Pruett. He sticks his nose in everybody's business. Anyways, he must of been drunk, because he made some joke about how you was indecently exposing yourself while Claude was overseas fighting for our freedom or some such. I guess he thought Claude knew. But when Pruett pulled out this here picture, your husband had himself a conniption fit. He went after Pruett with a busted beer bottle. Darn near killed him."

"Except Claude's the one who's dead."

"Killed defending your honor."

Belle picked up the photo. Sunlight seemed to glint off the black-and-white image. In 1914 she and her friend Rachel had gone down to New Orleans to attend a suffrage meeting, Belle's first.

Rachel had gone out of conviction. Belle had gone to get out of the house. But once she'd heard Constance Bancroft speak and the other women proclaim, "Failure is impossible," Belle became inspired. She loved being in the company of uppity women who spoke their minds and weren't afraid to stand up for their rights. She attended meetings as often as she could get away, which wasn't that often.

Claude didn't approve. He said she became impossible. He said the suffragettes put all kinds of ideas into her head. He was right about the ideas, but Belle had always been impossible. Most of the events were high-minded affairs, where serious matrons, in unfortunate hats, held forth.

But the meeting she went to all by herself four years later was different.

The speaker was young and beautiful. She'd gone to jail with Alice Paul. Her crime: petitioning President Wilson for the right to vote, standing in front of the White House holding a banner demanding suffrage while the country was at war. The police called it obstructing traffic and locked the women up.

The afternoon was hot, New Orleans–in–August hot. The roses filling vases around the room simply gave up and hung their heads. Above them, a ceiling fan turned, but it couldn't do much more than rotate the muggy air around the room, mixing the aroma of cologne with ladylike perspiration.

The lecturer told them about the shocking conditions in jail, where she and the other suffragists had gone on a hunger strike to call attention to their cause. She gave them a vivid picture of what it was like to be force-fed with tubes threaded up their noses until they gagged and vomited.

The crowd became intoxicated with the heat and dreams of equality. Around the room a murmur went up. "What have we been doing?" "Having meetings?" "Drinking tea?"

Afterward, with Belle leading the charge, a group of the younger suffragists decided to liberate the cooling waters of Lake Pontchartrain. They, too, would become pioneers. They, too, would blaze a trail for their sisters. Of course, it didn't hurt that they'd also get some relief from the steamy heat.

They would swim, actually swim, without being dragged down by those heavy skirts ladies were supposed to wear over bloomers and stockings. They became giddy at the thought of donning simple knit bathing costumes, the unencumbered kind, the kind their brothers and husbands wore, with trouser legs reaching only halfway down their thighs. Beryl Parkinson, one of the most daring girls, announced that she wouldn't even wear stockings. Belle thought that might be going too far, but she wasn't going to be the one to stop her.

Claude had taught her to swim in a secluded stretch of the creek when they were newlyweds. Alone, they always swam naked. She'd worn a boy's swimsuit when their close friends, Rachel and Abe Rubinstein, and their children, joined them for a picnic at their private cove. But Belle had never even been on a public beach. The thought of appearing with her sisters, wearing only a little knit covering, shocked but, at the same time, thrilled her.

They didn't expect to be arrested. After all, this was New Orleans, the city of Mardi Gras, jazz, and Storyville. Besides, they'd seen photographs of a Milwaukee ladies' swim team. They wore boys' suits. They even held public competitions in them.

The New Orleans suffragists wanted nothing more than to defy convention and set a new standard so their less daring sisters could follow them into the cooling waters. After all, this was a free country. They had as much right to swim as any man.

In the bathhouse, an indignant mother swathed in a high-necked, puffed-sleeve, navy blue taffeta bathing dress covered her daughters' eyes, assailing the suffragists for their scandalous disregard of modesty. She claimed they were endangering the delicate morals of her children.

Her sister, draped in layers of heavy cotton, berated them for betraying their brave men, fighting in foreign lands. Belle and Beryl exploded with laughter as the high-minded ladies stormed out, yanking their daughters with them.

A few minutes later, the noble Amazons sallied forth into the sunlight to reclaim their rights. They thrilled at the jeers and whistles of the men as they ran across lawn and sand and into the lapping lake. Some of the women dove and swam arm over arm, flutter-kicking across the tepid water, while others stood waist deep, splashing their sisters. Belle was trying to teach Beryl to float when someone pulled on her arm. "Look!"

Belle turned and saw a cordon of policemen in blue uniforms, standing between them and the offended citizens. Behind the police line, a photographer snapped shot after shot.

Photographs of the scantily clad suffragettes decorated the front page of the *New Orleans Times-Picayune* the next morning, to the acute embarrassment of their more serious sisters. "Arrested for nonsense! Don't you see how this sets back our cause?" Constance Bancroft had raged.

No pictures of Belle were published.

She paid her fine and went back to the farm. For the rest of the war, she behaved herself, more or less, performing only the most suitable suffragist activities, such as accompanying Constance and a delegation of large-hatted ladies to petition their representatives in Baton Rouge.

"Claude died fighting over this?"

"Yes, ma'am. Like I said, he died defending your honor."

A wave of nausea swept over Belle as the reality of what she'd done sank in. She clung to the edge of a chair. The sheriff helped her sit down. I murdered my husband, Belle thought. Those proper ladies, hiding their children's eyes in the bathhouse, tried to warn me. But I was too pigheaded to see.

"Now, we could go to trial, but it won't bring your husband back."

I murdered him, just as surely as if I'd held that knife myself. Then she thought about her daughter. Would Cady ever forgive her? How could she?

"All a trial would do is drag your name through the mud and upset Miss Effie, who's had enough upset, don't you think?"

Miss Effie. She'll hold me responsible and she'll be right. She'll never forgive me. I don't blame her. I won't be able to go back to the farm. But if I don't, where will I live? What will I do? People in the cities are starving.

All these thoughts were so loud in her head, she hardly heard the sheriff when he said, "Now, I'm going to let you burn this here picture, so we can put an end to this mess once and for all."

Belle could see his face, but it was flattened out. She'd lost her depth perception.

The sheriff talked about how Pruett Walker had felt so bad about what had happened he'd left town. As the sheriff spoke, he pushed a big, yellow, cut-glass ashtray across the desk until it was right in front of her. A cigar butt sat in the middle of it like a small turd. Its pungent odor made her want to gag. He dropped the photo into the ashtray and handed her a box of wooden matches. She broke one after another until the sheriff took them away from her.

Then, with a flick of his fingernail on the tip of a match, he rewrote her history. She watched the photograph curl up and turn black.

"It'll be our secret," he said, dumping the ashes. "You can depend on me."

That night Claude visited her in a dream. She was so happy to see him, even though she had to remind him he was dead. He said he'd come to warn her. "You're not out of the woods yet." Her eyes popped open. She sat up in bed. The moon, shining through the window, had a frightened face. Pruett Walker might have skipped town, but they hadn't burned the negative.

"WHAT DO YOU THINK?" The barber spun her around to face the mirror. A stranger looked back, a stranger with bobbed hair hanging around her ears and curling back up around her cheeks.

Belle had always had the good fortune to be not only pretty, but to have the looks that matched the esthetics of her day. In 1902, when she and Claude had started keeping company, she looked like a young Gibson girl, the early 1900s ideal. Tall and athletic, she had an eighteen-inch waist and a nicely rounded bust and hips, but her crowning glory had always been her dark hair, swept up in a pompadour.

Now. Now! The classic beauty had vanished. A new woman with strong cheekbones and a hint of mischief in her eyes looked back at her from the mirror. The barber spun her around again and held up a hand mirror so she could see the back. Her hair hardly grazed the top of her collar. She loved it. She felt wild and free.

Her hat was too big, of course. Even her hatpins wouldn't keep it on straight. She ran down Royal Street to Canal, holding her hat on, and dashed into Maison Blanche, where racks and racks of head coverings were waiting for her. A saleswoman led her to a vanity and sold her a chic little straw cloche with a bright yellow band. Then Belle bought a stylish yellow shirtwaist to match her new hat. She was finished with mourning. She was ready to get on with her life.

On the train back to Gentry, she enjoyed the buzz coming from the salesmen in their checked suits as they shot her suggestive glances. *Vogue* might have said that bobbed hair was the mark of the new woman, the height of fashion, the newest thing, but in 1920, in the more provincial parts of Louisiana, it was still a novelty.

Belle took a seat and began to plot out her new life. After her shopping trip, she'd taken a streetcar up St. Charles Avenue to show her brave new hairdo to Constance Bancroft. The suffragist said it suited her and then offered Belle a room in her big house on St. Charles Avenue whenever she wanted it.

Next year, when Cady was in college in the city, Belle intended to take her up on it. She would spend weekends there, if she could save up enough money. She had no intention of sponging off a friend.

She imagined trips to the theater, luncheons in fine restaurants, and evenings with women who believed change was not only possible, but probable. She turned to the window. Outside, it was night. Shadowy trees seemed to rise out of the swamp and rush past. But in the lighted train car, she saw the reflection of a woman of fashion, an emancipated woman. She touched her hair and smiled.

Chapter 2

"MAMA, HAVE YOU gone crazy?" Cady asked when Belle stepped off the train into the warm drizzle of the summer evening. The lights from the dining car lit the tiny droplets as they fell on her new straw cloche. Dark hair peeked out around her cheeks. "Don't you ever, ever think about what people will say?" Cady had a good deal to say, but Belle cut her off.

"Stop carrying on, honey. You act as if I'd taken up free love."

Iron brake shoes screeched against massive wheels.

"Ma-ma!" the girl wailed, elongating the two syllables. She glanced at the traveling salesmen eddying around them. The engine steamed and snorted.

Behind them, Jimmy Lee Cantrell, Cady's cousin twice removed, and her shadow, was unable to suppress a nervous snicker. The words "free love," emanating from the lips of the

woman he called Aunt Belle, made the blood rise over his large
Adam's apple, color his cheeks, and turn his pimples into
headlights.

A handsome young man, with black hair and steel blue eyes,
leaned against the depot wall under the dripping overhang. He
shot Belle a suggestive look and tipped his hat with a casual finger. She pulled herself up into her best imitation of a great lady
and strode off, with Cady running in her wake, trying to hide
her mother's embarrassing hairdo under her pink umbrella.

"You like my hair, don't you, Jimmy Lee?" Belle asked as she
led the way over the waterlogged planks of the wooden platform to their buggy.

Jimmy Lee's Adam's apple moved around in his neck a few
times before he managed, "It's different, all right."

"Is this one of your horrible suffragette ideas?" Cady asked.

"Don't be silly. I simply don't have time to mess with all that
hair, pinning it up and brushing it a hundred strokes every
night. I've got a farm to run." The train pulled out. Belle wiped
a hot cinder off her cheek and experimentally wound a short
lock around her index finger. "I feel so light and free without all
that weight dragging me down."

A familiar longing swept over her. She wished she were going
home to Claude. She wanted to find his big, quiet presence waiting for her at the farm. Well, maybe he wouldn't be so quiet tonight, not after what she'd done to her hair. A hint of a smile
tickled her lips when she imagined the scene he'd make and how
she'd have to gentle him with kisses. *Never let your husband go
to sleep angry* was a rule she'd made up for her Southern Girls'
Guide to Men and Other Perils of Modern Life. It was one rule
Belle had always tried to follow.

She'd been real good at making up in bed.

But it had been over three years since she'd slept with him or
any man. She'd had no trouble fending off the toothless vultures

who'd circled her while Claude was still cooling in the grave-yard. Recently though, she'd found her body responding most inappropriately.

She was sure there was a rule somewhere in the Primer of Propriety saying: *A lady should not have inappropriate thoughts about strange men.* A lady probably shouldn't have any thoughts at all about strange men. Or inappropriate thoughts about fa-miliar men either. But Belle figured, *as long as she stopped at thinking and didn't ease on over into doing, she'd be all right.* Besides, none of the men she'd grown up with aroused any in-appropriate thoughts at all. That should count for something.

The train took its smoke and roar up the tracks, leaving them in the hush of a rainy evening. Their buggy was hidden behind a big Ford truck. Loyal, Claude's horse of all work, stamped his foot on the muddy street when he saw them come into view.

"Where's Luther?" Belle asked.

Luther Collins had been on the farm all of her life, first as a sharecropper and more recently as an employee. He had chocolate-colored skin, white hair, and a deep, dignified voice. Before he went to war, Claude had asked him to take care of things. Belle, who'd known Luther since she was a little girl, promoted him to farm manager, or overseer, after Claude was killed. She might claim she was running the farm, but Luther did most of the work. And he knew all about growing straw-berries. She paid him a white man's salary, too. It seemed only fair.

At first it was their secret, but when his wife appeared in church in a brand-new, store-bought dress, and all his grand-children had shoes, and, finally, when he bought himself an electric clothes washer at Rubinstein's, there was grumbling in Gentry.

"It ain't right," Titus Pruett had said when he saw Luther and his nephew Curtis walk out of the store with the washing machine and put it in the back of the wagon. "How much you paying that boy of yours?" (He'd actually said "yourn.")

"Why you want to know, Titus? You fixing to hire him away from me?" Belle had asked, giving him a little smile and a toss of her head. *Only a fool answers every question a man puts to her.* And Belle Cantrell was nobody's fool. She added that as a rule to her Southern Girls' Guide.

"He's teaching his Bible study class tonight," Cady said. In his spare time, Luther was minister of the Hallelujah Chapel African Methodist Episcopal.

Jimmy Lee climbed into the wagon and took the reins. Loyal trotted down the street alongside the railroad tracks. In 1920, Gentry was a bustling farm town. The Nix Hotel, in spite of its relaxed standards of hygiene, was making Belle's stepfather rich. Every shop on Grand Avenue and beyond was occupied. They crossed the railroad tracks at Progress Street, where the windows of Rubinstein's department store were ablaze, offering merchandise imported all the way from Chicago. People used phrases like "up and coming" to describe their little city, or at least people on the town council used those words.

Belle, who'd lived here all her life, noticed none of it. Gentry was simply home. But after the glitter of New Orleans, she wanted something more. She rubbed the ends of her hair between her fingers like a talisman. *This can't be all there is to my life. I won't let this be IT.* She had a little money saved up. That was a start. She'd talk to Luther about turning some of their pasture into strawberries. That's where the money was right now. She'd make those brilliant weekends in New Orleans a reality. She might even meet an eligible man there. This time she thought she'd like to find a man who'd read a book, and not only that, actually planned to read another one. A man who could appreciate a woman with an independent spirit.

She was shaken out of her reverie by a sporty touring car splashing through the mud and coming straight at them. In Gentry this counted as an event.

The top was pulled up because of the drizzle, so Belle couldn't see the driver's face, but as he passed under the street-lamp, she caught sight of his hands, resting on the steering wheel. Long, beautiful hands the color of alabaster. A cigarette glowed like a jewel between his index and middle fingers. The word "graceful" sprang into Belle's head. And then "elegant."

He pulled over next to Jimmy Lee and asked for directions. She heard the rumble of his Yankee voice. It had overtones of faraway cities.

Belle suddenly felt her body becoming warm. It was responding inappropriately. She sat perfectly still. That's all it took? The sound of a man's voice and the sight of his hands! So what if his voice reverberated in her chest or his hands were nicely formed and well tended? She tried to get a look at the driver's face, but Jimmy Lee was leaning forward, blocking her view.

"Oh, boy! A Stutz Bearcat. Did you see that! Did you see that, Aunt Belle?" he asked as it drove away.

"I saw it," Belle said, and felt flushed under her crepe de chine traveling suit, as if the night with its persistent drizzle had suddenly turned hot.

THE STUTZ BEARCAT bounced through a particularly deep pothole. Rafe Berlin slowed to a crawl, as he'd done so often in the last ten days. The drive from Chicago had been an adventure, all right. He'd read somewhere that there were less than three thousand miles of roads fit for motor vehicles in the whole country. Obviously, none of them was anywhere near this God-forsaken place. Rafe had always had a memory for figures, and these days, numbers, dates, and cold, hard facts were all he could wrap his mind around. Since the war he'd had trouble concentrating on anything else.

He'd come back a hero, with medals and a field promotion to the rank of captain, but memories of mud so deep a man could hardly lift his leg, and the stench of men dying in that mud, had followed him back to Chicago.

The sign ahead said Grand Avenue. He wondered what fit of cheerful boosterism had induced the town council to name their main street Grand, and then neglect to pave it. The still wet gravel and muddy ruts glistened in the yellow light of the electric streetlamps.

He slowed to look at Rubinstein's department store. In the corner window, four badly painted mannequins in awkward positions modeled a cheap man's suit and three dowdy summer dresses. Above them was a display of ridiculous hats and a sign proclaiming "Rubinstein's Emporium of Fashion." Was this some kind of Southern irony?

How did his educated, refined sister stand her life in this hick town?

THE DRIZZLE HAD STOPPED. A full moon had risen and was playing hide-and-seek in the clouds. Belle inhaled the country air, fresh with rain and sweetened with the smell of the pine trees that bordered the highway. She reviewed her brave plans for the future. They'd need more men to work the strawberry fields, but since Luther was kin to most of the workers in the parish, that shouldn't be a problem. Maybe if the prices held up, she'd even have enough money to travel. She'd like to go somewhere cold. But that all depended on strawberries, and strawberries depended on Luther.

Loyal kept up a steady pace, his iron-shod hooves pounding

into the soft mud or clicking against the little mounds of gravel poured into chuckholes. Jimmy Lee was complaining to Cady about his algebra teacher, who'd had the gall to expect him to show up every single day with his homework in hand. Since Jimmy Lee had never once come to school with his homework in hand, the mathematical tyrant had had the effrontery to fail him, barring him from graduating with his class. "It ain't fair," whined Jimmy Lee.

"Isn't fair," Belle said automatically. Her mother-in-law had drummed the word "ain't" out of her when Claude had brought her home as his sixteen-year-old bride. Miss Effie couldn't abide bad grammar. There was a lot that woman couldn't abide.

As they reached the outskirts of the farm, they saw a mule cart filled with people heading the other way. It was going as fast as Belle had ever seen a mule cart go. Jimmy Lee cracked the reins, but he didn't need to. Loyal always picked up his pace as he neared home. As the horse trotted around the corner and into the long clay drive, Belle thought she saw dark figures running through the trees, but that didn't make any sense. Why would people be running around in the woods? And on such a muddy night?

An open car filled with white men roared out of the rutted lane leading to the little Hallelujah Chapel, where Luther Collins preached his weekly sermons. Luther had come to Belle a few months after Claude left for France to ask if he could build a chapel on the land he'd sharecropped for over thirty years. Belle had said she didn't want to stand in the way of the Lord, and the Hallelujah Chapel AME was put up with donated labor at night in little more than a week.

It was a pretty chapel. The outside was painted a simple white. The interior, decorated by the whole congregation, had taken them over a year. The benches and altar were hand hewn and varnished to a high gloss. They couldn't afford stained glass, of course, so one of the faithful, Sister Gertrude Moore, had painted big, primitive murals.

On the east wall was a giant Noah's ark filled with animals. A light brown angel in windswept robes stood watch on the bow. On the west wall Christ, with arms outstretched, stood on a mountaintop, preaching to a multitude of black faces. "The meek shall inherit the earth" was inscribed around his head. Although most of the parishioners were meek and would find comfort from the sentiment, few of them could read.

On the ceiling, above the altar, black and white angels floated together in harmony, blowing their trumpets as they flew in and out of plump, pink clouds. Miss Effie would have been scandalized if she'd known her daughter-in-law liked to slip in on Sunday mornings for the singing and the comfort of Luther's preaching.

When Miss Effie, who'd been spending a month in Baton Rouge visiting relatives, came home to find the chapel on her property, she'd had a conniption fit. "Nègres congregating on our farm! Nègres from who knows where!" Miss Effie always used the French pronunciation when referring to Negroes in polite conversation, and Miss Effie was always polite. That she didn't speak French and pronounced the final *s* gave her no cause for concern at all.

Belle nodded and tried to look sympathetic. *When dealing with the irredeemably hidebound, it's best to pretend to see their point of view.* Another rule for the Southern Girls' Guide. "Yes, ma'am. I see your point, but it'd be blasphemy to tear down a house of the Lord, don't you think? Even if it is a colored house."

Miss Effie was a religious woman and, as Belle was well aware, was not one to blaspheme. She thought about it for a day, and slept on it for a night, before announcing, "You got to fire Luther. That boy's grown too big for his britches. Imagine building a church, a Nègre church, on my property! I won't have it!"

"Miss Effie, you know we can't run the farm without Luther."

"Seems like it ran pretty well before he came."

That was back in the dark ages as far as Belle was concerned. But instead of pointing that out, she countered with, "Remember how he fixed the leaks after the pipes froze last winter?"

"Next winter we'll call D. T. Pruett. D.T.'s a real plumber and I'm sure he's up to fixing a few leaks."

Belle didn't like the way this was going. If Miss Effie was willing to lay out cash money to fix the plumbing, this was serious. "You think D.T. will stay up all night with a sick cow? Or help with that mare who's ready to foal? Or keep the books?"

"We can find somebody else."

Belle pulled out her last card. "Why don't we just wait until Claude gets back? He'll know what to do."

Miss Effie said nothing, and in the end she did nothing, which was what Belle had counted on.

As THEY NEARED the chapel, Belle saw more dark figures streaming through the woods. A picker Luther always hired at harvest time darted across the road. She called to him, but he kept his head down and quickened his pace as he disappeared among the trees. What was going on? "Jimmy Lee?" The boy had a sick look on his face. He clicked at Loyal to speed up. Suddenly Belle heard the crack, crack, crack of gunfire. She saw muzzle flashes behind the pine trees near the chapel. "Wait a minute!"

Jimmy Lee didn't wait. Instead, he whacked Loyal with the whip. "Jimmy Lee, you stop that right now, you hear?"

Over her voice came the roar of motors starting up. A Model T, filled with white men hooting and hollering, bounced out of the rutted lane. Someone called, "You been warned, nigger!" A bottle smashed against a tree.

A Ford Depot Hack barreled after them. Men hung on to the wooden posts of the open station wagon whooping like a bunch of desperados. As they rushed past, the night clouds parted. Belle saw a fat man, in a pool of moonlight. His legs, like big sausages, were hanging over the tail of the hack. He was blasting a shotgun into the night sky, as if he wanted to shoot down the moon. The sight of him left Belle stunned. "Jimmy Lee!"

"I don't know what's going on," he said, snapping the reins, urging Loyal on past the rutted lane leading to the chapel.

She looked back. The little church was now hidden in the woods. No lights shone. The only sounds were the squeaks and groans of the buggy. "Jimmy Lee, you stop this minute!"

"Aunt Belle, you don't want to do that!"

"Mama, let's just go home. Why do you always want to butt into other people's business!"

"Somebody might be hurt." Instead of stopping, Jimmy Lee cracked his whip. Belle yelled at him, "We've got to see what happened to Luther!" She reached over her daughter, grabbed the reins, and yanked. "You-all show up at those churches every Sunday morning. Don't your preachers ever teach you anything about Christian charity?" She swung out of the buggy.

"Mama!"

Belle ran through the woods, her high-heel, pointed-toe shoes sinking into the mud at every step. Brambles bit into her traveling suit and soiled her gloves as she clawed her way through the brush while visions of Joan of Arc leading a charge spun in her head. Joan had been canonized that May, a big event even for Protestants in Catholic Louisiana. Besides, Joan had been Belle's personal heroine for years, ever since she'd read Mark Twain's stories about her leading an army.

In the clearing in front of the church, a man was lying still in the moonlight. Belle crept out of the shadow of the slash pine. "Luther?" She reached out her hand and found he was shaking. She helped him sit up. "What happened? Why did they do this to you?"

Luther just shook his head. His mouth hung open. An acrid smell clung to him. The old man pulled away, ashamed, as Jimmy Lee and Cady brought up the buggy.

"Are you okay?" Jimmy Lee asked.

Luther just stared at him, as if he could ever be okay again. The moon lit up the chapel in back of him. The windows had jagged holes in them. The front door groaned and banged in the wind.

"Think you can walk to the buggy?"

The old man nodded and tried to stand, but his first attempt failed. Belle and Jimmy Lee helped him up. He was still trembling.

"Come on, let's get you up to the house. I think we can find some of Claude's whiskey."

"I been warned." The words came out tight, as if Luther hadn't started breathing regular yet.

"Jimmy Lee will fetch Ann Rose. He'll bring her up to the house, with a change of clothes. Won't you, Jimmy Lee?"

"Yes, ma'am."

Luther seemed to be able to take deep breaths once again, but his voice was strained. "I got to go away."

"Where?" Cady asked.

Luther looked lost. "It don't make no difference."

"All your people are here. It's not right," Belle said.

"No, ma'am. It's not right at all," Luther said, focusing on her for the first time. "But that never did make no difference, leastways not around here."

"This is the twentieth century," Belle said as she helped him climb up into the buggy. Luther said nothing. "Times have changed."

"If you say so."

"I'm going to see the sheriff."

Chapter 3

WE DON'T LIVE in the dark ages anymore, Belle told herself as she drove back into town. Night riding died out in the last century.

She was right. More or less.

Men on horseback, with masks under their hats, had faded away, but the bigotry that had motivated them was making a big comeback all over the world. Belle hadn't yet heard about the little man with a mustache who was electrifying crowds in a Munich beer hall with his harangues of hatred, but she'd read about race riots and heard rumors of lynchings in the United States. There were stories about colored soldiers home from the war, still in their uniforms, hanging from trees. She didn't know the numbers, or if anyone kept the numbers, but they seemed to be on the rise. Now, she wondered how many colored men were terrorized into quitting their jobs or, like Luther, driven out of their homes in the dark of the night. Their numbers would never be counted.

Belle didn't expect the sheriff to be in his office this late, but she knew his deputies would be. She wanted to report the crime right away. If she didn't protest, who would? The Southern Girls' Guide to Men and Other Perils of Modern Life said *A wrong which is not protested will never be righted*. She wasn't sure if she'd actually made that one up or if she'd heard it somewhere, but Belle was big on protests.

She hoped to use her feminine wiles on a simple deputy. Maybe she could get him so worked up, he'd go out and pound on doors, rousting the vigilantes out of their beds this very night. She wasn't a fool. She knew it wasn't likely they'd disturb the sleep of the mayor's son, but she had to do something. She had to try.

It was after nine o'clock when she finally got to the courthouse. The streets around it were deserted. The Nix Saloon, which had occupied the corner of Education and Grand, serving law enforcers and lawbreakers alike for forty years, was closed because of Prohibition.

The courthouse was set on a man-made hill in the center of a sweep of grass that took up an entire block. The architecture was Greek Revival, or at least that's what the city fathers called it. To Belle, it looked like a big brick box with four white columns out front, holding up very little. Over the main entrance the words "*Jus Est Ars Boni et Aequi*" were set into the cement. On their one and only high school field trip, Belle had learned that those fine words meant "Law Is the Science of What Is Good and Just."

Unfortunately, that entrance was locked.

She marched through a side door, the shreds of her torn jacket unfurled. Belle was ready for battle. A lone deputy manned the front desk. She didn't know his name, but from the way his teeth bucked out, she guessed he was a Pruett. They seemed to grow like weeds, all over the parish. She wondered if he'd be willing to arrest his kinfolks.

The deputy hung on her words. She told him how, alone and unarmed, she'd rushed through the woods. She put a frayed glove to her breast as she described Luther lying in the dirt in front of his church.

"Gosh," the deputy said, shaking his head.

Inspired by this reaction, Belle gave him a rousing description of the vigilantes racing around in their cars, shooting off guns. "I wouldn't be surprised if they were drinking illegal whiskey," she added.

"The sheriff's not gonna like this." He got up and headed for a shadowy corridor with empty offices on either side.

"He's here?"

"Oh, yes, ma'am, he's been here since suppertime."

Belle's spirits plummeted. She didn't think George Goode would be so easy to charm. There would be no pounding on doors tonight. But then she thought, maybe he'd gotten wind something was going to happen and wanted to be on duty. She was always surprised when elected officials actually performed the jobs they were paid to do. Surprised, but pleased. She thought she'd vote for him—if they let her vote—in the next election.

She heard a door open. Laughter bounced off stucco walls. A few minutes later, Sheriff Goode appeared.

"Hey, Belle—" He stopped short and a concerned look crossed his face. "What happened to you? Are you all right?"

"I didn't come here about me." She watched his tongue search around in his cheek as he stared at her. *A well-bred lady never makes a spectacle of herself.* Belle knew that, but here she was all tattered and torn, rushing around town in the dark of night, showing up at the courthouse looking like something even the cat wouldn't go near. If this wasn't making a spectacle of herself, she didn't know what was. Miss Effie would have a fit. Then Belle thought about all the spectacles she'd made of herself over the years. She decided to toss out that rule once and for all and make up one of her own. *If a lady doesn't make a spectacle of herself now and then, how's she ever going to get noticed?* That was a rule she could get behind, she thought. A rule worthy of the Southern Girls' Guide to Men and Other Perils of Modern Life.

Sheriff Goode pulled his tongue back between his teeth and rearranged his features. "Hope you don't mind if I continue smoking this fine cigar." (He pronounced it "see-gar.")

"Of course not, George. I find the smell—" Belle paused to heighten the impact of her words. "Manly." She watched him preen. She might be able to get around Cousin George yet. She imagined him and a whole bunch of deputies kicking down doors. Not likely. He hadn't even arrested Claude's killer, but then Claude had gone at Pruett Walker with a broken beer bottle. There had been witnesses.

The sheriff led the way. The dim hallway was lined with photos of himself in shirtsleeves shaking hands with farmers, accepting awards from the 4-H Club. Other pictures showed him dressed in his tailor-made suits defending the rights of businessmen. Clothes sure make a politician, she thought. Scattered among the photographs were framed awards for outstanding law enforcement.

No copies of her incriminating photograph had surfaced in over a year, she reminded herself. So he had taken care of her in his own way.

Sheriff Goode opened the door to his office. A little man jumped up out of his chair. "Belle! What in tarnation have you done to your hair?"

Belle stiffened at the sight of her stepfather. She'd forgotten all about her hair. It didn't seem important anymore, but she guessed there was no getting around it. It was the first thing everybody outside her own head saw. It added to the spectacle she was making.

A little smile played around the edge of the sheriff's lips. "You're not consorting with Communists now, are you?"

"You don't have to worry about Communists, George. You have enough homegrown troublemakers to keep you real busy."

"You got that right." The sheriff held out a chair for her and then went around to sit behind his big cherrywood desk. The office was large and well appointed, as befitted the sheriff and tax collector for the parish. An American flag hung behind him on his right, and on his left was the flag of the Confederacy. A brass chandelier, with a ceiling fan attached, cast a harsh downward light. The fan turned, but it couldn't rid the room of the smell of cheap cigars and raw alcohol.

Mr. Nix took his seat and licked his lips with a pale tongue, as if searching for stray drops of something stuck there. Belle suddenly got the picture. It wasn't overzealous duty that had kept the sheriff in his office late into the night. It was his wife, May Beth, who considered alcohol the devil's brew and wouldn't allow it in her house. Now that Prohibition had closed the bars, this office was the safest place in town for Deacons of Decency like her stepfather and the sheriff to drink.

"What can I do for you?" George Goode asked. Belle glanced at her stepfather.

"You can say your piece in front of me, sugar," Mr. Nix said. "I'm your daddy."

She glared at him and then turned her attention to the sheriff. To her surprise, he listened closely. He even took notes. When she was finished, he shook his head at the iniquity of the world.

"You said nobody got himself killed."

"No, but—" She had to make him understand this wasn't

about killing, it was about terrorizing. "They don't necessarily want people dead. At least I don't think they do. I mean, you know most of them aren't natural-born murderers. They just want to terrorize folks into toeing the line, their line—"

Mr. Nix broke in. "What I don't understand is, why are you so worked up over this here nigger?"

Belle bristled. She turned to her stepfather. "He's my nigger. And I want to keep him."

Mr. Nix nodded. So did the sheriff. Those were words these men could understand.

Belle turned back to the sheriff. "Luther's lived here all his life. You know his family. They've never given you any trouble."

The sheriff nodded. "It's a real shame." He sounded as if he meant it. He made another note on his pad.

"Ever since she was a little thing, Belle was always real soft on the niggers," Mr. Nix said.

The sheriff didn't honor that statement with as much as a nod. He looked at Belle and put down his pencil. His tone of voice was filled with sadness. "I don't expect you could see them real good. It being dark and all."

Belle was flooded with righteous indignation. "You know damn well who it was."

Mr. Nix's head shot up. "Belle! I'm surprised at you."

George Goode's look of concern vanished. "I'm going to have to ask you to refrain from profanity when you're speaking to an officer of the law."

Belle quickly veered off onto a different tack. "I'm sorry, George. But you can see how upset I am. I need you"—she looked up and fluttered her lashes—"to help me."

Sheriff Goode didn't disappoint her. His expression changed to benevolent attention. Good.

Mr. Nix came to attention too. The bastard.

She fixed her eyes on the sheriff and in her most helpless

voice said, "Luther's been running the farm ever since Claude went to war. I just don't know how Miss Effie and I can manage without him. You will help us, won't you?" She hesitated and added prettily, "George?"

The sheriff adjusted his pants. "Now, don't you fret. I'm gonna take care of y'all. That's what I'm here for."

She breathed, "Thank you." And a trickle of hope percolated up inside her.

George Goode smiled. An attractive dimple pitted his chin. "But you and I know that's no job for a colored. Not running a place as big as yours. Besides, I wouldn't know who to arrest."

The hope that had oozed up a moment ago became a choked river of rage. Her voice shrilled even as she ordered herself to control it. "How about starting with Titus Pruett?"

"Tell me again, what makes you so sure he was there?" The sheriff took a drag on his cigar.

"He was driving that old Depot Hack of his. And his cousin Pruett Walker was sitting in the back, blasting away at the moon. What's he doing back in Gentry, anyhow?" Belle had assumed, when he'd disappeared after knifing Claude, that staying away was part of the deal.

"Took over his father's sawmill," Mr. Nix said.

"That's not a crime." Smoke came out of the sheriff's mouth.

"How about beating up a citizen? That's a crime, isn't it? Desecrating a church? George, I saw his bald head in the moonlight. He's gotten so fat his stomach went halfway to his knees."

"That sounds like old Pruett," Mr. Nix said, slapping his thigh.

"It does, but there's more than one bald man in this parish, not to mention fat ones."

"I saw him."

The sheriff seemed to be taking her seriously. "I believe you, Belle, I do, but I need something that'll hold up in court. The

defense lawyer is gonna say it was dark and the car was speed-
ing away. Got anything else?"

"What about Titus's car?"

Sheriff Goode sighed. "There's more than one Depot Hack in
this part of the world."

"Old man Merkin used to have one," Mr. Nix said.

"He's nearly eighty years old," Belle protested.

"Still and all, a good lawyer's paid to bring that up." The
sheriff flicked the ash off his cigar. "Now, I don't like this any
more than you do. You think I want those boys running wild,
terrorizing the parish? But if that colored boy of yours has been
upsetting folks around here, maybe he's right to leave."

"George!"

"I don't think you should even try to stop him," he said,
pushing away from his desk. "I'm real sorry, but I can't watch
every redneck in the parish. It would only take one of them with
a shotgun to finish him off."

He opened the door, dimpling his chin, again. "Tell Cousin
Effie not to worry. I'll call her first thing in the morning."

Belle didn't remember leaving the courthouse. She didn't
want to go home, not until Miss Effie had gone to bed. She
couldn't face her tonight. The old lady might say something
about getting rid of that uppity Nègre, and if she did, Belle
didn't think she could remain civil.

She decided to visit the Rubinsteins. The two families had
been friends ever since they'd put their daughters in first grade.
Rachel Rubinstein had taught Belle about books and had seen
her through two miscarriages.

Abe Rubinstein understood politics, finance, and Southern
irony. He was quick to spot self-serving hypocrisy whenever a
politician proclaimed he was "fur virtue and agin' evil." Abe
was the one she'd gone to with any question Claude wasn't interested in or couldn't answer. It was Abe who'd shown her

how she could make real money in strawberries and had found buyers in Chicago she could trust. When Claude was in the service, Abe pushed her to negotiate with the owner of the cotton gin until he upped his prices. And when Claude died, it was Abe who took care of all the business and dealt with the funeral arrangements while the women wept.

Belle headed down Education and turned Loyal south on Hope. She pulled up under a giant live oak in front of a big antebellum house with white columns holding up the portico covering a deep front porch. It was almost ten o'clock, but lights were still shining through the long front windows.

Belle tied Loyal to the picket fence, opened the gate, and went up the brick walk. The living-room windows were open. "For Me and My Gal" was playing on the phonograph. The music flowed out over the grass and into the flower beds. Through the handblown glass panels in the front door, she saw her friend Rachel float by in the arms of a man.

A man who was not her husband.

The couple disappeared from view, but as Belle mounted the steps, they reappeared, gliding back and forth behind the long casement windows, moving as one. They could have been dancing together for years. The man held her lightly as they turned and dipped.

Where was Abe?

Who was this strange man her best friend was gamboling across the floor with? The music ended. A needle scraped on the center of the record.

Belle stepped onto the deep porch, wondering if she should interrupt, when their dog set up such a racket she had no alternative.

Rachel opened the door, flushed and beaming. She'd never been pretty, with her heavy figure and flyaway hair that was always coming unpinned, but tonight she seemed to glow. "Belle, come in. Flaubert, down!" she ordered, as the big, white, shaggy no-hunting dog jumped on Belle in a doggie frenzy, licking her hands and leaping for her face.

"Down, boy," Belle said, bending over the dog, who insisted on his right to gobble up everyone's attention. She ran her hands through his deep coat, calming him, and in doing so, calming herself. When she stood, Rachel let out a gasp. "What in the world happened to you? Are you all right?"

"No," she said, taking off her hat to brush away the moss and leaves still clinging to it. She was among friends.

"Your hair!" Rachel cried. "Belle! What did you do to yourself?"

Belle touched the dark lock swirling up onto her cheek. She'd thought it would be fun to be the first girl in Gentry to bob her hair, to be the center of attention. But now that she had more important things on her mind, she wished everyone would quit talking about it. "What do you think?"

Rachel opened her mouth. "It's—" Words failed her. She shook her head. "It's—"

"Very chic." Abe Rubinstein said, coming out of the bedroom wearing leather slippers and a cotton smoking jacket over pajamas. At forty-five Abe was getting thick around the middle and his head was shiny bald, but he was still big and handsome. He'd been in the hospital in New Orleans for weeks this spring after suffering a heart attack. He kissed Belle on the cheek. "You may be a little ahead of yourself down here, sugar, but soon all the girls will bob their hair and they'll look to you as an arbiter of fashion."

"If you ever let him go, I'll take him," Belle said to Rachel.

"You should have come around this morning. You could have had him," Rachel said, smiling at her husband.

Belle was glad she'd come. She always felt warm and taken care of around Rachel and Abe.

From the living room came the sound of a new record. "There's someone I want you to meet," Rachel said. Her face shone with pleasure.

A man turned as they entered. Belle had seen pictures of him, taken before the war, but the young man in the officer's uniform was fit and filled with youthful passion. This man seemed world weary, disillusioned, ruined.

Belle liked that. It matched her mood.

Everything about him was long and lean, his legs, his torso, his face with its high cheekbones and prominent nose. His dark, thick hair was short and combed back, but an unruly curl managed to fall onto his forehead. He had the saddest eyes she'd ever seen. Belle wanted to take him in her arms.

He was wearing gray flannel pants and an elegant blue-gray shirt of some soft material. Although he wasn't exactly handsome, the words "graceful" and "dashing" leapt into her mind. Suddenly, Belle felt ashamed of the disrepair of her clothes, her torn skirt, her muddy shoes, her dirty gloves.

"Belle, this is my brother Rafe Berlin. He drove down all the way from Chicago to surprise us."

"Mr. Berlin." Belle ripped off her soiled glove.

"Mrs. Cantrell, my sister has told me so much about you." As their skin touched, she realized his were the long, elegant hands she'd seen driving the touring car. She remembered the lit cigarette, glowing like a jewel between his fingers. She didn't want to let go.

They said all the usual things that strangers say. She'd heard so much about him. His sister had spoken of her in her letters. It was the sort of thing anyone might say, but as his deep, cultured voice resonated in her chest, Belle felt the warmth of inappropriate feelings sweeping over her. She was afraid she'd caught one of those Freudian complexes she'd been reading about in *Vanity Fair*.

"Did Mrs. Berlin come with you?" Belle asked at last, taking her hand back. Rachel had shown her pictures of her brother's brilliant wedding to the beautiful and wealthy Helen Herzog, the daughter of one of Chicago's oldest Jewish families.

"She'll be joining us soon," Rachel said. Brother and sister exchanged pointed looks. He said nothing.

What's happening to me? Belle wondered as the memory of Luther came crashing back over her. Does the mind always wander away from catastrophe?

Belle told them about the vigilantes. Rafe, Rachel, and Abe exchanged worried glances, as if they shared some silent fear. Rachel led her to a couch in the cool central hallway they used as a family room. She put her arm around her.

"I don't know what I'm going to do." Belle's plans for weekends in New Orleans came back to her. How can I be so selfish? My problems are nothing compared with Luther's. But they didn't feel like nothing. Tears were leaking out of her eyes. She hadn't cried before and she didn't want to now, but her friend's kindness broke the dam she'd built up with such care. Rachel stroked her short hair. Rafe handed her a handkerchief. "Thank you."

He seemed lost for a moment and then he said, "I never knew you Southerners cared so much for your darkies."

Belle looked up at him as if she'd been slapped. All the turmoil she'd bottled up suddenly bubbled up out of her chest and onto her tongue. "He's not my darkie! You think we still keep slaves?" Although she'd said something similar to the sheriff and her stepfather, she didn't want to hear this kind of talk coming from a Yankee.

"Rafe, would you mind making Belle a Coke? In fact, you could make one for all of us."

Rafe's relief was palpable as he disappeared into the dining room. Once he was gone, all Belle wanted to do was lay her head on Rachel's soft shoulder and weep onto her starched white shirtwaist. Rachel was so comforting, like the mother we all wish we had.

"Don't mind Rafe. He's a Yankee," Abe said, as if that explained everything. They heard the sound of an ice pick cracking a block of ice.

When Rafe returned, Belle managed a wan smile. "I'm so sorry, I didn't mean to be rude. This is very kind of you."

He nodded curtly as he poured the amber liquid over the chipped ice. The bubbles pricked her nose and the sweet taste calmed her down.

"What do you want us to do?" Rafe asked.

"Do?" Belle looked up. How like a man, she thought. While I'm weeping and wailing over losing Luther, and feeling sorry for myself, he wants to do something useful.

"He'll need cash," Rafe said, and looked at Abe, who nodded. Both men left the hall.

Abe came back with thirty dollars. "Stop by the store tomorrow. I'll be able to get you a little more."

"Thank you," Belle said, kissing him on the cheek.

Rafe returned with an envelope. His voice was distant. "This should help him get settled."

Belle opened the envelope and found a hundred dollars. Gratitude swept over her. "Mr. Berlin, this is too much. I can't accept it."

He didn't look at her. His voice seemed to be in a minor key, as if he were listening to other music. "It's not for you."

RAFE STOOD IN the doorway and watched Belle get into her buggy. "What do you think?" Abe asked. The sky was again thick with clouds.

"She's going to get caught."

Rachel moved quickly to the door. Worry carved lines between her eyes. She looked both ways for signs of vigilantes. The street was empty.

"In the rain. She's going to get caught in the rain." Rafe knew he was acting odd again. He could see it in his sister's face. He had to concentrate. He hadn't come down here to worry her. He closed the door, but he couldn't shut out the memories.

"She's a looker, isn't she? A real *shiksa* princess."

"Abe!"

"Sweetheart, every Jewish boy dreams about girls like Belle," he said, putting his arm around his wife. She slid away. "But we marry girls like you." He blew her a kiss.

Rafe watched them and thought how easy it was for them to laugh. Did he laugh with Helen before the war? He must have, but he couldn't remember. He felt as if he were locked out of the human race. He knew he was expected to say something, so he asked, "Who do you think terrorized that Negro manager of hers?"

"White trash, mostly," Abe said.

"Don't call them that! That's why they're so desperate to have someone to look down on."

"Lord help me. I had to go and marry a Yankee social worker, and a feminist to boot."

Rachel gave him a mock frown. "What was it Rebecca West said? 'People call me a feminist whenever I express sentiments different from a doormat.' "

"See what I have to put up with?" Abe said.

But Rachel was studying her brother. "Hey, big sister, I'm fine. Just tired from the trip."

"Of course," said Rachel, but she didn't sound convinced.

Rafe whistled and the big shaggy dog came bouncing across the room. "I think I'll take Flaubert for a walk before I hit the sack."

Bounding into the yard, Flaubert rushed this way and that, exploring all the alluring smells as if this were the very first time he'd ever been let out in this enchanting yard. Rafe picked up a stick that had fallen onto the brick walkway. He pitched it into the air. "Fetch!" The big dog watched the small branch sail by and then scrupulously ignored it.

Rafe opened the gate. There was no sidewalk. The wet earth squished under his shoes. He headed for the road, trying to beat back the memories of mud and war that came to him at night. The dog was running in circles around him.

Rafe stopped and took a deep breath. For the first time he noticed that the air, moist and warm, was filled with the rich sweetness of some unknown Southern bloom. Belle's face floated into his mind. Belle Cantrell. She was a beauty all right, with her short hair and her little straw cloche. So why didn't he feel anything?

He turned back to the house and wondered if he'd ever feel anything again.

Chapter 4

BELLE WAS EXHAUSTED when she got back to the farm an hour later. She'd stopped by Luther's house, but the wooden shutters were closed. No light seeped into the yard. She'd decided against waking them. He'd been through enough. Besides, she wanted to add to the money Rafe and Abe had given her.

She fell asleep as soon as she tumbled into bed, but awoke at three A.M. Memories of Luther looped and wheeled in the spaciousness of her mind. The scene played again and again whenever she closed her eyes. She rose before dawn and went downstairs to the office. She wrote Luther a check for all the money she'd saved, outside of Cady's college fund. It didn't assuage her guilt for letting him build that chapel in the first place, but it helped.

The sky was beginning to lighten when she stepped out the kitchen door. Dawg, Claude's black hunting dog, leaped around her in wild anticipation. "I wish something in my life gave me this much pleasure," Belle said to the dog, scratching him between the ears.

She saddled up Susan B. and trotted down the clay lane that led to Luther's cabin. Dew glittered on the grass alongside the road. The air was country sweet. Claude and his father and his father before him had always bred a few horses. It made the dull business of cows and cotton seem worthwhile. But now that everyone was so car crazy, Belle figured it was time to get rid of the horses. They were expensive to feed and never had paid their way, but neither she nor her late husband had ever been able to put a price on love.

Her thoughts circled back to what had happened the night before. Why hadn't she seen it coming? Claude would have known. One of the good ol' boys he drank with would have warned him so he could have gotten Luther out of town until whatever had riled up those men blew over.

It was one thing to talk about being a new woman, but when it came to what was really important, she was as helpless as a . . . as helpless as a . . . as a girl. Would it always be like this? Darn Claude. And then the guilt of his death coiled around her stomach like a snake.

Above her, live oaks—older than the nation itself—spread shady limbs, draped with long, floating sleeves of Spanish moss. She inhaled the cool fragrance of early morning in the country. The tap, tap, tap of a woodpecker echoed through the trees.

She let Susan B. have her head. For the first time in her life, Belle could feel the breeze on her scalp. I'd feel swell if I didn't feel so lousy, she thought as she slowed her horse to a walk. She turned onto the short path leading to the cabin Luther had lived in for forty years.

When he'd arrived, it had been nothing more than a dark, one-room shack, unpainted, with a roof sagging like a sway-backed old horse. Of course, in those days there was no running water or electricity. Over the years Luther and his wife, Ann Rose, had expanded the shanty into a cheerful yellow cottage, with three rooms covered by a fine roof of asbestos shingles. A big, black power line ran like a loose ribbon to the house.

Belle slid off Susan B. and opened the squeaking gate, making sure to keep Dawg out of the yard. A flutter of chickens ran around to the front of the house, clucking and chattering at her. She knocked on the front door.

Her heart was beating. Her sense of loss was swamped by her excitement at being able to hand Luther the envelope. Feelings are confusing, she thought. He'd have enough money to carry him and Ann Rose a long time, until they found jobs. She'd also enclosed a dozen letters of recommendation "to whom it may concern" and a personal letter to Constance Bancroft in hopes she'd be able to find work for the couple. She knocked again, but all she heard was the buzzing of insects and the clucking of the chickens. Where was their dog?

She cracked open the door. "Luther! Ann Rose!"

Nothing.

"Ann Rose!"

She took a step inside, afraid of what she might find.

The front room was empty and heartbreakingly clean. "Luther! Ann Rose!" Not even an echo. She opened the shutters and saw the floor had been swept, the table and chairs polished. She walked into the kitchen. Bags of cornmeal and sugar, along with jars of preserves and pickled watermelon rinds, were set out on the counter so neighbors could help themselves. Ann Rose knew people would be through the house and she was set on them finding it spotless.

Belle walked into the bedroom. The bed was stripped bare, the closets emptied out. She sat down on the striped mattress. She thought she might cry. God knows, tears were welling up inside her. They say it's easier to hard-boil an egg than a person, but Belle felt hard-boiled this morning. Tears were stuck somewhere deep inside her, a hard, desiccated mass, impossible to pass.

She went back to the kitchen, pulled out a bag of chicken feed, and scattered it around the yard before getting back on Susan B. and riding over to the chapel.

The front door was bouncing in the breeze. The bottom hinge was broken and the door made a whack, whack, whack sound against the wall. Inside, the hand-hewn pews were knocked over and smashed. Guns had blasted holes through the walls and windows. The faces in the murals Sister Gertrude had labored over had been used for target practice. In front of the altar, which looked as if it had been hacked up with an ax, a book was torn in half.

Belle stooped to pick it up. *The Souls of Black Folk*, by W. E. B. DuBois. She'd never heard of the writer or the book, but the vigilantes must have. That was strange. Belle figured most of them had finished reading about the time they'd finished fourth grade.

Torn pages were scattered around the floor. She picked up a scrap and saw what she assumed was a morsel of the table of contents. She read a couple of lines about spiritual striving and the dawn of freedom.

So Luther's Thursday-night Bible study classes were studying something besides the Bible.

She picked up half a page and read how racial prejudice would naturally engender self-questioning and self-disparagement. A third of a page fluttered across the floor. On it were the words "the ideal of human brotherhood." Belle couldn't bring herself to look any further. She knew the "ideal of human brotherhood" would sound like the flapping of the red flag of socialism to the good people of Gentry. And in their minds, socialists, anarchists, Communists, and bomb throwers were all the same.

The Red Scare was everywhere. It was bad enough when the Communists pulled Russia out of the war, but then the Red Army started fighting in places nobody'd ever heard of, and in spite of not having God on their side, they were winning!

Here at home, labor unions were organizing strikes, disrupting business around the country, and last year, some godless agitator had sent mail bombs to U.S. officials. One had exploded in the home of a Georgia senator. If it hadn't been for a vigilant postal clerk, thirty-six other bombs would have been delivered. A month later, a bomb was thrown at the home of Attorney General A. Mitchell Palmer, killing a passerby.

The nation was terrified. So on New Year's Day 1920, in the name of national security, Palmer retaliated by busting into the homes of thousands of labor leaders and Communist party organizers around the country and throwing them into jail without a warrant, along with any friends or relatives who happened to be visiting. The immigrants among them were deported at random.

When Belle asked how such a thing could happen in America, Abe Rubinstein had explained, Attorney General Palmer had invoked the Sedition Act of 1918, which made it illegal to criticize the war.

"But the war is over."

Abe had laughed. "You think a politician like Palmer is going to be deterred by mere facts?"

If Luther had been teaching farmhands and millworkers "the ideal of human brotherhood," Belle was pretty sure they were calling him a Communist agitator in town. At least those were the words they'd use when they were being polite. No telling what kind of fiend he'd turn into in the mouths of those whose main religion was bigotry.

Belle stayed a long time, grieving. If she hadn't let him build his chapel, maybe none of this would have happened. She thought she was so smart, tricking Miss Effie into letting him keep it. At first she tried to straighten up the mess, but the magnitude of the destruction defeated her. She sat on the side of a ruined pew and stared at the blasted mural of Jesus preaching his Sermon on the Mount. "The meek shall inherit the earth." Their inheritance is a long time coming, Belle thought. Must have got tied up somewhere in the celestial courts.

She'd never had the knack of belief like some people, like her mother-in-law, so she wasn't exactly praying. She was wishing. Wishing for a just God, who—against all evidence to the contrary—protected the meek and the decent. Usually she didn't think much about punishing the wicked, but today she wouldn't mind some Old Testament vengeance. If God wanted to smite the wicked, that would be just fine with her.

It didn't look like anyone around here would do it.

Subtly, without her really noticing it, her mourning for Luther and his loss slipped into mourning for herself and her own loss. How in heaven's name am I going to manage without him? she wondered. How are we going to keep the farm together? She was so sunk in her own misery, she didn't notice Dawg pointing at the door.

A low growl issued from the animal's throat. A long shadow fell over her. She spun around. The dark silhouette of a man blocked the sun. He wasn't tall, but she could tell by his shape that he was brawny. What was he doing here? Was he one of the vigilantes come back to loot what they hadn't destroyed? She stood as he came toward her. She tried to judge the space between him and the broken pews. There wasn't room to make it around him and out the door without risking his catching hold of her. She pulled herself up into an imitation of Miss Effie at her most imperious.

He took off his hat. When the sunlight caught up with his face, Belle saw his eyes were a startling blue. His hair was black and thick, slicked back with pomade. His jaw was square, his shoulders broad, and his lips, his lips even curled in a mocking smile, were perfect. In the shadows of the broken chapel, she guessed he was somewhere in his early twenties. He was the handsomest man Belle had ever seen close up.

A rule popped into her head. *Beware of men who are better looking than you. They think they're entitled.* Belle decided that was worthy of her Southern Girls' Guide to Men and Other Perils of Modern Life. She didn't bother to number it. Belle didn't bother much with numbers.

She caught the smell of damp moss in a dark forest and had a vision of some wild animal prowling there. He flashed white teeth in his suntanned face. "You must be Miz Belle." He turned her name over on his tongue as if he were about to eat it. "Name suits you. But I guess you know that, don't you?"

Belle flushed at his insolence. Who was he? How did he know her name? And most important, could she get around him and out the door, now? As if reading her mind he said, "Sheriff sent me. Said you ladies needed somebody to take care of the place. Looks to me like he was right." So that's how Cousin George is taking care of us, Belle thought. I should have known. "Them boys shot up this church real good last night." Belle shuddered. She reached down and touched Dawg's dark head. He was wary of the stranger.

"Name's Bourrée LeBlanc." The man held out his hand.

She hesitated, and then not wanting to leave his hand dangling in the air, she offered hers. "It was very kind of you to come all this way, Mr. LeBlanc—"

He trapped her hand in both of his and cut her off. "Call me Bourrée, chère." His hands were warm and calloused from hard work. There was a tracing of dirt under his blunt fingernails.

Belle pulled out of his grasp.

"Fine place you have here. I figure you've got what, about a hundred and fifty acres of cotton, am I right?" Belle nodded. "It's gonna need a lot of attention, to beat back the boll weevil." Behind his words, she heard the music of a Cajun accent, but it was a melody he'd worked hard to lose. "Haven't made a tour of your timber yet, but you got some trees out there that need cutting, bad."

"Thank you, I'll have to look into it."

His eyes gleamed, as if the idea of her looking into it was amusing. "You got what? Forty acres of corn?" Belle didn't say anything. "It's gonna need pulling in about a month. And those strawberries of yours are gonna need tending come fall. And of course somebody's got to look after all them cows."

"We'll be interviewing managers soon, Mr. LeBlanc. So why don't you let me know how to get in touch with you."

He studied her. Belle had the unnerving feeling he was considering a purchase. Then he smiled. "Miss Effie already took me on. She said I was a gift from God. That's what she said, a regular gift from God." He seemed to find that amusing. "I believe she's the owner of this here farm."

"Part owner." Belle had inherited an undivided fourth from her late husband.

"That so?" He looked at her with heightened interest.

"Excuse me. I have to get back. Come on, Dawg. We'll be in touch with you, Mr. LeBlanc." Dawg trotted after her, but when the stranger managed to brush against Belle in the confined space, the animal showed him his teeth.

Outside in the sunshine, Bourrée held her stirrup. As Belle swung her right leg over her horse, she felt Bourrée's stubby hand slide up the outside of her riding britches and boost her into her seat. She looked down at him, speechless.

"You be real careful now. That horse of yours looks like a handful." He winked.

Belle jerked Susan B. around. When they reached the lane,

she shifted her weight forward in the saddle until they were galloping. Her mind was in a tizzy. She didn't know if that was some Cajun way of helping a lady onto a horse or if he had just taken liberties. Then she thought, Maybe the Cajun way is to take liberties.

The Primer of Propriety was clear: *A gentleman may hold a lady's stirrup when helping her mount her horse, but he must avoid touching her body.*

Of course there was no reason to think a farm boy knew the Rules of Propriety. But still. At least she had nothing to reproach herself for, and that made a nice change. She hadn't broken any rules.

Except maybe one.

She'd enjoyed it.

I'm suffering from a whole outbreak of Freudian fever, she thought.

She urged Susan B. on, turning into the fields to see if any damage had been done to the crops the night before. She talked to the farmworkers. They were furtive and shaken. None of them knew where Luther had gone, or if they did, they weren't telling her.

It was almost noon when Belle got back to the house. A rusted Ford stood in the drive. Miss Effie must have company, she thought.

The Cantrell place was halfway between a farm and what people called a Southern plantation. At almost four hundred acres, they had a lot of land for this part of Louisiana, but the house itself didn't have any of the planter pretensions of Corinthian columns or winding staircases. It was a comfortable two-story home, with high-ceilinged rooms that rambled this way and that as bedrooms, a bathroom, and an office were added over the seventy years of its existence.

A wraparound veranda with Victorian gingerbread trim kept

the summer sun away from the windows and gave the family a cool place to enjoy spring days and summer evenings. Bowers of roses covered the trellises and cascaded down the front of the house.

Belle put Susan B. in the barn and went into the big old kitchen where Stella, Luther's sister, was making their midday dinner.

"Do you know where Luther went?" Belle asked.

"No, ma'am, I surely don't," Stella said, peering into the woodstove. She stood up, looking tired. "Lord, child, what did you do to your hair!"

Belle ran her fingers through the short hair at the back of her neck and shrugged. "Let me know as soon as you hear from him, because I have some money to help them get started and a whole bunch of letters—"

"Belle, is that you?" Miss Effie swept into the kitchen. "The most awful thing has happened."

"I know."

In spite of wanting to talk about this most awful thing, and Miss Effie had a lot to say on the subject, the sight of Belle's new haircut scattered all other thoughts. She stared. She opened her mouth, but only for a moment. Then she closed her lips and narrowed her eyes.

Belle stood up straight, ready to defend herself. On the train back to Gentry, she'd stockpiled an arsenal of good reasons for cutting her hair. She waited for the tirade to begin, but Miss Effie didn't give her the satisfaction. She just shook her head. "If you knew, why didn't you tell me?"

Belle was startled out of her defensive stance. "I wanted to see him first."

"Him?" Comprehension slowly crossed Miss Effie's face. She walked over to Stella. "I was real sorry to hear about what happened to your brother last night. Do you know what his plans are?"

"No, ma'am."

"Well, if we can help him get settled, you let us know, you hear?"

"Yes, ma'am."

Miss Effie, her duty to her servant done, turned back to Belle. "Somebody stole Loyal and took the wagon. I figure it must have been some of the white trash that was running around our woods last night."

Belle glanced over Miss Effie's shoulder at Stella, who had moved to the icebox. Her face had become impassive.

"I telephoned the sheriff. He said he'd send out a couple of his men."

"Oh, dear God."

"Belle! Watch your language! You know I can't have the Lord's name used in vain in my house."

"George say what he was going to do?"

"He sounded real concerned. But don't you worry, he knows how to take care of horse thieves."

Stella hacked angrily at the celery, hard-boiled eggs, and green pepper for the potato salad. The thud of steel on wood hammered in Belle's head. "Nobody stole Loyal and the wagon," Belle said.

"Well, they're not here," Miss Effie replied with implacable logic.

Belle sought Stella's eye. "I, er . . . I told Luther he could have it." Mute satisfaction flashed over Stella's face.

"You gave that boy my horse and wagon?"

"It's my horse and wagon, too." Belle always felt it was bad manners to remind her mother-in-law that she was now a fourth owner of the farm.

Miss Effie pursed her lips again. "Where'd he take it?"

"I expect we'll find it downtown at the train station." In

back of Miss Effie, Belle saw Stella shake her head. "In Hammond?" Stella nodded.

"Why on earth did he take it all the way down there?"

"After what happened last night, I don't think he felt very safe on the streets of Gentry." Miss Effie motioned for Belle to step out of the kitchen.

The dining room was weighted down by heavy Victorian furniture, a sure sign of nineteenth-century prosperity and self-satisfaction. Closing the kitchen door, Miss Effie hissed, "Mary Louise Pruett told me one of Luther's parishioners, if you can call him that, was agitating the workers over at Walker's sawmill. That boy's been nothing but trouble. I told you to get rid of him, but no, you wouldn't listen. Imagine building a church on my property for the sole purpose of getting the Nègres all stirred up. And now, now he's taken Loyal and left us stranded!" Her voice rose in pitch to martyrdom. "I'll have to miss my ladies' auxiliary meeting this afternoon."

"I'll catch the train to Hammond after lunch and pick up Loyal and the wagon."

"You don't have to do that, chère." Blunt masculinity churned up the still air as Bourrée LeBlanc walked through the doorway separating the dining room and parlor. Miss Effie suddenly became all fluttery.

"No sense in you clip-clipping over to the station only to hang around until a train comes through. I'll carry you to Hammond." Belle knew he meant in his car, but he looked perfectly capable of hoisting her over his shoulder and hauling her down there all by himself. Heck, he looked as if he could go out into the swamp with a hunting knife and come back with thirty alligator skins. He turned to Miss Effie. "Then I'll come back and carry you to your Ladies Auxiliary meeting, ma'am."

"Oh, Belle, in all the excitement I forgot to tell you the

news." Miss Effie turned to him. "I hope you'll accept my apologies. This is my daughter-in-law, Mrs. Belle Cantrell. Belle, I want you to meet Mr. Beauregard LeBlanc."

"Now, Miss Effie, you promised you was gonna call me Bourrée." Effie giggled like a young girl. He turned back to Belle. "I've already had the pleasure of meeting Miz Belle." He elongated the *z* and the *l*, as if he enjoyed the taste of them. Belle reminded herself he was just a few years older than Cady. Oh, Lord, he's just a few years older than Cady.

"When I talked to Cousin George this morning, he'd already heard we'd be needing a new overseer. He said Mr. LeBl—" Miss Effie caught herself and fluttered her eyes. "Bourrée had come to town just ten days ago and was looking for work. It's Divine Providence. That's what it is, Divine Providence. Luther is chased off in the night, and the next morning Bourrée appears."

"It's something all right," said Belle, but she doubted it was divine.

"George said he knew we couldn't handle this big old farm alone. That's George, always looking out for us."

"You know, I think Mr. LeBlanc would be more comfortable out on the veranda with a nice cool drink while we discuss this. Don't you agree, Miss Effie?"

Her words launched her mother-in-law into a flurry of gracious-hostess activities. Soon, Bourrée was seated in a cane rocking chair on the front porch, drinking a glass of sweet iced tea and nibbling on a plate of crackers, while the two women retreated into the parlor to decide his fate.

"We don't know anything about him."

"George wouldn't have recommended him if he weren't reliable."

At that moment a big Packard rumbled up to the front of the house. Nina Rubinstein, Rachel and Abe's daughter, drove up with a gaggle of girls she'd picked up earlier. There were five in all, counting Cady. Bourrée rose and walked out to them.

The women in the parlor stopped talking and watched the scene through the long casement window. Belle had a vision of a muscular animal stalking his prey. Five pretty young hands primped hair and covered giggling mouths. Eyes batted at the stranger, who had his foot on the running board and was leaning into the car.

Neither mother nor grandmother breathed when Bourrée gave Cady his hand and gallantly helped her down. They couldn't hear what she said, but they saw her giggle at his reply.

Belle stepped out onto the porch. "Cady!"

The girl waved good-bye to her friends and ran into the house. "Who's he?" Her face was flushed.

"Just someone your grandmother is thinking of hiring."

"Owww, you better watch out for Grandma. He's really handsome." Cady laughed and wiggled her eyebrows as they stepped inside.

"Cady, go wash up," Miss Effie said.

Belle watched her daughter run up the stairs. She turned to her mother-in-law. "I don't think he's going to work out."

"What do you want to do, make her walk around with a sack over her head? 'Good-looking men need not apply'? Cady's a sensible girl. I wouldn't worry about her."

"Well, I'm her mother and I do."

"That nice Thompson boy is paying her court. And if you haven't noticed, she's quite taken by him."

That was an understatement. Cady had talked of little else. It was Hugh this and Hugh that, ever since she'd met him at a church picnic the winter before. Belle didn't know the boy personally, but what she knew of the Thompsons didn't recommend him. She shook her head.

"Why, sugar, I never figured you, of all people, for a prude."

"I'm not a prude! But I know what can happen to a young girl who thinks she's in love." The word "thinks" was unfortunate. Love was the only excuse Belle had for her own impetuous youth. She knew Miss Effie had had other plans for her only son. The silence was thick between them. "I want her to go to college," Belle said at last.

"Where she'll find hundreds of attractive young men. Don't you worry about Mr. LeBlanc. I'll keep an eye on him."

He was still leaning on the door of the open car. Lily Moffat, pretty and plump, had taken off her glasses and found a strand of wavy blond hair, which she was twisting over her lips.

"He's awfully young."

"Young and strong. That's what we need around here, especially now that the white trash are making trouble again. Nothing in this world is worse than poor white trash."

"I think we should at least ask around before we hire someone. We can't just take the first young man who applies." Their choice of farm manager would determine not only their livelihood, but any chance Belle had of leading an independent life.

"Don't you think I've looked? Overseers for a place as big as this don't grow on trees. I've called everyone I know. Why do you think I let you keep that Luther so long?"

Belle let that sink in. "How long have you been looking?"

"Ever since that boy built that Nègre church. Now, Belle, tell me something. Do you plan to spend your summer standing out in the hot sun with a bunch of field hands?"

Belle had to admit that had not been part of her summer plans.

"Then I suggest we give Mr. LeBlanc a try."

"Okay, but only on a trial basis. Until someone better comes along." Belle knew she was grasping at straws.

STELLA ANNOUNCED DINNER was ready. Miss Effie said she'd invited Mr. LeBlanc to have a bite with them. "Are you planning to have him take all his meals with us?" Belle asked.

"Of course not, dear. But I'd think you'd want a good look at him."

Bourrée held Miss Effie's chair, barraging the dowager with compliments, until Belle told Cady to say grace.

Bourrée bowed his head and reached out his hands to Miss Effie and Belle, a custom in which the ladies did not usually indulge. The moment Cady said amen, Belle yanked her hand away, but she noticed Miss Effie gave up Bourrée's hand with reluctance. The old lady's flirting with him! Belle thought. She glanced over at Cady. The girl smiled back at her mother.

Belle studied the stranger as he devoured his salad of Creole tomatoes and cucumber. His black suit looked as if it was expensive, but had been bought for somebody else. The seams strained over his broad chest. Belle wondered how long it would take before his powerful arms ripped out those sleeves in an unguarded movement.

While the ladies picked at their salads, he endeavored to impress them with his knowledge of the latest advances in scientific agriculture. He explained how they could kill the boll weevil with nightly applications of poison dust and held forth on the importance of eradicating inferior livestock by getting rid of the runts before they had a chance to breed. "I'll boost your milk production one hundred percent," he boasted. When Belle brought the conversation around to strawberries, he suggested doubling the acreage. "We'll have to hire more workers, that's for sure. But don't you ladies worry about that. I'll get an honest day's work out of them."

When Stella brought out the meat and potatoes, Bourrée stopped talking. He filled his plate with roast veal, potato salad, mustard greens, and homemade biscuits. Then he bent over, sheltering his food in the curve of his left arm. Belle recognized in him a hungry child, shoveling the meat into his mouth first, beginning the next bite before swallowing the last, in case someone snatched the food off his dish. In spite of her attempt to be hard-boiled, she felt her heart stumble. She'd been just like him until she'd come to live with the Cantrells, until Miss Effie had assured her there would always be enough for her to eat, and taught her to sit up at the table like a lady.

Over bread pudding and coffee, Bourrée told them he was a proud member of the Woodmen of America and was going to stand for membership in the Gentry Boosters. Belle sipped her coffee and wondered what a farm manager needed with men's clubs. He'd just come to town and already he'd gotten to know the sheriff. Now, he was charming the widow who owned the biggest farm in the parish. Belle guessed he was what the businessmen in town call "a regular go-getter." That's not necessarily a bad thing, she reminded herself. But the question remained, What was he going after? And what would he get?

Chapter 5

THE ROAD FROM Gentry to Hammond was filled with bumps. Belle had heard that a Model T could reach a speed of forty miles an hour. Of course, without a speedometer there was no way of knowing, but they seemed to be flying. Belle took off her hat and let the breeze pick up her hair.

So as not to attract undue speculation, she sat regally in the backseat. Not even the most hidebound gossip could object to her hired man chauffeuring her about. She glanced over Bourrée's broad shoulders and watched his work-hardened hands grip the steering wheel. He turned his head. She regarded his chiseled profile and wondered if he was vain about his looks. She expected he was well aware of their effect on women.

He draped his arm casually over the top of the front seat. Belle saw his sturdy wrist and the dark hair sticking out of his sleeve. Of course, good looks aren't the worst thing in the world, she thought. A girl shouldn't be prejudiced.

The wind picked up her hair. She began to fantasize about what would happen if they just kept going past Hammond and headed for parts unknown, wild and free.

"Saw your picture over at the Nix Hotel," he called out over the rattle of the fenders. "Your daddy sure loves to talk about you."

Her wild-and-free fantasies slammed into the bumpy road. She wished Calvin Nix would stop telling people he was her daddy. Bourrée continued to talk over the sputter of the engine, the clatter of metal on metal, and the ups and downs of the road. Individual words somersaulted over the front seat, past her ears, but Belle had quit listening. She was lost in the past.

Her gentle father had died when she was only eight. Her mother found work at the Nix Hotel as housekeeper, supervising the cook and the colored maids. Within a couple of months, she was sharing Mr. Nix's bed. He married her soon after, saving him cash money and getting her services twenty-four hours a day, seven days a week.

He got Belle's services as well. "It's time she earned her keep," he'd say, along with "A little work won't hurt her" and "Teach her discipline." Calvin Nix was big on discipline. By her ninth birthday, he'd put her to work alongside the maids. They were real sweet to her, but Belle didn't think it was fair. They got to go home at night.

When she was twelve and starting to mature, he took to slapping her on the bottom every time he'd walk past. She told him to stop, but he only laughed and made fun of her, saying, "That was just a love pat, honey. Can't you tell love pats from slaps?" Then he started coming into the guest rooms where she was bending over, making the bed, and his slaps became more like slides. Finally, when he tried to kiss her, Belle ran to her mother.

"Now, you hush," Blanche told her. "Mr. Nix's been real good to us. I don't know what we'd do without him."

Belle figured she'd do real fine.

The next time he tried to stick his fat old tongue between her lips, she pushed him away with: "Brother Scaggs said this is a sin!"

"That's okay, honey."

"No it's not. We're gonna burn in the Lake of Fire!"

"He wasn't talking about me and you. I'm your daddy. It's only natural to kiss your daddy."

"Yes, sir, if you say so," Belle said. Mr. Nix smiled and tried to pull her toward him. "I'll ask him about it next Sunday."

Mr. Nix froze. His voice was even. "You don't have to ask him nothing."

"Oh, yes I do," Belle said sweetly.

After that, he quit trying to force himself on her, but he never gave up hope. Her mother watched their dance, refusing to admit, even to herself, that there was anything going on. How could she? As her daughter grew into a pretty young Gibson girl, Blanche found more and more to criticize, until Belle couldn't wait to leave home.

"HE'S A REAL Christian gentleman," Bourrée said when he stopped the car in front of the Hammond depot. The Model T let out a couple of coughs and died.

"Who?" asked Belle.

"Your father."

"My father's dead. Mr. Nix is just my mother's husband."

"Sorry to hear that, but you're lucky your mama married such a fine, upstanding citizen. He's the one who's putting me up for membership in the Boosters."

Belle watched Bourrée jump out and come around the car. It's not his fault, she tried to tell herself. To an outsider Mr. Nix looks like a pillar of the community.

"He's taking me to his church this Sunday. You hear they made him a deacon?" Bourrée asked as he opened the door.

A fire truck rushed down the street, clanging its warning bell. Belle's mouth filled with dust. "He still going to the Church of Everlasting Redemption?"

"Yes, ma'am, that's the one. I can tell you, I'm looking forward to it. I already heard Reverend Scaggs once in Atlanta. He preaches *The Fundamentals* like nobody's business."

"I'd have thought you'd be attending the Catholic church, Mr. LeBlanc."

"You can call me Bourrée, Mizzz Belle," he said, as if he were licking up her name. Belle's spine prickled. "But you got that right. I was born Catholic and my mama, well, she raised me Catholic, but after I heard Brother Scaggs, I saw the light, and praise the Lord, I have been born again."

"I'm keeping the books," Belle said as she swept out of the car ignoring his outstretched hand.

Bourrée started. "You don't have to do that, chère."

"Oh, yes, I do." Belle headed for her horse.

"I mean, I'll be happy to take that chore off your hands." When she didn't answer him, he added, "That's men's work."

"Nevertheless," she said, stepping on the hot gravel in her thin-soled shoes.

He followed her. "I wouldn't think that an intelligent lady like you would want to tire her eyes over anything so picayune as bookkeeping. I mean, a fine lady shouldn't have to waste her time with all them piddling numbers—" A car backfired, so Belle didn't hear the rest, but she noticed, in spite of all his work to rid himself of his Cajun accent, when he got going, "that" slid into "dat," and "think" became "tink."

She stopped for a mule cart. Bourrée continued his plea. "I mean, shouldn't you be doing good works or teaching in one of them new schools they're setting up to educate ladies on how to vote?" Belle crossed the street. Bourrée followed her. "We men need y'all to point us in the right direction. You're our better half."

"Thank you for your confidence and the ride into Hammond," Belle said as she untied Loyal. She stroked his nose and whispered in his ear, "Don't you worry. Food and water are coming up."

Bourrée tried to help her climb into her buggy, but she managed quite well without his assistance. His voice rose in pitch until it was almost a whine. "Do you know anything about bookkeeping?"

She turned back and, shielding her eyes from the sun, said, "Enough."

BELLE WANTED TO FLY back to Gentry, but after a trip to the local livery stable, where Loyal was fed, watered, and groomed, he set one foot in front of another at a slow clip and then a slower clop. There's nothing worse than your heart racing with impatience while your body is caught poking along at four or five miles an hour. She was afraid once Bourrée got his hands on the books, he'd be able to make the numbers dance a jig and they'd never know the difference. Miss Effie was mesmerized by him. Belle knew she had to take charge now, before it was too late.

She pulled into Gentry a little before six and tied up Loyal in front of Rubinstein's "Emporium of Fashion, Dry Goods, Grocery, Hardware, Feed, and Seed." Kicking the dust off her shoes, she entered the main department, with its dark-paneled walls and high ceilings. She wanted to rush up to the office and get Abe's help right away.

But Vince Stefano, who sold men's straw hats, stopped her to say hello. Then Angelina Monotti, who was measuring out a length of chintz, waved her over to ask after Miss Effie, while she and her customer gawked at Belle's cloche and the fringe of hair curling around her cheek.

Curtis, Stella's son, caught up with her in front of a display of men's work clothes. He hadn't been at the chapel, being less than enthusiastic about church attendance of any sort, but he'd heard how she'd tried to help his uncle. As she described what she'd seen and what the sheriff had said he'd do, they were joined by a janitor and a deliveryman who shook their heads and made humming noises over her story.

She was stopped again and again as she made her way through the store. She couldn't help but wonder if any of the genial men, who inquired so solicitously about Miss Effie and Cady, had been among the vigilantes.

The office was upstairs in an open mezzanine, where Abe and his staff could watch what happened on the sales floor. The girls in the front office were getting ready to go home. They gathered around Belle; asking after Cady and Miss Effie, all the while staring at her new bob. Mary Louise Pruett said the bob suited her. "Of course, I could never get away with it." The others laughed at the very idea of Mary Louise bobbing her hair. "But it definitely suits you."

"It's so modern," another said, in a tone of voice that indicated "modern" wasn't quite nice.

A third patted Belle on the arm and said nothing, although whether in mute encouragement or dumbstruck horror, Belle couldn't tell. Just then Rafe appeared in the doorway in his shirt-sleeves.

"Is Abe around?" Belle asked as the rest of the office staff fled before Rafe could think up some more work for them to do.

"He went home early."

"Is he all right?"

"Just tired. Is there something I can do for you, Mrs.

Cantrell?" His tone was polite, if a bit distant. He was standing on the step that separated the outer and inner offices. She had to crane her neck to look up at him.

"I thought maybe he could teach me bookkeeping. I'll come back tomorrow."

"Do you need a job?"

She heard the alacrity in his voice. *Got a problem? I'll fix it.* Just like a man, she thought. But on second thought she realized, *That's just what I like in a man. Claude was like that. Little talk, but big do.*

And yet she sensed a reserve in Rafe, no, something beyond reserve, that put her off. Did he think she was chasing after him? "We have a big farm. I want to be able to keep the books myself." Belle had never paid much attention to numbers at school, but then nobody ever expected girls to be any good at numbers. "It can't be that hard." Her voice wasn't confident, but it was hopeful.

"It's not," he said, noticing for the first time how tiny her waist was in her neat linen skirt and white shirtwaist.

She waited for him to say more, to make her an offer, but he didn't. "I'll give Abe a call, then. Good night, Mr. Berlin."

He watched her turn, listened to her heels click across the wooden floor. When she reached the stairs, he said, "Mrs. Cantrell, wait. I can teach you."

She smiled to herself. *Nothing like turning your back on a man to pique his interest.* That was an old rule from her Southern Girls' Guide to Men. But it took this one long enough. "I wouldn't want to impose," she said sweetly.

She'd been ready to flee, he thought. He wished he weren't so awkward these days. "I haven't exactly plunged into a whirl of social obligations."

In spite of his lack of gallantry—what can you expect from a Yankee?—she let herself be led into the main office.

A big silver fan whirred at them from the floor, pressing her skirt to her legs. He stared at them for a second before shifting his eyes, embarrassed. "Sit here." As soon as he said it, he could have kicked himself. He sounded as if he were talking to a dog. Sit. Trying too abruptly to recover, he all but elbowed her aside as he pulled out Abe's old desk chair.

Belle sat on the hard wooden seat and suppressed a silly desire to twirl around. The store was emptying out. Department heads waved good-bye from below. She watched Rafe walk over to a shelf and pull out a big black ledger.

He brought a straight-backed chair up to the desk and sat next to her. Sitting so close, he could almost taste her scent. He pictured wildflowers, woodsy and fresh, with a hint of jasmine and a sweetness all her own, a sweetness that stirred him in a nameless way.

She moved away from him. With her bobbed hair, she didn't want to risk giving him the wrong idea. Besides, she was here to learn bookkeeping. He opened the ledger and pointed to the debit column. "Debits are always on the left," he said, and began a dissertation. Claude had taught her some of the rudiments of bookkeeping before he went to war. She knew where the debits and credits went. From time to time he looked into her eyes to be sure she grasped what he was saying. She nodded. His voice grew warmer. *Men love to lecture to a captive audience,* Belle thought. *It makes them feel big and smart.* That was another rule she'd long ago found worthy of her Southern Girls' Guide to Men.

"You want me to lock up?" Harry Chambers, head of the men's department, asked as he came into the outer office. "Oh, hey, Belle. I didn't know you were still here." Harry had played baseball with Claude. They'd gone to the war together, and he'd been at that poker game the night Claude was killed. Harry was big, a real man's man. His customers liked the way he looked in his suits, and Harry always wore the best Rubinstein's sold. Abe gave them to him for free. He called it a promotional expense.

"Get that smirk off your face, Harry Chambers. Mr. Berlin has offered to teach me bookkeeping."

Harry raised an eyebrow, giving them an is-that-what-you-call-it? look. But all he said was, "Yes, ma'am." And then he said, "Like your new haircut. It's . . . uh . . . creative." Belle knew in Harry's world, "creative" was not a compliment. He went down the stairs whistling.

When he was gone, Rafe said, "I don't want to cast a cloud over your reputation."

Belle nodded. "You're right." As much as she wanted to learn what she needed to know to keep the books, the Primer of Propriety decreed, No *widow, especially if she's young enough to have her own teeth, can risk behavior the least bit unconventional without the Deacons of Decency descending upon her.* She'd just have to learn another day. She thanked him and clattered down the linoleum-covered stairs after Harry.

Abe would teach her. But when? Not during the day. He was always so busy with customers, visits from traveling salesmen, orders going astray, shipments coming in. She'd call and make an appointment to stop by the house after supper. That's what she'd do. Once he felt better.

But Belle hated to wait.

For anything.

She wanted to learn the basics now, tonight, before that Bourrée character started in earnest as overseer. She thought about his too handsome face, that square jaw, those steel blue eyes, and the effect he had on Miss Effie. All right, she had to admit it, the effect he had on her, too.

As she left the stairwell, she saw Harry approach the main entrance. He already had his straw hat on. His massive body was silhouetted against the glass door. He had broad shoulders, like Bourrée's. They cut out the light.

Harry raised a big brass key ring. Maybe she was overdramatizing her fears. Bourrée might be perfectly honest. She had to think about her reputation. She started to call out. Harry's keys chattered to one another as he opened the front door.

But what if Bourrée's plan was to take advantage of the poor widow women? It wouldn't be the first time a handsome young man came sniffing around a farm full of women. He didn't look like the type who'd be satisfied with farmwork for long.

Outside, a car backfired.

Belle watched Harry close the door behind him. As he turned to lock it, she stepped back into the stairwell. She doubted Harry would talk. He'd been friends with Claude. Not that that would count for much. He hadn't offered to testify against Pruett Walker. But he worked for the Rubinsteins. He wouldn't want to put his job on the line by bad-mouthing one of their kin. Besides, a woman's good reputation was supposed to protect her, not make her more vulnerable to exploitation.

Rafe had his hat in his hand when he heard her coming back. "You miss Harry? I'll let you out." He stood at the top of the stairs watching her mount.

"I want to learn tonight." She hoped she didn't sound desperate.

Rafe smiled for the first time. But his face didn't light up. It was a wry smile that covered acres of hurt. "You want to learn bookkeeping in a couple of hours?" Did she think he had some magic formula?

"As much as you can teach me."

He hesitated, but he might as well do this as something else. Besides, there was her scent of wildflowers and jasmine. "I'll do what I can." He ushered her into the executive office and once again held the chair steady for her to sit down. She bent toward the ledger. He began by itemizing all the things she should put in the right-hand column under credits. "Sales. Accounts receivable." She forced herself to listen. But as Rafe ran his beautiful long fingers down the right-hand column, she found it difficult to concentrate on his words. His nails were rounded and buffed and so very clean. Claude's hands had always had a trace of the earth in their rough cracks, no matter how often he washed. That had never bothered her. But clean male hands, really clean hands, without cracks or tears, would be nice, too. She wondered what these smooth hands would feel like if they happened to brush against her cheek or slide down her neck.

He's married! The Primer of Propriety practically shouted, *A well-bred lady would never allow herself to imagine secret pleasures with a married man.* On the other hand, Belle thought, *a girl can't be too hard on herself for giving in to the pleasure of imagination. As long as the pleasure stays right there in the imagination.*

He stopped and took a cigarette out of a silver case. "Do you mind?"

"Not at all. I find the smell—" Belle paused. "Manly."

She waited for Rafe to preen, but she was disappointed. What's wrong with him? she wondered as she watched his hands caress a silver lighter. She observed the way he stroked it until it fired. She imagined those hands stroking her. It's just in the imagination, she reminded herself. All in the imagination.

"Excuse me. May I offer you one?"

Without realizing what she was doing, she had wrapped her arms around herself. "I beg your pardon!"

"A cigarette, do you want a cigarette?"

No man had ever offered her a cigarette before. She knew what Gentry's Guardians of Goodness would say: *Decent women don't smoke. Them that do end up in a good-time house.* But she'd read magazine articles about girls smoking. All those liberated women in Paris and Chicago were probably puffing away like mad right now. She'd bet they had plenty of good times, without ever stepping inside a good-time house. She hesitated, and then, feeling very daring, said, "Thank you."

He flicked open his cigarette case. His movements are so graceful, she thought. She picked out a cigarette and held it between her fingers as she had seen him do.

He leaned into her and struck his lighter, noticing for the first time that her eyes were hazel, somewhere between green and brown and flecked with gold. He saw twin fires light up in them.

His eyes look like the river after a rain, she thought, warm and brown. You could get lost in eyes like those. She imagined him leaning just a little closer, their lips touching, his beautiful hands sliding down her body.

What in the world am I doing! This is carrying the imagination too far. Concentrate on the cigarette, she told herself. The cigarette. She held it to the fire. The tobacco flared, but didn't light.

He laughed. "Don't blow out. Suck in." He pursed his lips as if for a kiss.

She puckered up and inhaled. The smoke entered her throat. She began to choke. She threw the cigarette into the ashtray. "You do this for fun?"

He laughed again. "Maybe you've had enough accounting for one day."

"No!" Embarrassment swept over her. "Claude taught me some of the basic concepts, before he went away, but . . . now you're going to think I'm stupid, but I'm not." She could never abide women who pretended to be brainless to trap a man. She figured if a man wanted a brainless girl, there were plenty of them to go around. But she felt stupid when she had to admit, "I've always had a lot of trouble with arithmetic, adding up a lot of figures. I can handle two or three, but . . ." Her voice trailed off.

"Let's see." He took a piece of scratch paper and wrote down a column of numbers. He held out the page. Their hands brushed. They both drew back as if they'd been shocked.

Oh, Lord, she thinks I'm making a pass at her. I have to be careful, he thought.

He's a gentleman and doesn't want to lead me on. That's very nice, she tried to tell herself, but it didn't feel nice. She felt abandoned.

"Can you add this column?" She bent over the page. The collar of her shirtwaist separated from her neck. He caught a glimpse of the pale hair at the top of her spine. After feeling nothing for so long, he was surprised to find he had an urge to bend over that white neck and kiss it. He was examining this new impulse, rolling it around in his mind, when she sat up triumphantly. Her eyes were shining. She had the sum.

The wrong sum.

Belle felt as if her newly bobbed hair was drooping along with her dignity.

"Don't worry," he said, which was very nice of him considering what a fool she'd made of herself. "We're not stuck in the last century. We have machines for this now." He got up.

The sleeve of his jacket brushed her arm. The material was soft, as if silk were blended with fine linen. She wondered if he'd had the suit made for him in France or by some tailor in Chicago. She watched the way it seemed to flow over his long, lean body. All the middle-class men in Gentry wore suits, even the workingmen had one for Sunday, but none of them flowed. He picked up a boxy machine something like a typewriter, but with numbers instead of letters on the keys. He placed the contraption in front of her. She read the word printed on the side. "A 'Compto-meter'?" she asked.

"It rhymes with thermometer," he said.

The scent of his cologne was mixed with tobacco now. It was lovely. She decided to take up smoking, even if it made her sick.

"All you have to do is punch in the numbers."

"Do I pull the lever?"

He shook his head. "The lever clears it."

Belle tried to concentrate. But the figures on the page and the ones in her fingers didn't match. Numbers would get transposed, or worse, left out. He seemed baffled. "I'm not stupid," she said. She could see he wasn't convinced.

"Maybe you should leave the bookkeeping to someone else."

"No! I mean, I have to do it myself. My mother-in-law hired a new overseer. He wants to keep the books. And the men he's associating with—" She didn't tell him the men were her stepfather and Brother Scaggs, her childhood minister. "They could beat Mr. Houdini when it comes to making things disappear, especially other people's money."

Belle studied Rafe's face until she saw the look she was counting on. *Good men love to solve a girl's problems for her. All you have to do is ask sweetly and then wait until they've figured out how.* It was one of the first rules she'd discovered when she'd started her Southern Girls' Guide to Men and Other Perils of Modern Life, back in high school.

"I went to this progressive school in Chicago. They taught us a trick for adding up columns. Here, let me show you. Let's take this column of ten numbers again. This time just concentrate on adding the digits on the right. Okay?"

"Sure, but that's what I did before."

He seemed to ignore her and said, "Start from the bottom. What are the first two numbers?"

"Seven. I don't have any trouble until they hit twenty-seven or thirty-six or three hundred and ten and then I lose my place."

"It's the same with everyone."

"Even you?"

He almost laughed. "Even me. I'll teach you a way to keep your place."

She relaxed. Maybe she wasn't such an ignorant country girl after all. "Really?" He didn't grace that with an answer. She knew why. She was an ignorant country girl.

"The first number is seven and the next number is five, so that makes?"

"Twelve."

"Now, here's the trick. Put a mark on the right, next to the twelve. Now all you have to remember is the two. The next number is nine. What's nine and two?"

"Eleven. Do I put another mark?"

"Right! Now all you have to remember is one."

She looked up at him and was distracted by his long, black eyelashes. Inappropriate feelings began to snake up her thighs. Why did she have to have inappropriate feelings around a married man? It wasn't fair. She wondered if he was feeling them, too.

"You make a mark every time the numbers add up to ten or higher. This way you don't have to keep track of the second digit."

Obviously, he didn't have any feelings for her at all. She was simply a girl who'd flattered him. Concentrate on the numbers and not on his long, black eyelashes, she admonished herself. You've got to learn this. "So when I get to the top, all I have to do is count up the marks and add that number to the middle digit?"

"You've got it."

She raced through the column of numbers. "Five thousand two hundred seventy-three?"

"Perfect."

"Why didn't anyone teach me this before? It's fun, like doing a puzzle. Give me another."

Rafe crushed out his cigarette and watched her race through long columns of numbers, carefully checking digits. She was getting the sum right every time. Her wild scent seemed to enter his body. He wondered what she'd do if he leaned over and kissed her, licked his tongue over the pale hairs on the back of her neck. She'd probably scream, that's what she'd do. He could see the headlines now: "Depraved Yankee Jew Preys on Flower of Southern Womanhood." It had been only five years since Leo Frank was lynched.

"Twenty-two thousand, seven hundred and nine!" She looked up at him like a child. There was an adorable vulnerability about her. "Did I get it right?"

"You got it right."

Belle flushed with pride. She looked into those deep brown eyes and willed him to kiss her. She hadn't been kissed since Claude. Of course she knew all about what nice girls were supposed to do, and they were not supposed to kiss a man just because he'd taught them how to add up a column of figures. Miss Effie said, *A nice girl doesn't kiss a man until she's engaged.* Belle had somewhat reluctantly added that rule to the Primer of Propriety and had cautioned her daughter. But she didn't need a primer to tell her *A nice girl doesn't kiss a married man under any circumstances.* A girl could get into a lot of trouble by not being nice. She promised herself she was going to be nice from now on. However, she felt that part of herself that wasn't her body, exactly, but was linked to her body, lean forward.

"You're adorable," he said, and leaned forward to meet her. But as his lips brushed hers he pulled back. "Excuse me. I . . . er . . . I apologize. I shouldn't have—"

She sat up straight and patted her hair, surprised for a moment that it was so short. *A serious young woman does not mix business with pleasure.* She knew that. She started to say something, tried to think of something businesslike to say, anything, but the pain in his eyes stopped her. Wait a minute, he'd said, *You're adorable.* That sounded like something a soldier would say to a French floozy, didn't it? Just then the telephone rang.

Rafe reached for the receiver, pulling it and the tall mouthpiece to him in one hand. "Hello." Suddenly he became totally serious. "When?" And then, "I'll be right there." He hung up. "Abe had another heart attack."

Chapter 6

"COME ON, LOYAL. Get a move on!" Belle called as she snapped the whip over the horse's ears. Rafe had offered to drive her in his sporty car. Belle was tempted, but she didn't want to leave Loyal tied up on Grand Avenue, and she didn't want to give the Deacons of Decency any more to gossip about. The horse jogged for a few feet to show he could, and then settled into his usual clip-clop.

Belle cracked the whip again. This time Loyal ignored her and high-stepped regally down Grand Avenue, past Commerce, to Education Drive. Having been woken up before dawn and forced to stand for half a day at the Hammond depot without his morning feed, he was not in the mood to hurry just to satisfy some petty human concern.

Belle's heart was racing. Abe couldn't die. He was her rock.

She wished she had the knack of belief so she could pray for him. A good God wouldn't let Abe die. Not now. He wasn't even fifty. So for a second time that day, Belle wished. She wished for a good God, a God so good He'd keep Abe safe. She'd gladly sacrifice a sheep or a goat if that would help. She received no answer.

Loyal picked up speed when they turned into Hope, then stopped in his accustomed place in front of the fence. Belle jumped off the wagon and ran up the steps. She found Rachel in the long central hall. She was sitting on the couch, her arm around her daughter, Nina. The girl's dark curls had fallen across her face like a veil.

"How is he?" Belle asked, out of breath.

Rachel shook her head. "It seems to be milder than the last one. A sudden pain."

Nina unwound herself from her mother and went to Belle. "Dr. Vickerson kicked us out of his room."

"He did?" Belle said, hugging the girl who was in so many ways the child of her heart. Nina had her college all picked out, and after her father's first heart attack, she'd announced she intended to go to medical school.

"Do you think Dr. Vickerson knows what he's doing?" Nina asked.

"Of course he does," her mother snapped at the same time that Belle said, "I don't know."

Belle sat down in a big armchair. She wondered where Rafe was and figured he must be in back. Nina squeezed in next to her.

Buster Rubinstein, age fifteen, still in his baseball uniform, rocked assertively back and forth in a belle époque rocker, making it groan on the Oriental carpet.

"Stop it, Buster!" Rachel said sharply. The boy stood and stomped out. "Honey, come back. I'm sorry. Buster!" Rachel called after him. His only answer was the slamming of a door. The chair continued to rock.

"Nina, go talk to your brother. Tell him I still love him." The girl turned to Belle.

"Go on, honey. We'll talk later," Belle said.

"You'll tell me the truth?" the girl whispered. "The true truth?"

Belle hesitated. She didn't like to come between Rachel and her daughter, but she saw how frightened Nina was. Belle nodded. The girl kissed her on the cheek and followed her brother.

"What was that about?" Rachel asked.

"She's scared." Rachel raised her eyebrows as if to say, Who isn't? "She wants to know the truth about her daddy. The 'true truth.' It'll be easier for her in the long run."

"What truth? I want to know the true truth, too. Doctors—" She shook her head angrily and left the sentence dangling in the air.

Belle considered saying one of those phrases meant to soothe, one of those phrases Miss Effie would use, such as, "Don't worry. He'll be all right." But she knew better than to offer phony comfort. Rachel had every right to worry. Besides, Belle had seen too much in the last couple of years to be able to get her mouth around those empty words.

Rafe came in from the kitchen with a cocktail shaker and three cone-shaped glasses on a silver tray. A green olive resided in the bottom of each glass. He's always doing something, Belle thought. He smiled at her, his lips curving upward under sad brown eyes. In spite of her worry, she could almost feel those smooth lips brushing hers. This is no time for such mental pictures! she upbraided herself. But she felt herself lean forward.

"Would you care for a drink, Mrs. Cantrell?" He set down the silver tray and filled the first conical glass with a clear liquid, which Belle suspected was not water.

She'd only drunk liquor a few times in her life: a small glass of champagne on her wedding day, a swallow of bourbon once when she and Claude were cutting up at home and Miss Effie was out, a sip of raw moonshine at a juke joint where she and

Claude went to dance, and a glass of sherry with the ladies after his funeral. She'd never much cared for the taste, which was fortunate, because if there was one thing Miss Effie, the Methodists, the Baptists, and especially the Church of Everlasting Redemption agreed on, it was: *Drunkenness in a man is loathsome, but a gin-soaked woman is the devil's own playpen.* That was a rule from the Down-Home Primer of Right Behavior, a rule a Gentry lady broke at her peril.

Belle had never seen Rachel take a cocktail or anything else alcoholic. But this evening she picked up one of those funny-shaped glasses, looked at her brother, and merely said, "Thanks." She turned to Belle. "Rafe makes us martinis when we're alone at our country house outside Chicago. But you don't have to burden Abe with that information."

"This is a martini?" Belle had read about such drinks in magazines, but of course she'd never tasted one.

"My speciality." Rafe offered her a glass.

Belle hesitated. *If cigarettes lead to a good-time house, what in the world do martinis lead to?* She put that thought out of her head. If Rachel can handle it, so can I. Feeling very sophisticated, not to mention daring, she said, "Thank you." The liquid slouched a bit over the rim, imparting its pungent smell to her fingers as she grasped the stem. A whole new world was opening up for her.

"*L'chaim,*" Rafe said to his sister.

A tear welled up in Rachel's eye. She turned to Belle. "It means . . ." Her voice broke. She took a sip of her drink.

"To life," Rafe said. His voice rumbled in Belle's chest. She felt tears stick in her throat. Brother and sister sipped their drinks in silence. Belle put her glass to her mouth. The first taste was shocking. Her tongue recoiled. But as the cold liquid passed her throat, she felt a warmth settle in her chest and slide down through her body. As brother and sister brooded on Abe's condition, Belle took a second sip. "Waste not, want not" were the watchwords of her impoverished childhood. This time her tongue did not recoil. As the alcohol slipped down, she realized she didn't feel any different at all. She took another sip. She still didn't feel any different, except the anxiety that had been dogging her began to lift a little.

Rachel told them Abe had been in the kitchen tasting the redfish Creole Josephine was fixing for dinner when he'd felt a sudden burning in his upper abdomen. "It could be indigestion," Belle said. "I've had Josephine's redfish."

Rachel said nothing, but she seemed to admit to a ray of hope.

"I'm sure that's all it is," Belle said, squeezing her friend's hand. Belle's spirits had lifted. She was in a downright positive mood.

Rafe refilled their glasses.

Belle started to protest. *A gin-soaked woman is the devil's own playpen.* She giggled. She didn't feel gin soaked. She didn't feel drunk. She didn't feel anything.

Well, she felt good.

The martini shimmered. Little slivers of ice floated on the top. They glittered in the light. The cone sides of the glass sweated in the humid evening air. She reached for the glass. She could take one more sip without it affecting her. Her fingers made an interesting mark in the condensation. Holding the cold glass by the stem, she took another taste.

The world was looking up. Abe was probably suffering from nothing worse than indigestion, and she was having a martini. Two martinis, to be precise. But why be precise when she felt so warm and lovely?

She settled back in her chair. To take his sister's mind off Abe, Rafe turned the conversation to the suffrage amendment. "What do you think the chances are Tennessee will ratify?"

"Tennessee!" Belle said, and took another sip. She watched them turn to her. "Tennessee is . . ." But, although the thought made perfect sense in her mind, in fact, it was clear and eloquent, the distance from her mind to her mouth was too great. She stopped talking. Her cheeks felt numb. She saw Rafe and Rachel looking at her. Were they still waiting for her to speak? She licked her lips. They felt numb, too. Rachel took the glass out of her hand and set it on the tray. Belle didn't object.

The loud ring of the doorbell made her start. The beveled-glass insert in the front door revealed a tall, sweet-faced man.

"Hide the liquor!" Rachel said.

Brother Frank Meadows, the Methodist minister, was standing under the porch light.

"Too late, he's seen us," Rafe said.

Belle bumped the silver tray with her knee. Her martini shimmered. She didn't waste words; in fact, she had no words to waste. She put the funny glasses and the cocktail shaker back on the silver tray and stood up. It took her a moment to get her balance. When she had it, she headed for the dining room. She'd forgotten how far away it was.

"Won't he smell it?" Rafe asked, following her.

"Of course," Belle said, feeling the room sway. The shock of seeing the preacher hadn't sobered her up as much as it had jarred something loose. She still felt numb, but she was no longer paralyzed. "Brother Meadows," Belle said, and stopped. Did she say "brother" or "broder"? She didn't think she was slurring, but just to be on the safe side, she concentrated on her diction. "Brother Meadows is a man of high moral principles."

Rafe took the tray from her and placed it on top of the sideboard.

"Most of the men in his church drink. They just don't rub his face in it." Belle felt confident that she had gotten hold of her tongue. She wasn't so tipsy after all. She opened a door in the sideboard, held on to the top, and knelt down to find a place to stash the booze. The kneeling down gave her a little trouble. How was she going to reach the tray?

Rafe picked it up and knelt next to her. "That seems awfully hypocritical," he said as he slipped the offending drinks out of sight. They were on their knees, close together. Belle turned to him. Their faces were inches apart. She could feel the warmth of his breath.

"Of course it is. Don't you know? *The most important thing about virtue is to talk as if you're in favor of it.*"

"Did you just make that up?" He seemed delighted with her wit.

She preened. "It's pretty obvious, isn't it? I mean, life wouldn't be worth living if you actually had to *be* virtuous." What did I say? Oh, gosh, now he's going to think I'm a fallen woman. Why can't I ever keep my mouth shut?

He took her hand and helped her stand. "You have a very original mind." Belle nodded weakly and wondered if that was a good thing. "That's a good thing," he said. She wanted to kiss him for saying so.

Rachel had shepherded the minister out of the central hall, away from any fumes that might still be hovering there, and into the formal living room with its low art nouveau couches and curved end tables. A grand piano covered with a Chinese shawl stood in the corner.

"You know the whole congregation has been praying for Abe," Brother Meadows said. He pressed her hands in his.

"We do, and we appreciate that, Frank," Rachel said.

He looked up and saw Belle silhouetted in the doorway. "Belle. How nice to—" The minister paused, staring at her hair as Rachel clicked on a soft Tiffany lamp. Belle knew her bob wasn't a sin. At least she hoped it wasn't. How could a haircut be a sin? He couldn't actually preach against it in church.

Could he? She waited for him to speak. It took a while, which was unusual, because if there was one thing Brother Meadows enjoyed above all else, it was the sound of his own voice. "How . . . how very nice to see you," he said at last.

She fluffed her bob and floated into the room. She had nothing to worry about. She was Belle Cantrell, the woman with an original mind. The witty Belle Cantrell. She heard her shoe click once on the hardwood floor and then she felt her sole sink into the softness of the Oriental rug. She took a second step, but her high heel caught on the fringe. The rug captured her shoe. Belle stumbled headlong into the startled preacher.

He toppled back, catching himself on the mantelpiece, knocking over a cut-crystal vase. A profusion of wet hydrangeas soared onto silk cushions and rosewood tables. Water poured onto the hearth and Oriental carpet in rivulets.

Belle tried to hold her breath, afraid a miasma of gin and vermouth would envelop the minister if she opened her mouth. A blue hydrangea had found its way to the top of her head. Rafe and Rachel sprang into action. Rachel ran to the kitchen for towels. Rafe righted the vase and picked up the wet flowers.

"Are you all right?" Brother Meadows asked. His voice was filled with Christian solicitude.

Belle nodded encouragingly, still holding her breath.

She could feel her face turning red. Her head was ready to explode. Facing away from the minister, Belle pulled herself up into her dignity and took the blue hydrangea off her head. She tried to walk away with stately composure, but forgot she was wearing only one high-heeled shoe. She settled for hobbling and falling into the nearest chair. Afraid to go any farther, she looked up at Brother Meadows and smiled hopefully.

"We haven't seen enough of you in church this year." Had his voice slipped from compassionate to chastising? Did he suspect she'd been drinking? Brother Meadows was no fool.

Belle rearranged her composure. She was far enough away from him now to risk speaking, and after all, she was the witty Belle Cantrell. Paying careful attention to her diction, she said, "I'll be there next Sunday." Did she say next or *nes*? She covered by proclaiming, "It's always such a pleasure to listen to you preach."

Oops! Did that sound sarcastic? She didn't mean it to sound sarcastic. Brother Meadows had a good heart. He believed in Christian love and good works. She knew that, but once that man stood in front of an audience, it was darn near impossible to shut him up. Okay, the sentiment was sarcastic. She just hadn't meant it to sound that way. Where was The Primer of Propriety when you needed it? She picked a purple hydrangea off a silk footstool and handed it to Rafe.

Why had she drunk that martini? And why had she dipped into the second one? She was only a step away from scandal. A small step. A mere hop.

As Rachel mopped up the hearth, Rafe unhooked Belle's shoe from the carpet and slipped it on her foot. She hadn't meant to close her eyes when his hands caressed her arch and ankle. She pried them open and found Brother Meadows watching her. Adjusting her mouth into an imitation of a prune, she brought her handkerchief to it.

At that moment, Dr. Vickerson came in carrying his black medical bag. He was a short, round man, with thinning white hair and a cheery, can-do disposition. He loved marching into his examining room with all the majesty of medicine, and announcing he could fix whatever ailed the patient. He was Dr. Good News. But he was well aware of the limits of his profession, so he'd long ago bestowed upon his junior associate, Dr. Fulsom Pruett, most of those pesky house calls, letting him travel around the parish in all kinds of weather to deliver bad news, because except for births, if you had to call a doctor out in the middle of the night, there usually wasn't much medical science could do.

Dr. Vickerson made exceptions for patients like Abe Rubinstein. First of all, they'd become friends. Abe was a college graduate, and there weren't a lot of them in Gentry. Second, he lived only a couple of blocks from the office. Third, and perhaps most important to a country doctor, he paid his bills on time and in cash.

"He's doing fine. Nina's in with him now," the doctor said.

At that moment the doorbell rang again.

"I'll get it." Belle stood, a little too quickly. The room seemed to sway around her. Being extra careful to pick up her feet, she walked to the door. She didn't know she was tilting to the right.

Darvin Rutledge, of Rutledge Ford and Livery, and his pretty, blond wife, Debbie Lou, stood on the porch. He was big, with a ruddy complexion from too much duck hunting in inclement weather. Or maybe his complexion simply came from the home brew on which Darvin had grown up and to which he was immoderately partial. "Saw the doctor's car on my way home." His voice was hardy and concerned.

"We didn't want Rachel to be alone," Debbie Lou said. Carrying a home-baked pie, she leaned toward Belle for the obligatory Southern kiss on the cheek. Belle stepped back, but she must not have stepped back far enough, or the odorous fumes of gin still hung over her, because Debbie Lou paused and then her eyes lit up. She stepped up to Belle, gave her a hug, and whispered, "Honey, have you been drinking?"

I'm ruined, Belle thought. I should have followed those Priestesses of Prim down the straight and narrow, before it was too late. Miss Effie warned me. Heck, everybody warned me. But no, I had to do things my way.

Instead of censure, though, Belle caught a wicked gleam in Debbie Lou's eyes. She's envious. She thinks I'm wild and free!

If only. "Whatever gave you that idea?" she said in a voice of lofty propriety as the two women exchanged conspiratorial glances. She wondered if Debbie Lou shared her husband's enthusiasm for white lightning.

Belle took the pie, smelling of fresh-baked peaches, into the kitchen. She was tilting to the left.

"You better eat some of that pie." Josephine, the Rubinsteins' cook, had stayed late to help out. "You got to get some food in you, girl, before you go out there and make a fool of yourself."

"Too late for that," Belle said, plopping down at the kitchen table. She and Josephine had worked together at the hotel when they were both young. Josephine set a cup of coffee and a piece of pie in front of her and clucked about her hair. She made Belle take her hat off so she could get a better look.

Belle was feeling more like herself by the time she entered the front bedroom with its deep blue-and-gold, peacock-feathered wallpaper. Nina sat on her father's bed holding his hand. Over the mantelpiece was a painting of a serene woman standing in front of a bright yellow Chinese screen covered with white chrysanthemums. Next to it, a fragile milk-glass vase held a profusion of roses. They perfumed the air. White curtains floated in the breeze in front of a triple set of casement windows. This was not a room that welcomed death.

Abe sat up and smoothed down the sheet. "Belle! How nice of you to drop by. You're looking lovely, as always." She handed him a piece of pie and abruptly sat down on the bed. A wry look crossed his face. "My brother-in-law been plying you with liquor?"

Belle played with her hair. Her expression admitted nothing. "Why on earth would you say that?"

"You better watch out for him."

Changing the subject is the better part of valor, or something, Belle thought, but that didn't sound quite right. Assuming a

mock-censorious expression, she asked, "What do you think you're doing scaring us like this?"

His cheeks were white, his lips an unhealthy gray. "I just wanted to add a little drama to your lives. Don't you appreciate it?"

Belle glared at him. "Thank you very much, but when I want drama, I'll go to the picture show." Abe smiled as he leaned back into his pillows.

SHE RETURNED TO the living room to hear Dr. Vickerson tell Rachel, "The most important thing is to keep him calm. I don't want you-all to worry him about anything. Understand?"

"Tom—"

He didn't let her finish. "I've been reading up on heart attacks. Emotional strain can be every bit as dangerous as physical, so if you have any troubles, keep them to yourself. Think you can do that?" He waited for her to nod, but she shook her head. "Tell the children, if they have a problem, to bring it to you. Okay?" This was not a question, and he wasn't going to take no for an answer.

"I guess so." Rachel's voice was weak.

"Good!" Any victory, no matter how slight, was a victory in Dr. Vickerson's book. "Now, I don't want you to let him climb stairs or pick up heavy boxes."

"But that's what he does at the store."

"Well, get somebody else to do it from now on. He should take it easy, anyway, work part-time. Can you get some help?"

"I don't know. We're pretty stretched."

"I don't want him to be under any stress at all, you hear?"

Rachel nodded weakly. "Good. Now, you just do what I tell you, and Abe will be fine, you hear? Don't you worry, now." Belle could see Rachel wanted to scream.

"We'll all pitch in," Darvin Rutledge said, in his bluff, good-natured way.

"That's right," echoed his pretty wife.

Belle knew they meant well, but what could they do? For the rest of his life, what was left of it, Abe would be an invalid.

Rachel excused herself to sit with her husband. Belle watched Brother Meadows chat with Darvin. Picking up her feet with vigilance, she gathered the coffee cups. She was no longer tilting, but there was a definite lurch to her steps. Passing the hall door, she saw Rachel and Rafe talking softly. With tears streaming down her face, Rachel kissed her brother and went into the master bedroom.

Belle lingered in the kitchen. Josephine made her drink another cup of coffee. When she returned to the living room, the neighbors were leaving.

"Let me drive you home," Rafe said.

"I have my wagon."

"I don't think you should drive home alone tonight."

Belle always appreciated men trying to be gallant, even when it wasn't logical—especially when it wasn't logical. After all, he'd let her ride home in her buggy the night before. But maybe this wasn't gallantry after all. Maybe he didn't trust her to find her way after a martini. Okay, after almost two martinis. But she was sure Loyal would know his way home. Well, pretty sure. "I'll manage."

"He's right, Belle. You better let him drive you home tonight," Debbie Lou Rutledge said.

Motoring in the moonlight with a married man, especially this married man, is inviting trouble, Belle thought. Didn't the Primer of Propriety say: *A girl alone will have enough trouble knocking at her door, without inviting it in.* It was something like that. "I can't leave Loyal. He needs to be fed and—"

Debbie Lou turned to her husband and said sweetly, "You can take Belle's horse over to the livery stable, can't you?"

"Sure can. We'll take real good care of him. I'll come out and pick you up tomorrow morning. Might even sell you a car on the way back to town. It's time you got one, living way out in the country and all."

Brother Meadows looked uncomfortable. "Why don't you-all take Nina with you? Be good for her to get some fresh air." His voice had turned from compassionate to uncompromising.

"She has class first thing in the morning," Rafe said. Nina was taking a special college-prep math course.

"It's summertime. She doesn't need to go to school," Debbie Lou chirped.

"Her teacher will understand," Brother Meadows assured him.

Rafe looked at these people as if they'd lost their minds, but nobody was paying any attention to him. They had turned to Belle.

"Brother Meadows is right. Nina should come with us," she said.

Belle hung back from the long kissing and handshaking that marked Southern leave-taking. Even though she felt sober, she didn't trust how she might smell. She assured everyone, twice, that Nina would indeed accompany them to the farm.

"I expect to see you in church on Sunday, Belle. I'm planning to preach a sermon especially for you."

"I can't wait."

THEY DROVE THROUGH the moon-bright night with the top down. Nina, who had started the journey sitting between Belle's knees, fell asleep after Belle assured her that the adults weren't keeping secrets. "Your daddy pulled through again. We have to be grateful for that."

"I'm as grateful as I can be, but that doesn't cut it. I want to know what's going to happen to him."

"Honey, nobody knows the future, even a doctor who went to medical school at Tulane."

"I'm going to medical school in Chicago," said Nina with confidence and determination. "Then I'll take care of him." Belle kissed the back of her head.

Lulled by the motion of the car, the girl, exhausted from hours of anxiety, slipped downward, her knees spread apart, her feet turned in, her head lolling on Belle's chest. Belle held her tightly around the waist.

"I still don't understand why we had to drag Nina out. She's had a rough enough day."

"Mr. Berlin, to you this is simply a motorcar. To Brother Meadows and my mother-in-law, we are riding in a good-time house on wheels."

"Are you serious?"

"We natives have many quaint customs." Belle looked at Rafe's long, graceful hands. In the moonlight they were the color of ivory. She wanted to reach out and touch them. Forcing herself to be good, she turned away and watched the fence posts hurtle by. The car turned into the long clay drive. The ancient oaks closed their limbs over their heads, engulfing them in shadows. "Too bad you won't be here long enough to observe all our colorful rituals," she said. His going would leave an elegance void.

"Somebody has to help Rachel. I talked to our brother in Chicago. They'll get along without me for a while."

Her voice felt dry in her throat. "I guess Mrs. Berlin will be joining you."

Chapter 7

"MAMA! WAKE UP!"

Belle opened her eyes. Outside the window, the sky was beginning to lighten, but sunrise seemed far from certain. Cady continued to shake her. The girl's golden hair was in a tangle. On her face was a look of anguish and panic. "I have a sore throat!" she whispered.

Cady had been a member of the award-winning Methodist choir for the last two years, but this morning, she was to sing her first solo. Every evening for the last week, Miss Effie had pounded on the piano while Cady rehearsed and rehearsed the same hymn until Belle thought she would lose her mind. Cady attacked the job of singing with the same single-minded commitment she gave to anything she really wanted. She expected an A plus from life.

"It's probably just stage fright, honey," Belle said. But as soon as the words were out of her mouth, she regretted them.

He seemed to start. Belle figured it must have been her voice. She was pretty sure she hadn't slurred or anything. He kept his eyes fixed on the road. When he answered, his words were firm and strong. "No. She'll stay in Chicago."

"That's too bad."

"Yes."

She'll be there waiting for him when he goes home, Belle reminded herself. But the rumble of the engine seemed to hit a musical note and the moon came out from behind the dense canopy of leaves.

BOURRÉE WAS SITTING on the front porch of Luther's house when the Stutz Bearcat with the silhouette of two heads drove by in the moonlight. He narrowed his eyes and spat a wad of tobacco juice at the expensive car as it maneuvered over the bumps in the road.

Her daughter's panic began to bubble over into full-blown hysteria. "Or not," Belle added swiftly, remembering a rule from her Southern Girls' Guide. *Never resort to logic when speaking to a crazy person or an overwrought girl between the ages of ten and twenty.* "Come on, I'll fix you up."

Cady padded after her mother, into the kitchen, where Belle made her a soothing glass of warm lemonade with honey. When Miss Effie got up, she dosed her granddaughter with apple-cider vinegar and hot water. Stella arrived at six-thirty to fix breakfast and insisted Cady drink hot water laced with cayenne pepper. After a couple of glasses of Stella's remedy, Cady pronounced herself cured. "Yes, ma'am, it usually works that way," Stella said.

By seven o'clock, a full three hours before church services would begin, Cady had brushed out her hair and was tearing around her bedroom searching for hairpins. She was in full hysterics again by the time Belle found them in the drawer where they belonged. Next Cady popped a button off her shirtwaist. "I'll sew it on," Belle said, reaching for the blouse.

Cady clutched it to her breast. "I can do it! Shouldn't you be getting dressed? You're not going to make us late, are you!" Her voice marched up the scales with each sentence.

Belle almost made it to her own room before she heard the scream. She rushed back to find Cady had pierced her finger with a needle. An almost microscopic drop of blood had landed on the white cotton shirtwaist.

"I can spot it," Belle said.

But Cady insisted the shirtwaist was ruined. "Ruined!" To prove her point, she wadded it up and tossed it into the dirty-clothes hamper. Then she clawed through her closet and announced she had nothing to wear. "Nothing!"

"In that case, I'd advise you to keep your choir robe closed," Belle said.

SUNLIGHT STREAMED THROUGH the tall stained-glass windows, turning them into an exuberance of jewels, throwing a jigsaw of colors across the west wall of Gentry's most prominent church. Belle slid into the polished oak pew as the organ struck a chord that reverberated through the rafters and created sympathetic vibrations in her chest. She bowed her head and gave heartfelt thanks that both she and Cady had lived through the morning. She hoped they'd survive her daughter's last year in high school, but at this moment the outcome was uncertain.

Hugh Thompson, Cady's beau, had taken the train up to Gentry to be present at her debut. Belle scrutinized the boy from behind. With his thatch of unruly reddish brown hair perched on a skinny neck, he didn't seem like much. Of course, broad shoulders counted for something. But broad shoulders or not, he was too old to be sniffing around her daughter. He was already in his twenties and holding down a job. Belle knew an experienced older man could sweet-talk a young girl until she was so dazzled she'd lose her head. Claude had been older and Belle had been dazzled.

She wanted her daughter to lead the charge into the twentieth century, not get trapped into marrying a boy with a skinny neck. She didn't name her after Elizabeth Cady Stanton for nothing. A girl today could become a doctor, a lawyer, even an architect. She could build skyscrapers. She didn't have to follow some skinny-necked man around, picking up his underwear.

Hugh was sitting next to his brother, Tibor Thompson, and his best friend, Alton Jones. Belle had asked Miss Effie to invite them all for Sunday dinner. She wanted a good look at the boy and the fellows he hung out with.

Jimmy Lee had agitated to be there for his cousin's solo performance at the Methodist church, but since his grandfather on his mother's side was Reverend Scaggs, his attendance was required at the Church of Everlasting Redemption and at the preacher's home afterward for Sunday dinner.

The big moment arrived. The choir stood. Cady took her place in front of them in her maroon choir robe, her golden hair swept up and fastened with a matching maroon bow. Belle fanned herself nervously. Next to her, Miss Effie, in a hat that looked like a stack of black pancakes tied with a ribbon, leaned forward.

The organ played the introductory chords and Cady opened her mouth.

Her clear soprano sparkled with the stained glass. The notes circled the congregation, pure, bright, and joyous. When she sang, "Come home," and the choir echoed, "Come home," Belle felt as if her heart were expanding too much for her chest to hold.

She had produced a wonder.

The choirmaster asked the congregation to rise. Belle added her voice to the voices of the congregation. She was glad she'd come. She felt at one with this community of worshipers. She decided she would come to church more often. Miss Effie would be so pleased and it would go a long way toward mending her reputation with Brother Meadows.

As the final vibration of the organ vanished into the still air, Brother Meadows rose and asked the assembly to pray for their friend Abe Rubinstein, who'd suffered another heart attack. A murmur went through the church as the congregation bowed their heads. The organ played softly. The minister named other friends and parishioners who needed their prayers.

After the prayers the choir sang "Blest Be the Tie That Binds." When they had taken their seats, Reverend Meadows paused, looked directly at Belle, and announced that for today's sermon, he would be taking his text from Isaiah 28, verses one and three, "Woe to the drunkards of Ephraim."

Belle slid down in her seat. In rolling tones Brother Meadows went on and on about sinners reeling with wine and staggering with strong drink, "whose beauty is but a fast-fading flower." Well, Belle thought, I did it. No getting around it. I drank the devil's brew. *If you jump off the roof, you have to expect to hit the ground.* She figured that insight ought to be a rule for her Southern Girls' Guide to Men and Other Perils of Modern Life. Not only that, it was a rule she should actually follow.

Then she thought, I hit the ground, but I got back up. That's the important thing, I got back up. She fluffed out the fringe under her hat and pretended to take a pious, but impersonal, interest in the sermon.

Forty minutes later Brother Meadows was still enjoying the sound of his own voice and Belle was trying to balance a church fan on her knuckle. It fell to the floor with a crack. Parishioners turned. The preacher didn't pause, but the sight of her bending over to pick it up gave some slight respite to the bored church members sitting in her row.

The fan looked like a lollipop on a stick. Belle studied the badly printed picture of a rosy-cheeked Jesus suffering little children and small sheep. The rosy color was smeared upward, giving Jesus pinkeye.

The congregation shifted from buttock to buttock, shuffled their feet, coughed, studied their own fans, and Belle remembered why she'd so often skipped church. As the minister continued to inveigh against the evils of drink, she heard a congregant whisper, "I could sure use a stiff one right now." Stifled giggles bubbled up. A woman's voice whispered, "Warren!" And still the preacher preached.

Having finally wrung out every drop of shame a gin-soaked

woman could suffer, Brother Meadows must have felt he'd done his duty. Belle knew he preferred to leave vengeance to the Lord, but instead of letting them go home to dinner, he began to plow the more hospitable and familiar terrain of Matthew 22, "Thou shalt love thy neighbor as thyself," when a shaft of light hit him.

The congregation rejoiced in the interruption. They turned as one, to see three men in white gowns march down the center aisle in a column of sunlight. White curtains hanging from cone-shaped hats hid their faces. A chorus of excited whispers rose up around them. "What in the world?" "Klansmen." "Here in Gentry?" "I seen them at the picture show!"

As the masked men approached the altar, the last in line, a stocky man, tripped on the hem of his skirt and stumbled into the second in line, pushing him, domino fashion, into the first man, who barely missed toppling the minister.

It was at that moment a word slipped out from under a hood that was not usually heard in the House of the Lord. Titters broke out all over the church. Belle watched the man grab hold of his long skirt like a turn-of-the-century housewife and march up to the preacher. The Klansmen surrounded him in a semicircle.

"Brother Meadows, we of the All-Seeing Eye have judged your work and found it good," one of the Klansmen bellowed. Belle looked around at the congregation. After almost an hour of listening to the preacher, they seemed delighted by the theatricality of the diversion.

The only Klansmen she or most of the congregation had ever seen were actors in *The Birth of a Nation*. In the film, they were heroes, protecting their women and the fine traditions of the Old South against power-hungry carpetbaggers and former slaves gone wild.

The Klansman went on shouting about Brother Meadows's

compassionate heart, high principles, and courage in the face of
the immorality that besets society today. The curtain covering
his face floated in and out. Finally he got around to the main
event. "In appreciation, the Ku Klux Klan wants to make a donation to your church of one hundred dollars."

There was a hush and then a buzz. "A hundred dollars!"
"Oh, heck, if Brother Meadows don't take it, I will." "Shut up,
Leonard."

The first Klansman, who wore battered shoes but seemed
most comfortable in his robe, as if he'd worn it for a while, offered an envelope to the minister.

The choir and the congregation held its breath.

The minister appeared to be struggling with his conscience.
He looked at his parishioners for a sign, but they were watching
him. He was their moral leader. Then he examined the envelope
and ran his tongue over dry lips. He stared into the blank, white
masks. He gazed again at the envelope. A hundred dollars was a
month's wages for the underpaid clergyman.

"The Invisible Kingdom makes this donation out of Christian
charity, without reservation," the mysterious Klansman said in
a grave voice. It was a voice Belle thought she recognized, but
couldn't place. Brother Meadows looked up into the rafters as if
praying for divine guidance. The grave-voiced Klansman went
on, "All we ask is you continue with your good works."

At that, the minister snatched the envelope.

"Along with the money, you'll find a free membership in the
Gentry chapter of the Ku Klux Klan," the lead Klansman said to
the startled clergyman. All three hooded men saluted him. Then
they turned in unison and marched out of the church, careful
not to trip over their robes this time. A second buzz went up.
"There's a Klan chapter here in Gentry?" "The Ku Kluxers are
in town?" "When did that happen?" "I'll be jiggered."

The choirmaster asked the congregation to stand. Belle

opened her hymnal and inhaled mold and deteriorating paper. They sang the hymn scheduled to close the service, "Alas! And Did My Savior Bleed."

STELLA WAS IN the kitchen making Sunday dinner. Belle sat with her, shelling peas. As she described what had happened in church that morning, Stella shook her head.

"You were too young to remember them, weren't you?" Belle asked.

Stella opened the woodstove to baste the chicken. A blast of heat radiated out into the room. Sweat beaded her brow. She kept her back to Belle. The two women worked in silence for several minutes. Finally, Stella stuck a spoon into the crabmeat bisque and held it out as an offering. "You think it needs more salt?"

Belle tasted the hot soup. "It could use some."

Stella nodded and turned back to the stove. She picked up the bouncing lid from the pan of the potatoes she was boiling and poked them with a fork. Finally, she turned back to Belle. "They can say what they want nowadays, but my mama and papa told me what it was like back then." Belle handed her the bowl of peas. "We had us some hard times. Real hard."

When Belle stepped out onto the porch, Miss Effie was holding court from her high-backed rocker, fanning herself with a church fan. "Our plantations were in ruins. The freed slaves were running rampant."

Cady's black cloud of stage fright had blown over like a sudden summer thunder shower, leaving the sky bright and the air sweet. She had Hugh Thompson sitting next to her on the swing, and that was all she needed for happiness.

Belle studied the boy. Hugh was tall and had a nice, wide smile even if it was over crooked teeth. She had to admit his neck didn't look as scrawny when seen from the front. Still, he wasn't half as good looking as his big, blond friend, Alton Jones, who was already head of his own logging crew. The question was, what did this man in his twenties want with her seventeen-year-old daughter?

She watched them rock back and forth and remembered what it felt like to sit just inches from the boy you loved, while you pretended polite interest in the prattling of some poor, benighted soul too old to know anything about love. Hugh touched his knuckles to Cady's, rotating them on the back of her hand. Their faces shone.

There's no lust like unrequited lust, Belle thought. Determined to keep it that way, she wedged in between them, pushing Cady up against the wooden arm of the swing.

"Mama!"

"There's plenty of room for three, sugar." Belle smiled at Hugh.

"And there's a perfectly good chair over by Tibor," Cady said, pointing to an empty rocker.

Belle held her cardboard church fan in front of her face and hissed, "Don't make a spectacle of yourself." Once the words were out of her mouth, Belle thought, Oh, Lord, I sound like one of those Priestesses of Prim. But she immediately forgave herself, because, after all, it was for her daughter's own good.

Miss Effie went on talking and fanning herself. Her gray eyes stared straight into the past. "I was just a little girl, but I remember the excitement when the Ku Kluxers rode through town in their white robes. Even their horses were draped in white. Daddy held me on his shoulders and said, 'These men are our modern-day knights in the service of the South.' They were . . ." Miss Effie searched for the word and finally came up with: "Grand."

"It wasn't so grand for the colored folks," Hugh said.

Tibor Thompson, Hugh's brother, gave him a disgusted look. "You don't know what it was like for us back then, does he, Miss Effie?" Even though Tibor hadn't been born until the end of the nineteenth century, he had unshakable nostalgia for the romance of the Old South. Miss Effie patted his hand.

Hugh's good-looking friend, Alton Jones, said nothing, not that he could have said much with Miss Effie turning the corner into the humiliation the South had suffered under occupation. "I remember all those Yankee soldiers—" Suddenly her face lit up.

Bourrée LeBlanc was walking across the lawn. Belle had an image of a panther prowling his territory. His massive arms had already ripped his black suit coat. A little tongue of white stuck out at his shoulder. He tipped his hat to the ladies. Miss Effie batted her eyes and Cady, even though she was sitting next to Hugh, watched him and played with her hair.

Miss Effie invited him to join them for dinner. He sat down on the step, close to Cady's feet, and gave her a wink, which stunned Miss Effie into unaccustomed and accusing silence. Belle stood and gave the swing back to the lovers. So much silent disapproval was not lost on Bourrée. He got up and ambled to the other side of the steps, where he leaned against the post.

Miss Effie relaxed and continued her ramble down memory lane, but she kept an eye on Bourrée after that.

Belle watched Cady and Hugh move toward one another. Cady put her hand on the seat of the swing. Hugh put his hand next to hers and rubbed her little finger with his.

"If it hadn't been for those brave boys in the Klan, I just can't imagine what would have happened. You know, they've been around since biblical times."

Hugh shifted on the swing. Belle heard the chains moan and remembered Cady telling her he wanted to become a crusading journalist.

Miss Effie lowered her voice and said with considerable drama, "The Klan was originally a secret band of Israelites, who fought for freedom from Pharaoh's bondage."

Hugh couldn't stand it any longer. "Yes, ma'am, I heard that story, too, but the truth is, the Klan started in Pulaski, Tennessee, sometime early in 1866, when six bored Confederate veterans in their twenties decided to start a social club."

"Really?" Acid dripped from Tibor's voice. "Well, then how'd these Tennessee boys come up with a Hebrew name?" It wasn't a question so much as a challenge.

"It's not Hebrew. It's from the Greek *kuklos*. It means 'the circle.' The Confederates were all classically educated. Four of them became lawyers like you."

"You don't know what you're talking about," Tibor said.

"Do, too. I've been researching the Klan for the *Picayune*."

He told them that after a few drinks, the boys from Pulaski decided to change the name to Ku Klux so it would sound mysterious and added Klan because they were all Scotch-Irish. One of them said, 'Ku Klux Klan has the sound of bones rattling together.'

"That was all it took." Hugh leaned forward, eager to let them know how smart he was. "They raided the linen closet and started romping around in sheets. Then they galloped through town in their spooky costumes, busting into picnics and playing practical jokes on the guests. They gave themselves outlandish names, stuck silly symbols on their outfits, and improved their costumes, not to mention their height, with high-coned witches' hats."

As Belle watched him, she was reminded once again of the rule from her Southern Girls' Guide: *Men sure do love to lecture to a captive audience.* She glanced at her daughter. She was his captive, all right. She was looking at Hugh with the total admiration men dream of, but rarely find, in a living, breathing woman.

Encouraged by his girl's receptivity, Hugh continued. "Soon, wild gangs of armed men from all over the South started dressing up in sheets, calling themselves Klansmen. So the next year, they held a secret organizing meeting in Nashville and elected General Nathan Bedford Forrest, Grand Wizard."

"One of our greatest generals," Tibor announced.

"Oh, he was an officer and a gentleman, all right. Under him, the Klan became the *invisible army* of terrorists, whipping, mutilating, murdering. But for all the hoopla and romantic folderol, they only lasted three years. Congress shut them down by 1869."

Hugh was so enthralled with his own story, he didn't see the expression on Miss Effie's face. "Well, I think I'll see how dinner's coming," she said, getting out of her chair and going into the house.

"Now, see what you've done." Tibor didn't bother to hide his delight. "You've been so full of yourself ever since you got a job on that lousy newspaper. Excuse me, ladies." Tibor was in his first year of law at Tulane.

Hugh looked as if he had been set adrift on a foreign sea. He turned to Cady. "Maybe I better go talk to her?"

He started to get up, but Cady didn't want him to go. She put her hand on his arm. "She'll be all right. Mama upsets her all the time, don't you, Mama?" Belle gave her daughter a look. "Fortunately, Grandma's very forgiving." Hugh sank back down. Cady's hand was still on his arm. The lovers looked into each other's eyes, smiles fluttered across lips, and, at that moment, no one else existed.

Belle was in the chair next to Tibor. Bourrée had sat down on a step not more than a foot away. She thought she could feel his heat rising up through the folds of her skirt. Or maybe it's not coming from him at all. Maybe it's coming from me. She got up and took Miss Effie's imperial rocker. There was entirely too much heat on this porch, not generated by the noonday sun. "What about this new bunch? Are we going to see whipping, mutilating, and murder?" She thought of Luther lying on the ground.

"Gosh, I hope not." Hugh seemed less sure of himself since Miss Effie's departure, but he did want to make a good impression on his girl's mother. "All I know is, five years ago a drunken minister and failed garter salesman, by the name of William Joseph Simmons, figured that with the opening of *The Birth of a Nation* in Atlanta, he could make money by starting a new Klan."

"I remember reading something about that. They burned a cross, didn't they?" Belle asked.

Hugh nodded. "Funny thing. Cross burning had never been a part of the old Klan. Thomas Dixon, who wrote the novel the movie was based on, stole the idea from Walter Scott. Anyway, Simmons's campaign was a bust. He didn't have any idea what the revived Klan should do except line his pockets. He wrote ads soliciting membership into, I'm not kidding, 'A Classy Order of the Highest Class.'

"Then this June, when he was so broke he couldn't pay his rent, he went into business with a couple of publicists, Edward Clarke and a lady named Elizabeth Tyler, who'd been promoting the Anti-Saloon League and were looking for a new line of work. Now, suddenly, we've been hearing about the Klan popping up all over the country. That's why my editor asked me to look into it."

"I wouldn't worry about them," Tibor said. "They gave money to Brother Meadows so he can continue his good works."

"Never underestimate the ability of the hypocritical to hood-wink the sanctimonious," Hugh replied quietly.

Belle turned to him, stunned. The boy had a way with words. Maybe he'll become a real writer after all. *Never underestimate the ability of the hypocritical to hoodwink the sanctimonious.* That was a rule worthy of her Southern Girls' Guide to Men and Other Perils of Modern Life.

"Well, I for one was glad to see them," Tibor said. "Maybe you haven't noticed, but things are out of control in this country, what with the anarchists building bombs and immigrants swarming all over, and now, as if all that wasn't enough, now women think they can—"

"Vote?" Belle asked evenly.

"Yes, ma'am," Tibor said, not backing down. "The whole country's going to blazes, if you ask me. The Klan's the only one tough enough to take on the riffraff."

"Take them on? I figured they were signing them up," Hugh said.

Belle looked at Hugh with real respect. No wonder Cady likes him. The boy sounds like me.

Tibor leaped from his chair. Hugh jumped up to meet him. The porch swing bucked. Chains screeched. Doesn't take much to get those two at each other's throats, Belle thought.

The brothers faced off. Suddenly, Alton was in between them. Bourrée, who'd been sitting silently throughout the whole exchange, had jumped up, too. He put a hand on Tibor's shoulder.

"I'm sorry about that, ladies," Hugh said as he returned to Cady. "My brother and I don't see eye to eye about much these days."

Bourrée sat back down on the steps.

"I don't see why y'all are worried about the Klan anyway," Tibor said. "We're all white, Christian, patriotic Americans. They won't give us any trouble."

"I don't know," Belle said. "Once these good ol' boys start running around at night wearing masks, anything could happen."

Hugh turned to Bourrée. "Where do you stand?"

Bourrée looked Hugh up and down. "I'm sitting, son." He stretched out his legs and leaned back against the post.

As a muckraking-reporter-in-training, Hugh had learned not to let anyone get away with evasive answers. His voice was polite but persistent. "Where do you stand on the Klan?"

Bourrée took his time and took in the scene: The young lovers together on the swing. Belle, in her bright yellow shirtwaist, sitting in Miss Effie's high-backed rocker. The Jones boy not saying anything. Tibor agitated, standing above them. Bourrée's eyes followed a bluejay settling on the lush lawn. Then he turned back to Hugh and said smoothly, "I agree with Miz Belle, of course."

Sunday dinner was over at the Rubinsteins'. Buster and Nina had gone to a youth picnic organized by the Methodist church. At first, Rachel had been reluctant to consent to their going on church outings, but since the young people had no other organized activities, and Abe had survived them, she consoled herself with the thought that at least her children would be associating with well-behaved boys and girls.

Rafe and Abe were in the hall going over the books. Rafe's rich voice pierced the heavy door. "Of course you're in trouble. You can't keep on giving credit willy-nilly. Your suppliers aren't going to wait forever."

Rachel turned on the ceiling fan, unzipped her dress, and lay down in her slip. On the bedside table was *Madame Bovary*. She'd read it in school. Now she was tackling it in French. She loved novels she could fall into and had been looking forward to this afternoon with nothing else to do. She put her French-English dictionary on the pillow next to her and opened the book. Soon, she was deep in the French countryside with a small-town doctor's wife who longed for romance.

The loud ringing of the doorbell shattered the afternoon silence. Rachel returned reluctantly to Gentry and reached for her dress. After powdering her face and pinning up her hair in a manner that befitted the wife of a leading citizen, she went into the hall. Abe, still wearing his leather slippers and smoking jacket, was in the living room with a small, white-haired man whose posture was ramrod straight. Rafe was smoking on the screened veranda in the back, next to the children's bedrooms.

"What's that blankety-blank fool doing here?" Rachel asked.

"Beats me. He said he had to see Abe about something important. Who is he?"

"Belle's stepfather. Horrible old man. He owns the Nix Hotel and thinks a great deal of himself."

Rafe pulled out a deck of cards and dealt two hands of gin rummy on the white rattan table. A breeze sprang up and the air was filled with the sudden burst of Confederate jasmine. In the sweetness of the afternoon, memories of Belle sitting next to him, trying so hard to learn addition, came back to him. He recalled how he could almost taste her scent. He'd been taken with her, but other more disturbing memories preoccupied him. The same memories that had distracted him from Helen. Now he thought he'd like to see Belle again, but checked himself. It wouldn't be fair to lead her on and then leave her behind.

"Gin," Rachel said.

"How do you do that all the time?"

"I remember all the cards. You don't." He shook his head as he added up the score.

Rachel went into the kitchen. Rafe followed her. She took a

double-chocolate cake down from a shelf in the pantry and offered her brother a big slice. He shook his head. "Rafe, you have to start eating."

"I eat."

"At least have a glass of milk." He let her put the milk in front of him.

Abe came into the kitchen waving a brochure. "You won't believe it. That idiot just invited me to join the Ku Klux Klan. Said it would be good for business." His face was alive with cynical amusement.

"I thought they were supposed to be against the Jews," Rafe said.

"Some folks around here are so stupid, they don't know who they're supposed to be agin'," Abe said, slipping into country vernacular as he accepted a slice of cake. "He told me the Klan is sworn to stick together. When I told him I'd just as soon stick with the Rotarians, he got all huffy. Said since the Klan is a fact of life in Gentry, the better elements, I guess he meant him and me, ought to take control of it now and not leave it to the riffraff."

Rachel laughed. "As if that old coot wasn't a prime example of riffraff."

Rafe picked up the pamphlet Calvin Nix had left behind and looked it over.

"I wanted to tell him I had no intention of dressing up in sheets like some fool, and I didn't have anything against colored folks. They're some of my best customers."

"Oh, Abe, you didn't, did you?" Rachel asked.

"Of course I didn't. I said I'd think about it."

Rafe was reading the brochure. " 'Patriotic . . . fraternal . . . benevolent. Open to native-born white, gentile Americans . . . free of any foreign allegiance.' This doesn't look good."

Abe stopped eating. "My family's lived here for three generations. We never had any trouble except once, thirty-five or forty years ago, when the night riders were tearing through the parish. Since then, I guess I've heard a few remarks here and there, but nothing that would keep us from getting ahead."

Rafe found that hard to believe. He looked at his sister for confirmation.

"They were too busy hating the Negroes and the Italians," she said.

Chapter 8

JULY DRIPPED INTO August with temperatures hovering in the soggy nineties. Afternoons, Belle felt like wilted lettuce. She spent most days out in the fields, checking on the work. She had to admit Bourrée was doing a good job. Broken fences were mended, the cows were healthy, corn was growing, the cotton crop was coming up. Evenings she spent in the office, carefully going over all the expenses. Nights should have been a relief. But that was when the ghosts of Guilt and Opportunity Lost chose to pay their visits. They brought along their kinfolk, If Only, and Why Didn't You?, and the mother-in-law of all night sweats, What's Going to Happen to Me Now?

Often in the middle of these visitations, Rafe's long, sensitive face would appear and those inappropriate feelings would well up inside her so intensely, she'd throw off her nightgown and toss naked on top of tangled sheets.

She couldn't just stay on the farm watching the corn grow. She decided she had to do something. She picked up the phone.

The following Sunday afternoon, Bourrée was kneeling on his front porch, adjusting the electric fan so it blew straight at him, when he heard the rumble of a car. Through a gap in the leaves, he saw a black Packard driving down the clay lane, heading for the big house. Nobody in town except the Rubinsteins owned a Packard. Bourrée felt the fan turn his sweat cold. That rich Yankee, the one who drove the Stutz, was he with them, sniffing around Belle?

Bourrée waited until he couldn't stand it any longer. Then he followed the tire tracks on foot. They veered off before they reached the house and turned into a rutted lane that led through the woods. He found the car in a small clearing. Voices and laughter bounced through the trees. Bourrée crept down a foot-path until he spotted an isolated cove in the creek.

From his hiding place among the sawtoothed leaves of a hawthorn thicket, he caught sight of Belle cavorting in the water. That was the word, "cavorting." Her short hair was slicked back. She called to someone, but he couldn't see who it was. That Jew boy from New York, most likely. To Bourrée, they all came from New York.

He watched her swim to the shore. His father, his mother, hell, everybody he'd grown up with agreed: *Decent women don't swim.* But here she was, her breasts floating under her wet knit top. He watched her emerge from the water, her bathing suit stuck to her body, hiding nothing. She wasn't even wearing a knee-length skirt or long bloomers, as was fitting for a re-spectable woman if for some reason she should venture into the water. When she approached shore he saw her legs. They were bare up to the middle of her thigh. Good God, she wasn't even wearing stockings!

She bent over to splash someone. The Jew boy? Bourrée couldn't see. But he glimpsed a part of a woman that ought never be exposed to sunlight. He felt a burning in the pit of his stomach. His whole pitiful upbringing came back on him, sour and sharp, like a bad meal. It bubbled in his craw and stuck in his throat. She'd acted so offended when he'd given her a little boost onto her horse, as if she were too prudish to allow a man to touch her. And then she'd insisted on sitting in the back of his car, as if she were some fine lady.

He watched the Rubinstein woman lumber into the water like a sick cow, her wet suit rolling and creasing over the flesh around her waist. The whole tribe must be out here. He saw Belle splash her and dive into the water.

He watched her slap the logs and give her hand to someone. He couldn't see who it was without revealing himself. Where was the Jew boy? Was he holding her hand or was he back on the beach, waiting for her to kick again so he could stare up her legs?

Then he saw Cady and that little Rubinstein girl. They were running along the beach wearing those same indecent bathing costumes. He watched them jump into the water, screaming, with their long hair pinned and falling, their giggles disrupting the birds in the trees, their smooth young legs on display in front of God and man. Bourrée knew better than to mess with those girls, even though he was closer to their age than Belle's. The old woman would come down on him like a truckload of logs. His hands itched as he watched the Rubinstein girl grab Cady and duck her. Unfulfilled entitlement boiled inside him as he slipped like a wounded animal back into the forest.

AT FOUR-THIRTY A HORN sounded. That was the signal for the girls, their lips blue from the icy water, to hang a blanket over a tree limb and change into their dresses so that Abe, Rafe, and Buster, who'd driven out in one of Rubinstein's trucks, could take their turn in the icy water.

The swimming party had been Nina's idea. She'd begged for it when Belle invited them to a picnic. Belle had felt funny about wearing the same "indecent" bathing suit in front of Rafe that had caused her husband's murder. But if she was going to swim, and the icy, spring-fed creek was calling to her, she didn't want to be fettered and dragged under by layers of skirts and bloomers.

Rachel had the solution. "Let the men wait. They can swim after we're done."

But now they were here. Belle took her time adjusting the changing blanket. The Primer of Propriety had slipped from her mind. She'd forgotten her vow to be nice. She let Rafe catch an "unintended" little glimpse of her in her indecent swimming costume. Let him know what he's missing, she thought. After all, *the most important thing about virtue is to act as if you're in favor of it.*

Everybody brought food—Rachel, Miss Effie, who'd come for the picnic after everyone had finished swimming, even Jimmy Lee, who'd wheedled an invitation once he'd heard Nina Rubinstein would be there. But upon seeing her, he was struck dumb by the way her cotton dress clung to her still damp body.

As they packed away the dirty plates, Rachel told Belle that Constance Bancroft was going to Nashville on Monday to lobby the Tennessee legislature.

"It's a bunch of nonsense, if you ask me," Miss Effie announced while passing around plates of fresh blackberry pie. "A smart girl should be able to get what she wants without going into some dirty voting booth." She turned to Cady and Nina. "Remember, men don't like girls who have opinions."

"Miss Effie, you have opinions. You have lots of opinions," Belle protested.

"That's entirely different. My opinions are right. Cady, I'd like some iced tea."

While the others digested their food, Belle and Rafe took a barefoot walk along the beach, digging tired toes into the sand. Behind her she heard Cady say, "Grandma, don't you want to keep up with the times?"

And Miss Effie's reply: "Whatever for?"

Rafe talked about Paris, the lights, the Eiffel Tower, the sidewalk cafes, and winter evenings when the oyster men, with steam coming from their mouths, stand next to deep counters of shellfish set up in front of restaurants. Belle tried to imagine what it would be like to walk through a city where they didn't speak English and didn't even want to. Then she remembered Claude had walked down those streets speaking French. To Lisette.

As they disappeared around a bend in the stream, they couldn't see Miss Effie's eyes following them or hear Cady and Nina's excited whispers.

"Tell me about snow."

"What's to tell?"

"What's it like to walk through it, to feel it on your face?"

"Cold. Why?"

"Are you kidding? How could you go through a Louisiana summer without thinking about it? I used to spend my school vacations ironing sheets in the back room of the Nix Hotel, imagining snowflakes falling around me. Tell me, what's it like to stand in the middle of a snowstorm?"

"I can't describe it." And then he said with sudden bravado, "I'd have to show it to you." Once he'd said it, he realized how much he'd like to see something so ordinary through her eyes. Maybe her wonder would rub off. He held a long, flowery vine out of her way.

"You? You'd show me snow?"

He nodded.

"And Mrs. Berlin?"

Good Lord, she thinks I'm propositioning her.

She waited for a response. When one didn't come, she thought, Good heavens, does he think I'm flirting? Well, maybe I am. Nothing wrong with that. *Flirting promises pleasure, without demanding actual payment. A girl need not reproach herself, as long as the payment isn't given.* At least that is what Belle's Southern Girls' Guide to Men and Other Perils said. She brushed a flurry of little blossoms out of her hair.

She wondered why he never talked about his wife. Maybe they don't get along, she thought. Maybe that's why he's here. A bud of hope poked its head out of the ground. Belle stamped it down. She didn't need the Southern Girls' Guide to Men to tell her: *Only a fool messes with a married man. No matter what he says—and a man will say anything to get into your bloomers—you're always going to play second fiddle to his wife.*

Then she added, *A smart girl doesn't play that kind of music.*

"You seem so different from the other people around here," he said, staring at her.

"Because I'm interested in snow?" she asked, looking anywhere but into his eyes.

"That, and the way you treat people. I mean, you were pretty upset about your farm manager, what was his name, Luther?"

"You'd have been upset, too, if you'd seen him lying there on the ground."

The sandy beach ended. She led him into the cold, dark water. It covered his ankles. "But how many of your neighbors would? These people . . ." His voice trailed off.

Belle swung around and looked at him. "I heard you-all had a pretty good race riot in Chicago last year."

"That was different." The sand gave way to rocks. Rafe hobbled on city feet, trying to catch up with her.

"Was it? A colored boy swimming on a white beach?"

"The Negroes fought back."

"Well, whoop-de-do. That's why even more of them were killed. How many was it?"

"Thirty-eight." Rafe always knew the numbers.

"You-all always think, 'North good, South bad.' But it's not like that." She left the rocky water and stepped onto the rocky beach. "I think no matter where you live, there are always going to be a few people who are just mired in cussedness. They could live in Paradise and they'd find somebody to hate." She saw him struggling. She took his hand and helped him onto the soft sand. "Then there's going to be a few folks just brimming over with Christian love, and no matter what anyone else thinks, or how hard it is, they're going to be out there helping the downtrodden."

She dropped his hand and stood facing him. "The rest of us, most of us, are somewhere in between. We just go along and get along."

"Not you. You're on the side of the Christians."

"Me?" Belle exploded in laughter. He wanted to drink in the sound as it ascended the scale. "You better talk to Brother Meadows and my mother-in-law before you say that."

On the other side of the creek was a curtain of green. Trees reached toward the setting sun and spread out over the water. Leafy vines encircled them. Birds called from the branches. A fairyland of ferns covered the forest floor. She heard Cady's and Nina's voices singing about twilight, when the lights are low. The creek had twisted them around, but they couldn't be more than a couple of hundred yards away, straight through the woods. They should be getting back.

Instead she sat down on a log, splashing her feet in the water. "I grew up over there." She pointed across the creek.

"I thought you grew up at the hotel." He heard Abe's voice join the girls in the second verse of "Love's Sweet Song."

"That was later. For the first eight years, I grew up about a mile that way. My daddy was a tenant farmer. Forty acres of cotton, with vegetables growing next to the kitchen door and a little corn for the mule."

He didn't know what to say, so he said, "Sounds like a good life." He sat down next to her.

She studied him to see if he was making fun of her. To hell with him if he was. "It was all right until Daddy got sick. Then Mama just stopped."

"Stopped?" The singing was softer now. The cicadas were drowning it out.

"The whole year he was dying, all she did was sit next to his bed and rock. Half the time, I had to feed him and wash him, and I was only eight. By December we'd run through most of the food we'd stored up." She looked at the circles of splash her foot was making in the water. She wanted to hunker down, but at the same time, she had a wild urge to let him know, to let someone know, who she really was. Who she was before she became Belle Cantrell, one-fourth owner of the largest farm in the parish.

She saw black wings flying toward her. Crows wheeled over the creek, screeching to one another. "Stella, Luther's sister, lived down the road. I used to play with her kids. You might know her son, Curtis. He works for you-all, sometimes."

Rafe shook his head. He hadn't paid much attention to the people who worked downstairs.

"Anyway, by the time I was eight, I'd been two years in a white school and I'd been taught by the other kids, if not the teachers, that it was wrong to play with coloreds, and . . . and, well, you might play with them if they were close by and you didn't have anybody else, but you sure didn't eat with them. They'd call you a nigger lover. I never understood why, when Jesus said, 'Love thy neighbor,' being a nigger lover was such a bad thing, but it was. It felt awful when somebody called you that." She fell silent.

She remembered how her stomach had ached on that listless, gray afternoon, with dead leaves crunching under her feet. She couldn't look at Rafe. Would he want to have anything to do with her, once he knew how common her people really were? Her heart was pounding, but something compelled her to go on, to let him know the worst. She heard a raucous *caa-caa*. A solitary crow swooped onto a limb above them.

"I was walking home from school one afternoon when I saw Stella moving around her kitchen. I'd never been inside their house. I don't know what made me sneak up on her. I remember watching her lift the lid off a big iron pot. I couldn't see the mustard greens simmering with seasoning pork, but I could sure smell them." Years later, Stella told her how she'd looked, with her dress torn and dirty and her hair every which way, like some kind of bird's nest.

"I just stood there in the doorway, drawing a circle in the dirt with the toe of my shoe. Finally she asked, 'What you want, child?' " Belle stopped. It seemed as if it were the end of the story.

"What did you say?" Rafe asked.

"I've never told anybody before." Not even Claude. Especially not Claude. "I'd appreciate it if you didn't tell Rachel or anyone else." He nodded. If he was repulsed, well, then that was that. He'd be leaving soon. But she didn't believe he'd betray her confidence. "I said— I said." She stopped; she was ashamed even now. "I said, 'Pot liquor, please.' "

His face was impassive, as if he didn't understand the enormity of what she'd done. "Don't you see, I begged for pot liquor from a colored woman." She watched to see if he found her repugnant. She'd just admitted her people were as common as dirt, the very essence of poor white trash. Maybe even lower than white trash. So far below, there wasn't even a name for it.

"And she fed you?"

Belle looked away. It was so simple for him. Tears were forming somewhere behind her eyes and she'd be darned if she'd let him see that. When she'd gotten herself together, she went on. "She pulled me to her big bosom and hugged me." Belle shook her head, as if she could ever shake away those memories. Her voice was husky. "I kind of lived with them after that, only going home to sleep. My mama never even asked where I was. And Luther—"

"Your old foreman?"

Belle nodded. "Stella's brother. He was sharecropping for the Cantrells. Sometimes he'd bring over a pot of beans or a string of catfish. He was always a real good farmer. Once, it was Christmas Day, he brought a whole ham. He treated me just like the other kids, like his own kids. He used to read to us. He wanted to show us the way the world should be. So when I saw those horrible vigilantes—" She stopped.

The world shifted. He wanted to take her in his arms. He wanted to hold her and comfort her and let her comfort him. The sun had fallen behind the trees and the sky was suffused with a golden light. Tree frogs came out and serenaded them.

"I might as well tell you everything," Belle said, getting up and heading back. "I'm not one of those good Christians. When my mama married Mr. Nix and we lived at the hotel, I used to steal hams from the kitchen after Sunday dinner and take them to Stella and the kids."

BELLE WAS SLOW to grasp Rafe's acceptance of her and her secret. But that evening, when she brushed her hair, she realized she felt easier in her skin. "You're all right," she said to her image in the mirror.

"That Mr. Berlin is a very attractive man." Belle spun around and saw Miss Effie standing in the doorway.

"I suppose so," Belle said, enjoying the way her scalp felt as she gently stroked her hair.

"Rachel expects his wife to join them soon."

"That'll be something to look forward to." Belle slapped the wooden handle of the brush into her palm. She reached her fingers in between the bristles, pulled out dead hairs, and tossed them into the trash.

"Be careful, honey. You don't want to make a fool of yourself."

RACHEL RECIPROCATED FOR the picnic by inviting them to a musical evening the following Saturday night. At supper Belle sat between Abe and Jimmy Lee, who after jockeying for a seat next to Nina, became tongue-tied by the nearness of all that wild, tousled hair. Nina made a polite attempt at conversation with him, but getting no coherent response, she launched into an animated discussion with Cady about Hugh's visit the next day and the thrilling possibility of his bringing his handsome friend Alton Jones. Jimmy Lee suffered in silence, but a large pimple, which had bloomed on his nose that very morning, became redder and angrier as the meal progressed.

They moved into the living room where they reclined with their coffee on low couches under the big white ceiling fan. Rachel and Rafe led off the evening with a rousing piano duet of "By the Light of the Silvery Moon." Everyone joined in the singing. That was followed by Miss Effie playing "When the Sun Goes Down in Dixie" with great precision and a total lack of feeling. As she plunked out the second verse, Rafe perched

himself on the arm of Belle's curvy chair. He looked down and gave her a conspiratorial wink. He's married, she reminded herself, and then she reminded herself to breathe.

When Miss Effie's piece was over, everyone applauded as if she were America's greatest pianist. Belle clapped wildly, hoping it would afford her some relief. It didn't. She could feel Rafe's eyes on her. She wished he'd move. Where the heck was his wife? It wasn't fair. If she was coming, she should come.

Next Cady and Nina put on a record and danced to "Ballin' the Jack." When Nina pulled her knees together close, up tight, and swung them left and then over to the right, Jimmy Lee sat enraptured, in desperate silence. But when Nina spread her arms and shook the tumble of curls that had fallen out of their pins, he looked as if he were going to faint.

It was Jimmy Lee's turn next. He'd been at the farm all week practicing "When the Moon Shines Over the Moonshine." But Nina's presence had robbed him not only of speech, it had deprived him of the ability to perform on his banjo, which sat mute next to him. Unfortunately, by now his silent adoration was ignored. It wasn't that Nina disliked him. It was worse, much worse. He simply didn't matter to her.

Everyone turned to Belle. She protested she'd never had lessons and didn't have any natural talent. Rafe found her particularly lovely in her bright blue silk dress with the dropped waist and the blue band pulled low on her dark hair. Her eyes had picked up the color and turned a deep green-turquoise with glints of gold.

"She said she doesn't want to perform," Abe announced, and that would have been the end of it if Belle hadn't admitted that she had brought some sheet music, just in case.

Rafe smiled to himself.

Rachel took the music and played the introduction. Belle leaned an elbow on the fringed shawl draped over the piano.

But as soon as she sang the first two lines, she began to berate herself. What possessed me to choose this song? He'll think I'm singing for him! She'd picked "After You've Gone."

Her voice didn't have much range, but it had a sultry timbre that Rafe found moving. Would she be left crying over him? He told himself to stop being vain. It was just a song. She was performing. Besides, a girl who's gone through what she's gone through wouldn't cry over him. Southern girls are nice to everybody. They like to tease. It's part of their charm. She looked directly at him, and just as quickly looked down, fluttering those turquoise eyes demurely as she sang a line about him feeling blue and sad.

No, not me, he thought. The universal you in the song. But maybe he would feel sad after he'd gone. Maybe he would. On the second refrain he felt a pulsing, as if old feelings he thought had atrophied were beginning to bloom again. Of course he'd been moved by her story, anyone would have been. But he had a life, and that life was not in Gentry, Louisiana. He wondered if she smelled like wildflowers tonight. He was too far away to tell, but her lyric echoed in his head. Would a time come when he'd regret leaving her?

He stood and went to the piano. He needed some respite from this sudden cascade of emotions for a girl he hardly knew. A girl with no education. A girl who lived in a totally different world. He ran his fingers over the keys and began to pick out Rachmaninoff's Third Piano Concerto.

Belle hadn't heard much classical music. Of course, she'd been forced to listen to the Gentry High School Orchestra play on festive occasions. Their music always sounded big, pompous, and labored over. Rachel had taken her to a concert in New Orleans once, where someone famous played Chopin. At first Belle had been moved. Then pictures of her life intruded and romped around in her head. After that, she'd become desperately bored.

She'd never heard anything like Rafe playing Rachmaninoff.

He started by stroking the notes, slowly picking up the tempo, until Belle was filled with the most exquisite longing. But longing for what?

Suddenly, he attacked the keyboard. She watched his long hands strike the keys. Forget about him, a voice said. He's married. But how could she forget about him, with this music vibrating in her ears? She gazed at his lean, muscular body curved over the piano, the belted jacket of his linen suit flowing as he moved. As his right hand toyed with the high notes, Belle felt the pure, clear music pierce her body. Now he was probing a dark sensual resonance with his left hand.

He lingered over each passage, dark and light, slowly, as if he had all the time in the world. Now he was chasing the melody. It seemed to spill out under his fingertips. He pounded faster, faster, now softly, now pounding again. His hair flew. His body rose and fell. The music grew in intensity. His hands rushed on until just as he reached the crescendo, the front door banged open and Buster Rubinstein stomped into the hall. Rachel motioned for her son to join them, but he disappeared as the music became softer and softer and the last tender notes faded out.

The silence left Belle stunned.

Rachel went out into the hall to look for Buster.

Belle heard a door slam and Rachel's high heels on the wooden floor as she pursued her son down the long hall and into the back gallery. She heard a knock and then footsteps approaching as Rachel returned to the living room. "Abe, dear, why don't you see about your son?"

Abe looked pale, as if he were listening to the beating of his heart.

"I'll go," said Rafe. "It's always easier to talk to your uncle."

The evening broke up abruptly. They didn't linger at the door. Jimmy Lee tried to shake Nina's hand, but she put it next to her ear, waved her fingers at him, and said, "You-all be careful now."

"Stuck up, bi . . ." he murmured as he stalked across the porch.

Rafe came back in time to say good-bye. Belle felt the warmth of his hand and imagined she could feel the music flow into her. "I'll see you soon," he said.

"Soon," she echoed, and was halfway down the walk when she realized she hadn't told him how moved she'd been by his playing.

"Wonder what happened to Buster?" Cady asked.

"Who cares," muttered Jimmy Lee as he helped his great-aunt into the buggy.

"WHAT HAPPENED TO BUSTER?" Rachel asked Rafe when he returned to the living room.

"Just a fight."

Buster was plump and usually placid. "He doesn't fight," Rachel said. Her brother said nothing. "Did he tell you why?" Rafe shook his head.

"Somebody probably called him a dirty Jew," Nina said, looking down at a picture in the current *Vogue*, which she held in her lap. Three sets of adult eyes turned to her. She looked up. "He's so dumb, he doesn't know how to handle them. Do you think Miss Mary could make me a coat like this for winter?" she asked her mother, pointing to a picture.

"Did somebody call you . . ." Rachel stumbled and then went on. "A bad name like that?"

"Oh, sure." Nina was studying the coat.

"When?" asked Abe.

"Last week, I guess." She closed the magazine. She figured this was not the time to discuss fall fashions.

"And you didn't tell us?" Rachel asked, her voice on the edge of shrill.

"There was nothing to tell. That pasty-faced Dotty Lou Pruett came up to me right before math and said she didn't like Jews. That's all."

"That's all?" Rachel exchanged worried looks with her brother.

"Everybody knows how ignorant Dotty Lou is," Nina said, as if it was the most obvious thing in the world. Abe patted the plush arm of his chair. Nina sat down next to her father, snuggling against him as he held her around the waist. "I told her Jesus was a Jew, and so was his mother and all his cousins. Then I said I was pretty sure He wouldn't want her to go around bad-mouthing His kin."

Chapter 9

THE SUN WAS already blasting the earth at eight o'clock on the morning of August 18. So the stable was doubly dark when Belle led Claude's big stallion back into his stall after her morning ride. She called for Little Ricky.

He wasn't there.

At nineteen, Little Ricky was too slow for school learning, but he was serious about a clean stable and good with horses. He was good with the dairy cows, too. She called again. Bourrée must have him working the corn harvest.

She watered Jack herself, put him in his stall, and took off his saddle and blanket. She knew she should sell him. She'd gotten a good offer just last week, but she wasn't ready to let go of such an important part of Claude.

Not yet.

Suddenly she heard a crash. Jack reared. Belle looked up and saw his hooves poised above her head. She leapt to the side, hurtled out of his stall, and slammed the door behind her. "Little Ricky!"

But it was Bourrée who emerged from the shadows. "He's doing some work for a change." Through the partially opened stable door, sunlight fell on his back, making his white shirt glow around the edges. He smiled, and even in the shadow of his silhouette, Belle thought she saw his teeth glint.

"What are you doing here?" Bourrée had never had much to do with the horses.

"I wanted to see you in private." He hooked muscular thumbs onto his belt.

"In private?" His index fingers were pointed at that intimate structure of a man's body most often referred to by the plural of that word.

"I got something for you." He moved toward her.

"I'm in a hurry," she said, trying to move past him. She felt her heart pulsing in her ears.

He blocked her way. "Oh, this won't take long, chère." His dark eyes roamed over her shirt, open at the neck. He was so close she could feel his breath. "It won't take long at all."

Belle pulled herself up into her great-lady posture and said, "Why don't you come on up to the house. I'm sure Miss Effie would be happy to invite you to breakfast."

"What I got is just between me and you. You may have married up, but we're the same. I talked to your daddy, you grew up hungry just like me. You're still hungry, only now you got enough food." He pushed a strand of her hair gently in back of her ear.

She pulled away. "I don't know what you're talking about." She wondered what Mr. Nix had told him. How he'd saved her from a life of poverty, when the old coot wouldn't even buy her shoes for school?

"Wait here," Bourrée said. He went into the empty stall, next to the stable door. Belle was almost outside when he stepped out of the stall holding a large manila envelope. "This is for you."

Now that her back was to the door and she had a way to retreat, she didn't feel so scared. Sunlight fell upon his face and body. She realized he was wearing a new work shirt and pants. She took the envelope and turned to go. "Thank you."

He caught her wrist and pulled her to him. Close. "You don't want to take that up to the house, chère." His hand was hard and calloused, like Claude's. He was so close she could smell his new clothes. "You best open it here."

She stepped toward the light and ripped open the envelope. Inside she found a photo of a big policeman with a walrus mustache pulling her toward a paddy wagon. She was wearing her "indecent" bathing costume.

Belle's hands began to shake. She didn't remember that she'd been hanging on to the door of the bathhouse in the picture the sheriff had shown her, but she did remember hanging on to that door, when a policeman tried to haul her away. She felt her shoulders squinch up. Darts of white-hot pain shot into her temples. "If you think you can blackmail me, then—" What? What could she do? She wasn't sure, but she'd be damned if she'd let him know it. "Nobody, you hear, nobody blackmails—"

He put his finger to her lips. "I don't want to blackmail you, chère. This here's the only print and you got the negative right in there. If I was you, I'd destroy them both."

Belle put her hand into the envelope and pulled out the negative. She held it to the light. "How did you get this?"

"Friends." She thought about all those clubs he'd joined. "Friends ought to help one another, don't you think?" It took a few moments for his next words to wash over her, but when they did, the muscles of her neck and shoulders began to relax and the white-hot darts dropped out of her temples. "Nobody's ever gotta see this picture again," he said.

Tears filled her eyes. Anxieties that had been pecking at her since Claude's death flapped their wings and flew away, one by one.

"All I want is for you to be safe."

She found herself crying on Bourrée's chest. His strong, young arms wound around her. His left hand caressed her back. She felt comforted, taken care of, until she felt something rise between her legs. One hand held her tight, the other slid downward and cupped her buttocks in her beige riding britches. "No," she said, shoving against his chest.

"Mama!" They jumped apart. The girl glared at her mother. "Mr. Rafe's on the phone."

Bourrée's nose flared, as if he'd just caught a bad smell.

Belle bolted past her daughter and raced toward the house. Cady ran after her, calling, "Mama, how could you?" Belle had no answer for that one. She outdistanced her daughter. Cady never had been much of an athlete. As she ran, Belle rolled up the manila envelope and held it in front of her so Cady wouldn't see it. Or at least Belle hoped she wouldn't.

Belle sprinted into the house, slipped the envelope into the drawer of the telephone table, and picked up the phone. Through all her tumult, the memory of Bourrée's arms, the way they felt wrapped around her was still vivid. Rafe was no longer on the line.

Cady ran inside, panting. Before the girl had a chance to say anything, Belle took the initiative. "What did Rafe say?" Belle asked.

"Something about the Nineteenth Amendment."

Belle grabbed Cady by the arms. "Is Tennessee voting today?"

"I guess." Cady pulled away. She was still shocked by her mother's outrageous behavior. "Mama—"

Belle hushed her and picked up the phone again, but this time the party line wasn't free. Cady looked at her mother in mute incomprehension. Belle knew her daughter was a good girl. She actually believes in the Primer of Propriety. She thinks I believe in it, too. Well, I do, sort of. At least I know what rules I'm breaking. But I don't know how to handle a daughter who caught me in the stable in the arms of a hired man.

Since she couldn't tell her the truth, Belle began to talk about the significance of what was happening in Nashville.

The Nineteenth Amendment, giving women the right to vote, had passed Congress the year before. Thirty-five states had ratified it. They needed one more, but since the Tennessee legislature was the only one scheduled to meet before the November elections, the Anti-Suffragists hoped that the "Perfect Thirty-Six" would never be found and the amendment would die.

Belle and Rachel had planned to storm Nashville shoulder to shoulder with Carrie Chapman Catt and all the other famous suffragists, who were flocking there. But after Abe's heart attack, Rachel didn't feel she could leave him. And after Luther was run off, Belle was afraid to leave the farm in Bourrée's hands. So they were both stuck here in Gentry.

Belle tried the phone again and got through to Rachel. "It doesn't look good. As of last night, the count was forty-seven yellow to forty-nine red." Belle let out a little cry.

The legislators had taken to wearing roses on their lapels, yellow in favor of giving women the vote, red against. The newspapers were calling it the "War of the Roses."

"I'll be there as soon as I can," Belle said. Brave words, but what could she do? She couldn't do anything. But she didn't want to be alone, not today, not after all these years of meetings, protests, and even jail. She had to share victory or defeat with Rachel. "Cady'll be there, too."

"I have a tennis game!" Cady wailed.

"How can you play tennis today? The whole world is set to

change." Or not. She didn't even want to voice that last thought.

"But, Mama, today is the finals!" Cady was playing in a tournament at the Methodist church. "I'd be letting everybody down!" Belle could almost see the exclamation points dangling in the air as her daughter headed for the stairs.

"We did this for you, baby." If looks could whine, Cady's expression was high-pitched and steady. "Okay, suit yourself." Cady bounded up the steps, taking her exclamation marks with her.

Belle grabbed the envelope and ran into the kitchen. Stella had the woodstove going. Belle was stuffing the offending photograph and negative into the firebox when Miss Effie entered, the dining room door swinging behind her.

"Belle—"

Belle spun around. The envelope was still sticking out of the stove.

"Cady told me—"

What? Had Cady told her about catching her mother in the arms of the hired help? Miss Effie, the High Priestess of Propriety, would never forgive her. Belle wondered if the old lady would be a little envious.

The heat from the fire was burning Belle's backside. She longed to turn around and see if the envelope had caught. What if it hadn't? What if it had fallen out onto the floor and Miss Effie wanted to know what was in it? She had to hold her attention. "Did Cady tell you about Tennessee?"

Belle babbled on and on. Had the envelope disappeared or had the heat spit it out? She glanced down between her feet. No sign of the envelope. "Just think, if we win today, you and I will be able to march arm in arm into the polling booth in November and cast our vote for the next President and sheriff and every dogcatcher in the parish. They'll have to pay attention to us then."

"They pay attention to me now. And they pay entirely too much attention to you. Cady told me you were planning to go into town."

Out of the corner of her eye, Belle saw flames lick the envelope.

"Now, I'm willing to give you Loyal and the buggy, but you have to be back by noon."

The heat was searing Belle's calves and the backs of her thighs. She sneaked a look and saw the paper blacken and curl. "Noon? I'll have to leave town by eleven. What if they haven't taken the vote by then?"

"You'll just have to wait for the morning paper like everyone else. There's a meeting of the church auxiliary at two. You're welcome to accompany me. Or you can take the milk wagon."

BELLE THOUGHT ABOUT clip-clopping into town in the wagon in back of the mule or one of the old nags they used for farmwork. It would take more than an hour! She could make it in less than half that on horseback. But the Primer of Propriety said: *A lady shouldn't make a spectacle of herself.* She'd never gone into town in riding britches. They weren't considered indecent. Lots of girls wore them, now. They were considered merely inappropriate for street wear. But no one will arrest me for them. What the heck is liberation for if I can't gallop into Gentry on Susan B., today of all days?

The envelope disappeared. Belle slammed the firebox door shut and turned back to her mother-in-law. "It's a new day, Miss Effie," she said as she kissed her mother-in-law on the cheek.

"Belle Cantrell, you're not thinking of going into town dressed like that, are you?"

But Belle had already fled.

———

SHE SLID OFF Susan B. and tied her up in front of Rubinstein's. As she ran through the main department, she saw Vince
Stefano selling a hat to one of the Pruetts. Vince was wearing a
yellow rose on his lapel. He waved at Belle as she flew by. Angelina Monotti had a yellow rose, too. But hers was wilting on
the counter next to her.

Belle took the stairs to the office two at a time. Rachel came
out to meet her. She'd brought in a big bouquet of yellow roses
from her garden and had distributed them to all her employees.
She pinned one on Belle's shirt. The secretaries in the front office were all wearing them, but whether from a desire to vote or
a desire to keep their jobs, it wasn't clear.

"And?" Belle asked. "Did they take the vote?"

Rachel nodded.

"And?"

"It was a tie." Belle made a little groan and collapsed into a
chair in the back office.

"Don't you see? That means one of the legislators switched.
We haven't lost yet."

Rachel had met both north and southbound trains and had a
stack of newspapers on her desk, where she was working almost full-time to learn the business in case Abe became com-
pletely incapacitated.

The two women pored over the papers. Belle tried to ignore
the warm feeling that stole over her at the sight of Rafe entering
the office. She was a feminist, she reminded herself. This was no
time to think about men. To stop the chatter in her head, she
read aloud, " 'Women have never needed to vote, and they don't
need to now. They should do their duty before God and save
their energy for their husbands and children instead of gallivanting around, messing with things that are none of their business.' "

Belle wadded up the paper and hurled it across the office into the wastebasket.

"It's true," Rafe said, turning to Abe, who was working mornings. "Women don't have the intellectual discipline to vote. They're too emotional." He sneaked a pleased peek at Belle.

She rose to the challenge, lobbing a rolled-up paper at him, missing his head by inches. The miss was intentional. As a girl she'd been a star at baseball. That is, whenever the boys allowed her to play.

"Guess she proved your point," Abe said to Rafe.

Rachel picked up a rolled paper and threw it at her husband. But Rachel had never been any kind of athlete. The paper missed Abe by a couple of feet and sailed, end over end, out of the mezzanine and down into the men's department where it hit Harry Chambers on the head as he was selling a customer a new pair of overalls.

The two women ran down the stairs to tend to his wounds. When they found he'd survived, they took their papers to the Country Kitchen, across the tracks, to study over coffee and plates of fresh-baked biscuits with butter and syrup. They read aloud to Selma, the waitress, who was illiterate but became caught up in their excitement. She swore she'd register no matter what her husband said. Rachel promised she'd personally escort her to the courthouse and, taking her yellow rose off her blouse, she pinned it on the girl.

Selma admired it against her navy blue uniform. "Nobody ever gave me a flower before."

Above the blue-and-white curtains that covered the bottom half of the window, Belle spotted the head of Righteous Diggs, the telegraph runner, bobbing in the direction of the *Gentry Post*.

Belle leapt up and dashed out to the sidewalk. "Have they taken a second vote?"

"Now, Miz Belle, you know this here's a private telegram," Righteous said, "and it's addressed to Mr. Floyd."

"Righteous!"

He looked at her, opened his mouth, decided against speaking, and ducked into the newspaper office.

The *Gentry Post* was housed in a storefront on Grand Avenue. It had three desks in the front office. The printing press was in the back. The only desk occupied today was that of Floyd Taggert, publisher, owner, and editor in chief. His sole reporter was out covering the Methodist tennis tournament. The other empty desk belonged to Floyd's brother-in-law, who traveled around the parish selling advertising and print jobs.

Floyd was in the middle of designing an ad for "the purest drugs in Gentry" with Francis Hopper, owner of Hopper Drugs, when Righteous, pursued by Belle, entered the office. The newsman looked up, gave the boy a nickel, and threw the telegram into his in-box. Floyd Taggert was a tentative man with a receding hairline that matched his receding chin. His journalistic motto was "If you can't say something nice about someone, don't say anything at all." Although this philosophy might have been scorned by journalists across the country, it endeared him to his advertisers and printing customers.

"Be with you in a minute, Belle," Floyd said.

"Do you think that telegram might have the results of the voting in Tennessee?"

"I don't know."

"Aren't you going to open it?"

"In a minute. Right now I'm helping Mr. Hopper. That story's not going to run until tomorrow." Just then the wife of his biggest advertiser appeared in the doorway. Floyd stood. "Hey, Miss Rachel, come on in. What can I do for you?"

"You can open the telegram, Floyd," Belle said.

"That would be nice," said Rachel. Francis Hopper shrugged.

Floyd tore open the envelope, pulled out the telegram, and read it.

"Is it from Nashville?" Rachel asked.

Floyd nodded.

"Did they take a second vote?" Belle asked.

Floyd nodded, again. He was a slow and careful reader.

"What does it say?" Belle was ready to scream.

"Looks like another tie."

Belle made a noise halfway between a groan and a scream. "At least it didn't go the other way," Rachel reminded her.

"How can you be so positive all the time?"

"Life doesn't always live up to your deep cynicism, Belle."

"It does its best."

Francis Hopper left, wishing the women good luck, and Floyd turned to Rachel. "Anything else I can do for you ladies?"

"We'd like to wait here until the vote comes in," Rachel said.

Floyd glanced nervously at Belle in her riding britches and then he looked back at Rachel. Dismay spread over his bland features. He'd never ventured an opinion on suffrage in print, but Belle guessed in his heart he felt it somehow went against nature, although she doubted he was firm in that belief. Floyd wasn't a firm man.

"Well now, ladies, you know this here's a place of business."

Belle sashayed over to him. She watched his eyes rove down the length of her leg, unshielded by the folds of a skirt. She leaned over his desk until she caught him looking down the open collar of her shirt. "This is such an important day for us. I know Mrs. *Rubinstein* would appreciate it if we could rest here awhile. I'll be happy to sit behind that empty desk so no one can see my inappropriate attire, if that's the problem." She watched sweat pop out on his forehead. He wiped it away with his pocket handkerchief.

"That'll be fine." He jumped up and held out a chair for Rachel. Belle slipped behind the reporter's desk. *A man will generally give you what you want, if you can figure out how to ask for it in a way that will further his self-interest.* She made that a rule in her Southern Girls' Guide to Men. She'd told Rachel about the guide and quoted some of the rules. Rachel had chuckled and said it showed her natural cynicism. Belle figured she was right. She'd tried to share some of the wisdom with Cady, and looked forward to the day when the girl was old enough to know she didn't already know everything.

An hour later Rafe stopped by with sandwiches and Cokes for everyone, including Floyd and his pressman. "What's happening?" Rafe asked, perching on the edge of Belle's desk, blocking her view of the front door.

"The politicians are probably out in the hallways, wheeling and dealing and getting hot under the collar," Floyd said as he put down the phone. His fellow newspapermen in Hammond and Amite hadn't heard yet, either.

Just then Belle's mother, Blanche Nix, swept in with a bulletin. "I got some news for you, Floyd." She plunked down a sheet of lined notebook paper with the handwritten announcement. "The Nix Hotel is gonna be serving dinner on Sundays, soon as church lets out."

"Hey, Mama."

Blanche turned, surprised to see her daughter sitting at a desk in a newspaper office. Belle got up to give the older woman a familial kiss, but Blanche stepped back.

"What in tarnation are you doing downtown dressed in men's pants?"

"Oh, Mama, they're my riding britches. I came to town on my horse."

Blanche looked her daughter up and down. "First you cut your hair like a man's. What you gonna do next, grow a beard?"

"Mama!"

"Do you enjoy making a spectacle out of yourself? Or do you do it for the sole purpose of embarrassing me?"

Rafe watched Belle wilt as all the excitement drained out of her. He suddenly understood her bobbed hair and bids for attention. He wanted to take her in his arms and soothe her. He watched her pull herself up in an attempt to replicate Miss Effie's effortless demeanor of a great Southern lady.

"I don't think you understand. We could get the vote today. This is a great moment for our sex."

"Our what? Tell me something, what good is it gonna do me or you to vote? You think it'll matter which one of them crooks we send to the capitol? They'll pick our pockets just the same."

Belle turned and walked out the door. Rafe followed her out.

"I know, I know, since Daddy died she never had a chance. She's a pathetic old woman, married to a horrible old man, but still . . ." She was silent for a moment. "Why is it no matter how old we get or how much we know about them, we still care?"

"Nobody can hurt you like your family."

As they were talking, Reginald Scaggs, minister of the Church of Everlasting Redemption, saw them standing together on the street. "Belle!" His disapproval rolled over her.

Belle pulled herself up. "Afternoon, Brother Scaggs. Have you met Mr. Berlin?"

But Brother Scaggs was in no mood for pleasantries. " 'The woman shall not wear that which pertaineth unto a man.' Deuteronomy twenty, verse five." With that he entered the newspaper office.

"That's the church I was brought up in. Just filled to the brim with Christian love," Belle said in answer to the question she saw forming on Rafe's lips.

When they entered the newspaper office, they heard Brother

Scaggs telling Blanche, "A woman's mission is to fulfill the noble office of wife and mother. Don't you agree, Brother Floyd?"

Floyd looked at Rachel and Rafe and then back at the minister. He made a quick calculation, gave them both a sort of constipated nod, and ducked his head. The preacher had handed him a pencil draft of a flyer he wanted printed, announcing a big foot-stomping revival meeting. Floyd was going over it for spelling, grammar, and some semblance of sense when the telephone rang.

He picked up the receiver. "I don't have time to take the vote right now. Why don't you send me a telegram after they finish."

"No!" yelled Belle.

Floyd turned to her, distressed. "Belle, I'm sorry, but I've got to work on Brother Scaggs's announcement right now."

"I'll take the call," Rachel said, rising smoothly from her chair and holding out her hand for the receiver. Blanche puckered up her lips as if she'd eaten a green persimmon.

Reverend Scaggs, who was in no way beholden to the Rubinsteins or their store, stepped in front of Rachel and said, " 'Thy desire shall be to thy husband and he shall rule over thee.' Genesis three, verse six." Blanche nodded in approval.

"Sixteen," Rafe said. Reverend Scaggs turned to him. "Genesis three, verse sixteen," Rafe repeated. Belle stared at him. He shrugged. "I remember numbers." The minister glared at Rafe with unconcealed hatred, but he risked no other biblical quotations. "Give her the phone. We all want to know what's happening." Captain Berlin's voice was deep and commanding.

Rachel stood with the receiver to her ear and called out the votes as Belle wrote them down on a pad of paper. Rafe again perched on the edge of her desk. Suddenly Rachel let out a shriek. "A legislator named Harry Burn just changed his vote. He's voting to ratify."

Reverend Scaggs looked as if he'd joined Blanche in her diet of green persimmons.

"Let's just hope none of ours changes his vote and sides with the reds," Belle said.

Suddenly everyone in the newspaper office heard screams coming from the receiver. "What's going on?" Rachel called through the mouthpiece. She turned to the people in the newspaper office. "They're chasing Harry Burns around the chamber. What?" she asked the stringer. She turned back into the room. "They're trying to kill him."

"Serves him right," the minister proclaimed.

"Good heavens, he just disappeared out the window. The third-floor window. Belle, what's the count?" Rachel asked.

"I'm adding as fast as I can."

Rafe leaned over her tally. "You won." His voice was quiet.

"Are you sure?" Belle asked.

"We won!" Rachel proclaimed as the stringer announced the official results. Floyd grabbed the phone.

"We won!" screamed Belle, jumping up, and in the excitement that followed, Rafe picked her up and twirled her around. Belle was perfectly aware that a primary rule of the Primer of Propriety stated: *No lady deserving of that name would ever indulge in a public demonstration of affection.* But some rules are just made to be broken. She didn't even think about it. She simply threw her arms around him and kissed him on the lips.

"You're a disgrace to the family!" Blanche shrilled.

"What did I tell you?" Brother Scaggs snorted. "Give women the vote and you'll corrupt the morals of the country!"

When you can't do anything about impending doom,

a girl might as well dance.

THE SOUTHERN GIRLS' GUIDE TO MEN AND
OTHER PERILS OF MODERN LIFE

Chapter 10

THE NEXT MORNING, when Rachel picked up the newspapers at the depot, she read that Harry Burns, Tennessee's youngest legislator, the man who'd changed his vote and America forever, had crawled out onto the third-floor ledge of the capitol, picked his way around the building, and hidden in the attic until the other legislators had cooled down.

When he spoke to reporters that evening, he explained it was true he'd worn a red rose on his lapel, but in his coat pocket, next to his heart, was a letter from his mother. It said, "Don't forget to be a good boy and help Mrs. Catt put the 'rat' in ratification." Harry Burns had been a very good boy.

BELLE STAYED OUT on the farm. Not only had she embarrassed herself by a public display of affection, she'd kissed a married man.

In the middle of the day.

On Grand Avenue.

In front of a preacher.

Would she never stop making a fool of herself? Good thing Cady hadn't been there. She'd think her mother was a tramp.

But the memory of Rafe's long, lean body pressed to hers lingered no matter how hard she tried to banish it. It snuggled into her bed at night when she tossed and turned, chasing sleep. It reappeared during the day in quiet moments around the farm. She wished his wife would come and get rid of the temptation.

Friday morning she rode Susan B. out to the end of the lane to pick up the mail. She passed the Hallelujah chapel and decided to go in. She could use a little spiritual uplift. But when she came into the clearing, she saw the little church that had once hosted such riotous singing, now had the aura of a bad dream. She'd thought the congregation would look after it, but the smashed windows hadn't even been boarded over. An angry buzzing filled the air. A hornet's nest clung to the eaves. No one had cut the grass. Brambles had sprung up, along with bushes, ferns, and sprouts that would soon become trees. The forest was taking back its own. She turned her horse around and cantered to the mailbox.

There, she found an invitation to a private victory celebration at Constance Bancroft's house in New Orleans. That evening, Belle ran up a dress for Cady in layers of peach-colored silk. As she pumped the pedal of her sewing machine, she thought about Rafe and wondered if he'd be at the party. If he were, what would she say?

She hadn't heard from him since she'd kissed him in public. She hadn't heard from Rachel, either.

Maybe I'll meet someone single at Constance's. Belle stopped sewing and laughed out loud. I'm really desperate if I'm hoping to find an eligible man at a suffrage party!

———

THE BANCROFT FAMILY home was set back from the traffic of St. Charles Avenue, amid trees, lawns, and gardens. It had Corinthian columns in front and wide galleries on the sides. The long casement windows were open. Music spilled out and mingled with the soft beat of the summer rain.

Cady, in the frothy layers of silk, chirped like an excited sparrow as the taxi pulled up to the house. The front porch was guarded by a battalion of veteran suffragists. These were noble ladies, well into middle age and beyond, who'd braved the jeers and condemnation of their families and society for decades. Some of them had marched arm in arm with Susan B. Anthony and Cady's namesake, Elizabeth Cady Stanton. But in their mannish shoes and dreadful hats, they offered little inspiration for Cady's blithe generation of girls who wanted nothing more than to dance the night away and kiss boys in the backseats of cars.

Constance stood in the receiving line at the door. "Congratulations," Belle said, inhaling the scent of face powder as she kissed her friend on her dry, crinkled cheek.

"Don't expect to rest on your laurels, Belle. You, too, Cady. The real work is just beginning!" Cady's eyes sparkled, but it wasn't in anticipation of voter-registration drives. Hugh Thompson had found her. I should have known, Belle thought.

Belle entered the front parlor and discovered a celebration far removed from the constraints of Gentry's Deacons of Decorum. It was the kind of party she'd dreamed of attending when Constance had offered her the possibility of weekend getaways in New Orleans. The rug had been rolled up. In the corner, a Negro band played ragtime, while a singer in a bright red dress wiggled her ample bottom and belted out a naughty song about her man's "sweet jelly roll."

Hugh met Cady at the door and swept her onto the dance floor. Even though women outnumbered men three to one, boys soon lined up to cut in on her. Cady waved at her mother, who watched the boys vie for her daughter's attention and wondered if she realized how lovely she was.

Beryl Parkinson, one of the young suffragists who'd been in the forefront of the failed liberation of Lake Pontchartrain, ran over and gave Belle a hug. "Where've you been? I haven't seen you since we went to jail!" Belle glanced at her daughter, who was now waltzing around the floor with some unknown boy while Hugh cut in on Nina.

Beryl, in her early twenties, was pretty in a distinctly bohemian way. She'd thrown a fringed shawl over her shoulders, cut her black hair into a severe bob, and even painted her lips. "Didn't we have fun!" she exclaimed. Beryl was an inveterate exclaimer.

"I hope you won't—" Belle began when she saw her daughter leave the dance floor, but she never got a chance to finish.

"Hide me," Cady laughed to her mother. She was flushed and out of breath. "Those boys just keep cutting in."

"Oh, the boys here are impossible, aren't they?" said Beryl. Cady nodded in agreement. "I find the best thing to do is to step on their toes." Cady stared at her blankly. Belle could think of no way to avoid introducing Beryl to her daughter.

"Your mother and I are comrades in arms," Beryl said, shaking Cady's hand with a firm grip. "But I guess you know all about it."

"About what?" Cady turned to her mother.

"Nothing," Belle said, giving Beryl a hard look.

"She didn't tell you? It was our finest hour!" More exclamation points amid a cascade of well-rehearsed musical laughter.

"I don't think we need to go into this right now," Belle said.

But Beryl barreled on. "We were arrested for indecent exposure! We went to jail!" Her voice shrilled around the room.

Now Cady was staring at her mother as if she'd never seen her before.

"You didn't tell your own daughter!" Beryl shrieked. "I intend to tell all my children!"

"Good for you," Belle said between clenched teeth.

"Of course, I expect to have them out of wedlock. I believe in free love. Don't you?" she asked Cady.

Cady stared at Beryl as if this red-lipped creature were from some distant and distinctly hostile planet. Then she turned to her mother. "What—?" But before she could say any more, Hugh reclaimed her. Cady allowed herself to be led to the dance floor. However, she looked back at her mother as if to say, We'll discuss this later.

Hugh's best friend, tall, blond Alton Jones, smiled his slow smile at Beryl. She shimmied over to him. Belle heard her proclaim, "I believe in free love, don't you?" Alton said nothing, but his face lit up. He pulled her close and let her chatter away, leaving Belle to wonder what she was going to tell her daughter about her arrest for indecency. The truth would be best. She could even cast herself as something of a heroine for the cause, but jail, even if it was for only a few hours, wasn't the sort of thing a mother wants to admit to her carefully raised daughter. Or have that daughter blurt out to her grandmothers. Miss Effie would be a nightmare if she found out that Belle had been arrested for indecency, but if Cady told her maternal grandmother— Belle thought her mother might disown her, and although Belle tried to convince herself she didn't care, deep down she knew that wasn't true.

The singer in the bright red dress was belting out "Alexander's Ragtime Band." Belle couldn't stop her feet from tapping.

She made up a new rule on the spot for her Southern Girls' Guide to Men and Other Perils of Modern Life: *When you can't do anything about impending doom, a girl might as well dance.*

"Come on along, come on along." A young trumpet player put aside his horn and sang. Belle looked around. Wasn't anyone going to ask her? She loved to dance, even though she'd never had much opportunity. Most of the ministers in Gentry were four square against drinking, dancing, and going to the picture show on Sundays. But after they were married, Claude had taught her to dance at a little juke joint deep in the woods, where a Negro band played and Miss Hattie May, light skinned and beautiful, sang naughty songs about how she loved her handyman. Ministers of both pigmentations described it as a sinkhole of sin and degradation, which made it ever so much more fun. They went several times a month until Cady started school and the obligation of becoming responsible parents and setting a good example weighed down upon them.

The band was playing "No Wedding Bells for Me," and Belle was still not dancing when Rachel, Nina, and Abe came through the door. Rafe was not with them.

"Good," Belle said to herself. But she didn't feel good. She didn't feel good at all. She pushed through the crowd and kissed Rachel on the cheek, saying softly in her ear, "About what happened at the newspaper office. I'm so embarrassed. You understand, it was the excitement of the moment, don't you?" Rachel patted her on the hand. Belle waited for her to tell her where Rafe was. She didn't. So Belle was forced to ask, "Will he be here tonight?" She tried to sound offhand.

Rachel said something about their brother, Gabe, in Chicago, needing ad copy for their new fall line, but Belle knew the real reason he hadn't come. She'd scared him off. Another rule for her Southern Girls' Guide to Men popped into her head: *A man would rather face early death than risk embarrassment.*

She and Rafe hadn't talked about that all-too-public kiss. They'd gone back to the store, where a spontaneous celebration had broken out. Even the employees who'd been against suffrage were in favor of celebrating.

Miss Effie said a lady doesn't kiss a man until she's engaged, or better yet, married. Why didn't she ever listen to Miss Effie?

Of course, Rafe was married.

Just not to her.

She told herself to stop thinking about married men and find herself someone eligible.

It was then that the trumpet hit a sour note and a short man with too much hair oil appeared. "I'm Victor Skuse, wanna dance?" He steered her onto the dance floor. The music, which only a few minutes before had set her foot to tapping, tumbled around her, stacking up on the floor to be tripped over. Victor led her with soft insecurity, usually half a beat behind the music.

As he stumbled over her feet, he said, "Always been in favor of women getting the vote" and "You gals have to show us the way" and "You're our better half."

Belle guessed he was one of those men who haunted suffragists' rallies hoping to find a woman who believed in free love. "You ought to meet Beryl Parkinson."

"Oh, her. Already had the pleasure," he said, and stepped on Belle's soft evening slippers. From his tone of voice, she guessed that Beryl's love wasn't free enough to include Victor Skuse. He launched into his favorite topic, his many resentments.

Girls, young and pretty, were standing in a clump around a waiter, as if what they really wanted were cups of punch instead of a dancing partner. You're welcome to mine, Belle thought as Victor launched into an enumeration of all the women who'd treated him badly.

The waiter stepped away from the girls. His white coat showed off his deep chocolate skin. "Luther?" Belle said.

"No, Victor. Victor Skuse," her dancing partner replied, stepping firmly on her left foot.

Belle pulled away from his grasp and limped over to her old overseer.

"Don't you look fine." He seemed to want to drink her in.

"I went to the sheriff the night you left, but . . ." Her voice trailed off.

"But you found the world don't work like it should," he said in his deep, rich voice. Belle nodded. "And you weren't able to fix it all by yourself?" He talked to her as if she were still the hungry little girl he'd read to so long ago.

"I miss you," Belle said.

In the kitchen, Luther's wife, Ann Rose, was placing rings of shrimp around a plate of cracked ice. She screamed with delight and, wiping her hands on a dish towel, hugged Belle, careful not to touch her green silk dress.

"Heard you got yourself a new overseer. A white man. Living in our house." Luther's voice cracked and a world of hurt leaked out. He'd worked that land since he was a young man. His children were born in that little cabin. "Why didn't you take on the job yourself?"

"Me?" That was just like Luther, Belle thought, always pushing her to take on more than she could handle. "Are you-all getting along okay?"

"Oh, yes, ma'am. And we want to thank you for the money you sent and for writing Miz Constance, too."

The week after Luther had been driven out of Gentry, he'd written Belle to apologize for taking Loyal and the wagon as far as Hammond. He'd sent her his temporary address and she'd sent him the money and letters by return mail.

"She's been real good to us," Ann Rose assured her.

"Are you working for her full-time?" If so, Belle hadn't heard about it.

Husband and wife exchanged looks. Ann Rose said, "We work all her parties and for her friends and for Mr. Abe's family too. And then Luther, well, you know Luther can do anything, so when any of these New Orleans ladies has a problem, or something gets broke, they just call up Luther and he goes over and fixes it. We got us a phone and everything now."

At that moment Constance appeared in the kitchen. Her expression was disapproving, her voice firm. "Ann Rose, are those shrimp ready yet?"

"Oh, yes, ma'am." Ann Rose put the finishing touches on the platter and handed it to Luther. Belle followed him into the dining room.

"What happened to my church?" Luther asked while he arranged the platter on the buffet table.

"It's pretty run-down. I think folks are afraid to go out there. I can send some men over after the corn harvest to chop the weeds and fix the windows."

"No, ma'am. I don't want nobody else preaching there. You just let the Lord take it."

Constance, who wanted her staff to attend to their work, saw them together and grabbed the first unattached man she could find. "Belle, there you are. There's someone I want you to meet." Belle turned away from Luther, who hurried back to the kitchen. "Mrs. Cantrell, may I present Mr. Skuse?"

"Mr. Skuse and I have already met."

The band struck up "Shake It and Break It."

"Wanna dance?" Victor asked.

"I'm afraid it's against my religion," Belle told him, and tried to join a group of women bunched around the punch bowl, but Victor followed her, reminding her that she'd danced with him before, and befouling the air with his disgruntlements.

She was reaching for a cup of punch when she heard the sax sound a long and lonely note. She looked up and found Rafe standing between her and Victor. Belle felt as if she'd been freed from captivity.

"Dance with me," Rafe said, and she could feel her chest resonate to the timbre of his voice. He swept her onto the dance floor. He had a strong lead, so she was able to give herself up to him. She felt as if her body were a reed as he bent her this way and that with the gusts of music. The beat picked up as the band segued into "Dark Town Strutters' Ball." She felt gay laughter swelling from her diaphragm, up through her chest. Words came through the laughter and Rafe's neutral face opened. A beautiful smile wreathed his lips as he twirled her around. She glanced over at her daughter dancing with Hugh's friend Alton. Nothing to feel guilty about, Belle told herself. We're just dancing.

On the next song, the tempo slowed. Rafe pulled her close. She could feel the linen of his cream-colored coat through the bright green silk of her dress. They moved together, her hips following his hips. He spoke into her ear, but his words flew away. His breath was warm and calling to her. She remembered she was a woman, not just Cady's imperfect mother, not just Claude's guilty widow, not just a suffragist, but a woman with possibilities unfolding.

She lay her cheek on his shoulder, breathing in the scent of expensive cologne and the elusive, delicious musk his skin threw off. Thoughts that weren't even alluded to in The Primer of Propriety swirled in her head. The piano player soloed, soft and cool. The drummer came in next. Rafe kept time with a soaring heartbeat. The bass plucked, low and insistent. Rafe pivoted Belle to the wail of the trumpet. She looked up at him and found he was smiling down at her. For one suspended moment, she knew what bliss was.

The moment cracked when Victor Skuse tapped him on the shoulder and said, "My turn." He grabbed her and pushed her into the middle of the floor. "Thought you said dancing was against your religion."

"I've been converted," Belle said, watching over his shoulder for Rafe to cut back in.

"Let's get a breath of air." Which one of them had said that, Belle or Rafe? Later, neither would remember.

The front porch was still thick with dowagers in hats, huddled together, planning their assaults on the parish voting machines. Around them, young girls in clusters giggled about their latest conquests.

Belle and Rafe retreated, through the living room to the dining room. He opened the door to the side veranda. The smell of rain and fresh grass rose to meet them. A soft, moist breeze caressed their overheated bodies. No words upset her ears, which were filled with rain and music and the beating of her heart.

He bent to kiss her. What does it feel like to be really and truly kissed for the first time in years? Not a kiss on the forehead. Not a demonstration of public exuberance, but a real kiss, a long, sexual kiss. When you're fifteen, you're aware of lips and noses and how everything seems to fit so miraculously. When you're a woman of thirty-three, who's been married and widowed, clutching your pillow in your solitary bed, for such a woman the first real kiss is like an alarm going off, waking up sleeping cells, reminding the blood to pump through your body, reminding you, you still have a body.

"No. This is wrong," she managed to say. "You're married."

Rafe let go, but he stared at her in a kind of shock, as if he didn't understand. It was a moment before he said, "My wife and I are separated. Since last summer."

"But Rachel said she'd be joining you."

"Wishful thinking." Now it was her turn to stare at him. He added quickly, "On Rachel's part."

"Separated?" Belle felt wave after wave of happiness sweep

over her. They were separated. Then the waves hit the shore
with a splat. Separated meant they were still married.

"The war left me . . ." He paused. "Distracted. I don't blame
Helen. She met somebody else while I was over there."

Belle knew separations were common, but divorce was rare.
Families intervene. Husbands have second thoughts. Wives
change their minds and plead for a reconciliation. *A girl's a fool
to get caught in that push-pull game.* Belle was sure the Primer
of Propriety would agree.

"I'm so sorry," she said, and meant to say more, but she
found her mouth unexpectedly occupied. Okay, it wasn't entirely unexpected.

He was kissing her again and she had to admit, she was kissing
him back. The Southern Girls' Guide seemed to be saying, *Virtue
may be its own reward, but sometimes that's just not enough.*

Of course, she knew what they were doing was wrong on so
many levels. Her head was filled with rules from the Primer of
Propriety. It screamed, *There are dozens of people who might
wander out to the veranda at any moment.* It cautioned, *For
God's sake, don't create a scandal.* And finally it fulminated,
*You're kissing a married man, no matter what he says about his
wife.* But her heart, or that part of our anatomy for which the
heart is a metaphor, didn't hear a word.

IN THE LIVING ROOM, Rachel looked around for her
brother. She went out onto the front porch, but he was nowhere
in sight. She remembered he'd been dancing with Belle, but they
weren't dancing now. Nina was fox-trotting with some boy
Rachel had never seen before. Cady was standing at the punch
bowl with Hugh, away from the boys who would cut in if they
went anywhere near the dance floor. Rachel questioned her. The

girl didn't remember seeing her mother or anyone else. But then, she couldn't be expected to, not when Hugh was around.

"I saw them go into the dining room about fifteen minutes ago," Abe said.

In the dining room, Constance was supervising the refilling of refreshments. She hadn't seen them at all. Rachel went out to the side veranda. It was empty.

People were scattered all through the house. Although the main party was downstairs, upstairs, behind closed bedroom doors, the fast young set was smoking cigarettes and sneaking swigs of liquor from pocket flasks.

Cady and Hugh went into the kitchen to chat with Ann Rose, who was arranging a platter of cookies.

"You're getting so grown up. I'm gonna have to start calling you Miss Cady."

"Don't you dare!" Cady said, popping a cookie into her mouth.

As soon as the older woman took the platter into the dining room, the young couple made a dash for the back stairs.

"Where do you think you're going?" Ann Rose asked, her fists on her hips.

"Shhh, Ann Rose." Cady's face was glowing. "Hugh and I . . ." She said the word "Hugh" with reverence, as if he were a prince, a saint, a god, not simply a tall young man with unruly reddish hair and crooked teeth. ". . . We were just going to look around upstairs."

Ann Rose, who was as susceptible to young love as anyone else, smiled and said, "Yes, ma'am." And added, "Don't you-all get in trouble, now." She watched them mount the stairs, their arms around each other, and remembered how she'd felt when she was young and Luther was the strongest, smartest, handsomest man she'd ever met.

The upstairs hall was lit by one dim bulb and papered in tiny
flowers. Dark, badly painted portraits of ancestors looked down
on them. Rubber plants stood at attention next to glossy white
door moldings, but Cady and Hugh saw none of it. He had his
arm around her. His fingertips brushed the side of her breast,
and even a tiny bit more if she turned away from him. And she
just had to turn a bit from time to time.

They opened the first door. A group of young people, sitting
on the bed and on the floor leaning against the bed, waved cigarettes and flasks, calling to them. Hugh and Cady waved back
as Hugh closed the door.

They were lost in the perfection of two. Sometimes Hugh lec-
tured her on news stories he was writing and Cady thought how
lucky she was to have found such an intelligent man. But he
wasn't talking tonight. They were filled with silence.

They opened another door. A girl Cady's age was being sick
in the toilet. She waved them away.

"Mama's right. This is a new day," Cady said, shutting the
door.

Hugh grasped the handle of a third door. He opened it a
crack. The room was dark. He turned to Cady. She nodded. The
hall light cast a dim ray on a walnut dresser standing against
the opposite wall.

"Get off me! I mean it!" emanated from the shadows. The
voice sounded like that of Beryl Parkinson. Hugh and Cady
backed out. "If you don't stop this minute, I'm going to spit in
your face!" As Hugh closed the door, they heard a phhht and
the sound of bedsprings recoiling.

"Think she needs our help?" Hugh asked.

Suddenly the door banged open. Alton Jones emerged, his
jaw clenched. He looked at Cady and Hugh, nodded slightly,
and charged off.

"I guess free love doesn't extend to Alton Jones," Cady said.

Music floated up from the jazz band. The singer belted out a song about careless love.

"Maybe we should go downstairs," Cady said.

"Maybe we should," Hugh agreed. But he pulled his girl to him as they approached a fourth door. It was smaller than the others and looked more like a hall closet than a room. Hugh was the kind of young man who respected a girl. No girl would ever have to spit in his face. And he respected Cady most of all. But he was only twenty-two, and they were engaged, weren't they? Well, maybe not officially. No sense in giving Miss Belle conniptions before it was absolutely necessary, but as soon as Cady graduated from high school, they planned to tie the knot. He'd had a couple of cups, well, maybe four cups, of moonshine and he just wanted a nice quiet place to kiss his girl. Was that too much to ask?

He put his hand on the doorknob and looked at his sweetheart. It was a look filled with dogged longing. A look Cady couldn't resist. She nodded. It was an imperceptible nod, but Hugh knew an affirmative when he saw it. He wasn't slow to act.

He swung the door open.

A whiff of camphor wafted out. Half hidden between the winter coats and woolen dresses, he saw the back of Belle's head. And then he saw Rafe's hand half hidden in her hair. His other hand was caressing her bare thigh, above her stocking. Her green silk skirt was bunched up.

They sprang apart as much as they could spring with winter coats and suits bunched up around them. Belle's skirt floated down. Hugh tried to shut the door, but Cady had already seen them. She screamed, "Mama!" Her voice was high and strained. Belle stepped out of the closet. Rafe followed, his jacket mussed, his tie askew.

Cady faced them. Her lips moved, but her shock was too deep for words. She ran down the hall.

Hugh looked at Belle and Rafe. Then he turned and ran after Cady.

"What can I do?" Rafe asked.

"Sometimes there's nothing you can do," Belle said, watching her daughter disappear down the stairs. "This is just my luck. After three long years, I finally get to kiss a man and my daughter thinks I'm a tramp."

Chapter 11

BELLE AND CADY spent the night at the Monteleone Hotel in New Orleans. Even when they bumped into each other in their tiny room, the girl refused to speak to her mother.

Belle watched her daughter slip out of her dress and take down her hair. She remembered when Cady was a little girl and she had to remind her to hold her arms up so her mama could pull her dress over her head.

As Cady brushed her hair one hundred strokes, Belle thought about how her little blond curls used to peek out from under a lacy bonnet when they sat in the garden with Cady's books spread around them, the little girl pointing to the pictures and proudly reciting the nursery rhymes to her mama. Belle taught her to read before she entered school. She wanted her daughter's childhood to be filled with all the books and pretty things she'd longed for when she was growing up.

That suited Claude and Miss Effie, who both doted on the

girl. Belle remembered Miss Effie teaching her granddaughter table manners and how pleased the little girl was to sit up straight and get her knives and forks just right. Claude adored her, their only child to have been born alive. He bought her a pony when she was still so little she was afraid to ride it, and he loved to take her fishing. Belle could still see them rising before dawn, Claude always so quiet as he assembled his lures and tackle, while Cady chattered away about her friends and her imaginary games.

Now, this same daughter slipped into the bed in silence and pretended to go to sleep. Belle remembered their weekly visits to the cemetery during the first year after Claude's death. Cady planted forget-me-nots on his grave and visited it alone almost every day after school. Belle found her there one afternoon, telling him about her day, telling him how much she missed him. She thinks I've betrayed her daddy, Belle thought.

THE NEXT MORNING she woke Cady up. "Come on. Let's go for coffee and doughnuts at the French Market."

"No thank you." There was a righteous primness in Cady's response.

"Please."

Cady was not to be moved. Belle tried an impersonation of Miss Effie. "Now listen to me, young lady." And: "You get up this minute, you hear?" Finally: "I have something important to talk to you about."

Belle didn't want to have this conversation in the cramped, stifling hotel room with its scattering of rumpled bedclothes. The truth was, she didn't want to have this conversation at all. What mother who's spent seventeen years convincing her daughter about the importance of chastity and self-restraint wants to admit her own failings?

"I promised Hugh I'd meet him at noon," Cady announced.

Belle knew she'd promised no such thing. In fact, they'd planned to take the twelve-thirty train back to Gentry. For a fleeting moment, Belle considered letting her daughter have her way. Why have a confrontation when it can be avoided? After all, plenty of people live perfectly well without ever discussing anything deeper than what they want for dinner. Husbands and wives, even mothers and daughters, can go on that way for years. But Cady wouldn't look her in the face and Belle couldn't bear that. "If you get up right now, you and Hugh can have all afternoon and early evening together in the city."

Cady stared at her mother. Her look said, Do you really mean it?

Belle nodded. "We'll catch the seven-thirty train tonight."

The prospect of so many hours in New Orleans with Hugh broke down Cady's resistance, but it didn't change her shock and shame. Soon, mother and daughter were sitting at iron tables across the street from Jackson Square.

It was a glorious New Orleans morning. Around the square, artists had set up easels displaying bright watercolor portraits and scenes of the city, painted with agility, technique, and that complete lack of originality so comforting to shoppers who need to fill a space on their wall, but don't want to be troubled by newfangled art. Or oldfangled art, either.

Cady examined her mother as if she'd never seen her before. But when Belle looked up, her daughter shifted her eyes away. Belle cast around for ways to launch their what? Discussion? Confrontation?

Cady spoke first. "It's not fair. You and Grandma taught me how to behave." Belle nodded, afraid of where this was going. "I've always tried to follow your rules."

"I know, honey, and you've made me very proud."

Cady didn't want to hear how proud her mother was.

"Weren't you supposed to follow the rules, too? I thought you did." She stopped and reconsidered as she looked at her mother's bobbed hair underneath her cloche. "I mean, I knew you were crazy, but I thought, well, I thought you paid attention to the important ones."

Belle nodded. "Sugar, life is long."

"That's no excuse! What were you doing in that closet with Mr. Rafe?"

At that moment a waiter in a long white apron brought them steaming cups of café au lait. Cady blushed a deep pink. "No, never mind," she said when the waiter had gone. "I know what you were doing. I saw you." She took two spoonfuls of sugar and stirred noisily.

Belle knew exactly what her daughter was feeling. She remembered her own devastation when she'd found out her mother had taken up with Mr. Nix. She didn't know if she could make Cady understand, if a mother could ever make a daughter understand that besides being a mother, besides being the wife of her father, she was also a woman.

"It hasn't even been two years since Daddy passed away."

"And before that I waited a year and a half, worrying about him, dreaming about him, until on the very night he came home—" I killed him, Belle thought. What she said was, "I never even looked at another man until Rafe came along."

Cady's voice quivered with indignation. "That's not true. I saw you in Mr. Bourrée's arms Wednesday morning." Somewhere deep in the French Quarter a church bell tolled.

Oh, Lord. I'd almost forgotten about that. And last night that horrible Beryl told her I'd been arrested for indecency.

"I don't know you anymore," Cady said. She wasn't avoiding her mother now. She was glaring at her. "Maybe I never did."

"I wasn't in Bourrée's arms, honey, I was crying on his shoulder."

"You didn't look like you were crying to me." Cady crossed her arms.

Belle put the white cup to her lips. The coffee tasted bitter. "We'd been talking about your daddy and . . . and how he died." Which was true. Sort of. We teach our children never to lie to us and then, as good parents, we lie to them "for their own good." But even that's a lie. We lie to them because it's easier. Because we don't want to admit we're not perfect. "I'm not attracted to Bourrée." Belle couldn't believe what she'd said. She'd just told her daughter another lie. "I mean, he's a very attractive man. You know that. You said so yourself, but I'm not having a physical relationship with him."

Cady sat back in her chair and stared. "I can't believe you're even thinking about . . . about things like that. I mean, Mama, you're over thirty!"

"A woman always thinks about 'things like that.' At least I believe she does, even at my advanced age." She's seeing me as a real person, not simply her omniscient, controlling Mother. Belle felt a little twinge of regret at having to give up that role, but it was time they were friends. She wished she could have that relationship with her own mother.

"So you're thinking about things like that with Mr. Rafe?"

What could Belle say? Cady had seen them in that damned closet.

"But, Mama, he's married."

A barge on the river behind them blew a long, plaintive blast. Belle took a deep breath. "He and his wife are separated."

"But he's still married. Mama! Why?" Cady's wail merged with a second blare of the barge.

She might as well know now as later, Belle thought. It was the last thing a mother wants to admit. "Because I'm human."

They talked for a long time after that. Their waiter set a plate of beignets in front of them. Cady reached for one of the little puffs of dough, sizzling hot and dusted with powdered sugar.

"So you love him?"

A wagon heaped with shiny, green-striped watermelons stopped in front of the outdoor cafe. "Watermelon, luscious red watermelons. Get yourself a sweet, juicy watermelon," the vendor sang.

Belle remembered, when she was Cady's age, love excused everything. She bit into one of the little beignets and licked the powdered sugar off her lips before answering. Were the emotional storms that buffeted her when Rafe kissed her love? Or were they, as she suspected, just loneliness, or worse, lust? For Cady's sake, she had to say, "I think maybe I might love him." Once the words left her lips, she felt they could be true.

"Do you think he'll divorce his wife for you?" Cady's voice was eager.

"Honey, it was only a kiss."

"Only?"

"I don't want to be a home breaker."

"But you said they were separated."

Mass had let out at St. Louis Cathedral and Jackson Square was filling up with people in their Sunday clothes. Belle watched them for a moment before turning back to her daughter. "You like him, don't you?"

"I don't know. I guess he's all right, if you like him, I mean."

Belle stood and kissed her daughter on the top of her head. "Come on. Let's let Hugh know about your date. It's a beautiful day for a stroll along the levee."

As mother and daughter walked through the crowd in Jackson Square, Belle talked about the day she and the other suffragists stormed the beaches of Lake Pontchartrain. She managed to make their escapade sound brave, noble, and even funny.

When she briefly put her arm around Cady's shoulders, her daughter didn't shrug it off.

THE FOLLOWING EVENING after supper, Rafe came out to the farm. Rachel had a standing order with a bookshop in Chicago. They'd just sent her a box of new books and Rafe had brought several out for the Cantrell ladies to read first: *Main Street* by Sinclair Lewis for Belle, and for Miss Effie a mystery by a new British writer people were talking about by the name of Agatha Christie. While they were in New Orleans, Nina had seen a book of collected poetry she'd wanted. Rafe had bought it for her and an extra copy for Cady. "I hope you don't think I'm presumptuous," he said.

Cady didn't say anything. She looked at her mother.

Miss Effie, surprised by her granddaughter's lack of manners, jumped in and said, "How very thoughtful, Mr. Berlin. I know Cady will cherish it." Then she glared at Cady, who thanked him, shyly. She was still wary as she accepted the book, but Belle could see she appreciated Rafe for trying.

Belle walked him out to his car. The cicadas shrilled around them in the starlight. He pulled her to him, but she pushed him away. "No, not here."

"Where?" She shook her head. "I want to be with you."

"It's a lovely dream, but I have my reputation to think about and you—" She was going to add "have your wife." But he was running a long finger over her cheek.

"What about a romantic weekend in New Orleans, just the two of us? I'll get us a room at the Roosevelt Hotel. We can—"

She cut him off. "We can't. I'm sure to run into someone I know."

"Baton Rouge?"

She shook her head. "Miss Effie has kin there."

Rafe cast about for another place. "How about Jackson, Mississippi? I stayed in an inn out in the country on my way down here. It was a beautiful old plantation house. You know anybody in Jackson?"

Belle shook her head. She'd never been out of the state. She'd never been anywhere. How could she even consider such an adventure? But as he talked, she thought about the thrill of driving north in his little car with the wind in her hair. Then she thought about the pleasure of sharing a bed with a man again after all this time. The pleasure of this man.

"Should" warred with "could."

An unmarried woman who travels around the country in the company of a man sets forth on the Road to Perdition. She knew that. It was a hard-and-fast rule from the Primer of Propriety. I'm old enough to know right from wrong, and this is wrong. On so many levels. He's still married to another woman.

But this may be my only chance for an adventure. Nobody ever need know about it. It would be our secret.

"What do you say?" Rafe asked.

She knew she ought to say no.

Then she pictured her life, days of nothing much turning into weeks, weeks turning into years, years of nothing much. Just growing old on the farm with Miss Effie. And then I die. To hell with it, Belle thought, and made up a new rule for her Southern Girls' Guide. *Life is uncertain. A girl has to grab hold while she still has a firm grip.*

THEY PLANNED THEIR ASSIGNATION for the following weekend. Belle was in a state of feverish anticipation. She didn't yearn for the mechanics of sex as much as she ached for that deep tenderness between a man and a woman, which had abandoned her after so many years, leaving her restless and sad.

Of course, she had to admit, a little sex wouldn't be bad either.

This time she was determined to be sensible. She wrote to a pharmacy in New Orleans for one of those contraceptive sponges Margaret Sanger kept alluding to in her speeches, but was not allowed by law to promote or even describe. Belle's suffragist sisters had long known where to obtain them, and by return mail. Before she put her letter in the post, she stopped, thought about what she was doing, ripped open the envelope, and ordered a second sponge.

All the sneaking around and buying illegal contraceptives heightened Belle's sense of sin. There's nothing like a little sin to get the juices flowing, she thought. All she had to do was think about Rafe for her body to light up in a most agreeable way.

Of course, they couldn't just hop into his car and drive off, waving to friends and relatives. They had to devise an elaborate plan. She concocted a story about Constance Bancroft organizing voting schools for ladies and the need for her to stay overnight in New Orleans. Saturday morning, she'd buy a ticket on the southbound train, but instead of going all the way to New Orleans, she'd get off in Hammond. He'd pick her up there and drive north to Jackson, where they'd register as man and wife. They'd mapped out their whole itinerary via back roads.

SHE CLIMBED UP onto the train, wearing a prudish gray traveling suit with little blue flowers over the diaphanous, clingy red undergarments she'd made for Claude's homecoming and never worn again. Until now. She could feel her silk bloomers swish when she walked. A wave of anticipation washed over her. She sat down on the aisle, closed her eyes, and let herself float in a soup of feelings.

"Hey, Belle."

Her soup splashed over its rim. She opened her eyes to see Sheriff George Goode swing his heavy body into the seat across from her. "Miss Effie told me you'd be going down to New Orleans today." The steam whistle screamed and Belle saw her first real adventure slipping away. "Said something about you starting one of them schools to teach ladies how to vote."

The train jerked forward. "You'd better be on your toes, George. You know, I can vote for you now. Or—" She paused and gave him a sultry look. "Your opponent. I've been hearing a lot of talk about him."

George Goode pulled on his collar. "I always did admire a woman who takes her civic responsibilities seriously." He launched into a monologue about the upcoming election and its challenges for right-thinking people. Belle realized for the first time someone was courting her vote. It would have felt grand, if she hadn't been thinking about Rafe sitting in his Stutz, with the sun beating down, waiting for her.

As the train clattered and swayed, the sheriff warned her about the Italian problem. "Are the Italians having a problem?"

She let him fulminate about how they were all forming criminal gangs, taking jobs from one-hundred-percent Americans, and receiving their orders directly from the pope. "You don't say?" She had to keep him talking until she worked out how she could get off in Hammond without his seeing her.

Unthinkable with him sitting next to her.

There was only one answer.

She couldn't.

She brushed some cinders out of her eyes. George had left the Italians and was on to taxes. He was against them. What he was for was business and protecting family morals. "Morals are the bedrock of our civilization. Don't you agree?"

"Of course," she said.

Belle had always known how to handle the boys, how to flirt with them, how to hint at adventure without ever promising to be really bad. She'd enjoyed being seen as a rebel, not one of those boring girls who followed all the rules and missed out on most of the fun. She liked the attention, took it as admiration, but she'd been careful to walk that thin line. Even when she and Claude were having their wild love affair, she knew they'd be getting married. So it was just a matter of time until he made an honest woman of her.

But if George Goode found out about her immoral plans for the weekend, she'd go from being "our Belle, always a bit of the rebel" to "that fallen woman." Ladies would quit inviting her. She'd be the butt of men's dirty jokes. What would she do after she'd burned her bridges and Miss Effie threw her out of the house?

When the train stopped in Amite, the sheriff stood up and began shaking hands hither and yon with every voter and potential voter in the parish. He even kissed a drooling baby.

Suddenly Belle knew how to handle him.

As soon as he sat back down, she said, "I'll always remember Claude Senior's advice to me if women ever got the vote. He said, 'Vote for your relatives first, your friends second, and after that you can vote for the best man.' Now, George, you're Miss Effie's cousin and that makes you kin as far as I'm concerned. I'm always delighted to hear your views, and I am just as flattered as I can be that you want to sit next to me, but your time is too valuable. Elections are just a few months away. I can't let you waste another minute. Don't you want to tackle those undecided voters in the observation car?"

He stood and looked at her with new respect. "Belle, if all women had your sense, I'd a been in favor of giving you-all the vote a long time ago."

BELLE LEFT HER SEAT before the train rolled into Hammond. She knew once the sheriff got to smoking cigars and swapping stories with the boys, he wouldn't be inclined to return to her, but she had to clear the platform and get into the depot before the train started and swept the observation car forward. She didn't want the sheriff observing her.

Unfortunately, before she reached the front of the car, an enormous farm woman rose to her feet, blocking the aisle. The woman waddled slowly, collecting and cuffing a whole litter of children along with their many bundles and baskets. Belle turned and darted for the back of the car, but a porter helping a crippled veteran board thwarted her quick getaway.

By the time she made it down the steps, the "all aboard" had been called. The other porters were throwing their footstools back into the cars and swinging onto the iron stairs. The train started to roll. Belle wanted to fly, but had to run on tiptoe across the wooden platform, so as not to catch her tapered heels in the spaces between the planks. She scampered into the depot, seconds before the observation car swept by.

Hyram Pruett, one of the Hammond Pruetts, was at the ticket window picking up a train schedule. He invited her to come to the house for lunch. Belle thanked him and said she was real sorry, but she'd made other plans, and then without spelling out exactly what those plans were, she slipped out the door and made her way down the block, ducking under awnings so she wouldn't perspire through her prim traveling suit.

At the end of the block was a hardware store. She walked around it and spotted the Stutz parked in the alley in back. Rafe was in the driver's seat. The top was up. Belle looked both ways. No Pruetts in sight. Now her heart was pounding like a jazz drummer. Stumbling on the gravel, she rushed to him.

THE COUNTRY INN outside Jackson was set in the middle of rolling lawns surrounded by deep woods. Rafe had reserved a large corner bedroom with high ceilings. It opened onto a covered veranda. Electricity hadn't reached the old plantation house. Candles were set out on tables and in sconces on the walls, ready to be lit. Lace curtains floated in the afternoon breeze.

Rafe watched her sit gingerly on the strange bed, as if trying out the springs. "Come here," he said, and his voice was hoarse.

He stood in front of a mirrored armoire. She could see him front and back. Who was this tall beanpole of a stranger?

She thought of what lay ahead, all the buttons to be unbuttoned, the laces to be untied, the hooks to be separated from their eyes. It seemed impossible. Belle had known only one man in her whole life. Claude was big and strong. In bed he was a substantial bear, hot and always eager to get the job done.

"Come here," Rafe said again. This time his voice was sure. She hesitated and then went to him, because after coming all this way, what else was there to do?

Belle didn't remember the mechanics of what happened next, but she remembered certain details and she remembered her feelings. She remembered him unbuttoning the pearl buttons of the high lace collar of her flowered traveling suit and continuing down until the buttons gave out at her waist. He slipped off her jacket and ran his hands over her neck and shoulders, letting the straps of her red silk chemise fall until he'd bared her breasts. She remembered him looking at her as if he wanted to drink her in.

She remembered his smooth piano-playing hands trembling when they slid across her chest. She remembered how her breasts tingled when his beautiful, clean fingers cupped them and how with the flick of his fingernail he made her nipples stand up and sing hallelujah. She remembered how much she wanted him at that moment before the world, the room, everything fell away under those hands.

Next, she remembered he did something she'd never even heard of. He fell to his knees in front of her, his lips warm on her bare breasts, sliding down her stomach. Belle felt embarrassed. What was he doing down there? She wanted to lift him up. She'd read about foreplay in a marriage guide. She'd even pointed it out to Claude once, but he figured walking across the room was foreplay enough for him.

Rafe pulled up her skirt, untied her bloomers, and pressed his mouth to places no man had ever ventured before. At first she was confused. Then she cried out with the wonder of it. If this was the way they made love in Chicago, what the heck was she doing in Gentry?

He stood before she wanted him to. They both fumbled with his buttons until she saw him long and lean and naked in front of her. She remembered touching him. She remembered him moaning as he took her face in both his hands and pressed her lips to his.

How did they get to the bed? She didn't remember, but she remembered the way his wavy hair felt in her fingers as he bent over her breasts. And she remembered his lips on her breasts. She remembered crying out as his naked skin slid against her naked skin, and the taste of his lips and tongue. She remembered the feeling of him entering her, their bodies moving together. He was tall and angular. She was soft and curvy. They fit each other to perfection.

He turned her until she was on top. Belle had never been on top before. She wasn't sure it was right for a woman to be on top, but she soon found pleasure in it as she squinched around, moving over just the right spot. It seemed strange to her to take the lead, but he didn't seem to mind at all, so she stopped worrying about what was right and simply abandoned herself to those delicious arrows of pleasure shooting through her. She remembered crying out and his hand covering her mouth as a million, trillion arrows shot through her and took her to a place of pure feeling.

Had she ever experienced lovemaking like this before? She couldn't remember. She couldn't remember anything. Everything was now. He must have been waiting for her, because he cried out soon after.

They lay on their backs holding hands.

Rafe turned, bracing himself on his elbow. He looked at her lying there amid the rumpled sheets. His taste for women was back. And in dazzling color.

He slid his palm over her rounded belly, ran his fingers lightly through her soft hair, and caressed her thighs. Soon they were making love again, this time slower, longer, even better.

The lace curtains changed from white, to rose, to gray. The room filled with shadows, but Belle and Rafe never noticed. They were too caught up in the wonder of each other. Their pleasure radiated out until it encompassed the whole world.

They ignored the chimes rung by a maid outside their room at six and seven. But by seven-thirty they were starving. They felt like naughty children scampering down the spiral staircase. They didn't hold hands, but managed to bump into each other numerous times on their way down. The touch of Rafe's arm against her shoulder sent waves of happiness through Belle.

The proprietor of the inn greeted them at the foot of the

stairs and hurried them into the dining room. They walked through the double doors with as much dignity as they could muster and found twenty eyes looking up at them.

On his way down to Gentry, Rafe had pulled into the hotel late at night. He remembered its isolated setting, beautiful grounds, comfortable accommodations, and excellent late breakfast. He hadn't thought to inquire about the seating at dinner.

The polished pecan wood of the buffet and china cabinet glowed softly in the candlelight from the brass chandelier. In the center of the room, ten guests were seated around a big table covered with a white linen cloth. They studied the new couple. The proprietor introduced them as "Mr. and Mrs. Brown," and hurried into the kitchen to alert the staff.

The other guests had finished their soup and started their main course. They put down their forks to introduce themselves. Belle sat back, relaxed, as the conversation eddied and flowed around her.

"And where do you-all come from, Mrs. Brown?" a white-haired woman asked Belle.

"Cincinnati," Belle said, and wondered where that had come from. She'd never been to Cincinnati, she'd never wanted to go to Cincinnati, she'd never even thought about Cincinnati. Rafe gave her a pained look.

"What a coincidence," a plump little blonde squealed.

A pretty colored maid, in a starched white apron, her hair covered with an old-fashioned tricorn scarf, brought in a tureen of soup.

"You sound like a Southern girl to me," said the white-haired woman.

Belle froze and then said, "I guess a Louisiana girl never loses her accent, but I'm from Cincinnati now."

"What part of town do you live in?" the little blonde, whose name was Mrs. Farbler, asked. She wore a small hat of peacock feathers and a silk dress with a feather motif. She looked like a little bird perched on the limb of her big, gruff husband, who was dressed in a rumpled, bark-colored suit.

Farbler Warbler, Belle thought as she concentrated on ladling out a creamy orange soup. "This looks delicious," she said, feeling like a perfect nit. "What kind of soup is it?"

The maid gave her a look, as if to say, Some white people are too dumb to live. "Cream of tomato."

"Of course. I should have guessed. Don't you-all just love tomato soup?" Belle asked the assembled guests.

The answers were various. As the maid passed the soup to Rafe, Mrs. Farbler resumed her interrogation. "What part of Cincinnati did you say you lived in?"

Rafe had chosen this inn outside Jackson because it was less than a day's drive from Gentry and the roads were relatively good. They hadn't planned on meeting anyone. They would be away only one night.

Now he realized what a damn fool thing he'd done. He could see the headlines: "Lascivious Jew Transports Flower of Southern Womanhood Across State Lines for Immoral Purposes." Just three years before, two prominent Californians had been convicted under the Mann Act when they took a couple of girls to Reno for a fling. The case became a nationwide sensation. Rafe could go to federal prison for five years. Belle would be ruined.

Rafe had never been a liar. He'd never been any good at it. Never wanted to be. He turned to Mrs. Farbler and said suavely, "Actually, we're moving there from Chicago. Perhaps you can give us some advice."

Mrs. Farbler's little bird face lit up and she let out a chirp. "I think there's a house for sale down the street from us, isn't there, Fred?" The songbird turned to her dark husband.

"Yes, indeed," Fred said. "What brings you to Cincinnati?"

As Rafe tried to create a new business venture that he hoped would fit into the Cincinnati economy, the little bird turned to Belle. "It's a perfect home for a big family. Do you have any children, Mrs. Brown?"

The maid brought Belle a plate of pale lumps. If she'd bothered to inspect it, she might have been able to identify baked chicken, mashed potatoes covered with flour gravy, creamed corn, and stewed onions. Only a dab of turnip greens contrasted with the ashen food.

Belle shoveled it all into her mouth without tasting, pointing to her lips when asked to elaborate on the threads that were being woven into her sham life. She'd always figured a lady has to lie for a good cause from time to time, but that evening her mouth hurt from it as Mrs. Farbler pecked at the crumbs of her story.

Rafe tried to bring the conversation around to baseball, the war, anything but Cincinnati, but the Farblers were relentless. "Best little city in the country, if you ask me," Mr. Farbler said. "You planning on joining the Chamber of Commerce? How about the Boosters? I can help you there."

The arrival of the lemon meringue pie was a great relief. Belle almost slumped into it. By the time they'd had their coffee, Fred Warbler had given Rafe his phone number and invited him to the next meeting of the Boosters. Mrs. Farbler, who by now insisted on being called Vera, had shown Belle pictures of her many children and offered to sponsor her for membership in the Ladies Assistance League. "They're a wonderful group of girls."

"When I get to Cincinnati," Belle promised, "you'll be the first person I'll call."

Belle and Rafe went upstairs without speaking. All the lying had fouled their great adventure. When they got to their room, they realized it was raining. They sat out on the veranda and watched it fall.

THEY CROSSED BACK into Louisiana after dark the next night. Rafe put the top down and they drove under a clear sky studded with stars. He talked about Chicago. He told her about ice skating in Grant Park, and once again he promised to show her snow. This time she believed him. She took off her hat to enjoy the night wind flowing through her hair and pictured herself in this rosy future, walking down Lake Shore Drive with him in a swirl of snowflakes. She touched his knee. He picked up her hand and brought it to his lips.

A sign said, "Welcome to Farabee."

"Let's not drive directly through town," Belle said.

"It's night."

"Too many Farabee Pruetts. They'll recognize your car."

"That damn family is everywhere."

"You know where the Bible says, 'Be fruitful and multiply'? Well, the Pruetts take it personally."

Rafe turned off onto the back road they had driven up on. What houses they passed were small, set back behind fields and pastures.

They came across a line of parked cars, trucks, and wagons stretched around the bend in the road. In the distance, they heard "Onward, Christian Soldiers" sung by what sounded like an all-male choir. Belle looked for a church, but could only make out a small shack on a little hill.

Suddenly, a blast of dynamite shook the ground. Rafe jerked back the brake lever, slammed on the foot brake, hit the clutch, and shifted into neutral. The engine snorted and popped as the car came to a standstill.

Next to the road, burlap sacks soaked in kerosene ignited. Fire darted over heavy timbers until a huge cross blazed against the night sky. Figures dressed in white, with cone-shaped hats and arms outstretched, turned toward the Stutz, now clearly illuminated by the flaming cross.

"Who goes there?" a voice called.

Belle felt as if she'd been caught in a spotlight. She grabbed her hat and tried to duck, impossible in the low-cut car. Men in white gowns ran toward them.

Rafe stood on the clutch, pressing it all the way down until it clanged against the aluminum floorboard as he slammed the car into first gear. He mashed down on the throttle and let out the clutch. The engine roared. Rear wheels fishtailed across the loose soil on the high-crowned dirt road.

Behind her Belle heard voices, calling, threatening. She came close to praying as she tried to strike a bargain with God. "Oh, please, let us get out of here. I'll . . . I'll . . ."

Sparks shot out from beneath the car. Rafe wrenched the wheel to the right. A cloud of dust kicked up from the blast of the exhaust. They were off, climbing to thirty, forty, fifty, sixty miles an hour. The car jounced over the washboard road with a rat-ta-tat-tat that sounded like a machine gun. Belle clutched the door with one hand and her hat with the other. Suddenly a giggle bubbled up from deep inside her. For the first time in her life, she felt wild and free. Her giggles turned to chuckles, and before long full-fledged laughter spilled out into the night. Her gaiety infected Rafe, who began to chuckle with her. Their hilarity grew, feeding off each other's until they were howling into the wind.

A white-robed figure stayed in the middle of the road, watching them disappear. He stood there, eyes narrowed under his mask, even after the others had turned back and joined hands to sing "The Old Rugged Cross."

Chapter 12

AT LUNCH ON MONDAY, Miss Effie asked Belle, "Tell me about your weekend, dear. Anything exciting happen?"

"Oh, you know," Belle said, reaching quickly for the corn bread, a little smile inching over her lips.

"Did you have a good time with your friend?" Belle took a very big bite of corn bread. "What's 'er name?" Miss Effie pressed. Belle pointed to her stuffed lips. "Don't take so much in your mouth, Belle. I shouldn't have to tell you that after all this time."

"Is Miss Constance going to open one of those voting schools in Gentry?" Cady asked.

Belle swallowed at last. "I don't know, sugar." She spooned black-eyed peas onto her plate, and before Miss Effie could inquire further, Belle said, "Stella, these peas look wonderful. Did you do something different?"

"No, ma'am." Stella set a pitcher of iced tea on the table.

She'd rinsed out Belle's red silk undergarments that morning, and she was pretty sure Belle had not spent the weekend doing good with a bunch of women.

"I saw D. T. Pruett in town this morning," Miss Effie said, cutting a small piece of catfish.

"Did you?" Belle reached for the pitcher of iced tea.

"He said his brother Titus saw you driving around in Rafe Berlin's fancy car somewhere outside Farabee last night."

Tea overflowed Belle's glass and poured onto her knuckles.

AFTER LUNCH, BELLE MARCHED into Rubinstein, wearing a navy blue skirt and high-necked, starched shirtwaist that was a model of both propriety and discomfort. What she wanted to do was run up the stairs and leap into Rafe's lap. Instead she forced herself to stop on the sales floor and discuss wool flannel with Angelina Monotti.

She knew Rafe could see her from his desk in the mezzanine. Minutes passed. Where was he? Angelina took down bolt after bolt of the scratchy material. Still Rafe didn't appear. Belle was reduced to asking, "Don't you have a gray with a little more blue?" when she noticed Angelina's attitude change. It went from a dealing-with-an-impossible-customer stance to a the-boss-is-watching posture.

Belle turned and tried to stop her face from lighting up. She wasn't at all sure she succeeded. A misty glow seemed to float in the air between them.

"Mrs. Cantrell."

"Mr. Berlin, how nice to—" Belle paused. "Run into you."

Rafe seemed to be casting around for something to say. "That piece of farm equipment—" Belle looked at him blankly. He went on. "The one you inquired about, is in."

Belle took a moment and then said, "Really? I'd appreciate it if you showed it to me, Mr. Berlin. Excuse me, Mrs. Monotti."

He made a slight bow to Angelina. Belle turned, brushing her exposed elbow on his suit coat. Shivers fluttered up her arm. As they headed into the hardware department, she said, "Titus Pruett recognized me last night."

"Are you sure?"

Belle nodded. "Miss Effie told his brother that was impossible, because I was in New Orleans. Of course they couldn't help but recognize your car."

Rafe looked worried. "Do you think he believed her about New Orleans?"

"Probably not." The Primer of Propriety stipulated: *A lady's reputation is her most prized possession.* When that's in jeopardy, the Southern Girls' Guide to Men and Other Perils of Modern Life advised: *Suspicion isn't knowledge, so lie through your teeth.*

"It would help if you'd drop a couple of hints about some other woman. Ask Mary Louise Pruett if she knows a florist who'll deliver flowers to a lady in Farabee. That should start the rumor mill working overtime."

Rafe looked uncomfortable with the subterfuge. "But whom would I say I was sending flowers to?"

"Why, darlin', a gentleman like you would never divulge that information."

He smiled. "Of course. How foolish of me. I think it would have been safer for you to have told me this on the phone."

Belle laughed. "Over our party line? You might as well print it in the *Gentry Post.*"

"Belle, I want you to be extra careful. I don't think you should come here alone anymore. I read where the Klan whipped a couple of girls for riding in a car with boys."

"So that's what those benevolent heroes are up to. Whipping colored girls." She shook her head.

"White girls."

"You must have gotten that wrong."

"No."

"But that's been their whole justification, protecting white women. What are they protecting us from now? Our own children?"

"Apparently, they're only interested in protecting what they call 'innocent' girls."

Belle gave a little laugh-snort. "And Miss Effie called the Klan 'modern-day knights in the service of the South.' "

"It happened in Oklahoma."

The whole world's gone nuts, Belle thought. Rafe stopped to let her go through the doorway first. She stepped down into the hardware department, turned the corner, and came face-to-face with Titus Pruett. He was buying a gun.

She turned back and bumped into Rafe.

"Hey, Belle, what you been up to?" Titus asked, his voice booming off the light fixtures. He grinned. He knew what Belle had been up to. At thirty-three, Titus was a man of strong beliefs and weak intellect. He was stocky, like a football player gone to seed, with reddish hair, a loud voice, and a bottomless pit of righteous indignation.

His companion turned, and for the first time in a year and a half, Belle came face-to-face with Pruett Walker, the mayor's son, president of Walker Sawmill and the man who'd killed her husband. He'd gained at least a hundred pounds. She hoped it was from guilt.

"Hey, Belle, never got a chance to tell you how sorry I was for what happened to Claude." Pruett Walker's voice was as soft as his flapping jowls.

"Not as sorry as I was," Belle said.

"We all miss old Claude," Titus said, glancing at his corpulent cousin, who was having a squint at Rafe and then at Belle.

In her best imitation of Miss Effie at her most imperious, Belle said, "You-all know Mr. Berlin, don't you?"

"Can't say I've had that pleasure." Pruett Walker rocked back on his heels and stuck his thumbs into his suspenders, displaying his pendulous belly. He pointed it left and right while Belle made the introductions. She wondered if Sheriff Goode had told him she'd demanded his arrest.

"You Miss Rachel's brother from New York?" Redheaded Titus fingered the shotgun on the counter in front of him.

"Chicago," Rafe said. The cousins exchanged a smirk, as if making the distinction was somehow funny. "If you'll excuse us, I was just showing Mrs. Cantrell some farm equipment she'd inquired about."

Pruett Walker picked up a deer rifle and sighted through it. "Just what kind of equipment would that be, Mr. Berlin?"

Rafe looked blank. Farm equipment was not his specialty. Belle came to his rescue. "I'm looking for a poison spreader, Pruett. We've been having trouble with rats."

Rachel intercepted them on their way to the poison spreader. "Oh, Belle, Angelina said I'd find you here."

"Hey, Rachel." She kissed her friend on the cheek. Pruett Walker and Titus Pruett were still watching. Belle was glad to have a chaperone.

"Debbie Lou Rutledge and I were trying to get up a bridge game Saturday afternoon. Miss Effie said you were in New Orleans. Something about the ERA Club and voting schools or was it registration?"

Belle looked at Rafe. He remained impassive. How do men do that? she wondered.

Rachel put her arm around Belle. "Will you and Cady be able to come over to the house Friday evening?"

"Sure."

"I want to do a traditional Shabbat dinner in honor of my brother." Rafe looked surprised, but not pleased. Rachel ignored him and went on. "We used to celebrate every week when we were growing up. Friday night is the beginning of our Sabbath."

"That would be lovely. Of course, we'd be delighted to come."

"You'd better talk to Abe. He's not exactly observant." Rafe's voice was cold.

"Oh, Abe will humor me this once."

Belle witnessed a silent standoff between brother and sister and wondered what was going on. Why was Rafe set against her sharing Sabbath dinner with them? After several silent moments, Rafe turned to her. "Don't worry, we won't boil any Christian babies."

"What a shame," Belle said. "And I was so looking forward to the spectacle."

DURING THE NEXT WEEK, Belle was flooded with fantasies. Mornings she worked with Bourrée preparing for the cotton harvest. Evenings she spent in the office, going over all the receipts, making sure everything checked out. But during the long afternoons, she retired to the chaise longue in her bedroom and gave herself up to reveries. Wearing only her undergarments in the darkened room, she rolled a glass of iced coffee across her forehead and thought about Rafe. She imagined him sitting next to her, his long hands caressing her, slipping into her camisole.

She relived the conversation she'd had with Cady. "Do you love him?"

If this wasn't love, it was a darn good imitation. Rafe was like no man she'd ever met. And because Belle wasn't nearly as wild as she thought she was, she began to dream about marriage. Why not? Love meant marriage, didn't it? They might even have children. It wasn't too late. She'd like to have a baby again. Give Rafe a son. She thought about the miscarriages she'd had since Cady. But maybe it would be different in Chicago, with a Yankee doctor. They were learning things all the time.

If Bourrée brought in the cotton harvest as well as he'd brought in the corn, without even hiring any extra workers, she'd be free. They could get someone at the bank to watch the books, or Abe, if he were well enough. Cady would be away at college next year. Miss Effie had her clubs and her friends. Belle figured it was her turn.

His divorce couldn't take forever.

She let her mind play around with the idea. She and Claude grew up together, they knew everything about each other, but marriage to Rafe would open up a whole new world, a world Rachel was inviting her to enter. She wasn't just giving a Sabbath dinner for her brother. She wanted them to become sisters. But why had Rafe been so set against it? There was only one obvious answer, but it was an answer Belle did not want to face.

As PART OF her newfound commitment to live her own life, Belle decided to give herself a present. She was tired of clip-clopping for an hour every time she wanted to go into town.

But she knew that among the many things Miss Effie would never countenance, a car, that good-time house on wheels, was first and foremost.

So Belle decided to buy herself a truck. A truck wasn't built for a good time. It was a serious piece of farm equipment. At least that's what she told Cady that Friday afternoon when she dropped her off at the Rubinsteins' before driving the buggy around to Rutledge Ford.

Darvin had taken a 1918 truck in trade. It was washed and waiting for her. Jim, the mechanic, came over and admired it with her. "It's a swell truck."

"You really think so?" Belle was nervous in the face of such a monumental purchase. She knew it would change not only distance but time. And forever.

Instead of an hour to get to town, it would cover those five miles in just over ten minutes.

If the weather was dry.

"Golly, yes. I'd buy it myself. I got it running real slick. Look here, Darvin even put in a windshield. He didn't want you to get wet when it rained." The metal hood over the motor and the fenders was black, but the wood chassis had a fresh coat of bright yellow paint. It took her breath away. "If you don't like yellow, we can paint it some other color. It was red when it came in, but Darvin didn't think that was a respectable color for a lady."

"Yellow's fine." She stepped up onto the running board and slid into the cab. There were no doors. Four metal posts held up the canvas roof. Jim told her the tires were solid rubber and then said something about cylinders and a compression ratio. Belle stroked the steering wheel.

"Will you show me how to drive it?"

"The boss likes to do that himself. He should be back anytime."

They went into Darvin's office, where the mechanic handed her a brochure on the operation and maintenance of her wonderful new machine—a very dull brochure on the operation and maintenance of her wonderful new machine. It was filled with words she'd sort of heard of but couldn't make sense out of by the time she got to the end of the sentence. Soon she was using the brochure for a fan.

Still Darvin didn't show up. On his desk was a magazine, *The Dearborn Independent,* Dearborn Publishing Company, Dearborn, Michigan. Belle picked it up.

What she expected was information on Ford motorcars or the latest maintenance tips. What she found was something quite different. "The international Jew, the world's foremost problem," the magazine proclaimed. In small type and dense print, Belle read how Jews planned to take over Christian states, how they already controlled the means of commerce, how they were loyal only to their race.

"Hey, Belle, sorry I wasn't here when you came in. Want to take a spin in your new truck?"

Belle tossed the magazine onto his desk. "You subscribe to this?"

"Me? No. It's just something Henry Ford sends out for free to all his dealers. Don't mean a thing."

"Listen to this: 'If fans wish to know the trouble with American baseball, they have it in three words: too much Jew.' Baseball, Darvin, he's talking about baseball!"

"I never had time to read it." He took it from her and tossed it into the wastebasket.

"You and Debbie Lou took Abe a pie. She and Rachel played bridge just last week."

"Honey, Rachel and Abe aren't Jews. They're neighbors. Now, you know there's good and bad all over. Let's go and have a look at your new truck."

Belle hesitated. "Maybe I'll go to New Orleans and get me something else. A Packard maybe."

Darvin's ruddy complexion became suddenly ruddier. His beefy body became beefier as he launched into his role as car salesman to Gentry. "Hey, be sensible, girl. You can't afford a Packard. Besides, you're buying this truck used. Henry Ford's not gonna make a darn penny off it. I bought it for you, and Jim out there, he's been working on it all week so it'd be in tip-top condition." Still Belle hesitated. "If you don't buy it, I'm the one who's gonna be out. Old Henry will do fine either way."

Belle made Darvin sweat for a while longer before she handed him the ninety-five dollars she'd taken out of the bank that afternoon. She really, really wanted that yellow truck.

After receiving a fifteen-minute lesson, she drove away as big, fat drops of rain began to fall. The truck shuddered over the tracks on Grand Avenue and rumbled over the ruts on Commerce Street, but it carried her down Hope to the Rubinstein's. Nina and Cady met her at the door.

Belle had often stopped by for supper on Friday night with Rachel and Abe, but tonight, for the first time, Rachel had brought out the lace tablecloth she'd inherited from her German grandmother. She'd set the table with china Belle had never seen before, china with real gold around the rims.

Abe wandered into the dining room and shook his head. "Think the good Lord is going to shine His Countenance upon you because you brought out the family Limoges?"

"Abe, hush. Go put on your new suit," Rachel said as she placed candles, grape juice, and a twisted loaf of bread on the table. She was wearing Rubinstein's finest dress, slung low over her ample hips.

Abe groaned. "All right, but no hat. I'm not wearing a hat to the table. And neither is Buster."

"All right, no hat."

———

RACHEL TOLD BELLE to sit next to Buster and tried to put Nina and Cady with Rafe, but he was having none of it. "Let the children sit next to each other. Belle can sit next to me."

Belle watched her best friend put a shawl over her head and light a couple of candles. She was fascinated by Rachel's mysterious hand gestures and wondered why she'd covered her eyes. Her attention to the ceremony was diverted, however, when Rafe slid his foot over hers. Even though she felt a thrill rise up her calf, she was careful to pull her foot out from under and slide her toe over his. Romance was all very well, but she had splurged on a new pair of twelve-dollar shoes for the occasion and made herself a silk dress to match. The shoes had blue trim and tapered heels and she was determined to protect them.

Rachel seemed to be blessing all sorts of things, the candles, the children, the bread, and a big goblet full of grape juice, but Belle wasn't sure, because she was doing it in a foreign language. She also passed around a crystal finger bowl and a little pitcher for the ritual washing of hands. When she opened the Bible and started reading a passage, Abe said, "Enough, already. Let's eat."

Rachel glared at her husband and concluded her prayer. Then she said to Belle, "I hope this doesn't seem too strange to you."

"We say grace before every meal," Cady piped up. "It's really not that different, is it, Mama?"

"Not very different at all. And I think getting dressed up once a week and making a family dinner a special event is a wonderful tradition. I'm so glad you included us."

Rachel looked strangely displeased. "We call this challah," she said, passing a twisted loaf of bread around the table.

"Challah," Belle repeated. Suddenly the windows were

flooded with a flash of light. Rachel seemed irritated and corrected Belle's pronunciation as thunder rumbled through the
house. Flaubert crawled under the table. Belle slipped her free
foot out of her pump and rubbed the big dog's shaggy coat.

Rachel's irritation increased when Cady enthused over the
pot roast with prunes and asked for the recipe. "I bet Hugh
would love it." The hostess became even more cranky when
Belle praised her noodle casserole.

"Sugar, are you feeling all right?" Belle asked her.

"Of course I'm feeling all right. Why shouldn't I feel all
right?" The wind had picked up. A tree limb banged against the
house.

When Josephine came in with the fresh watermelon Belle had
picked that afternoon, the electricity went out. Nobody was
very concerned. Electricity failed all the time during a storm. Besides, the dining room was beautiful in the dancing candlelight.

Rafe pressed his leg next to Belle's as he dug into the melon.
He'd forgotten how sweet fruit could be.

Abe went into the back closet and brought out a couple of
storm lanterns. Rafe handed him a cigarette lighter. "Don't
light those!" Rachel exclaimed.

Abe froze. "Why not?"

"It's Shabbat."

"Enough superstition!" Abe roared, and the sky roared with
him. Belle had never seen him so angry. He lit the lanterns, putting one on the sideboard and taking the other to Josephine in
the kitchen.

They finished dinner in silence. The electrical storm outside
provided the entertainment.

After dinner Rafe took Belle out onto the back porch to look
at the storm. Water poured off the eaves. The air smelled of
rain.

Rafe held her close. "Thank you."

"For what?"

"For bringing me back to life."

Before she could ask him what he meant, he kissed her. She thought about Cady and Nina, but she didn't pull away. Rafe's arms felt too much like home.

The door was flung open. They were silhouetted against a blaze of lightning. "Excuse me. I thought we might have our coffee out here," Rachel said as the sky growled.

The storm began to let up while they were drinking their coffee. Belle crossed her feet at the ankles and pushed them forward. When the lightning flashed again, she wanted to show off her new shoes.

Rachel turned to Rafe. "Abe promised to take Cady and Nina to a slumber party, but I don't want him driving around all alone in this storm."

"Nonsense," Abe said. "I'm perfectly capable of driving the girls a few blocks."

"Please, Abe, humor me." She turned to her brother.

"Of course." Rafe rose. Belle rose with him. "I'll be back in a flash." His voice was so intimate, it made her tremble.

"I'll be here," she promised, and was glad she'd worn her contraceptive sponge, just in case something unforeseen happened. She couldn't imagine where that unforeseen event might take place, but she was prepared.

When the men had gone, Rachel invited Belle to sit out on the front porch with her. Belle was light-headed with the thought of Rafe's return. Rachel settled down on the swing and patted the seat next to her. She looked troubled. "What is it? Not more bad news about Abe?"

Rachel shook her head and looked out at the rain. "You know how much I care for you?" She stopped and waited for Belle to nod. "I don't want to see you get hurt."

"What are you talking about?"

"Rafe, of course." Belle laughed, but Rachel went on scowl-ing. "Last weekend did you . . . I mean, did he . . . ?"

Belle felt as if she were in one of those Victorian novels Rachel had loaned her. "Compromise my virtue? How could you think such a thing?"

"Listen to me, dear. I'm only telling you this because I care for you. Don't get involved with my brother."

"I don't see—"

Rachel cut her off. "He'll break your heart."

"My heart's pretty strong. I think I'll take my chances."

"Belle! He'll never marry you."

What the heck was going on? Rachel was her best friend, or at least Belle thought she was. "I'm not chasing after your brother, if that's what you're afraid of." Does she think I'm a gold digger? Belle pulled herself up into her great-lady posture. "If anything, he's chasing me." She wasn't sure that was true, but it felt good to say.

"I know. He's not being fair to you."

"You think he's leading me on?" The whole idea seemed comical. She wasn't some young virgin. She could take care of herself.

"Not on purpose, perhaps. I'm sure he doesn't think of it that way, but he'll leave you all the same. My brother would never marry outside his faith." Belle felt as if her heart had just been stomped on.

She didn't remember what she said next or how Rachel replied. What she heard was, My best friend doesn't think I'm good enough to marry her brother. And I was ready to be her sister!

"You think you could make him a Shabbat dinner?"

"You mean could I light a couple of candles and say a prayer? You bet I could. And I could learn it in Hebrew, Latin, or Aramaic. But you're wrong. Rafe's not any more religious than Abe is."

"Our religion has a strange hold on us."

Belle's voice was tight. "I haven't noticed you running down to New Orleans to go to your church." They didn't call it church, did they? "And Abe—"

Rachel cut her off. Her voice was soft, caring. "Abe went all the way to Chicago to find a Jewish bride." Belle expected to hear a crash of thunder. There ought to be thunder at a moment like this. But the sky was silent. The only sound was Rachel's voice. "My brother might contemplate marrying outside his faith. He might even get engaged, but he'd never go through with it. The children wouldn't be Jewish."

"So what? If there's only one God, like you-all say, you really think He cares which house He's worshiped in? I figure He visits them all."

"It would kill our parents."

There was more before Belle stormed out to her truck and cranked it up with one hand, holding her umbrella in the other, trying to keep her silk dress dry. There had been words friends don't say to one another, words that couldn't be taken back, words that would never be forgotten.

Belle didn't want to believe her. Rafe wasn't prejudiced. She idled at the end of the street with the rain blowing in on her, waiting in the truck for Rafe's return. She rehearsed what she was going to say, but she had to admit he'd never actually mentioned marriage. So what was she going to do, propose to him?

Nothing in her upbringing would let her do that. But she had to get to the bottom of this. She'd ask him straight out what his intentions were. She thought about the heat in his voice when he'd looked down and said, "I'll be back in a flash."

Lightning zippered through the sky. The crack of thunder

brought her back to her senses. The Southern Girls' Guide to Men and Other Perils of Modern Life warned her: *A man will say anything. And when the sap is rising, he might even believe it. But once his bodily fluids take their natural course, his memory of those fine words will become impaired.*

Suddenly, Belle knew it wouldn't make any difference what Rafe said. Not tonight. Maybe not any night. They don't want me, she thought. They don't think I'm good enough.

They've all gone to college.

Up North.

She tried to imagine what that must be like. She pictured Tulane, but in the snow. Excited students walking and laughing, carrying books and discussing lofty ideas between stone buildings. Vast libraries filled with fireplaces and snow falling outside the windows. College dances. Afternoon teas with brilliant professors.

She thought of all the books and magazines she'd read since she'd met Rachel. I'm just an ignorant country girl with no education and no experience of the world. She felt tears waiting in back of her eyes.

Through the rain, she saw the Packard coming up Hope Street. She put the truck in gear and drove away from Hope, down New Century.

Damn him, damn him, damn, damn, damn, she thought as she bumped over the country highway, back to the farm. Her faint headlights illuminated the rain and not much more. She tried to push the words from *The Dearborn Independent* out of her mind, but they kept crawling back in. "The Jew is loyal only to those of his own race." No, she wouldn't believe that slander. But still and all—

She was overwhelmed by a sense of betrayal and loss. Rachel had been her friend and teacher. She'd opened her mind, given her a glimpse of life outside the confines of Gentry. She'd felt at home in their house. She'd depended on Abe. Now she wondered what she'd been to them. A social-work project? Someone we can help, but not really one of us?

Wait a minute, Belle thought. I'm the one who's supposed to be prejudiced against them, not the other way around. I'm the one who's being magnanimous.

She opened the throttle and let the clutch out all the way. She was flying! Rain smeared across the windshield. The truck rocked and gamboled over the ruts in the road. They think just because they're Jews, it's all right for them to be prejudiced? She splashed a mule cart going the other way. Well, it's not. Prejudice is prejudice and it hurts.

Suddenly she realized she'd almost missed the turnoff to the farm. Loyal knew the way. She wasn't used to looking for the driveway herself.

She wrenched the steering wheel around to the left and stepped on the brake pedal. The truck bucked and choked. Good grief, I forgot to push in the clutch! She stamped on it with her left foot. Was that halfway? It was more than halfway, wasn't it? A man had to have invented this thing. No woman would have made it so complicated! She felt the truck bite into the turn, but the rear wheels were skidding out.

She stood with her whole weight on the brake pedal, but the truck kept on sliding. She yanked up on the brake lever. The truck continued to spin over the wet gravel, bouncing like a girl doing a shimmy. Were they going into the ditch? She peered into the dark rain. The ditch was getting closer. She tried to twist the heavy steering wheel the other way. But it was too heavy. Why was it so heavy now?

Suddenly she felt the truck lurch sideways and roll. What am I supposed to do!

Oh, God, oh, God!

Chapter 13

BELLE WAS FLUNG into the steering wheel. Pain shot through her. The truck lurched. She slipped down across the bench.

The engine stalled.

Dead.

But Belle didn't die. She knew this because she heard a jack-hammer she figured must be her heart pounding between her ears. She said a shaky thank-you to Whom It May Concern and pulled herself back up behind the steering wheel. Her arms screamed. Her ribs throbbed.

The truck was tilted, so the driver's side was open to the sky. Rain pelted her. She grabbed her umbrella, climbed painfully out onto the running board, and jumped to the ground. Pain shot through her ribs and thighs.

She felt the tapered heels of her new pumps sink into the mud. She eased over, pulled them out of the muck, and slipped them back on, squishing over the ground on her toes. Spasms shot through her legs. The right-rear wheel had plunged into a ditch. She smacked the darn truck with her fist, but all she accomplished was to hurt her wrist.

Belle, who'd been so hard-boiled, so filled with righteous anger a moment earlier, started to cry. Big, fat tears ran down her cheeks and mixed with the rain.

She threw her umbrella into the truck bed, and pressing her shoulder to the rear frame, tried to roll the damn thing out of the ditch. It didn't budge, but her new silk dress was ruined and her twelve-dollar shoes vanished beneath the muck. She stepped out of them, pulled them out again, and hurled them into the dark.

That's when Belle started to swear. She knew The Primer of Propriety forbade vulgarity, and she didn't have a lot of obscenities at her command, but if there was ever a time to bring them out, this was it. She yelled every expletive, every oath, every four-letter word she'd ever heard. The wind whipped around her. Lightning flashed across the treetops. She cursed the sky. Thunder shook the ground.

She was trying to crank up the engine while screaming at the rain when an old rusty Model T stopped next to her.

Bourrée LeBlanc jumped out. "What you doing out here all by yourself, chère?" His pale eyes sparkled in his dim headlights. She thought of him as a knight errant seeking to rescue a damsel in distress. His quest has succeeded, she thought. I'm nothing if not distressed.

He examined her wounded vehicle. "You just buy this here truck?" Belle nodded her miserable head. "I love to see a woman drive." He made it sound downright sexy. The rain plastered his shirt and pants to his body. She felt as if she were seeing him naked. She had to admit, it was a pretty good sight.

He returned to his car, where he retrieved a heavy plank. He must keep it there all the time in case of emergencies, she thought. That's when Belle realized ownership of a motor vehicle is a mixed blessing. Sometimes, it's your friend. Sometimes, it tries to kill you.

"Come on." Without thinking, she followed in her stocking feet and watched him set the plank in back of the wheel. "I'm going to try to lift the back of your truck. When I do, I want you to shove this here plank under the wheel. Okay?"

"Okay." She eased herself down, feeling her muscles complain and her wet dress hug her breast and legs as she squatted in the mud facing him. She took hold of the plank.

The gas headlights from his old Model T scattered radiance onto the gray raindrops. They haloed around him. She saw the muscles of his thighs bulge under his drenched pants. Through his white shirt, she watched his chest expand, biceps balloon, shoulder muscles swell. His neck strained. A vein protruded and beat in and out. He lifted the wooden bed of the truck away from the wheel and then slowly the wheel itself began to rise out of the mud. She shoved the plank under the wheel. "I got it!"

He let the truck drop and grinned at her. She felt as if they had fought a battle together. The joy of victory was intoxicating.

He licked the rain off his lips. "Get in the passenger side."

They were fellow warriors now, battling the elements together. "You sure you don't need me?"

"Oh, I need you, chère, but there's no sense in us both standing out here in the rain." He picked up the crank. The rain slackened. In the truck lights she watched his massive shoulders hunch over. He shook his hair out of his eyes, and droplets of light seemed to fly off his head. His whole body surged until the damp engine caught.

Then he jumped into the driver's seat. He did mysterious things to the throttle and the spark-control lever while playing the foot pedals like an organist, making the truck rock backward then forward with a lover's frenzy, until he could drive it right out of the ditch.

The word "masterful" leapt into her mind. My knight errant.

He continued driving. "What about your car?"

"I'll pick it up in the morning."

He drove the truck right into the barn. Then he turned off the motor. "Stay there," he said, leaping out and shutting the door.

The barn smelled of hay and the comforting scents of cows and milk. The rain beat on the roof. Belle stepped out onto the running board of the Ford. Bourrée turned off the headlights and the world went dark.

She felt him next to her, but he was invisible. His blunt hands clasped her around the waist and lifted her down. His breath was hot and excited. She put her hand on his chest and realized she could feel the beating of his heart.

His lips brushed her cheek and sought her lips. In the disorienting darkness where touch was all, she could feel her body responding. The real world was elsewhere. They were locked in a cocoon of shadows. "We've had this date for a long time," he said, grabbing her rain-soaked breast. Belle jumped, but at the same time a thrill shot through her.

She thought about pushing him away. Her brain told her, You must push him away. Then her brain said, You should push him away. He's not the man you love. This isn't right. But the voice was faint after all she'd been through this evening. Somewhere deeper, much deeper than the voice of her brain, somewhere beneath speech, she was still sobbing from rejection.

She wrapped her arms around Bourrée.

He metamorphosed into a wild animal. There was nothing tender about him. She felt his rough hand pull up her wet skirt, and although she was sore, sore all over, the pale hair on her skin searched for him. Comfort me.

Her mind disconnected in the absence of light as his hand

slipped between her legs and rubbed until she couldn't help but move with him. She felt him unbutton his fly. He's going to take me right here. Her thoughts were a muddle of frenzied desire, rebellion against Rafe, and distaste for what she was doing. Could she still stop him? Was it too late?

He pushed her up against the truck and yanked down her bloomers, ripping them in his haste. Now he was rubbing against her with his body, but he couldn't get a proper angle. He roughly turned her around and went at her from behind.

Belle's mind cleared as he slammed into her. She tried to move away, but he didn't loosen his grip. She told him to stop, but he kept on banging and banging, tearing at her. Her ribs hurt. Muscles she'd forgotten she had cried out. But in a perverse way, the pain only intensified her erotic craving. Rain beat on the leaky roof, falling all around them. Thunder rumbled and the barn shuddered and still he slammed against her, hammered into her, faster and faster. Then just as suddenly as he started, he was finished.

"That was beautiful," he whispered in her ear. "Just like you."

Belle pulled away from him. The rain was falling between them. She didn't know what she was feeling except she wanted to get out. She straightened her clothes, but he slid his arms around her. "Hold on, little sugar. Just give me a couple of minutes. It's always better the second time."

"I've got to go," Belle said as she slipped out of his no-longer-desperate grasp.

"What's your hurry, chère? I told you, I still got some life in me yet."

Miss Effie came out of her room when she heard Belle hobbling up the stairs in her torn stockings. "Good heavens, child. What happened to you?" Belle shook her head. Words failed her. "You get yourself into some dry clothes before you catch your death. I'll make you some tea."

Death was sounding pretty good to Belle at that moment. "Do you mind if I just take a hot bath? I don't feel like talking tonight."

SHE DIDN'T FEEL like talking the next day, either. She wasn't about to tell Miss Effie she'd bought a truck and then run it into a ditch. Let Cady or Bourrée or someone else tell the old lady. Belle was indisposed.

She announced she'd caught a summer cold, didn't want to infect anyone, and then, like a nineteenth-century heroine, she took to her bed. But the heat was relentless. Even the breeze had abandoned her. The only movement outside her windows were the flies throwing themselves against the screen.

She lay on her chaise, wearing only a soft cotton chemise trimmed in lace and silk ribbons. A mosquito got into the room. It flitted about, sticking close to the ceiling, but as soon as she got settled, it attacked. She flailed at it with a sore arm. *Men are like mosquitos, best slap them down early, before they get a chance to torment you.* She decided that should be a primary rule in her Southern Girls' Guide to Men and Other Perils of Modern Life. She promised herself she'd follow it in the future.

If she had any future.

Rachel had lent her a copy of *Wuthering Heights*. Belle had been reading it. Now she threw it across the room. She'd thought Heathcliff wandering around the moors yelling for Cathy was pretty silly. She'd wanted to give him a good swat and tell him, "Get a grip on yourself." But the narrator, the narrator who stayed in bed for a year, now he deserved more attention.

A year in bed sounded pretty good to her.

Stella hefted her large body up the steep steps to bring Belle her meals on a tray. Bourrée came to the house. She sent down word she was too sick to see anyone. Rafe called every few hours. Rachel called too. Belle refused to talk on the phone. Cady and Miss Effie hovered over her. She sent them away. With admirable self-discipline, Miss Effie refrained from commenting on the muddied, dented truck gracing the barn.

As Belle lay on her chaise, old guilts began festering. If she hadn't killed Claude, none of this would have happened. Claude. A silent movie came to life in her head. She saw him on his first day back from the war, in a fury over her field of strawberries. She saw herself burning the evidence of her complicity in her own husband's death. The pictures played over and over in a silent loop inside her agitated brain.

She picked up an old issue of *Vanity Fair*. The sentences curled around each other. What did she care about what rich people did in cities she'd never see?

On Sunday, both men presented her with flowers. Rafe came out to the house with an elaborate bouquet. He'd managed to get the local florist to open up his shop. Bourrée had picked a profusion of pink and yellow roses, lilies, passionflowers, and great stalks of orange bird of paradise from the garden. He brought them to the house. Belle refused to see either of them. She even refused to have the flowers in her room. Their cheer distracted her from the angry depression she was wallowing in.

On Monday, Rachel sent over a box of expensive candy. Belle gave it to Stella. "For your grandchildren."

Belle wrote Rafe a terse thank-you note and asked Stella to put it in the mail.

"You're not going to thank him in person?" Stella asked.

"Nope," Belle answered, handing her a second note. "This one's for Mr. Bourrée. I don't want to talk to him either." She hadn't bothered to write Rachel.

That afternoon, after Miss Effie had set off for her United

Daughters of the Confederacy meeting, Belle stole downstairs in her silk wrapper. Her sore legs cried out with each step. She stood at the kitchen door and whistled for Dawg. He came bounding out of the woods, his black ears flapping with joy. He was excited and nervous about venturing into the forbidden house. Stella caught them on the stairs. "You know what Miz Effie's gonna say if she catches that dog in her house."

"I do. So we're not going to tell her."

"Miz Rachel called."

"I'm sick."

"You ain't that sick."

"I'm sick of the Rubinsteins."

In the relative safety of her room, Dawg rested his head on Belle's thigh and groaned. She brushed his dark coat and thought about what her life was going to be like without Abe and Rachel.

Belle fell into a deep pool of sadness and loss. She struggled to the surface on a wave of anger. She submerged her longing for Rafe in the acid stream of: He just wanted to use me. I was only a little country fluff he could amuse himself with before he went back to the city and his real life. Damn him. Damn him to hell! The repetition of his damnation brought her to a smoldering shore. She climbed out on the hard rocks of righteous indignation.

Her dog turned over onto his back. Belle eased herself down next to him on the rug and scratched his stomach until his hind leg jumped. Her thoughts quit pestering her, or at least pestered her with less insistence. Claude had raised Dawg from a puppy. She felt as if she had a part of her husband with her. Near sundown, when the dog began to pace and moan, she sneaked him outside.

On Tuesday, Stella didn't make the climb to the second floor with a breakfast tray. Nobody else came up with it either, so

Belle pulled her wrapper around her and clumped down to the kitchen. The soreness in her legs had eased. She didn't want to eat, but she was longing for a cup of Stella's Creole coffee.

"I got too much to do to carry trays up and down those stairs," Stella said, chopping green peppers. "You ought to be ashamed of yourself, lying up there, making everybody worry."

Belle poured herself a cup of coffee. "I'm feeling poorly."

"What you need is a good whipping and to be sent outside to play." Belle managed a weak smile. Stella set a plate of biscuits and fig preserves in front of her. Belle drank the hot café au lait and poked at a biscuit.

"Poking at your food ain't eating. I didn't stand over a hot stove for you to disrespect my cooking."

Belle put a crumble of biscuit, sticky with preserves, into her mouth. The taste inspired her appetite. When she'd finished the biscuit and eaten a second one, she began to feel a little better.

"I'm sorry I gave you extra work." Stella didn't honor her with an answer. After a minute, Belle said, "I should never have hired a cook who knew me as a child."

Stella moved her heavy figure around the kitchen, clanging iron pots. Finally she turned to Belle and said, "You got what you deserved. Now go on outside and get some fresh air."

"Maybe tomorrow." Belle swept out of the kitchen and into Miss Effie.

"Why, sugar, I'm so glad to see you up."

"Thank you." Belle sighed as she headed toward the stairs.

"Still feeling peaked?"

"Yes, ma'am."

Belle's hand had just touched the banister when Miss Effie said, "I think I'd better call your mama."

Belle spun around. "What for?"

"Why, honey, you've always been as healthy as . . . as

healthy as that horse of yours. If you're this sick, Blanche and Calvin should be with you."

"I'm not that sick."

"That's good to hear. Nevertheless—" Her hand hovered over the telephone. She picked up the receiver.

"I'm just . . . I'm just getting ready to take Susan B. out for a ride. She hasn't been exercised in days."

"Are you, now?" asked Miss Effie as she put the receiver back on its cradle.

DAWG RACED ACROSS the yard the moment Belle stepped out of the house. He bounced around her in celebration of such a marvelous event. Belle did not share his enthusiasm, but it felt good to be outside.

The cotton harvest had started. She knew she should be there, watching the workers drag their heavy bags down the furrows, keeping an eye on Bourrée as he weighed the bags, making sure he weighed them properly.

The truck, washed but battered, was parked next to the barn. Oh Lord, she thought. She'd have to call Darvin and have him do something about it. She promised herself she would as soon as she got back to the house. She mounted Susan B. with an aching body, but she found she could ride without too much pain. She walked her horse into the blazing fields. Bourrée stood on the wagon, next to the scales, silhouetted against the bright sky. He waved as if he were expecting her.

Belle wheeled her horse around and rode back toward the house. Susan B. wanted to gallop when they hit the drive, but Belle couldn't take the pounding. Instead, she turned her into the deep woods, with its merciful shade broken up by holes of intense sunlight. The scent of pine and bayberry was everywhere, but Belle didn't notice. As she passed through light and shadow, all the ways she'd messed up her life flashed through her mind.

She followed a narrow path through the hardwood near the creek. She planned to wade into the shallow water. Maybe the shock of cold would adjust the chaos in her brain.

Dawg led the way. Thickets and thornbushes reached out for her. A crow watched from a high branch. Suddenly it flapped its wings and sailed along the path in front of her, screeching. Belle yanked Susan B. to a sudden stop. In the shade of a ridiculously romantic live oak festooned with garlands of Spanish moss, Cady was kissing Hugh.

"Cady Cantrell, you stop that this minute!" The tone of Belle's voice was not pleasing.

They wrenched themselves apart in horror. Cady's lips were pink and sore. There was a raised mark on her neck. Several buttons on her shirtwaist were open.

"Hey, Miss Belle," Hugh said sheepishly. His lips were swollen.

"I won't have this."

Cady was indignant. "Now you're being all moral. What about you and Mr.—"

Belle cut her off. "Don't you talk back to me, young lady!" Oh, Lord, Belle thought, I sound just like my mother. She tried a different tack. "Cady, you're only seventeen. Young girls make decisions that can mess up their whole lives, before they have the sense God gave butter beans." She said the last to herself, but Cady grabbed hold of it.

"Is that what you really think? You don't think I have the sense God gave butter beans?"

Belle didn't know where all her righteous indignation was coming from. She doubted it was from a good place, but she couldn't stop herself. She just couldn't bear to see Cady and Hugh together. "I will not have you ruin your life like I did mine."

"You mean by marrying Daddy?"

Is that what she meant? Did marrying Claude ruin her life? At the time, she thought he'd saved it.

A look of sudden realization came over Cady's face. She started slowly. "You and Daddy, you—"

Belle cut her off before she could say, "Had to get married." There are some things a child doesn't need to have confirmed. Instead, she changed the subject by going on the offensive. "Hugh, I have nothing against you, but you're a grown man. I won't have you taking advantage of my daughter."

When they got back to the house, Belle was feeling sheepish. She shouldn't take out her own suffering on her daughter, but she didn't want her to do something foolish. She took her into her bedroom and opened her armoire. On the back of a shelf, Belle found a little silver box covered in white tissue paper and tied with a pink ribbon. She gave it to her daughter. Cady tore it open. Nestled in the deep recess of this pretty box was the second contraceptive sponge Belle had sent away for. At first, Cady didn't know what it was. Then her face turned red. "What makes you think I'm that kind of girl?"

"We're all that kind of girl, sugar."

"Well, I'm not! I believe *a lady should never have intimate relations with a man outside the blessed state of holy matrimony.*"

Good Lord, Belle thought. She has her own Primer of Propriety. I guess we all carry something like that around in our heads. What she said was, "Looked like your relations were getting pretty intimate out there in the woods."

"We weren't going that far! And we're not going to until I've finished high school and we're—" She stopped suddenly.

"Until you're in college, right?"

Cady said nothing. She plonked the box in front of her mother.

"Honey, virtue is a worthy goal. I'm in favor of it. All I'm saying is, if you slip, you don't have to be stupid."

Cady studied the box, and then picked it up. "I'm just taking it to humor you."

"Fine," her mother said. "I could use a little humor."

Beware of men who think they're

on speaking terms with the Almighty.

THE SOUTHERN GIRLS' GUIDE TO MEN AND
OTHER PERILS OF MODERN LIFE

Chapter 14

RAFE PUT DOWN the phone. "Why won't she take my call? What did you say to her?" He and Rachel were alone in the office overlooking the store. After a bout of angina, the doctor had put Abe on bed rest.

"Rafe, you come from different worlds."

"Yes, you made that abundantly clear to her."

"Because it's true. Belle never finished high school. She never read a book I didn't give her. What are you going to do? Teach her to play mah-jongg and take her to the country club? Introduce her to Aunt Sadie?" Rafe didn't say anything. "That's the problem with men. They don't think about anything but their own feelings." He started to protest, but she cut him off. "You're on the rebound. It's only natural for you to fall in love with the first pretty girl you meet, but Belle's my friend. My only real friend here. We'll make up eventually, if you don't break her heart."

"Why are you so sure I'll break her heart?"

"You haven't thought one second about her or her reputation. People see you together, they'll say she's carrying on with a married man. She kissed you in public! You can't keep encouraging her, for her sake."

Rafe didn't say anything. He was afraid she was right.

"I can't tell you how much I appreciate your coming down here and helping us out. I don't know what we would have done without you. But you have your own life. And as soon as Abe is well enough, I think you should go back to it. Once you're in Chicago, you'll see how impossible it would be for you to take Belle up there. This way, she'll fade into your memory as a lovely summer romance, another road not taken."

He was silent. He got up and pulled out their latest account book and took it to his desk. Rachel called home. He heard her say, "Good," and thought Abe must be resting comfortably. Then she said, "Dr. Vickerson wants you to wait at least two weeks before you tackle these stairs again." Abe must have protested, because her voice became strained. "Abe, you know what he said about overdoing it!"

She hung up and put her head in her hands, shielding her eyes. He remembered her sitting like that when they were children and she didn't want the family to know she was distraught. At that moment, she was his big sister again, the one who'd always looked out for him on the playground, the one who'd taken him on adventures. He reached across the desk and touched her arm. "Before I go back to Chicago, I want to leave you with a business that runs like a business."

BY THE END of the week, Belle's angry depression had lifted. She'd survived the humiliation and become bored with the pain. She'd even forgiven herself for giving in to Bourrée. I may have slipped, she told herself, but at least I wasn't stupid. Besides, the experience wasn't so bad in the contemplation of it. In fact, it was kind of exciting.

She rode into the fields again, to see how the cotton harvest was coming. A dozen pickers were in the furrows, but Bourrée was not on the mule cart weighing their bags. The workers were sitting on their sacks in the hot sun. Where was he?

SHE FOUND HIM in the cool dimness of the parlor with Miss Effie, sitting on the velvet sofa amid the flotilla of lace anti-macassars. He was wearing a work shirt so new it still had the creases from the package. He stood when she entered the room.

"Why aren't you in the fields, Mr. LeBlanc?"

"Belle!" Miss Effie gave her daughter-in-law a you-*could*-be-civil look. The dowager was less fluttery around her handsome foreman than before, but Belle could see his masculine presence was still having an effect on her. "Bourrée invited us to a picnic at the fairgrounds next Sunday."

This was the first time Belle had come face-to-face with Bourrée since the night of the truck. He turned his broad smile and blue eyes on her. Just because she'd slipped, it didn't make him a bad man, she reminded herself. "Now, don't you worry about respectability, Miz Belle." Her face became hot. "This is gonna be a real old-fashioned family affair."

"He's offered to drive us there in his new car. And he wants me to invite Jimmy Lee, too. Isn't that nice? I know Cady will be glad for the company."

"You have a new car?"

"Yes, ma'am. A Crow-Elkhart. Wait'll you see it. You-all are gonna be real comfortable."

"They've asked Cady to sing. She's going to lead off the program," Miss Effie said.

"Then we'll have to go, won't we?" Belle's heart was pounding. Fear, attraction, distaste, and a shameful thrill were playing leapfrog on the grassy lawn of her mind.

SUNDAY AFTERNOON AT THREE, when Belle and Cady stepped out of the house, Jimmy Lee was already there examining the inner workings of Bourrée's car. "Got a twenty-horse-power Lycoming engine," Bourrée said. Jimmy Lee whistled, so Belle figured that must be a good thing.

The car was royal blue. The top was down. Sunlight glinted off the chrome instruments. Two spare tires in a white case were strapped smartly to the rear. The seats and steering wheel were covered in the softest leather.

"Gets twenty-five miles on a gallon of gas," Bourrée said. Belle examined some wires attached to the back fender. "My golf-club rack."

"When did you take up golf?"

"Haven't yet, but you never can tell. Good way to meet the right people." Cady moved to the car and stroked the upholstery.

Belle had a bad feeling. "That's a fine car for a farm manager."

Bourrée examined her. She felt as if he were peeling each article of clothing off her body and tossing them aside. The car's blue enamel reflected in his steel blue eyes. "It's three years old. Fellow offered it to me at such a good price, couldn't afford not to take him up on it."

When Miss Effie came out of the house, Bourrée slipped into his jacket and Belle saw he was wearing a new suit. This one fit. Where was he getting all his money? She was keeping the books and writing the checks. Had he been cheating the pickers? Was someone at the cotton gin, someone in one of his clubs, slipping him money on the side? Or had he made a deal at the feed-and-seed store to overcharge them and give him a kickback? She'd checked the books. She'd have to go over them again. Then she remembered she wouldn't be able to show them to Rafe. Or Abe. Damn them.

Bourrée opened the door and gave his hand to the older woman. He helped her into the backseat, where she sat regally under her big black hat. I guess not all cars are good-time houses on wheels, Belle thought. Jimmy Lee got into the front. Bourrée continued to hold the door. The expensive car sparkled in the afternoon sunlight. There wasn't a speck of dust on it, even though it hadn't rained in days and dust was everywhere. He must have polished it in front of the house. "Cady? Miz Belle?" He drew out the "Miz" until he hissed, and then rolled "Belle" around on his tongue as if he were licking candy.

Cady skipped toward the car, but Belle grabbed her arm and held her back. She didn't want to be beholden to Bourrée or have to depend on him for a ride home. "We'll take the truck."

"For goodness sakes. Why do you want to show up in that old rattletrap?" Cady complained. Darvin had sent his mechanic out. The truck was running, but the fender was dented, the yellow chassis was scratched and patched, and the new wheel didn't match the others.

"Sometimes a lady wants her own transportation," Belle said.

WHEN BELLE AND CADY arrived at the fairgrounds, they were greeted by the sweet smell of barbecuing pork. They'd been slowed when the truck stalled twice, once on the railroad tracks. Belle had had to get out both times to crank it up. Her dress was damp under the arms and smudged with dust. Cady wanted her to go home and change, but Belle said it was a proud mark of a liberated woman and she wouldn't change for anything. The reality was, the second time the truck stalled, a farmer saw her wrestling with the crank. He jumped out of his own truck, got hers started, and gave her driving tips so it didn't happen again. But reality did nothing to dampen Belle's pride in her own resourcefulness. Cady in her white skirt and blouse had refused to have anything to do with the dirty work of operating a truck and was spotless, as always.

The Gentry marching band, sweating profusely in their bright red costumes with gold braid, paraded through the crowds playing "The Stars and Stripes Forever." A line of tow-headed children marched behind them. Men and boys played baseball or beat the heat by leaping from the high bank into the river below, splashing and screaming, while little girls in patent-leather shoes and starched pinafores or barefoot and in dresses made from flour sacks watched with equal envy.

In the shade of a giant live oak, church ladies, wearing hats that looked like flower baskets, were bunched around a long table, accepting entries for the baked-goods competition. Belle saw Miss Effie enter her fresh blackberry pie. It was favored to win the blue ribbon. Only Cady and Belle knew it had been baked by Stella, who'd ignored Miss Effie's recipe, which, at any rate, she couldn't read.

Belle looked around for Bourrée. Not that I care, she reminded herself.

"You missed the most exhilarating ride. That car practically floated over the bumps," Miss Effie effervesced when they caught up with her.

"See, Mama. What did I tell you? You always have to be so proud."

Belle brushed the dust off the front of her skirt and wondered if perhaps she'd been foolish to insist on her independence. Would it have hurt her to ride to the picnic in a fancy car?

They passed a man-made hill. Boys on bicycles and roller skates were hurtling down it, competing for the most serious injury. One of the first rules Belle had ever entered into her Southern Girls' Guide to Men and Other Perils of Modern Life was: *Before they're old enough to flirt with girls, little boys insist on flirting with death.*

A three-legged race was spurred on by a fiddler sawing away at "Turkey in the Straw." From a distance Belle thought the contestants looked like aberrations out of a freak show with two heads and three legs as they staggered clumsily toward the finish line.

Then she saw Bourrée step out from behind the racers. He was surrounded by a covey of fluttering females. She recognized one of Cady's friends, pretty, blond Lily Moffat, cooing for his attention and saw him wink at her. He stopped every three or four feet to shake hands, slap backs, admire babies, or tip his hat. He looked like a mayor among his constituents. Not wanting to seem as if she were waiting in line for his attentions, she took Cady's arm and steered her toward some kind of science booth.

Her mother, Blanche Nix, stepped out of one of the exhibits.

"Hey, Grandma." Cady skipped over to the older woman and kissed her on the cheek.

"Well, I certainly didn't expect to see you here," Blanche said to Belle. Then she turned to her granddaughter. "I'm glad your mother has come to her senses. I expect we have you to thank."

Belle felt uneasy at having inadvertently done something of which her mother approved. "How are you, Mama?"

"I'm fine. Just fine. You know Mr. Nix is gonna speak tonight."

"Well, that should be a real treat."

"I don't know how you can still be so disrespectful after all he's done for you."

Or to me, Belle thought, but she didn't say it. What was the point?

"I'm going to sing," Cady said.

"I know, sugar, and I'm as proud as I can be. It was real obliging of your mama to let you."

"What are you talking about?" Belle asked.

Blanche paused, examined her daughter, and then said, "You-all go on and see the exhibits. I know you'll find them educational."

Belle had never seen science exhibits at a picnic before, and these weren't much, just a couple of rough, three-sided shacks. Above the first, a big red, white, and blue banner announced, "Enter the Perfect-Baby Contest. Find out if your baby has a goodly inheritance." Inside, Fulsom Pruett, Dr. Vickerson's dour young associate, was dressed in his white coat lest someone forget he was a doctor. A mob of women surrounded him, waving babies.

On the side of the booth, Belle spotted a large poster listing the enlightened states that practiced forced sterilization. Apparently Indiana led the pack, extending altruistic gelding to orphans, ne'er-do-wells, tramps, and paupers. Belle thought of her own impoverished childhood, blessed with church baskets and charity shoes. If she'd grown up in Indiana, would her own sweet daddy have been considered a pauper?

Cady spotted Jimmy Lee. He was looking up at some blinking lights in a second booth. A banner over the entrance announced: "The Science of Eugenics and Health."

"What's eugenics?" asked Cady. She pronounced it "e-ugenics."

Belle opened her mouth and then realized she didn't have a clue. She glanced across the fairgrounds. Bourrée and his flock were making their way toward them. A leapfrog of emotions hopped around in her head—all right, in her body—as she watched him glad-hand Floyd Taggert, the editor of the *Gentry Post,* and clap him on the shoulder. So he's intelligent and ambitious? Nothing wrong with that, she told herself, but where was the money coming from? What had she missed?

Cady had joined Jimmy Lee. They were reading the signs tacked up along the walls: "The Peril of Unchecked Breeding Among the Genetically Defective." Underneath this provocative headline she read, "Some people are born to be a burden to the rest."

"Ain't that the truth?" said Jimmy Lee. Belle didn't venture a comment.

A red light flashed at forty-eight-second intervals to show how often a feebleminded child is born in America. Next to it, another light flashed at fifty-second intervals to show how often a criminal goes to jail.

Not often enough, Belle thought as she caught sight of Pruett Walker, the man who'd knifed her husband. Pruett was enjoying a large plate of pork.

A third light was supposed to flash every seven and a half minutes when a high-grade person was born, but unfortunately, the bulb was missing.

Belle noticed a subtle change in the atmosphere. A young mother, with a baby in her arms, bent over and cooed at her child while looking up through her lashes at someone standing in the entrance of the booth. Two young girls clutched each other and giggled. An older woman casually smoothed her hair.

Belle turned and saw Bourrée LeBlanc standing in the entrance. His legs were spread apart, as if he were astride the world. His slick, blue-black hair glistened in the sunlight. He spotted her in the crowd and strode to her side.

"Having fun, chère?"

Belle caught sight of an exhibit of dead guinea pigs, black, white, and mixed, glued to a board. "A laugh a minute." She couldn't take her eyes off the dead guinea pigs. They were starting to smell. "Did you organize this?"

"Just helped out here and there. Miz Belle," he said for Cady's and Jimmy Lee's ears as he guided her out of the booth. "How about you and me having supper together out by the river?" He gave her a seductive look, which Belle figured probably worked on that gaggle of women she'd seen in his thrall, but wasn't going to cut it with her. Actually, she had to admit it did cut it with her. A little. "Yes, ma'am. You and me, we need to go off someplace quiet and discuss the cotton harvest." His blue eyes twinkled mischievously, but underneath Belle glimpsed something raw and vulnerable.

It was this vulnerability that touched her. As they walked toward the high riverbank, she could feel the envious eyes of Cady's friend Lily Moffat following them. "What we did was wrong," she said as gently as possible.

"What we did was beautiful," he whispered.

That kind of beauty is in the pants of the beholder, she thought. She moved away so she wouldn't feel his hot breath in her ear. "It's not going to happen again." She wondered if she'd really be able to hold out against his persistence. And then she wondered how she'd feel about him if the sex had been better. It's funny how the mechanics of a thing can change the way you see a person, she thought.

"My intentions toward you are honorable, chère. I love you."

Oh, Lord, she thought, love. She couldn't help noticing how good looking he was at that moment, with his pale eyes undefended. "You're just a kid. You'll find plenty of young girls—"

"Don't you think I've found me plenty of young girls? I don't want 'um. I only want one thing."

Her emotions were not only leapfrogging, but grappling with one another. He could learn to become a better lover, she thought. And then she remembered the money.

"Bourrée, we got to get some things squared away for tonight," said a voice behind them.

Belle turned and saw Pruett Walker eating a piece of blackberry pie. Dark syrup dribbled out of the corner of his mouth. He started. "Hey, Belle, shoulda recognized you from behind." His voice was soft and friendly. She didn't return his greeting. "You ever get that poison spreader?"

"I'm considering it." Belle's eyes were steady on him as she reviewed her options. Unfortunately, it was too late to sterilize his mother.

He put his pie plate and fork in one hand and reached into his pocket. His pendulous belly rippled at the displacement. He pulled out a handkerchief and wiped his forehead. Pruett had always been heavy. Now, his midsection dripped over his belt. Maybe he'd eat himself into an early grave. It couldn't be too early for her.

God, she missed Claude. Life would be so easy if he were here now. At least that's what she told herself.

Pruett muttered to Bourrée, "The boys got some questions, about our—" He stopped himself, looked at Belle, and continued with, "Surprise entertainment."

They're like little kids playing conspirator, she thought. Bourrée turned to her. "I'll meet you out on the riverbank for supper."

"I wouldn't dream of depriving Miss Effie of the pleasure of your company. I know how much she's been looking forward to it."

As she watched him swagger away next to the purling figure of Pruett Walker, she couldn't remember what it was about Bourrée she'd found attractive.

AT SUNSET, CADY STOOD onstage looking lovely in her white middy blouse and white skirt. Her honey blond hair was pulled back softly at the nape of the neck with a circlet of flowers. She was wearing Miss Effie's pearls.

Belle and Miss Effie had been with her in the dressing area for an hour, fixing her hair, allowing her a hint of face powder, and mostly calming her down. By the time they finished, there was only one seat left. Belle gave it to her mother-in-law and prowled around in back of the crowd, which far exceeded the folding chairs set out in front of the bandstand. Cady sang "Shine On, Harvest Moon" with Jimmy Lee accompanying her on the banjo. Belle applauded wildly.

Cady was followed by Dr. Fulsom Pruett, who explained how science could make the United States into a paradise in only three generations. "Our beloved nation is at a turning point. The dangerous and the defectives are reproducing in droves." He expostulated on the need to eradicate them. Belle figured he'd wipe out half his audience.

He introduced Brother Scaggs, minister of the Church of Everlasting Redemption. The doctor called him God's spokesman. The preacher rose and began speaking in rolling tones about God's will. The way he talked, it sounded as if he had personal knowledge. According to him, God wept at the evil incarnate in our jazz-mad world, filled with wild women and wayward men. But what the Lord abhorred most was mixing the races. "Race traitors," he called them. "God loves the white man and God loves the black man, but only Satan, himself, can abide the half-breed."

Beware of men who think they're on speaking terms with the Almighty, Belle thought, and wondered if Brother Scaggs had made that last up himself. She remembered he was often venomous, but rarely original.

She looked around and saw Bourrée in back of the bandstand, huddled with a group of men, but when the sky darkened and the electric lights came on, he and his crowd disappeared. She wished she could disappear. If only Cady weren't scheduled to sing the last hymn.

Titus Pruett stepped into the spotlight. His voice boomed. With his deep faith and shallow intellect, the man was a bottomless pit of indignation. His brain swarmed with enough facts and figures to bewilder the simpleminded. He extolled patriotism, true-blue, one-hundred-percent American patriotism. Morality was big with him, too. He was "fur" it. Pretty soon little snakes of hatred began to slither out of his mouth, hissing about Catholics, union organizers, and the ever present danger lurking in the darker races. Belle wanted to grab her daughter. She tried to make her way through the crowd, but a knot of admirers had gathered in front of the stage. As she pushed into the press of humanity, the snakes of hatred multiplied, twisted, and rasped until Titus's red face became a nest of vipers.

Suddenly, the lights went out. Trumpets sounded. The Gentry marching band played "My Country 'Tis of Thee." Folding chairs tumbled. The crowd turned as one toward the music, to see Klansmen on horseback carrying flaming torches. They trotted out of the woods and circled the audience. Belle spotted Pruett Walker right away by his airship of a stomach bouncing over his saddle. The son of a bitch was leading the white-robed crowd up the man-made hill.

Suddenly, a strange roar was heard in the east. The crowd looked up. Fire flew across the heavens. A biplane, the first Belle had ever seen, circled above them. A burning cross swung from its undercarriage.

Horses spooked by the flames and noise shied and reared. Pruett Walker fell off his steed, howling like the stuffed pig he resembled. He tumbled down the hill, with his skirts wrapped around him. The plane swooped over the fairgrounds, dripping little fireballs.

Screams went up from the crowd, who began jumping and slapping themselves. All the while, the choir, led by Cady, sang "Onward, Christian Soldiers." Belle fought her way through the agitated mob. By the time she reached her daughter, Cady was into the second verse. " 'At the sign of triumph, Satan's host doth flee . . .' "

"Cady, I will not let them use you or the Lord like this! This is blasphemy!"

Cady sang, " 'Hell's foundations quiver . . .' "

"Hell's foundations are gonna quiver all right if you don't get off this stage this minute!" Belle was furious.

Chapter 15

THE NEXT MORNING, Belle saddled up Susan B. and rode out into the fields. Bourrée wasn't there. She waved to Stella's son, Curtis, who always helped with the cotton harvest. "Haven't seen him, today." Curtis's words were polite, but his face was sullen.

"Who's weighing the cotton?"

Curtis shook his head. "We just been sitting around, waiting until he gets it into his head to honor us with his presence. Been that way most of last week. I thought you knew."

When Claude went to war, Miss Effie hadn't wanted to let Luther weigh the cotton. "It's not fair to give that man so much temptation. He's got to be kin to half the pickers," she'd said.

"You know how to work the scales?" Belle asked Curtis.

"Course I do."

"You take over, then."

Curtis's face broke into a slow smile. "You mean it?" Belle

nodded. Miss Effie's going to have a conniption fit, she thought. Curtis's smile disappeared. "What happens when Mr. Bourrée comes back?"

"You let me worry about Mr. Bourrée, you hear?"

BELLE CHECKED THE BARN and stable. Bourrée wasn't there. She searched the cornfield. Still no Bourrée. She even checked the parlor. Finally she rode over to his house and saw his car parked in the yard. His front door was open. She heard him whistling as she crossed the porch.

Through the screen she saw him writing something in a ledger with his right hand, round, awkward letters, as though some first-grade teacher had forced him away from writing with his left. A half-full glass of something was at his elbow. His black hair, not yet greased, fell over his eyes. He shook it out of his face when he saw her.

"Hey, Belle, come on in. I just need to finish up a little paper-work." As he stood to greet her, a little brown pharmacy paper fluttered in his wake. The screen door bounced and closed behind her. "Sit down, chère. Sit down." He walked around the table, glass in hand. He motioned for her to sit on the daybed. His voice was warm, excited. "I thought you'd come to me today. At least I'd hoped you would."

"We need to talk." She did not sit down.

"Well, there's no one in the world I'd rather talk to. That was some show last night, wasn't it? Miss Effie and Jimmy Lee, they had themselves a time." He took a sip from the glass.

"That's what I came to talk to you about."

"You don't need no excuse, chère." His voice caressed her. "I know why you're here." He put the glass down, but instead of offering her whatever he was drinking, he grabbed her and kissed her hard. She tried to push him away, but he was too strong. He ran a hand down her back and over her buttocks, encased in her tight riding britches. "And don't you worry none. You're not gonna leave unsatisfied today, I guarantee." (He pronounced it "gar-ron-tee.")

"Cut it out!" She struggled against him, but his massive arms and chest were hard with work and youth. *Once a man has had your favors, he thinks he owns you.* Belle added that to her Southern Girls' Guide to Men. "I mean it, Bourrée, stop it."

"I love it when good girls say no but mean yes." He nuzzled his face in her neck. They were still standing. He rubbed the back of his thumb between her legs, sawing. She had a vision of a Boy Scout trying to light a fire.

She tried to kick him in the shin. "Stop it!" But he was wearing boots.

"Don't you worry none, little sugar, I know what you want and I'm just the man to give it to you. It won't be quick like the last time, neither." The Primer of Propriety was clear. She shouldn't be here. *No respectable woman enters a bachelor's living quarters alone.*

He pushed her backward, until she found herself under him, lying across the foot of the daybed. She didn't believe in rape. She'd never thought it was possible. She hadn't been able to visualize the positions. The undressing. How a man could hold a woman down.

Until now.

He was pinioning her with his weight.

"God, I feel like a million dollars!" he brayed.

"Stop it! I mean it, dammit!"

He laughed a low laugh, fumbling with the buttons on the side placard of her britches. "You're a regular little spitfire, aren't you? I just love that in a woman." He drew out the word "love" and mushed it around his mouth as he opened the first button, the one at her waist. Then he ripped the rest. He slipped a rough hand inside her bloomers, probing, arousing. She had to think. She couldn't just react.

"Get off me, you goddamn louse!" She wanted to be clear. She started to cuss, using all the vulgar language she'd ever heard, but all he did was chuckle. She ran out of swearwords.

"Oh, Miz Belle, you are some woman." When he eased away enough to unbutton his pants, she managed to slip her right hand out from under him.

"Are you so pathetic, the only way you can get sex is to rape a woman?"

The word "rape," accompanied by a swift jab to his Adam's apple, got his attention. He choked and blinked as if he didn't quite understand. "Get off me!" she screamed, giving him a shove and rolling out from under him.

He got up grudgingly, rubbing his throat. His voice was strained. "You didn't have no cause to do that." He seemed honestly confused by her rejection. "My intentions are honorable." He went over to the table and took a couple of quick swigs from his glass. His eyes were bloodshot. "Most girls want what I got."

"Then I urge you to find one of them. Please, dump your affections on her."

"You don't have to act like some great lady with me. I know you, Belle. You and me. We're just alike."

"Stop saying that! I may have started as trash, but I tried to rise above it. You, you're wallowing in it."

"That's where you're wrong. I got prospects, too. I'm not gonna be stuck doing farmwork all my life, no sirree bob." A proud smile flashed across his lips, as if he had a delicious secret he was dying to share.

"You knew that was a Klan picnic, didn't you?" Belle asked, pulling her blouse together.

"Darn tooting I knew it. I was in charge. Chère, I'm the organizing Kleagle for this whole area. And lemme tell you, kleagling is a gold mine. I get to keep four dollars out of every membership I sell."

Belle buttoned the top button on her pants, the one that still held. "What are you talking about?"

"Kleagling, it's like being a salesman for the Ku Klux. And believe me, it's one of the great business opportunities of our time, maybe the greatest. A man has to have real get-up-and-go to be a Kleagle. You know, people think of the Klan as a white supremacist organization, which it is. I mean, we got to stand up for the white race." His Cajun accent had begun to reassert itself. "Think" became "tink." "That" became "dat." "But the real genius of Mr. Clark, he's our Imperial Kleagle, is he realized that some towns don't even have a nigger problem, so we sell them on going after the union organizers or the Jews or the Catholics. Great thing about Catholics is, they're everywhere." His words were flying now, bumping into one another. "Then you got your foreigners, your bootleggers, your wife beaters, and, of course, wild women. We take care of them all—"

Belle managed to interrupt his outpouring. "Do you honestly believe in all that?"

He paused for a moment, the cadence of his pitch broken. "Well, I have to admit, if it was up to me, I'd let the bootleggers go." A sly smile curled his lips. "And maybe a few wild women," he said, winking at Belle. "But it's not about what I believe. That's what I'm telling you. It's business." He picked the pharmacy paper off the table and shook a few grains of white powder into his glass. "It's about get-up-and-go, hustle, pouncing on an opportunity when you see one." He downed his drink. "We're not sticking to the South like the old Klan, neither. No sirree, we're expanding into the Midwest and California. And I'm gonna be right there with them. California is ripe for the picking. Mr. Clark says, folks out there, why, they hate just about everybody. The opportunities are . . ." He fumbled for the right word. "Unlimited. That's it, unlimited! So when I tell you I love you, it's not just because you're a rich widow. I mean, I appreciate what you done for me. Gave me a place to live, helped me get established. I couldn't have done it without you and Miss Effie." He took a step toward her.

She didn't want him to demonstrate his appreciation. "Bour-rée!" He stopped moving, and looked at his empty glass with regret. "What are you drinking?"

"Nothing. I just made me a little tonic, that's all. I was feeling a bit peaked after last night. I mean, I had to do something if I was gonna give you an honest day's work." He flashed his most seductive smile. "You want me to make you one?" He hunkered down in front of his icebox and pulled out a bottle of Coke. Six years before, you could find cocaine tonics in every pharmacy and most grocery stores. People drank it as a pick-me-up. Coca-Cola had removed it from their secret formula, and cocaine was illegal now, but it wasn't hard to get, if you knew where to look. Belle figured Bourrée knew where to look.

He stood and moved toward her, the bottle in his hand. "Want some?"

"No." Belle backed out onto the porch.

He followed her outside. His voice was soft, caressing. "Of course, a man looks for other opportunities besides business. Now, I know you're almost ten years older than me, but I'm willing to overlook that. I want to marry you, Belle. You're the most fascinating woman I ever met. I'll order us up a Klan wedding with all the trimmings. I can even get us an airplane. What do you say?"

"You're fired."

A woman's place is in charge.

THE SOUTHERN GIRLS' GUIDE TO MEN AND
OTHER PERILS OF MODERN LIFE

Chapter 16

"YOU'VE OVERSTEPPED YOURSELF, missy! You can't fire my overseer."

"He made indecent advances." Belle left out any mention of having once succumbed to them.

"Humf!"

"I had to fight him off."

"Where?" Suspicion seemed to sizzle from her hairpins.

"He was all over me!"

"Don't play innocent with me, young lady. Where did it happen?"

There was a long pause, during which Belle considered shaving the truth in self-defense. She understood the necessity of it. She just hated doing it. "In his house." Her voice was thin.

"Well, what did you expect? Going to a man's house alone. I never heard of such a thing." Miss Effie fretted and fumed until

Belle wondered if she was disappointed Bourrée hadn't made indecent advances toward her.

"We could promote Curtis. I've known him since I was a little girl, and he's as honest as—"

Miss Effie cut her off before she could finish the cliché. "His
uncle was bad enough."

They called everyone they knew, but they couldn't find an experienced white farm manager in the middle of the cotton harvest. Meanwhile, the pickers either had to sit idle or they had to
trust Curtis. Finally, in a moment of bravado, Belle offered to
take on the job herself.

Miss Effie was angry enough to let her.

*IF YOU JUMP off the roof, you've got to expect to hit the
ground.* But once in a while I could look first. It might make a
nice change, Belle thought as she drove her truck into the cotton
field. The sun was just coming up and it was already almost
eighty degrees. She stopped the truck and slapped the first mosquito of the day.

The work was hard and physical, men's work, but as the days
shuffled into one another, Belle discovered the great secret, the
secret men had kept hidden. It wasn't so hard a strong woman
couldn't handle it. And although she may not have loved the
work itself, she loved herself for being able to do it.

She found if she did simple, innovative things like bringing
jugs of water or lemonade into the field, the workers harvested
more cotton in less time. Evenings she pored over her ledgers.
For the first time in her life, she was earning her keep and, to
her surprise, Miss Effie began to defer to her.

A woman's place is in charge, Belle decided.

At night, she fell into her bed ready for sleep, but all too often, a memory of Rafe, long and lean, snuggled in with her. She

wondered if she'd been fair. She hadn't even heard his side. Maybe she should call him. Then she remembered he hadn't even wanted her to share their Sabbath. And Rachel's words would come back to her. *He might even get engaged, but he'd never go through with it. The children wouldn't be Jewish.*

To hell with them. Belle forbade herself to think about them and their narrow-minded intolerance. She took deep breaths, concentrated on pretty thoughts, and fell asleep. But Rafe had a way of invading her dreams.

TWO WEEKS LATER, on September 16, just before eleven o'clock in the morning, Belle stood on her truck bed and hauled yet another thirty-pound sack of cotton onto the scales. Her shoulders ached. Her hair was matted with perspiration under her wide-brimmed hat. Rivulets of sweat ran down her cheeks. She held her arms out and twisted her body, while a thousand miles away a rickety cart clip-clopped through lower Manhattan. The driver got out on Wall Street, near the offices of J. P. Morgan, and disappeared.

Moments later, a sudden flash of flame shot up. The air trembled. A yellowish-green mushroom cloud rose between the skyscrapers. The huge windows of the New York Stock Exchange crashed onto the trading floor. Automobiles were tossed into the air. Awnings twenty stories up caught fire. Glass shards from hundreds of windows and shattered chunks of stone rained down on the street. Five hundred pounds of metal fragments flew like shrapnel into brokers, clerks, and stenographers on their way to lunch. Thirty died on the spot. Two hundred lay wounded. Ten more would die in hospitals.

The next day, half of Gentry flocked to Rubinstein's as people have since the Greeks crowded into the agora, to make sense of a public tragedy. They savored the horror and told each other stories they'd read in the newspapers, smug in their distance from New York. They agreed they were glad to live in Gentry and not some dangerous Yankee city, packed with foreigners, Communists, and Lord knows who. Only those citizens who came from what Miss Effie called "obscure families" put any stock at all in the account of one eyewitness, who claimed he'd heard the driver speak with a Scottish accent. They knew what type of person would commit such a crime, and he wouldn't be Scottish.

While Rachel commiserated with customers on the floor, Rafe stayed in the office dictating letters. He'd read that crowds trampled the bodies of the dead and wounded in their terror. He didn't want to talk about it or what it must have been like to be there. He was afraid he knew.

He concentrated on business. Facts and numbers. In his letters he asked deadbeats to pay their bills. Rafe did not think this was an unreasonable request. He didn't threaten any action, except to cut off future credit until the bills were paid. Again, this did not seem unreasonable.

To him.

He'd been sending out collection letters for several weeks, ever since he'd promised to leave his sister a business that ran like a business. And they were having an effect. The farmers were proud men. They didn't want to owe anyone. Most of them were glad to be able to pay their debts, especially after they talked to Rachel. She knew how to calm their suspicions and help them work out payment plans they could afford, even if it was only twenty-five cents a week.

Between Rafe and Rachel, the store was turning the corner. They'd been able to pay off some of their suppliers, and the bank had agreed to extend them more credit. Rafe was heartened by the prospect of leaving his sister provided for.

Suddenly he broke off dictation. He'd spotted Miss Effie on

the floor talking to Reverend Meadows. He dashed down to intercept her.

The three of them engaged in a repeat of the conversation everyone had been having all morning. "Isn't it awful!" one of them said. The others nodded. It was indeed awful. They speculated who could have done such a terrible thing. They shook their heads.

Reverend Meadows said, "We have so much to be grateful for."

"Amen to that," Miss Effie said.

When they'd exhausted those topics, Rafe asked after Belle.

"She's just fine," Miss Effie said.

"We haven't seen her around." Rafe tried to sound casual, but he'd hoped she'd come in with everyone else.

Miss Effie didn't lie, but she had no intention of telling him or anyone else, and certainly not her minister, that her own daughter-in-law was working out in the sun alongside the field hands. "She's been so busy these days with one thing and another."

What Rafe heard was Belle was avoiding him. He wanted to be with her, especially today, when the whole world seemed so unsafe. He knew he'd be leaving Gentry soon and he had to find out what had happened after that Sabbath dinner, why she'd suddenly bolted without even saying good-bye. Mike O'Malley, the crippled vet, would soon give him the opportunity to find out.

The afternoon papers were filled with more eyewitness accounts. Although Rafe tried to bury himself in work, he couldn't help glancing at the news or hearing the secretaries chatter about a woman's head, with her hat still attached, rolling across the pavement, or an eyeless clerk who crawled on his knees because his feet had been blown off. Memories of the trenches came swimming back. Sweat glowed on his forehead and soaked his shirt under his light jacket.

He found Mike O'Malley stomping around the hardware department on his wooden leg. The two men shared a silent bond of having seen more than any man wants to remember. For the first time, Rafe invited Mike for coffee.

They went across the tracks to the Country Kitchen. For a while they sat in a booth playing with their coffee cups, watching the steam rise. Selma, the waitress, brought them plates of fresh-baked biscuits with butter and syrup. "What do you-all think about that there bomb in New York City?"

"It's awful," Mike mumbled. But when she left, he and Rafe started talking about all the things the newspapers reported and what they must have left out. They talked for over an hour.

Vince Stefano stopped Rafe when he returned to the store. "Titus Pruett's in the men's department. He's asking for you."

Rafe nodded and turned to go, but Mike rubbed the stump of his arm, hidden under the pinned-up sleeve of his jacket. "I'd be careful if I was you." He looked around and motioned for Rafe to step into a quiet corner, where he whispered, "Titus was just elected Exalted Cyclops of the Gentry Klan." Rafe stared at the boy. "Or so I was told."

Before Rafe reached the men's department, he heard Titus's booming voice. He was telling Harry Chambers and everyone else within earshot about "the importance of practical benevolence."

Whatever the hell that means, Rafe thought. He said, "What can I do for you, Mr. Pruett?"

Titus dropped the sweater he was fingering and swung around. His reddish hair became unstuck and flopped in a kind of thin frizz over his forehead. His bluff good nature fell away. Harry Chambers, head of the men's department, stepped back to watch. Mike lurched into the department and slipped in back of the counter, shielding himself behind a heavy brass cash register. Around the edges, next to the walls, a silent audience was gathering.

Rafe was wary. Was Titus armed? The man was overfed without being fat. His seersucker jacket bagged. A good-size lump protruded from his right-hand pocket. A gun? It was impossible to tell.

Rafe saw Mary Louise Pruett looking down on them from the office. Was she a sister? Cousin? How many Pruetts were there in this damned town? He scanned the crowd for armed confederates.

"You write me this here letter threatening to cut off my credit?" Titus boomed, playing for the crowd. Nervous titters fluttered around the walls. Rafe stepped in close to take the letter.

"We have bills we have to pay, too, Mr. Pruett," Rafe said, sticking to Titus's right side, ready to snatch the gun if Titus pulled it out. "I'm writing all of our customers who've been in arrears for over two months, and it looks like you've been in arrears for, what?" He scanned the letter. "Four years?"

"That ain't nothing. I been trading with Abe Rubinstein for nigh onto fifteen years."

"And we appreciate that," Rafe said as two boys in overalls wandered into the department. No one was leaving. "But you know at some point you have to pay for the merchandise you take home." Chuckles darted up to the high ceiling. Damn, Rafe thought. He hadn't meant for them to laugh.

Titus didn't seem to notice. "I know that," he said with a note of dogged stubbornness. "I run a business myself." He puffed out his chest and slipped his thumbs under his suspenders as he proclaimed himself a businessman, even though his business was a failing bicycle shop that he ran out of the back of his brother's plumbing-and-electrical-supply warehouse.

"Then you understand our situation," Rafe said, staying

tight on Titus's right-hand side, even though a spray of liquor-scented breath assailed him with each of Titus's speeches. "If you'll just come upstairs to my office—" Rafe wanted him alone. He didn't want to risk some innocent shopper getting shot. "I'll be happy to arrange a payment plan for you."

"What the hell are you talking about?"

"A small monthly payment. Something that won't leave you strapped and won't leave us strapped either." Rafe saw his sister come into the men's department. Had she lost her mind? Had they all lost their minds? Why didn't they get out of here? "I'm sure we can work out something." Rafe gestured in the direction of his office.

Titus eyed him. Rafe felt he could almost hear the cogs groan as the gears in Titus's brain turned ever so slowly. A look of suspicion spread across the face of the Exalted Whatsis. "Hell, no. I know about you people. You don't get Titus Pruett that easy." He smiled his little half smile to the spectators as he reached for the lump in his right pocket.

Rafe grabbed Titus's wrist before the hand cleared his pocket.

"What the hey! You people just can't wait to get hold of my money, can you?" Titus's face was red with anger. What he'd pulled out of his pocket was not a gun, but a wad of cash. Rafe stepped back as Titus threw the bills onto the counter. "There it is. All seven hundred and fifty-three dollars. Now you tell Abe Rubinstein I'm through. You hear? From now on, from now on," he repeated, playing to the crowd, "all my trade with you-all is gonna be in cash!"

With that, Titus turned on his heel and stormed out of the store. Rafe picked up the money and headed for the cash register. Only Mike saw his hand was shaking. He took the bills from him and rang them up. "Thanks," Rafe said, his hand on Mike's good shoulder. Then, as the men's department cleared out, Mike confessed something he'd meant to bottle up for the rest of his life. He told Rafe what had really happened the night Claude Cantrell was killed.

THE FOLLOWING SUNDAY, Belle lay in a hot bath until the water turned cold and the skin on her fingers puckered. Cady and Miss Effie had taken the train to Amite to visit relatives, leaving Belle alone in the house with nothing to do.

She emerged slowly and stretched. She looked at her reflection in the plate-glass mirror as she lengthened her arms toward the ceiling. Stomach still flat, waist small, breasts full, hips soft and round.

She wondered if anyone would ever see her naked again. The current ideal of womanly beauty had turned from Gibson girl curves to the straight lines of a preadolescent boy, but Belle knew there were plenty of men out there with old-fashioned tastes. A memory of Rafe hovered in the shadows of her mind. He hadn't minded a few curves. History, she reminded herself. Ancient history. No sense dredging up the past. Her mind drifted to the terrible bombing of Wall Street. She'd wanted to go into town with Miss Effie to talk about it with Abe, to spend time with Rachel, and, most of all, to be with Rafe. Well, she'd just have to find someone else to talk to. That was all there was to it. Besides, she was too busy to go gallivanting around the countryside just because of something she'd read about in the paper. It was harvesttime. She had the cotton crop to bring in.

She rubbed jasmine-scented skin cream all over her body. Would she be alone until her breasts sagged, her tummy bulged, and her hair turned white? She looked at her hands, which she'd kept so carefully manicured ever since her marriage. They'd become rough with work and freckled in the sun. Unladylike, Miss

Effie would say. But Belle was secretly pleased with their new strength.

She smiled at herself in the mirror while she slipped into her clothes. She'd ceased to be some nit who had to get into a man's good graces and then spend all her time worrying about keeping him. She was equal to any of them. It felt good. Damn good. And if her breasts started to sag or her belly bulged, what the heck.

She didn't need anybody.

She went into the kitchen and made herself a chicken sandwich with thick slices of Creole tomatoes and Stella's homemade mayonnaise. Then she padded out to the screened porch in hopes of a breeze. Her bare feet slapped the sloping hardwood floor. Sitting with one leg bent under her on the blue-and-white-striped glider, she held her sandwich in one hand and in the other a new book she'd sent away for, *This Side of Paradise*. Rachel had offered to lend it to her in the days when she was talking to Rachel. Now, she had her own copy.

The phone rang. Belle ignored it. She was reading the part where these rich young people went to petting parties and kissed whomever they pleased. She wondered if kissing was Mr. Fitzgerald's genteel term for sex in general. The thought of it, and all that sophisticated life going on somewhere else, made her nervous. She remembered her dreams of a life with Rafe. "Forget it," she said out loud. Dawg came up to the door and whined to be let in. She decided to take a swim.

RAFE DROVE OUT to the farm. He hadn't seen Belle since he'd kissed her on his sister's veranda back in August. He thought about Christine Winthrop, the girl he'd had a crush on in college. Christine, with her golden hair and exquisite manners, had jilted him as soon as the society parties started.

Maybe Belle jilted him when things began to heat up between them. Maybe it had nothing to do with Rachel. His mother had warned him about gentile girls. Rafe wondered if he was simply a slow learner.

He turned into the long drive. Dust flew up around the car in clouds. It settled on his white shirt and linen pants. The trees, still thick with foliage, were just beginning to turn.

He pulled up in front of the house and got out expecting to be confronted by her dog, but everything was quiet. He climbed the steps, crossed the front porch, and lifted the brass knocker. The sound echoed through the silent house. He heard no answering footsteps, only the buzzing of flies and the mooing of a cow somewhere in the distance in back of the house. Her truck was parked in front of the house. She must be around somewhere. He sat down on the swing to wait.

Red roses bloomed on the trellises framing the porch. The air was sweet with them and the white blossoms of the Confederate jasmine that twined around the posts and curled into the gingerbread trim. He was surrounded by the soft, country stillness of the South, where time itself is languid, and sitting on the porch seems like a worthy occupation even to a Yankee. The side yard was shaded by a giant oak. Clumps of moss and little white flowers grew in the shadows around roots and rock.

Then the mosquitos came out to greet him. They landed on his cheeks and on his hands. After minutes of slapping, he stood and paced back and forth across the porch, his footsteps breaking the silence.

Maybe Belle had gone somewhere with her mother-in-law and daughter in their buggy. He should be getting back to town, but the thought of spending another long, muggy Sunday with his sister and her ailing husband didn't appeal to him, not after he'd come all the way to this sylvan outpost.

The air seemed to have turned to liquid in the heat. His shirt, starched and pressed when he'd started out, was sticking to his body. What he wanted was a swim. He thought about the clear water of the spring-fed creek, icy on his sweaty skin. Why not? He'd come this far. No one was around. Maybe Belle would be back here when he'd finished.

He found the path leading down from the house. A fat brown squirrel leapt into a tree and scurried to safety. Rafe was soon confronted with divergent paths. They both seemed to head toward the water. Above him he heard the echoing tap of a woodpecker. He chose the path covered with pine needles. His feet trod softly.

He remembered a broad beach. But when he reached the creek, there was only a small cove of sand next to a green, mossy bank. He dropped his clothes on the moss and walked down onto the little beach. His shoe-cramped feet reveled in their freedom as he stepped into the icy water.

CURTIS HAD FOUND Belle an old, patched inner tube several days before. She lay in it now, enjoying the cool water on her backside and the beauty of the Spanish moss hanging from the cypress limbs shading the creek. She let her hand trail. She didn't know what heaven was like, but she wouldn't mind if it were something like this.

She ought to turn around. She couldn't let herself drift too far downstream, not wearing this indecent bathing suit. She didn't want to pass the farm sharecropped by those crazy country Pruetts.

But it's hard to leave paradise.

Just a little more, and then, she promised herself, she'd start the slog upstream. Dawg alternated between swimming next to her and running along the bank.

The bushes were high. She couldn't see what was waiting for

her around the bend, but here in the middle of the stream, she surrendered to a lazy country solitude.

Suddenly, Dawg gave a sharp bark.

Belle turned and saw Rafe. He was standing ankle-deep in the water, naked as a jaybird.

Rafe searched wildly for his clothes as the dog bounded up to him, tail wagging in glee. He had a mental picture of how he'd look, trying to cover himself with one hand, pushing the slobbering animal away with the other, all the while bent over and foolish as he rushed across the beach and up the bank.

Instead he dove into the deep water. The shock of the cold took his breath away.

Belle watched him swim out to her. Memories of their trip to Jackson flashed in her head. She had to remind herself that this man thought he was too good for her. What the hell was he doing here? Trying to get a little action before he went back to his glamorous life?

He was up to his chest when he caught hold of her inner tube. "What do you want?" she asked, as if she didn't know.

"I needed—" He stumbled. She figured she knew what he needed, but she wasn't his for the asking. How dare he come out here naked. What did he think she was?

"I have something I wanted to tell you." He could see the way her breasts swelled, full in her soft, knit bathing suit. She was so womanly. Her legs were bare up to the middle of her thigh. They dangled inches from his face. In spite of the cold, he knew he couldn't get out of the water in the state he was in.

"I'm listening."

His fingers touched her naked flesh. She slapped his hand away. Her legs were served up to him at eye level, so he couldn't help noticing her smooth thighs were covered in little goose bumps.

He tried not to look, but he'd never wanted a woman so

much. The ribs of her chest moved when she breathed beneath the wet knit. "It's about your late husband. How he died."

"I know how he died," she said, looking away from him. Guilt fluttered in her stomach. Why did he have to dredge that up today, when she'd been so content?

"You don't know everything."

Her teeth began to chatter. "I want to get out. I'm cold."

"I'd better get dressed," he said.

Their eyes met. "All right." She watched him head for the shore until she saw his lean buttocks with their muscled indentation leave the water. She slipped out of the inner tube and stood, looking away from him, her toes digging into a patch of fine white clay on the bottom of the creek. A flock of tiny birds ran along the sand on the far-side shore. A white-tailed doe poked her head through the underbrush, startled, and ran away. Belle wanted to run with her. At least a part of her wanted to run, the guilty part. The silly, female, nit part wanted to stay with this beautiful naked man.

When she turned around, he was standing on the sand, tall and wet. His sheer linen shirt and faun-colored slacks embraced his body like a wrinkled skin. Dawg was standing next to him, pointing at her.

She walked out of the creek. Rafe watched the sun sparkle on her wet skin. She looked like a Greek goddess, Venus, perfectly formed, strong, effortlessly graceful. A dove coo-ooed in the leaves above her. She shielded her eyes with her hand, looking up at him. She's so self-contained, so calm, he thought.

Belle had to remind herself to breathe. Here she was exposing herself in the same indecent bathing suit that had caused Claude's death. Of course, Rafe had seen her in her altogether, so it wasn't . . . Wasn't what? Her mind was a jumble. What could he have discovered now? Guilt was caught in her throat.

She didn't want to hear any more about how Claude had died, or about what she'd done to provoke it.

"You know Mike O'Malley?"

She nodded. Poor Mike. It must be awful, she thought, going through life stomping around on a wooden leg. What we do to our young men in the name of glory.

"He was there the night your husband died."

"You don't have to tell me. I know all about it. He saw a photograph of me being arrested for indecent behavior. Now you know it, too. Let's just drop it. Okay?"

"But—"

She cut him off. "I said drop it."

"Belle, he didn't see any picture." She shrugged. So not everybody saw it. Good, but what difference did it make, really? "There was no photograph."

"Huh?" She knew that was vulgar, but it just came out.

"Your late husband caught the mayor's son, Pruett somebody—"

"Pruett Walker."

"It seems Claude caught him marking a card. When he challenged him, this Pruett character pulled a knife and stabbed him. It was over before Mike knew what had happened."

Belle was staring at him as if he were speaking a foreign language. Finally she asked, "What about the broken beer bottle?"

He shook his head. "There was no broken beer bottle, no photograph. The sheriff and Pruett cooked up that story between them. The others didn't see the pictures—"

Belle cut him off. "Pictures? There were more than one?"

Rafe nodded. "But the men at the poker game didn't see them until a couple of days later, when they all swore to tell the same story."

"To protect the mayor's son?"

Rafe nodded again. "Apparently the sheriff had gotten a call about you from the New Orleans police when they hauled you in. So he made some phone calls after Claude's murder and found out there were several pictures the paper hadn't printed. He had copies sent up from New Orleans."

It took a moment or two for Belle to understand. "That son of a . . . Excuse me."

"He's a son of a bitch, all right. No excuses necessary."

The picture was supposed to make everything go away, she thought. And damn me, it worked! Suddenly her first meeting with Bourrée flashed in her mind. He'd come to them on the sheriff's recommendation. There were more pictures. They could have used them against me for years. "Well, we'll see about that."

"Belle, listen to me. Mike said he has enough problems just getting around. If he's called to testify, he'll deny he ever said anything."

"Then why did he tell you?"

"He didn't want you to go through life blaming yourself."

Belle was in a gumbo of boiling emotions. She knew white people had been killing each other in Gentry for decades without ever going to jail. Colored people, too, as long as they just killed each other and didn't kill whites. There was always self-defense or temporary insanity or some such when the power structure was involved, or felt sorry for the perpetrator, or the killer was kin.

Even if she could get the DA to indict, a big if, what good would it do to bring on some long, useless, court battle? A local jury would never convict Pruett. They'd find a loophole. Cousins would testify. The Cantrells' forest would go up in an unexplained fire. None of it would bring Claude back. No sense starting a battle she couldn't win. An old rule from the Southern Girls' Guide came to her: *Lawyers are bad for your health.*

But as the knowledge sank in that she wasn't responsible for her husband's death, she felt as if she'd cast off a veil. The sunlight became brighter, the colors more vivid.

He watched her struggle with herself. Now was the time to ask her, because wasn't that the real reason he'd come out here instead of writing her a letter? "What happened? Why did you leave so suddenly? Was it something Rachel said?"

"Ask her."

"Don't you think I have?" He waited for her to speak. When she didn't, he pleaded, "For God's sake, Belle, this isn't fair to me."

For the first time, she saw this tall, elegant man not as a prince from a wondrous faraway country, but as a vulnerable, shell-shocked vet whose own wife had deceived and abandoned him. "She said you could never—" Belle stopped herself. It would sound like a proposal. She tried again. "Rachel said you would never be serious about a girl who wasn't Jewish."

"Damn her! Excuse me, but she had no right to say that."

"Unless it's true." She waited, watching him. He pushed back his hair. His response wasn't fast enough. "You-all think you're too good for me, don't you?"

"No. Of course not."

"What am I to you, just poor—" She stopped herself before she said "poor white trash." She should never have told him. "Just some poor ignorant country girl?"

"No. It's not that. It's—"

"What?" She heard her voice become steely.

What is it? he wondered. He wasn't religious. What is it that keeps us separate? Fear of rejection? Certainly. Fear that it will mean the end of Our People? Fear of the unknown? The image of Christine took shape in his mind again. Christine, with her golden hair and impeccable manners. He heard his father's voice: "Marriage is hard enough when you have the same back-

ground. Why make it harder?" And Rachel: "What are you going to do? Teach her to play mah-jongg and take her to the
country club? Introduce her to Aunt Sadie?" But what did he
care about the country club or Aunt Sadie? If we don't want
people to be prejudiced against us, we can't be prejudiced
against them. "I thought the Shabbat dinner might have scared
you off."

"Did Rachel say that?"

"Not exactly." He tried to explain. "She doesn't want me to
get a divorce. I'll be the first in the family to—" He stopped
talking and watched a glittering droplet of creek water fall from
her bobbed hair onto her shoulder, slide down her chest, and
head for the scoop of her bathing suit. "Oh, Belle." He reached
out for her.

She felt his long hands encircle her waist. She still had reservations, but they were hard to hold on to when his fingers slid
up her back under her long bathing-suit top. He looked down
and gently kissed her lips. Rachel said he'll break my heart,
Belle reminded herself. But when he laid her down on a bed of
yellow leaves, her heart felt strong enough to take him on. Sunlight splashed on his wavy hair. He bent over her. She remembered crying out as his beautiful wet skin met her skin. She
tasted the creek on his lips and neck and chest.

Afterward, they lay together as the shadows lengthened. She
didn't pay any attention when Dawg barked. He barked at
squirrels. He barked at shadows. He barked for the ferocious
pleasure of barking.

She didn't even hear the crunching of leaves and twigs under
heavy boots. But Rafe did. Suddenly the trees exploded with
gunshots. He rolled over to protect her with his body. Wings
flapped. Squirrels scattered. Dogs barked.

"Pruetts!" She pushed out from under him, looking for her
bathing suit. Dawg came rushing out of the woods.

"Jesus Christ, is there no end to them? Isn't this your farm?" He was sweating. His breath was short. She saw his hands tremble.

"They don't care. They hunt wherever the spirit takes them." She wanted to put her arms around him and hold him until his breathing became normal and his hands stopped shaking, but there was no time. "They can't see us together. Not out here alone." She found her bathing-suit top and slipped it on, but the bottom, where was the bottom?

Another shot, closer this time. More barking. She was scuttling around on the sand. In spite of the beating of his heart and the dryness in his mouth, he couldn't help but admire the view. He found her gray bathing-suit bottom thrown against the roots of a tree.

"Call to them as soon as I'm out of sight. Tell them you're lost. You're a Yankee. They'll believe it." She slipped on her bathing-suit bottom and splashed into the creek. When she turned back, she saw Rafe buttoning his pants. No Pruetts in sight yet, but the joyous barking of their dogs was echoing through the trees. She called for Dawg.

A flight of doves sailed across the creek as shot after shot chased them.

How could she have done this in the middle of the afternoon? What had possessed her? Well, she knew what had possessed her. When you've been dozing for years, only dreaming about a life, and a man—who bares a striking resemblance to Prince Charming—wakes you up, how can you tell him no thanks, sorry, I'm going back to sleep?

Belle's arms sliced through the water. Her feet kicked frantically. She thought about her Margaret Sanger sponge. It was safe and dry in her lingerie drawer at home. She was unsafe and wet in the middle of the creek. This was a fine time to think about that.

She heard another shot. Something splashed into the water behind her. Then she heard the howling and the yelping of the dogs. She reached the edge of the creek and started running upstream. She'd have to douche with vinegar and water when she got back, but that was far from being surefire. What if I get pregnant? He's still married. Why didn't I have more sense?

Out of sight of the Pruetts and their dogs, she slowed to a walk through the shallow water. Dawg bounced around her. Prince Charming had taken Sleeping Beauty back to the palace to live happily ever after. But Rafe hadn't even mentioned any such intentions before taking his pleasure with her. She wasn't Sleeping Beauty, *la Belle Dormante,* as Claude's father had sometimes called her. She was *la Belle Stupide.* But just as she started to dwell on that and on Rachel's predictions of heartbreak, she realized she hadn't told him her intentions either.

She wasn't some nit who could leave home because a man crooked his finger. She had a farm to run. She didn't need a man to take care of her anymore. A slow smile lightened her face. She was an independent woman. She could take her pleasure wherever she found it. Just like a man.

As long as she didn't get pregnant.

RAFE WAITED UNTIL she was out of sight, then he called out to the hunters. At first his throat was so dry he could only cackle. He called again. A dry roar. The shooting stopped. The thin, mangy dogs came first. They jumped around him, barking, until he felt like a treed squirrel. Then three generations of armed men, rangy and tough, came out of the woods, trampling any buds and shoots that found themselves beneath their heavy boots. Shaving didn't seem to be a priority among the country Pruetts, but only the eldest had a real beard. He compensated by having no teeth. He nodded to Rafe and gave out a suspicious, "Afternoon."

Rafe introduced himself in a rough voice, holding his still trembling hands together. He'd seen them around the store, when the farmers came in on Saturday.

"You the one threatening to cut off our credit?" the middle Pruett, whose name was Jake, asked, shifting his shotgun. In spite of his many good teeth, he rarely smiled, at least not at strangers.

Rafe's panic cleared as he assessed his chances. Not good if they wanted to take him. They had a rifle and two shotguns between them. He'd survived in forests thinner than these, but he guessed these men were more expert at shooting in the woods than the German recruits were at the end of the war. "I'm the one," Rafe admitted.

He heard a moan. Something inside Jake Pruett's hunting sack jerked and bled. Rafe wondered if he should give them an extension on their bill or make a run for it.

Moses, the bearded, elder Pruett, spat out a mouthful of tobacco juice. His voice had the rattle of gravel. "You Miss Rachel's Yankee brother?"

"Yes." Rafe saw the middle one squint, saw his thumb move a little over the stock on the other side of his rifle. Did he just flick on his safety? Or did he flick it off?

Moses turned to his son. "A man's got a right to collect his debts."

"I expect," said Jake, raising his gun. Rafe could almost feel the trajectory of a bullet moving up from his groin, to his heart, to his head. A powerful crash shook the woods. A wild turkey flapped ungainly wings and fell into the creek behind him. The dogs rushed headlong through the current.

"Scare you?" asked Jake with a satisfied grin.

As the younger Pruetts retrieved their prey, Moses showed Rafe how to get back to the Cantrells. "You say hello to Abe for me, you hear? Tell him we're praying for him."

Rafe promised he would. But as he headed into the trees, he heard the middle Pruett say in a hard voice, "Wonder which one of them Cantrell women that Yankee Jew boy is sniffing around."

"Miss Effie probably," said the youngest one.

This was followed by a "Hush up, you fool!" and an explosion of snide laughter.

Chapter 17

IT WAS LATE Saturday afternoon. Bourrée LeBlanc was getting a shave and a shoeshine when he caught sight of Rafe walking up and down the platform in front of the depot. Bourrée checked his watch. The Panama Limited was due in a few minutes. He'd heard about that all-Pullman train, where a man could eat a first-class dinner served to him on a white linen tablecloth, sleep between fine sheets in a comfortable bed, and wake up the next morning in Chicago with his shoes shined. If things went his way, he'd take that train himself, someday. His eyes narrowed at the thought of the Jew boy being able to step onto that train this afternoon.

What the hell, he was leaving.

Good riddance.

Arnold tilted Bourrée back and wrapped his face in hot towels. Bourrée inhaled the steam and began to relax. All in all, it was a fine end to a fine week.

He'd be leading a church visitation to Ticfaw in the morning and wanted to look his best, not that the congregation would see him under his hood, but the other Klansmen would. A Kleagle can't afford to look like a bum. He'd found a particularly friendly minister at the Church of Everlasting Redemption outside LaGrace. After receiving a donation of a hundred dollars, he'd told his congregation, "If Jesus came back today, he'd join the Klan." Bourrée expected he'd be able to charter a new Klavern there in record time.

The main problem he was having was right here in Gentry. The picnic was fine, but it hadn't brought in enough new members. Except for a damn good cross burning in Butlertown to put the fear of God into the jigaboos, and a fund-raiser when Hiram Pruett's widow needed money to bury him, the Gentry Klan had been real quiet, which was fine with him, but without the romance of the Knights in combat against the forces of evil, new members weren't signing up and the old members were getting antsy. They were agitating for action.

Bourrée advised caution. The wrong kind of action could bring in the authorities. Besides, there was no money in it. The money was in those ten-dollar membership dues and, of course, Klan paraphernalia.

Arnold had tilted him back up, slapped lather all over his face, and begun to shave him when Bourrée heard the whistle of the Panama Limited coming into the station. Good-bye, Jew boy. Guess you'll ship that fancy car of yours up north. Bye-bye. Go pester the Yankees now.

He saw the locomotive charge into the station from the south amid clouds of smoke. He heard the brakes scream and saw the Berlin boy cross the platform. Bye-bye. A satisfied smile settled on Bourrée's lips as he watched the porters jump down with their little step stools.

It was then that Bourrée noticed Rafe didn't have any luggage. Maybe the rich had it sent on ahead. As Arnold shaved his right cheek, Bourrée rolled his eyes toward the window. He saw Rafe approach the train, but instead of climbing aboard, he stopped and held out his hand. A lady placed her white-gloved hand into his.

"Son of a bitch!" Bourrée spat out as he jumped up, kicking the shoeshine boy crouched at his feet. He didn't even feel the razor cut into his cheek. He stood at the window. Globules of blood and lather fell onto the black-and-white-tile floor. He saw Rafe help Cady off the train, saw him pick up Belle's package, and saw her smile up at him like some fine lady, as pure as the driven snow. That was a laugh. He thought of her in the barn with him, the two of them going at it, grunting like animals. Jealousy bubbled up, hot and sour, in his throat until it choked him. Wonder what that rich boy would do if he knew he'd been sharing her with me? he thought. Words for an informative letter were taking shape in his mind when Calvin Nix entered the barbershop from the lobby.

"Hey, Bourrée. What's going on?"

Bourrée didn't turn. He simply motioned with his head. "That Yid yonder's got your daughter."

"WHAT ARE YOU DOING HERE?" Belle asked when Rafe picked up her package.

"Meeting your train."

"But we didn't know ourselves when we'd be coming back."

"Mental telepathy," he said, tapping his forehead. "I had this vision: Belle and her lovely daughter will leave New Orleans on the Panama Limited."

Cady's eyes opened wide. "Really?"

"Really." His voice was deep, rich, sincere.

"You met every train, didn't you?" Belle asked.

A smile lit up Rafe's face. "Caught. Now you'll have to let me take you and Cady to dinner."

"Why don't you come on out to the house? Miss Effie just loves to feed handsome men, doesn't she, Cady?"

Cady inspected this man her mother had taken up with and said warily, "I expect Grandma would be pleased to have you."

Rafe turned to Cady. "I don't see how a gentleman could decline an invitation like that."

WHERE RAFE SUGGESTED they could be alone the next evening was tacky, sleazy, and, Belle had to admit as she crossed Grand Avenue, downright thrilling. Her high-heel pumps clicked on the iron railroad tracks like the tsk, tsk, tsk of the Deacons of Decency. She looked around. *If a lady wishes to gain the respect of the world, she must be respectable.* That was a prime commandment of the Primer of Propriety, but since no Watchdogs of the Wicked were liable to be running the streets at ten-thirty on a Sunday night, Belle figured, *What they don't know can't hurt me.* She made that a rule in her Southern Girls' Guide.

She entered the shadows of the long awning in front of Rubinstein's department store. A chill draft of night air tickled her bare arms. She thought about Brother Scaggs, the minister of the Church of Everlasting Redemption. If he ever got wind of what I'm about to do, he'd call me a harlot and proclaim my future address to be the Abode of the Damned.

In the gloom, she made out Rubinstein's Emporium of Fashion. Wooden mannequins with dead eyes and painted smiles held out their arms to her. Suppose it actually existed, the Abode of the Damned.

Belle tried to picture it. There wouldn't be any preachers, of course, and none of those upright Deacons of Decency. Just an eternity with the folks who didn't follow the rules. Nothing but wild women and rowdy, passionate men.

Didn't sound so bad, not nearly as bad as Gentry, come to think of it. Taking a quick look around, she slipped into the alley behind the store, where Rafe was waiting on the loading dock. He held the door open. It creaked when he closed it. Suddenly, they were plunged into total darkness. She heard the key turn in the lock.

"I'm afraid we're going to hell," she told him.

"I've already been there," he said as he ran his fingers through her freshly shampooed hair. "It was nothing like this." The scent of wildflowers mixed with jasmine surrounded him. Miracles are real, he told himself.

He turned on a big flashlight and guided her through the stockroom, past a rack of suits and boxes of shirts. He'd have to speak to Harry Chambers. This merchandise should have been put out on the floor Saturday. You can't sell it if the customers can't see it.

He guided her through the hardware store and into the ladies' department. Belle was reminded of her childhood dream of having the run of the store, especially that first year with Mr. Nix, when she'd outgrown her shoes and had to go to school barefoot.

Rafe's light looped over a display of new hats. There was a darling blue cloche with some kind of exotic feathers on it. She couldn't help touching it.

"Go ahead, try it on."

She looked at him. He nodded. A naughty smile crossed her face. After the cloche, she tried on sunbonnets and rain hats, knit caps, and a huge vermilion going-to-church-on-Sunday hat sprouting a ridiculous bouquet of flowers and feathers. He handed her a bowler.

"What do you think?" she asked. Her short hair fell around her ears.

He examined her critically. "Fetching."

He led her to the lingerie department. "Let's see how you look in ready-made lingerie."

"No, Rafe, I'm—" Thirty-three, she thought. Already middle-aged!

"Never going to look more beautiful than you do now."

Belle considered that. He was right. *A girl has to enjoy what she's got while she's still got it to enjoy. After twenty, life is one downhill slide. The only thing a girl can do is lean back and enjoy the ride.* If that wasn't a rule for her Southern Girls' Guide to Men and Other Perils of Modern Life, she didn't know what was.

He shone his flashlight on her. Belle felt as if she were on a stage as she slowly unbuttoned her shirtwaist and let it fall to the floor. Underneath she wore her red silk camisole. It's a good thing Miss Effie can't see me now. She won't be joining us in the Abode of the Damned, Belle thought.

But Rafe will.

A great exchange, if you ask me.

He handed her something soft and lacy. It was one of those new, patented Warner bras she'd heard so much about. It looked like two handkerchiefs sewn together with baby ribbon.

She was alone in the spotlight. She unbuttoned her camisole and pulled it off over her head. She slipped into the new contraption. It separated her breasts and held them up. She felt like a young girl again.

Belle looked at herself in the three-way mirror and saw Rafe sitting in back of her in the shadows. He had one leg crossed over his knee as he held the light.

I'm making a spectacle of myself, Belle thought. It gave her a funny thrill. It's not often a girl gets a man's undivided attention. She'd be a fool not to make the most of it. She turned and blew him a kiss. He handed her a pair of matching flesh-colored panties made of China silk. They were loose and stopped at the top of her thighs. She blushed, deeply thrilled.

She unhooked the waist of her silk bloomers. She pulled up one leg, balancing on the other like a dancer. He marveled at her flexibility and had to hold himself back from taking her right there. She extricated one bent leg, then the other. He glimpsed dark pubic hair against pale skin and wondered if she had any idea how beautiful she was to him. She had begun to pull the little panties over her ankle when he heard a noise.

She started to say something. But he hushed her and cut the light. The building was fifty years old. He'd heard it groan and wheeze when he worked late, but this sounded different, more like metal on metal. It sounded like a key in the lock.

They held their breath. Then he heard a groan of a wheel that needed oil as the loading door slid open.

He helped her gather up her clothes in the dark and, feeling his way, led her to a recessed rack of dresses. She stepped into her skirt. Then she slipped her arms into her shirtwaist, while he held the dresses apart for her. Her bloomers and camisole had disappeared into the darkness.

"Step over the bottom panel. You can lie down and hide beneath the dresses," he whispered.

"But—"

"Shhh," he breathed, and feeling his way, he headed for the hardware department.

A dim light coming from the stockroom was reflected in a display of mirrors. Something was moving around. There had been "slippage" (the word Abe used for theft) for over a year, but Abe couldn't or wouldn't do anything about it.

Rafe stumbled in the gloom. His hands were trembling. A loose board creaked under his foot. The sounds from the stockroom stopped. He held his breath. For several moments, all he could hear was his own blood pumping. Then the squeak of wheels on concrete.

Rafe moved through the darkness toward a faint glow. He hit his shin on the rounded leg of a woodstove. It hurt like the devil, but he kept going, feeling in front of him with his hands as he moved forward. Echoes of a stupid, wasted raid through no-man's-land came back to him. A severed head screaming silently in the mud. He'd fought the war to end all wars. They'd won. Why did he have to do this? His next step almost took him into a barrel of nails. He caught it and set it upright before the nails could spill out.

He listened for voices. Nothing. That could mean one man was working alone, but he had to be sure. He looked around for a weapon. There were dozens of guns, but they were locked in display cases. The key was upstairs in Abe's desk. However, the hardware department was filled with metal rods, axes, knives.

He ran his fingers lightly along a display until he found a sugarcane knife with a sturdy wooden handle and a fifteen-inch blade. Holding it down by his side, he edged toward the stockroom. He didn't notice that his tremors had stopped. He was focused. He was taking action.

He saw the rack of men's suits wobble out to the loading dock. A bulky figure, silhouetted by dim headlights, grabbed an armload of the suits and carried them to a Model T. Was there only one or were there more?

The man came back. He didn't look armed, but Rafe couldn't be sure. He waited until the thief had a carton of shirts in his arms, then he clicked on his flashlight.

Harry Chambers, the head of the men's department, was caught in the spotlight. "Put the shirts down, Harry."

Harry put up a hand to shade his eyes. "Hey, Rafe, I was just—"

He didn't get a chance to finish. "Bring the suits back." Rafe kept the cane knife down at his side and followed Harry to the truck, watching him to be sure he didn't pick up a gun.

Harry brought the suits back and hung them carefully on the rack. "Good as new." He patted them.

"Now give me your keys."

Harry had a sheepish grin on his face as he handed them over. "Times are tough, you know."

"They're even tougher when your employees steal from you. Now, get out."

"Wait a minute, I understand about the keys, but you can't fire me."

"The hell I can't."

"Not without talking to Abe."

"I'll tell you what. If you go quietly, I'll talk to Abe before I call the sheriff."

"Son of a bitch! You people are all the same. The only thing you think about is money! You don't give a damn what happens to the rest of us. Well, you better watch out, you hear? You just better watch out!" Harry called after him as he cranked up his car and roared off.

"YOU CAN'T FIRE Harry Chambers!" Abe said, swinging his legs to the floor. He'd been in bed all day on orders from Dr. Vickerson after a bout of tachycardia that had lasted twelve hours. "He's kin to everybody in town except the Pruetts."

"In that case, why don't you invite his kinfolks in and let them steal from you, too?"

Abe slipped into his silk robe and slid his feet into his slippers. "You don't understand."

"You can say that again. You don't have to call the sheriff, I will."

"What's going on?" Rachel asked, bringing her husband a cup of tea. "Honey, what are you doing out of bed?"

Rafe walked out into the hall and picked up the phone. Abe followed him and pushed down the hook before the operator came on the line.

"Will somebody please tell me what's going on?"

"Rafe caught Harry stealing." Before she could say anything, Abe continued, "He's learned his lesson. I want to give him another chance."

"Are you out of your mind? The man's a thief!"

"Rafe, stop it! You want to kill him?" Rachel's voice was shrill.

Rafe looked at his sister, and forced himself to calm down. "Hire him back, go ahead, but if you do, I'm leaving."

"I won't stop you," Abe said.

Rachel glared at her brother. Then she turned to her husband. "Come on, honey, let me help you into bed. We don't need to make any decisions tonight."

Suddenly Rafe felt bereft. He didn't want to stay in this hick town, but how could he leave Belle?

He went into his bedroom. A cut-glass vase filled with blue hydrangeas and yellow roses greeted him from the mantel. We don't have to make any decisions tonight, he reminded himself, taking off his jacket and hanging it over the walnut valet stand. Things will look different after a good night's sleep. The big, canopied bed had been turned down. The yellow chenille spread had been taken off and folded. A pale blue summer blanket lay on top of the crisp, white sheets. He didn't think he'd get much sleep tonight. He hung his pants over the pants press and thought of what he would be going back to. His empty bachelor's apartment was still empty. A table, a few chairs, a bed. He'd let Helen keep the big house in Hyde Park. He hadn't had the heart to shop for furniture.

Rachel knocked. Rafe slipped into his dressing gown and opened the door. "Is Abe all right?" He thought about apologizing, but the words wouldn't come.

"He's resting," Rachel said, walking into the room and sitting on the blue damask sofa. "I talked to Helen tonight."

"You had no right to do that!"

"She's still my sister-in-law. I can talk to her if I want to. Rafe, I think she's prepared to take you back."

Chapter 18

MONDAY EVENING, SHERIFF George Goode drove Harry Chambers to the courthouse in his official car. Harry was dressed in one of Rubinstein's finest ready-made suits, but he seemed slumped into his big body.

They skirted the entrance over which the Latin words for "Law Is the Science of What Is Good and Just" were carved, and entered through the back, near the jail. The sheriff led Harry down a short and shadowy hallway. No pictures of smiling public servants shaking hands with happy businessmen graced these dingy walls.

Sheriff Goode opened a door and ushered Harry inside.

Already assembled were Bourrée LeBlanc; Calvin Nix, Belle's stepfather; D. T. Pruett, president of Pruett Plumbing; the corpulent Pruett Walker, mayor's son and now president of Walker Sawmill; and Titus Pruett, who pumped bicycle tires by day and was Exalted Cyclops of the Gentry Ku Klux Klan. Mr. Nix and

D.T. had the fanciful titles of Kligrapp and Klabee. Potbellied Pruett was Klaliff, a sort of vice cyclops. He'd actually won the election to become the Exalted Cyclops, but Bourrée didn't think it sent the right message to elect as Klan leader a man who'd murdered a leading citizen.

And Bourrée had counted the votes.

None of them wore white robes or cone hats. This was a meeting of the executive committee. "We got to go get us a nigger. Give the folks some excitement, otherwise they're just gonna drift away, and sure as shooting, we ain't gonna get nobody new." Titus's sonorous voice was filled with conviction. He rarely lacked conviction. What Titus lacked was sense.

"The coloreds are keeping real quiet," Pruett Walker said, passing around a greased paper filled with pork cracklings.

"One of them might could be going after one of our women," declared Titus without wavering.

The sheriff sat down behind his walnut desk. "Now, Titus, listen up. I don't want you provoking a race riot like they had over in Knoxville, you hear?"

"That would be real bad for business," Calvin Nix said. His clean white hair shone in the overhead light.

D.T. Pruett nodded. He wanted no interruption in Pruett Plumbing and Electrical Supply.

Titus sat back like a scolded schoolboy and ran his fingers through his rust-colored hair.

"Besides, you start agitating the niggers and they'll stop coming to work," Calvin Nix said. He leaned over and flicked his cigar into a big glass ashtray standing on the floor between him and D.T.

Bourrée pulled out a flask. "Now, George, you know I'd hate to break the law, but I got me some pretty good moonshine here."

Titus's laugh boomed. "Yeah, it wouldn't be right for the sheriff to associate with no lawbreakers."

"You aren't selling or manufacturing it, are you, boy?" the sheriff asked. An expectant smile half formed on his lips.

"No, sir."

"Then I assume this liquor was in your possession before the law was passed."

"Oh, hell yes," Bourrée said. The other men laughed, all except for Harry.

"Well, far be it from me to arrest a man for sharing his private stock with a few personal friends," Sheriff George Goode said, taking glasses out of a drawer in his desk and handing them around.

Harry Chambers kicked back his drink and held out his glass for more. Bourrée obliged. "What's up, Harry? You look down tonight."

"Son of a bitch fired me. After I put in ten years at that store."

Bourrée's eyes lit up. When opportunity knocks, it behooves a man to open the door. It looked like he might be able to run that rich boy out of town and have a chance at Belle and that big farm of hers yet. When he spoke, he betrayed none of his eagerness. His voice had a slow, sardonic drawl. "Well, what do you expect from a bunch of clipped dicks?"

"Clipped what?" Titus asked.

"Oh, come on, Bourrée, there's no call for that kind of language," D.T. said.

"Hey, boys, I'm not prejudiced against anyone, but you-all gotta admit, they do business different than we do. That's why they're so rich."

"I went to school with Abe," D.T. said.

"His father gave the land for the baseball field," the sheriff said.

Calvin Nix's sharp eyes darted from speaker to speaker.

Bourrée knew he was watching which way the conversation was going. Calvin ventured, "His brother Leon died in the war."

"Oh sure, if they can't get out of it, they go to war with the rest of us. And sometimes they even donate a little money to charity, but that's just a cover. The truth is, every last one of them are members of a secret, international conspiracy." Bourrée could see they weren't convinced. "There's a book. It lays it all out."

"What book?" D.T. asked.

"It's called the something of the elders of Zion. I don't have a copy of it here, but I seen it when I was back in Atlanta." He leaned forward and lowered his voice. "You know that fellow who bombed Wall Street? He was a Jew."

"Where'd you hear that?" the sheriff asked.

"Atlanta. I got it straight from the Imperial Wizard himself." This wasn't true, but Bourrée figured it wasn't an actual lie unless someone caught you at it.

D.T. and the sheriff exchanged looks.

Seeing his arguments weren't gaining traction, Bourrée veered off in another direction. "Now, you-all say Abe's family have been here for a while?"

"Must be fifty years," D.T. said. "My granddaddy worked for his granddaddy after they got back from the War Between the States."

"Brother Meadows had the whole congregation praying for him when he had his heart attack," the sheriff said.

"Well, that explains it! Abe's become sympathetic to our ways. That's why they sent his brother-in-law down here to bring him back into the fold."

"Abe's been sick," Calvin Nix said. "His brother-in-law came down here to help out."

Bourrée flashed his white teeth. "They go after their own,

when they're weak. I know you-all may be partial to Abe Rubinstein, but think about what that Berlin fellow's been doing.
Dunning us for money in hard times like these. Cutting off our
credit when we need it most."

Titus Pruett jumped in, "I told that som' bitch I was closing
my account."

"See, here's a man of principle," Bourrée said.

Titus beamed. "I told him from now on, anything I buy at
Rubinstein's is gonna be for cash money."

The sheriff coughed. Bourrée wanted to kick himself for
making Titus Exalted Cyclops. Crawfish had more sense. But
there was nothing he could do about it now. "You-all know as
well as I do, their business practices don't harmonize with our
Christian ideals. Look what they did to Harry here."

"Why'd Abe fire you?" Pruett Walker asked. Pork cracklings
hung from his flopping jowls.

"It weren't Abe. It was his damn brother-in-law. Abe just let
him do it."

"See what I been telling you!" Bourrée brayed. "That's why
he came down here, to put folks like Harry out of work. You
watch, next thing he'll be hiring more of them Italians and Abe
Rubinstein will let him do it."

"You know why? You really want to know why?" Harry was
becoming excited over the unexpected prospect of getting revenge. Bourrée poured him another drink. Harry leaned forward. "One night, when I was locking up, I caught that Yankee
all alone in the office with Belle Cantrell."

"My Belle?" Calvin Nix asked. His back became ramrod
straight.

"Said he was teaching her bookkeeping."

Bourrée sounded shocked. "Bookkeeping! That's what he
called it?" Titus sniggered. Calvin Nix's nose flared. D.T.

shook his head. Pruett Walker stuffed another handful of crack-lings into his gaping mouth.

Bourrée stood. "Brothers, we are Knights sworn to protect the chastity of our women. How long are we going to let that lecherous Jew remain in our city to lure innocents into his fancy car? How many daughters are we willing to sacrifice to his lust? How many names are we going to let him add to his—" Bour-rée paused dramatically before whispering, "Ledger book?"

"Not a one!" said Titus, standing up.

"You know I'm with you," said Harry, standing with him. The prospect of revenge shone on his face.

"Nobody takes advantage of my Belle and gets away with it," Calvin Nix said, getting up.

Pruett Walker put down his cracklings and pushed himself out of his chair. "We can't let that Jew boy mess with a hundred-percent American womanhood."

Bourrée glanced over at the sheriff and said, "Not much chance of a race riot over one little family of Jews." George Goode nodded, giving his consent, as Bourrée had expected he would.

Bourrée put his arm around Harry's shoulder. "We're stand-ing with you, Harry. We're sworn to come to the aid of our fel-low Knights! Aren't we, fellows?"

"You betcha," and "Sure are," and "You can count on us, Harry" were heard around the room.

"Besides," said D.T., coming to his feet. "If we run them off, won't nobody around here have to pay their bills."

"Looting might could break out," Titus said, with a gleam in his eye.

"A man could buy up that store for a song." Pruett Walker's piggy eyes were shining, even as crumbs fell from his lips.

"Anything's possible," Bourrée said. "I say we plan our

festivities for Friday night. I have it on good authority that the Jew can't so much as turn on a light switch after dark."

Tuesday morning was one of those clear, crisp autumn days that make you glad just to be aboveground. Belle awoke smiling.

Sunday night, after Rafe had chased away the intruder, he came back to her a hero. In the soft light of a hurricane lamp, he set up Rubinstein's best Victrola and they danced around the empty store, casting wild shadows on the walls and over the merchandise. What they did after that started her heart beating just thinking about it.

One of Belle's most constant fears had always been that on her deathbed she'd look back and find she hadn't lived. But Sunday night she'd grabbed life in both hands. Two days later, she was still a little sore, although the dull pain was an exquisite reminder.

The cotton harvest was in. They'd made a profit. Curtis was working with three of the farmhands, clearing pasture, getting it ready for new strawberry beds. Suddenly Dawg leapt at her, barking.

Moments later she heard the unmistakable roar of the Stutz. A lovely melody she couldn't name played in her head as she tucked her white shirt into her loose-fitting denim pants. Combing her fingers through her dark hair, she flew toward the driveway, hardly aware her feet touched the ground.

Rafe climbed slowly out of his car. Dawg jumped wildly around him.

Belle pulled the dog away. "Planning any new adventures?" she asked.

She must have had a smudge of dirt on her cheek, because he

wiped it away with his thumb. His eyes didn't meet hers. "We have to talk."

Belle didn't like the sound of that. If there was one thing she knew about men, it was they hated "to talk." Lecture. Yes. Pontificate. Absolutely. But actually want "to talk" to a woman? Rare as a two-headed pig.

He looked at her briefly, as if he wanted to ask her something, and then seemed to drop it as he led her to the front-porch steps. She sat. He stood above her, leaning on one leg, and began his speech. There was a long preamble filled with digressions. What she heard was "I'm leaving."

"What'll happen if Abe has another heart attack?" she asked, but Belle wasn't thinking about Abe or about Rachel. She was thinking, What about me?

"They'll be all right. Rachel has learned the basics of running the store and she understands the people around here. God knows, I don't." Belle felt something cold and damp settle over her. "Abe has a different"—he paused—"philosophy of business." He seemed to have found something to study in the dirt.

"Well," Belle said. Neither of them spoke for a while. "I guess you have to go, then." Heaven forbid you-all should have a difference in philosophy.

"Looks like it." He glanced up at her as if that unspoken question was plaguing him, but he said nothing.

"When?" Her voice was hoarse.

"I made reservations for Saturday on the Panama Limited."

Belle felt as if she'd been slugged. Of course she knew he had to leave sometime. He couldn't stay in Gentry forever. But she hadn't expected it so soon, or that it would hurt so much. Rachel had warned her he'd break her heart. Well, I have plenty to do around here, Belle thought. A broken heart isn't such a big thing. Not the way people think. There are people a lot worse off. The Armenians, for example. A broken heart would look like small potatoes to them, what with starving and running away from the Turks. They wouldn't worry about a little thing like a broken heart. Besides, I'm an independent woman. I have my own life. But she felt a squinching up in her chest. She patted the step next to her. Dawg lay down, his head on her lap.

"You could visit me," he said after a pause.

Could? Yes, I could visit you, she thought. I could do a lot of things. I could jump off the barn roof. I could sing in the opera. "You forget you're still married?" she asked. Darn shame I forgot it.

"That's what I wanted to talk to you about."

That's what you wanted to talk to me about! Telling me you're leaving on Saturday isn't enough? He went into a long preamble about how much he cared for her.

Swell, Belle thought. That's a word every girl longs to hear. "Care." I care for my aging aunt. I care for my sick cat. I care who wins the pennant.

He gave her that suspicious look again, then seemed to stifle it once and for all. He launched into how he'd felt dead inside until he met her. He couldn't relate to people. Everything was gray. "You brought me back to life."

She smiled.

"You must know how much you mean to me."

Belle waited for the "but." When it came, it was a doozie. The rich and beautiful Helen Herzog wanted a reconciliation. She and Rachel had been exchanging letters and now phone calls. He said it was something he had to "handle." That was an unfortunate choice of words. She imagined him handling Helen, his long, elegant fingers fondling her. It was not a pretty picture.

"I'd—" He hesitated and then said, "I'd like you to come for a visit as soon as the divorce is final."

If it's ever final, Belle thought. She still has to agree to give you a divorce. And why would she, after I brought you back to life? You're fine now. Better than fine. All these feelings for your lovely wife will come bubbling up. I've made a real contribution to your wedded bliss, haven't I? Well, I never wanted to be a home breaker, anyway, she assured herself.

"I'm sure my brother and his wife will be happy to put you up."

Suddenly, she just wanted him to go. She'd never cried over a man, certainly not in front of him, and she wasn't going to start now. She scratched Dawg between her ears.

He was saying, "I know it'll be a big change for you. So I don't want you to feel that you'd be under any obligation."

No, no, we couldn't have that. Don't want anyone to feel obligated, even if he danced you around a department store in the middle of the night and took you on a pile of down comforters and never told you about his reconciliation. "We'll be planting strawberries soon," she said.

"Later?"

"Sure, later." She didn't ask him to stay for lunch. She didn't even walk him to his car. She sat on the step and stroked her dog. The Down-Home Primer of Right Behavior said: *Any fool knows a man won't buy a cow if the milk is free.*

Here's one fool who didn't pay attention, Belle thought. The sky darkened with rain clouds. She heard the blast of a shotgun.

BOURRÉE LEBLANC WAS WALKING through the woods with the Pruetts and their pack of mangy dogs. Deer-hunting season had begun, not that it made much difference to the Pruetts. They shot all year long and at anything that moved.

"Thing is," Bourrée was saying, "you-all are gonna have it easy. Now, I'm not supposed to tell you this, but your cousin Titus is the Exalted Cyclops."

Old man Moses Pruett snorted. "He's a what?"

"That means he's got one eye," said Jake Jr., who'd been as far as fifth grade and was brighter than he looked.

This was not going well, Bourrée thought, what with the damn dogs making a racket and the guns going off and the Pruetts whooping about who shot what and who was bagging the most game. Bourrée had gotten a letter from the Imperial Kleagle the day before. Said some boy in north Louisiana was beating him out in memberships and if Bourrée didn't get a move on, this other boy would become King Kleagle before Christmas. The King collected a dollar for every membership sold in his whole state.

Bourrée didn't know if the boy really existed or whether the whole thing was one of Clarke's schemes for motivating the troops. Imperial Kleagle Clarke was big on motivation.

He turned to Moses because Moses was the elder and leader of the family. "See, with Titus head of the Gentry Klan, you boys get in automatically. What do you say?"

Moses wasn't saying anything, he was sighting a squirrel scampering through the underbrush. Three guns converged on the scared animal. When the squirrel was thoroughly shot to pieces, Moses grabbed what was left of it by its tail and turned to Bourrée. "I never did think much of Titus and his projects. None of 'um have ever come to anything yet." He tossed the remains of the dead animal into his bag.

"Hey, that one's mine. I got him with the rifle," Jake Sr. said.

"Uh-uh, Daddy, I'm the one that blasted him to kingdom come."

"And I'm the one that got him in my bag," said Moses in his gravelly voice, spitting tobacco juice between the gaps in his teeth.

Bourrée reviewed his options. He couldn't tell them joining would be good for business. The Pruetts were tenant farmers. It wouldn't help their business at all. He doubted whether the promise of good fellowship would be a lure. They seemed to like to keep to themselves. Finally he said, "You're native-born, white, gentile Americans. It's your patriotic duty to join the Klan!"

"Oh, hell," said Jake, "if I'd wanted to be patriotic, I wouldn't slip into a white dress like some damn fool and parade around nigger neighborhoods starting fires. If I'd wanted to be a real patriot, I'd quit making moonshine."

BELLE WAS SUPERVISING the preparation of new strawberry beds when Rachel called to invite them to a farewell dinner for Rafe the following evening. Miss Effie picked up the phone and accepted for them all.

"You have to go," Miss Effie told Belle at supper.

"Mama, how's it going to look if you stay home?" Cady said.

Belle didn't need much persuading. Rachel hadn't been prejudiced against her after all. She really had wanted to protect her. Belle saw the years stretching out in front of her. How could she bear Gentry if she was exiled from Rachel and Abe? A rule from her Southern Girls' Guide came to her: *No sense in holding a grudge. It just adds ugly pounds to your soul.* Besides, she didn't want to let Rafe go away without seeing him one last time.

JOSEPHINE'S FRIED CATFISH and sweet potatoes tasted like ashes in her mouth. She watched Rafe's long fingers turn the food over on his plate. Rachel talked about autumn in Chicago, the clear, crisp days, the trees wild with color, the smell of smoke drifting from hundreds of backyard fires. Nina said she was going to visit him over Christmas, when the snow would be falling and the city covered in white. "It'll be just like a Christmas card." She asked if Cady could come, too.

"I don't see why not," Rafe said, seeking Belle's eyes. She saw the same expression he'd had Tuesday morning, when he'd come out to the farm to tell her he was leaving. It was as if he had a question for her. No, not just a question, a suspicion. But a suspicion of what?

"Can I, Mama. Can I?"

Belle turned to her daughter. "Sure, honey, I think it'll be a wonderful experience, riding the train through all those states, getting a chance to see snow." He promised to show me snow, she thought. A man will promise anything when the sap is rising. I'm just a cow, a cow who's fool enough to give away free milk. It serves me right.

As they were finishing dessert, Flaubert got to his feet. Belle felt his shaggy coat brush against her legs under the table. He growled. They heard footsteps on the porch. The growl turned to full-fledged barking as the big dog ran from the dining room.

Suddenly, they heard a loud thump. It was followed by more footsteps, running. When they entered the hall, they saw a Model T racing away and a sheet of paper fluttering against the glass inset of the door.

Rafe opened it to find a rusted hunting knife with a broken handle lodged in the door frame, cracking the wood. He pulled out the knife. The note was printed on lined notebook paper.

"What does it say?" Cady asked.

Buster peered over his uncle's shoulder and read, " 'Get out of town, you and your hole tribe.' " He laughed. "The fools spelled *whole* h-o-l-e!"

No one else was laughing. "Who's it from?" Abe asked.

"It's signed 'The Invisible Empire,' " Rafe said. "Have you ever gotten anything like this before?"

"Who's the Invisible Empire?" Nina wanted to know.

"That's what the Ku Kluxers call themselves," Cady told her.

"This can't be from the Klan. Someone must be using their name," Miss Effie stated categorically.

"It's probably some nut with a big bill who'd love nothing better than to scare us into leaving. Josephine," Abe called, "we'll take our coffee in the living room."

Rafe took the note into his bedroom. When he returned, Belle had just picked up her coffee.

"Belle, can I see you for a moment?" Rafe was standing in the doorway.

"Sure," Belle said, getting up. She could feel everyone's eyes on her.

He led her out to the screened-in veranda next to the back bedrooms. "Do you know a Bourrée LeBlanc?"

Belle's heart pounded. Her mouth felt dry. She nodded. "He worked for us; why?"

"I think he may have written the note."

Rafe produced a letter. The envelope was postmarked the previous Saturday. It was written in Bourrée's awkward hand. Rafe must have gotten it sometime Monday or Tuesday morning, she thought. Was this the reason he was so willing to leave? She looked at the note. Even though it was printed to disguise the handwriting, it seemed to be written in the same round, awkward hand of a lefty who'd been forced as a child to write with his right hand. Belle's stomach fluttered. Guilt came riding in on a broomstick. This is because of me, she thought. She pulled out the letter. Rafe snatched it away. "No." He stuffed it and the envelope into his pants pocket.

"What did it say?"

Rafe's face became wooden. His eyes looked past her. "Slander. No gentleman would repeat it."

Once a man has had your favors, he thinks he owns you, Belle thought. "Rafe," she said, then stopped. The Southern

Girls' Guide was very clear: *A smart woman never confesses promiscuously to bad behavior*. He turned to her and she realized the letter was the cause of all those searching looks, his wanting and not wanting to know.

Finally he had to ask, "Did you and he? Were you two—?"

Answering a direct question was not a promiscuous confession, but she didn't say anything.

Rafe had expected more than a vehement denial. He'd expected revulsion at the mere suggestion. When she didn't say anything, his expression changed from inquiring to disappointed. He shook his head and turned to go back into the living room.

Belle caught his arm. She thought about denying it, but when she saw his face she realized it was too late. She'd missed her chance. He wouldn't believe her now. It was all so crazy. One night in the dark of the barn, when she was grieving over him, she'd made a mistake. The whole thing hadn't taken five minutes. It meant nothing.

To her.

But she knew it would mean something to Rafe. *Men are like dogs. They mark their territory*. They'll kill each other over a woman they think they own. "Talk to Abe. Make him take this seriously. Bourrée LeBlanc is some sort of salesman for the Klan."

He pulled away with distaste and went back to the living room. Belle watched him go. He's through with me. Well, what did I expect? I brought it on myself. As she came into the hall, she heard Rafe say, "Why don't you come back to Chicago with me, all of you?"

"What about school?" Nina wailed. "I'm graduating this year."

"You can go to school in Chicago."

"Swell!" said Buster.

"Nobody's going anywhere," Abe said. "My father didn't run thirty years ago when those crazy night riders were terrorizing the parish, and we're not going to run now." Even after Belle returned to the living room and tried to reason with him, he refused to change his mind.

Chapter 19

"AUNT BELLE, I gotta talk to you," Jimmy Lee said Thursday morning, when he came out to the farm to fix a leaky pipe. Although Jimmy Lee hadn't managed to graduate from high school, he'd found a job as an apprentice plumber with D. T. Pruett. With his first paycheck, he'd bought himself his very own used car. It not only gave him transportation, but afforded him occupation for all his leisure hours. He'd spent a most enjoyable week under it, just getting it to run. Now, he was looking forward to fixing the brakes so it would stop. "You've been seen shopping at Rubinstein's."

"So?"

"I was told to warn you."

"From shopping?"

Jimmy Lee looked impatient. "You best patronize one-hundred-percent stores from now on."

"What are you talking about? One hundred percent of what?"

"American."

"Listen to me, Jimmy Lee. That kind of talk turns patriotism into a cussword."

"Aunt Belle, don't ever say that! Not even in fun. The All-Seeing Eye is watching you."

"Have you joined them, you fool?"

A smug look of superiority crossed the boy's face. "I can't tell you that, but for your own good, you better stay away from them Jews. They're out to get you."

"They're not out to get me." Good Lord, she thought, it's not just Bourrée. What did they say at that stupid picnic? Something about race mixing being a sin? "What do you know about that note Rachel and Abe got last night?"

"I'm sworn to secrecy," Jimmy Lee said, acting very important.

My bad behavior caused this, Belle thought. So why didn't I behave? Because I can't follow anybody's rules but my own. And even then it's iffy.

She turned her attention back to Jimmy Lee. "You're keeping bad company, boy." But she couldn't get through to him. He was too pumped up on the romance, the adventure, and having grown men accept him as one of their own. As he repeated old invectives against the Rubinsteins and their "tribe," she wondered what part Nina's rejection had played in his newfound bigotry.

Miss Effie came out to the porch and hugged her great-nephew. "I swear, you get handsomer every time I see you. And now you're fixing the plumbing." She turned to her daughter-in-law. "Don't worry about that message last night, sugar. I just got off the phone with the sheriff. George was very concerned. He promised he'd handle it."

"Look what I got!" Jimmy Lee's Adam's apple bobbed with pleasure as he pointed to the driveway in front of the house.

"Well, I'll be. You went and bought yourself one of those good-time houses on wheels!" His great-aunt frowned at him in a most satisfactory way.

Jimmy Lee grinned. "You want a ride?"

"I guess I better get used to it," Miss Effie said as she walked down the stairs. Jimmy Lee helped her into the car, then turned back to Belle. "Remember, you been warned."

Belle thought, I should never leave my room.

THURSDAY AFTERNOON, AFTER his nap, Abe went out to the front porch in his leather slippers. A second letter had been slipped under the door. This one consisted of two new sentences: "You have failed to heed the warning sent to you. Be prepared to meet your maker." It was signed "The All-Seeing Eye." Abe rang up the store.

"I want you-all home. I'll pick up Buster and Nina."

THE RUBINSTEINS ASSEMBLED around the art nouveau dining-room table. Abe sat at the head, dressed in a dark suit. He'd put away his slippers and smoking jacket.

"Do you think it's real this time?" Rachel asked.

Abe shook his head. "I don't know. It could be a bluff. Someone who just doesn't want to pay his bill." He turned to Rafe. "I told you not to push these people, but oh, no, you wouldn't listen. You had all those big-city theories of how a business ought to be run."

"You had thousands of dollars in receivables and you couldn't pay your suppliers."

"They'd wait. It wouldn't be the first time."

"Let's not fight among ourselves." Rachel's voice was tense.

Rafe took the letter from his sister and studied it. "How soon can you be packed?"

"You want us to run away?" Abe asked.

"I want you to make a tactical retreat until this boils over."

"How long you figure this tactic is gonna last?"

"How the hell should I know?"

Abe stared out the window. His mother's garden was in full bloom. Red roses and pink and white hydrangeas graced the mantel, perfuming the room. A blue Tiffany vase filled with silvery plumes of pampas grass stood on the graceful Gaudi sideboard. He took two pecans from the sterling-silver centerpiece and rolled them around in the palm of his hand. They came from the tree his grandfather had planted the day his father was born. "What'll I do in Chicago? Wait around until my heart gives out?"

"You can't be thinking of staying," Rafe said. "Remember what they did to Belle's farm manager."

Rachel put her hand on her husband's arm. "You know what the doctor said about stress."

Abe crushed the pecan shells. "When my grandfather came here, Gentry was nothing but a watering stop for the railroad. We spent our lives building up this town. We own buildings up and down Grand Avenue. I'm not going to cut and run just because of a couple of anonymous letters. Besides, I've got forty employees who depend on the store for a paycheck. What's going to happen to them?"

"At least let Rachel and the children come with me."

"I'm gonna stay and fight," proclaimed Buster.

Abe turned to his daughter. "Nina, I want you to go up to Chicago with your mama and Uncle Rafe."

"Why, Daddy? If it comes to a fight, I can shoot better than Buster. Remember when we went hunting last year? Who got the most ducks?"

Rafe saw the excitement shining on Buster's face. He thinks fighting's about shooting. Rafe knew better. It's about dying.

"I can't leave them," Rachel said to her brother. Her voice was quiet.

Memories of the trenches flooded over him. He could almost see that German boy, not much older than Buster, running low across no-man's-land. Rafe had shot him down, but the boy's cries went on and on through the dark hours of the night, until the mists of dawn rose over the battlefield. He couldn't bear the thought of his sister or her children being shot by some bigot's bullet. "I'll help you fortify the house."

BELLE WAS OUT on the back porch with Stella, shelling peas, when she heard the phone sound three short rings. She picked it up and heard Rachel's voice. It was as if their friendship had never suffered. "Belle, thank God you're there. I don't know who else to turn to. We got another message this afternoon."

"Oh, Lord."

"I'm scared to death, but nobody can reason with Abe and I can't leave him, not when he's so sick."

It's my fault, Belle thought again. Guilt clawed at her. "What can I do?"

"I thought maybe you could find out what, if anything, is going to happen. If I knew what and when, I might get Abe to leave, at least until everything blows over."

I'm the kiss of death, Belle thought. "How was the note signed?"

"Very dramatically. 'The All-Seeing Eye.'"

Just then the voice of Jimmy Lee's mother, Kirksey Cantrell, came over the party line. "Belle, you stay out of this, you hear? This isn't your fight."

"Who's that?" Rachel asked. She lived in town and could afford a private line. In her distress it had slipped her mind that Belle lived in the country, where lines were shared.

"She's right, Belle," said Thelma, the telephone operator, who liked to keep up on all the latest gossip.

The gravelly voice of Moses Pruett came from out of the ether. "Belle, don't you go messing with the Klan, you hear? Them boys mean business."

"Moses, who's Belle talking to?" a fourth voice asked.

MISS EFFIE WAS HOOKING her bulging figure into her corset when she heard Belle's knock. She slipped into her dress and opened the door. "I swear, the older you get, the longer it takes you to look less and less good."

Belle told her about the second letter.

"But George promised me he'd take care of it."

"The main thing George Goode takes care of is George."

Miss Effie nodded with resignation. "I know." Belle stared at her. "I didn't just fall off the turnip truck, Belle. I know more than you give me credit for. But I didn't think he'd let anything happen to Rachel and Abe. Why, if old man Rubinstein hadn't given George's father credit in ninety-four, they'd have lost the farm. They'd have become sharecroppers." She stopped for a moment, as if considering whether she should admit, "So would we."

Belle hooked up the back of her mother-in-law's dress. "You think he'll stop this mess?"

"He should, but whether he will or not—" Miss Effie did not finish the sentence.

Belle had a plan, but it was one she was afraid her mother-in-law would disapprove of. She searched for the right words. Nothing spectacular came to mind. "I thought I might talk to some of what you call the 'better elements' and ask them to find out what's going to happen and stop it, if they can."

"You're going to what?"

"I thought I might talk to Brother Meadows and Tom Vickerson—" Belle didn't get a chance to finish.

"If those hotheads around here are planning an attack—" Miss Effie stopped. "Those men are crazy. You know, if you stir up trouble for them, they could come after us next."

"I know." Belle hesitated and then blurted out, "You want me to get a room at the hotel, so you're not involved? I could tell everybody we had a fight, and that you threw me out. That way you and Cady would be safe here." Belle didn't realize she was biting her lip. She didn't like the idea of spending even one night under her stepfather's roof, but she was willing to stay as long as necessary. She peered into the long, wavy mirror and scrutinized her mother-in-law's face for a sign. The older woman said nothing. Belle went on. "I can't just sit out on the porch and do nothing."

Miss Effie turned to her. "Belle, this is your home. Whatever happens, this is where you belong."

Tears welled up in Belle's eyes. The old lady seemed blurred when she reached out and took her daughter-in-law in her arms. It was then she spoke the words Belle had yearned to hear ever since she'd come to live with the Cantrells as a sixteen-year-old bride with bad grammar and a worse attitude. "I'm so proud of you, sugar."

"BROTHER SCAGGS IS YOUR PATIENT. So's my stepfather." It was early Thursday afternoon. Belle was sitting on an uncomfortable wooden chair in the office of Dr. Thomas Vickerson. She'd put on a wasp-waisted skirt that showed off her curvy hips and a cornflower blue blouse that turned her eyes aquamarine. She fluttered them at the gray-haired doctor, who loved nothing more than to march into his examining room and say: "Don't worry, I can fix it."

He didn't say that today. "What makes you think either one of them has anything to do with those anonymous letters?"

"They both spoke at the Klan picnic, along with your own associate, Dr. Fulsom Pruett."

The doctor's swivel chair groaned. A yellow skeleton dangled on a stand behind him. "I appreciate your faith in me—"

Belle heard a "but" coming and rushed to cut it off. "All I'm asking is for you to talk to them. Find out if the Klan really means to attack, and when, and maybe, if they are, you could try to talk them out of it."

"That's all?" The skeleton swayed in the breeze coming through the window.

"Abe's your patient. You owe it to him to try."

"I'm sorry, honey, but I'm too old to get messed up in something like this." He stood. His chair sighed. When Belle didn't take the hint, he walked around his desk and, giving her his hand, he escorted her to the door. "Talk to Rachel. See if she can get Abe to leave town for a while." When Belle started to protest, he cut her off. "Listen to me, Belle. If those jackasses start shooting guns, the strain alone could kill him."

"IT's UP TO THE GOOD PEOPLE of Gentry to stand together for what's right." It was late Thursday afternoon. Belle was sitting on a cheerfully flowered couch in the office of the Methodist church, sipping iced tea with Brother Meadows. Her white gloves were folded neatly on her knee. Through the open windows, she could hear birds chirping and the plop, plop of tennis balls. It seemed strange to her that the world was proceeding as if this were just an ordinary day. "Sheriff Goode and D. T. Pruett are members of your church."

"They haven't been to services in a while. I don't think I'd have much influence over them."

Belle wasn't ready to give up. "The Klan gave you an honorary membership. Use it. Go to their next meeting. They must be holding them, if they're planning some kind of attack."

"You came here to ask me to get up and speak at a Klan meeting?"

"You're a very strong speaker."

Brother Meadows sighed. "Belle, you have a good heart, and I know you're trying to do the right thing, but I'm a minister of God. I can't get involved with violence."

"But you can stand up against it, can't you? You're their moral leader." He looked out the window. "They'll listen to you."

"I'd like to help . . ." His voice trailed off.

"Rachel and Abe are your neighbors."

"And I'll pray for them."

"YOU KNOW AS WELL as I do Titus Pruett doesn't have the sense God gave butter beans," Belle said.

"That's a fact," Darvin agreed. "In any kind of mental test, butter beans would probably come out ahead."

It was early Thursday evening. Belle was paying a visit to Darvin Rutledge in his modern brick house on Hope Street. His wife, Debbie Lou, brought in a tray with big slices of chocolate layer cake. Their daughter, Virginia, followed with steaming cups of chicory coffee.

Belle could hardly choke down a forkful of cake, but she declared it delicious. Debbie Lou squeezed Belle's shoulder in encouragement and sent Virginia to her room.

"All I'm asking you to do is talk to him," Belle said when the adults were alone. She told them about Titus's speech at the Klan picnic, his face contorted by the hissing snakes of hatred. "I mean, if you could talk him into buying that Depot Hack, you can talk him into anything."

Belle and Debbie Lou watched Darvin eat a huge slice of cake, chewing each bite slowly. Then he ran the tines of his fork around the edges of his plate, scavenging for crumbs. Finally he spoke. "Belle, I'd like to help you, I really would, but I have a business to run. I can't afford to antagonize my customers."

Chapter 20

FRIDAY MORNING, WHEN Belle drove into town, the heavens opened up. Darvin had installed a windshield and wiper, but since the truck had no side windows or doors, her only protection from the wind-driven rain was a piece of canvas, rolled halfway up on the sides. It wasn't much protection at all.

She was sopping wet and shivering when she arrived at the Nix Hotel. Her stepfather greeted her heartily, but when Blanche Nix saw her daughter dripping on the tile floor of the lobby, she was anything but gracious. "What in tarnation are you doing out in this weather? Have you lost your cotton-picking mind?"

"Glad to see you, too, Mama."

They exchanged cold kisses. Mr. Nix led the way into their private apartment, behind the front desk. Belle thought he looked like an evil little elf prancing into his den. Her mother followed heavily in her high-necked dress and high-buttoned shoes. She was a good head taller than her husband.

Their sitting room was crammed with dark, heavy, oak furniture. Belle had to turn sideways to move through it. Some people eat when agitated. Calvin Nix bought furniture. "Can always use it somewhere in the hotel," he'd say. He threw nothing away.

The gray walls were punctuated with small windows that let in a view of the gray sky.

"What a pleasant surprise!" Calvin Nix said, rubbing his hands together. He sat down in a wingback chair upholstered in dirt-colored velvet. Belle noticed his feet hardly reached the floor. Mrs. Nix went to the hotel kitchen for coffee.

Belle made the mistake of asking him if the Klan was planning an attack and, if so, when. She saw his eyes narrow, his back straighten. He professed ignorance. She quickly changed direction. She appealed to him as a leading businessman to come to the aid of a fellow businessman. Mr. Nix was not moved. "You and Abe are both Masons. Aren't Masons pledged to help one another?"

Mr. Nix darted across the room and sat down next to her on the hard Victorian sofa. His voice was intimate. "You've been seen consorting with that Berlin feller." His toes tapped the polished floor as he began an impassioned performance, his logic spinning out of control. He was like a crazed dancer who misses every other beat while stepping on his partner's toes.

He fox-trotted out with an evil Capitalist sucking the blood of honest, hardworking men, but came waltzing back with a Godless Communist who wanted to overthrow the natural order and "everything we hold dear." Then he tangoed around and around with an immoral lecher preying upon the virtue of innocent Christian girls. Patting her rather too high on the thigh, he said, "You best stay away from those Jews."

She slapped his hand away. She might have been able to get around another man, let him think he could get another feel, maybe, if he'd only do what was right. She knew how to hold out vain hope as well as the next girl, but Mr. Nix was her step-father! It was too disgusting to contemplate.

Her mother came back with the coffee service. When she saw them sitting next to each other on the couch, her mouth turned sour. Mr. Nix rose. He was a busy man. He couldn't sit around all day, chatting with a bunch of women. "It was good of you to drop by," he said as he leapt out of the room.

"Mama," Belle said, when they were alone. "I need your help." She told her about the threats and her fears. She re-minded her, "They gave us credit when no one else would."

Blanche Nix put down the tray and looked her daughter in the eye. "Don't embarrass the family."

EVEN THOUGH THE RAIN had cleared and the sun had come out by the time Belle returned home, she was in a black mood. She scolded Cady over nothing, announced she wasn't hungry for dinner, and went straight to her room.

When she'd started working in the fields, she'd worn dresses, which were nice and cool, but made it hard to climb over fences or step up onto the back of a mule cart or truck. Then, as the weather cooled down and the rain turned the ground into mud, which often captured her shoes and always ruined them, she found, in spite of Miss Effie's disapproval, boy's work boots, denim pants rolled up at the ankles and gathered at the waist with one of Claude's old ties, a man's collarless shirt, and a broad-brimmed hat made her life easier.

Miss Effie and Cady found her on the kitchen steps, dressed for the fields, angrily pulling on her boots. For once, the older woman didn't make any disparaging remarks about her daughter-in-law's appearance. "What happened?"

The Primer of Propriety said: *Never speak ill of your family. It shames your name and establishes you as an ingrate.* Belle shook her head. She knew Miss Effie was aware she wasn't close to her mother or stepfather, but Belle had never bad-mouthed them. She'd always maintained she'd come from poor but honest folks. There was no advantage in coming from such a family, but at least there was no disgrace.

"Cady, honey, would you please get me my lavender shawl and let me talk to your mama?" When Cady had gone, Miss Effie asked, "What did they say? Is Calvin Nix going to put a stop to this nonsense?"

Belle's good intentions began to slip. She told her about Mr. Nix's wandering hand and her mother's response. As she talked, the misery of her childhood began to leak out. When she'd finished, she was mortified. *I've destroyed every shred of whatever tattered esteem she held me in. Why did I have to open my mouth?*

Miss Effie pursed her lips. "Listen to me, Belle. We all think we deserve perfect parents. Well, we don't. If we did, God would have provided us with them. Now, it's a shame your stepfather's a scoundrel and your mother isn't as strong as you are, but there it is. You'll just have to get over it." To Belle's surprise, Miss Effie leaned over and kissed her. Belle held her tight.

The shadows were lengthening as Belle stomped into the muddy chicken yard. Little Ricky was supposed to keep it clean, but as much as he loved horses and put up with cows, he hated chickens. She was surrounded by a flurry of feathers, clucking, squawking, and menacing each other.

No matter how much feed she tossed out, the first priority of the hens was chasing the weaker of their species away until the queen anointed the "best" pile and took first peck. Even though these birds had been well-fed from birth and not one of them had ever gone hungry, their principal concern was status. Maybe Brother Scaggs is right when he says people didn't descend from apes; but we sure as shooting descended from poultry, Belle thought. The rooster stood on tiptoe and crowed.

While the chickens were busy fighting over the best pile of identical feed, Belle went into the henhouse. She had to stoop to enter its interior, lit only by the sun shining in through the open doorway and gaps in the siding. She picked her way over the dirt floor, nasty with white droppings and feathers. Little Ricky had to take care of this today.

She walked along the three tiers of roosts, carefully placing eggs into her basket, but when she reached up to the top roost, something smooth and scaly began to rise under her right hand. In a bright slat of light, she saw it uncoil. She yanked her hand back, but she was too late. A huge snake whipped out and wrapped itself around her arm.

Belle screamed.

A man appeared in the doorway.

But Belle elbowed him out of the way as she emerged from the henhouse with a six-foot black snake writhing in her grip. As the fowl squawked and cackled, Belle whirled the serpent around her head, again and again, and threw it out of the chicken-wire enclosure. She knew chicken snakes weren't poisonous.

"You're one tough woman, Miss Belle." Bourrée had come to her rescue once again. Only this time she didn't need him.

"What do you want?" She shifted the basket of eggs on her arm.

He stepped forward, but Belle held her ground. "A word to the wise, chère. People have been talking about you and that Yankee." He picked up his foot and carefully brushed chicken feathers off his cuff. She saw he was wearing a new, tailor-made suit. It looked expensive. "I'd stay away from the whole tribe, if I was you."

"Is the Klan really planning to go after Rachel and Abe?"

"I expect so. Folks around here are pretty worked up."

Guilt wrapped around her chest just as the snake had wrapped around her arm. Her mouth was dry. I'm the kiss of death, the kissing killer, she thought. "This is crazy. What are you-all planning to do, just light a cross and sing a few hymns?"

Bourrée smiled. "We already done that over in Butlertown. Some of the boys feel this is more serious."

"When?" He said nothing. "When are you planning your attack?"

His tongue came out of his mouth. He licked his lips. "Why don't you and me go somewhere and talk. I hear my old house is just lying empty. I still have a key. What do you say?" The light shifted, playing on the subtle black-and-brown weave of his suit coat.

"If I say yes, you'll call off the attack?"

"Well, that would depend on the upshot of our conversation, wouldn't it, chère?" He rolled the word "chère" around in his mouth. His steel blue eyes looked into her. No doubt about it, he was handsome. "Don't pretend to be a great lady with me. I know you better than that."

Her heart started to pound. Is this what she had to do to save her friends? It wasn't such a big thing.

"Come on," he said, grabbing her left arm. She covered her eggs with her right hand so they wouldn't fall out.

At that moment she saw in his face the half grin of a conqueror. He was playing with her. If she gave in to him, he'd lose all respect for her, and worse, she'd lose respect for herself. The irony would be, of course, it wouldn't put an end to the attack. It might even spark it. She was about to tell him no thank you,

when he passed a hand over her breast and gave her nipple a little pinch.

Belle jumped and smashed an egg on the lapel of his hand-
made jacket. The yolk sank deep into the fibers. White mucus
slid down his chest. "Gosh, I'm sorry," Belle said. "You
shouldn't have startled me. I do hope I didn't ruin your nice new
suit. I know how hard it is to get egg off fine wool."

BELLE WATCHED BOURRÉE pull out in his fancy car, blasting his horn, almost running an ice truck off the clay drive.
Every Friday, Stella's cousin J.B. delivered ice and the latest gossip circulating in Butlertown. Stella was standing on the kitchen
steps looking after him, when Belle approached the house with
the eggs.

"You know J.B.'s mother, Aunt Sarah, don't you?" Stella
asked, taking the eggs from her and waddling into the kitchen.

"Sure, she let out Cady's velvet party dress last winter."

"Well, Dr. Pruett went over to her house last night and told
her to sew up his white dunce cap, but not to tell nobody."

Belle could never understand why the bigots expected the colored folks to be loyal to them. But of course she knew, *Expecting bigots to be rational is like expecting cow pies to sing.*

"When's he picking it up?"

"This afternoon."

BELLE RAN INSIDE and grabbed the phone, but Moses
Pruett was on it. She hung up and saw Hugh come up the drive,
his wheels churning in the mud. Cady ran to meet him. But even
with his arm around Cady's waist, his face was grim. Belle
opened the screen door.

"They're going to attack your friend Nina's parents tonight," Hugh said to Cady.

"But why?"

Hugh shook his head. "Because they can, I guess." He looked up at Belle. "I heard they're bringing guns."

Belle ran back through the darkened parlor. The flotilla of white antimacassars seemed to sway precariously. She picked up the phone and asked Thelma to connect her to the Rubinstein residence.

"Sure, honey." But the voice on the other end of the line wasn't Thelma's. The operator on duty was new.

Abe answered the phone.

"Listen, the Klan is coming for you-all tonight." Belle heard breathing, but Abe said nothing. "Abe, can you hear me? They're bringing guns. You've got to get everybody out." Silence on the other end. "Abe? Abe, are you there? Abe?" She waited for an answer. "Abe!" When had they been cut off? Had he heard her warning? Somewhere down the line she heard a snigger. "Don't you-all have any decency!" she screamed, and then she heard a click.

WHEN BELLE STEPPED OUT onto the front porch, Miss Effie was already there. "Oh, Belle, I just hate to see you going around looking like that. Why don't you go back inside and change your clothes?"

"No time," Belle called as she ran toward her truck. Turning back to Hugh she asked, "Will Cady and Miss Effie be safe out here?"

Miss Effie's head shot up. "Safe?"

Belle willed her not to get hysterical.

"I wouldn't want to risk it. Once those boys get together and get themselves all liquored up, there's no telling what they'll do," Hugh said.

"Can we go to your house?" Cady asked.

A pained look crossed Hugh's face. "Not tonight, honey. Daddy and Tibor might not be so sympathetic." Cady looked at him, her mouth open.

Oh, God, what have I gotten my family into? Belle thought. "Cady, why don't you go to Darvin and Debbie Lou's? Virginia is in your class. You-all get along, don't you?"

"Sure, but what about Nina?"

Belle shook her head. Tears were forming in Cady's eyes at the unfairness of the world and the sudden meanness of the people in it.

Belle reached into the bed of the truck. "Hugh, you can take her, can't you?"

"Of course."

"Miss Effie, why don't you let Hugh drop you off at Dr. Vickerson's? I'll bet he and Mary Ruth would enjoy a visit tonight."

Miss Effie pulled herself up into her indomitable grand-lady posture. She betrayed no hint of hysteria. "I'll visit with Brother Meadows and Gayle Ann, if it's all the same to you."

"Fine," Belle said, picking up the crank from the truck bed.

"What about you?" Hugh called.

"I've got to warn Rachel and Abe." Belle slipped the crank into its socket and put her body behind the handle, hoping, as she always did, that the truck wouldn't backfire and break her wrist.

Hugh took the crank from her. "You're going to make one heck of a mother-in-law, you know that."

"Who said I'm going to let you marry my daughter?" Belle asked as she leapt into the truck and headed out.

Chapter 21

BELLE'S WHEELS BIT INTO the soft earth, splattering mud onto the orange and golden leaves carpeting the edges of the driveway. Having made daily trips to the cotton gin during the harvest, she'd grown accustomed to driving. Above her, the ancient oaks reached their limbs into the red-rimmed sky. She knew she was breaking yet another rule. The Primer of Propriety said, or should say: *No intelligent woman would rush impetuously into action. She would stop for a sober consideration of all the consequences before proceeding.*

But here she was, rushing impetuously as usual, without considering anything, much less soberly. What else could she do? She had to warn them. She felt like her heroine, Joan of Arc, riding into battle, her steed rattling and bouncing beneath her. If St. Joan were alive today, wouldn't she be galloping to the rescue? But of course Joan didn't personally cause the English to invade France. *Sometimes a girl has got to stop thinking and get going.*

She passed the Hallelujah Chapel. Its front door still flapped on its broken hinge, like the wing of a wounded bird.

The sun was setting as she turned onto the highway. The sky had deepened to the color of fresh blood. A jerry-built car with an exposed engine and no fenders roared up behind her, honking madly. A recent load of gravel had smoothed out the road, so they were flying. The two vehicles raced past a field of dead cornstalks and hurtled through a dark forest of slash pine.

The car darted into the middle of the road and pulled alongside her. Maybe she was overdramatizing her own importance, Belle thought. After all, Rafe had sent half the town collection letters. And he did look different from everybody else.

The jerry-built car cut in front of her, throwing up chunks of gravel. Still, if she hadn't been running around with him, kissing him in public, maybe Bourrée would have left the whole family alone. She thought about the poison letter Bourrée had written. How would Rafe feel about seeing her again?

A sudden rock stopped all speculation. A blizzard of shattered glass flew around her. Splinters bit into her hands and face. Her shirt and pants were covered in shimmering shards.

Belle veered and almost smashed into a mule cart coming at her in the dark. She swung onto the left shoulder and jammed on the brakes as the jerry-built car disappeared down the highway. The mule cart stopped. Two men jumped out. In the fading light, their skin looked almost black. They were dressed in raggedy clothes and looked as if they might be father and son.

The older man tipped his hat. Belle could see his mouth moving, but her heart, beating like a crazed drummer, was so loud she could hardly hear him. He seemed to be saying something about bleeding. She looked down at her trembling hands and saw poppies of blood.

"You want us to carry you to the doctor, ma'am?" the old man asked. Belle shook her head.

"We can pull you out, if you're stuck," the younger one said.

The engine had died. Belle tried to pick up the crank, but she kept dropping it. The older man took it from her. "I got it." He fitted it into the socket. Then the younger man turned it until the engine started up and Belle was able to drive off the soft shoulder and back onto the highway. Her heart had slowed a little, but her hands were still shaking when she looked into her purse. She pulled out a dollar.

The old man's eyes grew big. She knew he'd expected a nickel, a quarter, maybe. "That's okay, ma'am," he mumbled, but his hand was already reaching for it.

The road ahead of her was clear. She brushed her cheeks and forehead and ran her fingers through her hair. Fragments of glass blew out and fell around her.

A spiky mountain range clung to the bottom of the windshield frame. She wondered how fast she could go before those spikes flew into her face. She should stop and pull them out. That was the only sensible thing to do, but if she stopped she might not make it in time to warn Rachel and Abe to get out, tonight. She slowed and tried to knock the glass loose with the crank handle.

Bad idea.

Glass shards flew at her.

She saw flames in the distance. A burning cross? But as she passed a huddle of shacks, she realized it was only a trash fire.

Were Rachel and Abe boarding up their windows? Was Rafe loading guns? Or were they sitting down to supper? Maybe they'd already left town? Oh, God, let them have left town. It was a little late to pray for that, she realized, but she couldn't help herself. She felt as if she were a little girl again, kneeling in the safety of her bedroom with her daddy by her side. It felt good to pray. Was Someone out there to hear her? Oh, God, make them leave town now, if they haven't already gone.

She sped up when she saw the lights on the outskirts of Gentry. Dark shacks lined the road. A barefoot child threw a ball into the street. Don't run out in front of me, Belle willed. The little boy ran to the road and stopped. That was a good sign. Maybe luck was with her tonight.

She entered Grand Avenue and drove along the tracks past Park Lane, although there had never been, nor would there ever be, a park in Gentry. She passed Homestead and picked up speed, hoping against hope the windshield would hold. Only seven and a half blocks to go. Enterprise, Progress, turn on Commerce, go over three blocks and then a block and a half on Hope.

Without a speedometer, she didn't know how fast she was going, but her speed surged to match her anxiety. No one was on the street tonight. The town seemed to be holding its breath.

Shops flew by. A greengrocer. A butcher shop. A little furniture store. Suddenly she felt a jolt and heard a loud crack. She was thrown forward toward the spiky windshield, but the steering wheel saved her from crashing into it.

Thank you, God.

The truck hadn't stalled. Her good old truck hadn't stalled. It had only hit a pothole. Her faithful truck bounced up and was back on the road.

But it was wounded.

Its nose dropped forward. A spring had broken. The front fenders skimmed the wheels, sending clouds of black, pungent smoke into the darkness. She tried to keep driving straight, but she was slueing to the right. She couldn't muscle the wheels back onto the road.

Suddenly she slammed into another pothole. The recoil tossed the front of the truck into the air. The broken spring rebounded enough to clear the fender and she was able to straighten out the wheels. Thank you, Lord! Would the wooden wheel spokes break? Don't let the wheel break, she begged. Would the truck overturn? No. She seemed to be going straight!

Then the nose of the truck sank again as she drove past Enterprise.

Deliver me from evil.

The fenders dragged on the tires, braking the truck to a crawl. The motor stalled and died. To hell with it. She jumped out and left the damned machine in the middle of the road.

She ran down Grand Avenue, past Rubinstein's, its plate-glass windows tempting passersby. Why the heck hadn't they taken the merchandise inside? What were they thinking? Oh, Lord, they're still here. Still planning to open the store again tomorrow morning.

Across Grand Avenue, Arnold's Barbershop was dark and shuttered. But the electric sign above the Nix Hotel would burn like a beacon all night, just like any other night, luring drummers into dim rooms with dirty sheets.

As she ran across the street, a stitch grabbed her side. She stopped for a moment in front of Darvin Rutledge's Ford dealership, doubled over with pain. Four and a half long country blocks to go.

She hobbled across the tracks and headed up Commerce, past Justice Avenue. Holding her side, she began to jog over the broken brick sidewalk. Pushing through the pain, she passed pastel houses with big yards, flower gardens, and leafy trees. How could this be happening here? In a lighted window, a mother was sewing while her children played quietly at her side. In another, a man was sleeping in a chair, his newspaper fallen over his chest. In the second block, two children ran after her.

Finally, she saw the redbrick school set back among the pines. Hidden in the dark were double doors, flanked by pilasters and surrounded by cement curlicues and the words *"Mens sana in corpore sano."*

The pain in her side had slackened. She turned away from the school and ran down Hope toward Rachel and Abe's white-columned house. The yard alone took up a quarter of the block. A white picket fence separated it from the street on two sides. In the back, hedges sheltered it from its neighbors. But fences and hedges would be no protection tonight. The Methodist church loomed on the opposite corner. Both the church and house were dark.

She walked up the steps to the porch. Behind the beveled glass on the front door she saw heavy boards. The long windows on either side of the door were boarded up, too. She imagined the pain it must have caused Rachel to make holes in her beautiful woodwork.

She heard the sound of hammering coming from the front bedroom. "It's me, Belle." The casement windows were all open in front of the thick boards. "Rachel! Abe!" she called, and thought, Rafe!

The door cracked open and Rafe pulled her inside. Nina was right behind him. The only light came from the front bedroom. "What the hell are you doing here?" He didn't seem pleased to see her. Before she could answer, Flaubert was on top of her, jumping up, clawing her clothes, barking wildly. He wouldn't stop even when she ran her fingers through his thick white fur. In the front bedroom, Abe, Rachel, and Buster were boarding up the windows.

Nina pulled the big shaggy dog off Belle and put him out on the screened porch next to the back bedrooms. "He's been like this all evening," she shouted over the noise of the hammering.

Belle was still trying to catch her breath. "What happened to you?" Rafe asked, picking a tiny glass sliver from just beneath her eye. "My God, you're bleeding."

Rachel rushed in from the front bedroom. "Belle, what happened to your face?" The hammering paused.

"They're coming tonight," Belle said.

"I thought that's what I heard, before the phone was cut off. I just wasn't sure," Abe said, coming in from the bedroom. "What do you think they'll do? They lit a cross in Butlertown a few weeks ago, but all they did was parade around in their nighties and sing a few hymns. Nobody got hurt."

"This time they're bringing guns."

Abe's face turned ashen. He looked as if he were having trouble catching his breath.

"Why don't you-all get in the car right now? Come back in a week, when they've cooled off," Belle said.

Rachel threw a pleading look at her husband, but before he could say anything, Rafe said, "It's too late. They'll recognize our cars. We don't want to be caught in the open by some hothead who's trying to make a name for himself." That made sense, Belle thought. There was only one decent road through town. The rain had turned the rest into mud holes.

"Sometimes you just have to stand up to these fools," Abe said. His color was coming back. They all moved into the bedroom.

"We're fortifying ourselves here, so at least we'll have the advantage." Rafe looked grim. The stench of fear permeated the air.

On the floor around the white mantel, against the deep blue-and-gold, peacock-feathered wallpaper, was an arsenal of guns and ammunition. It looked to Belle as if they'd emptied out the store. She glanced up at the painting of the serene woman smiling in front of the chrysanthemum screen. Next to it was the milk-glass vase filled with fresh roses. Did Rachel cut them this afternoon and then come inside to board up the windows?

Abe placed a nail between his fingers and slammed it into the board.

"You were very brave to come here tonight," Rafe said to Belle. "Now, go home."

The hammering had started again, louder than the pounding of Belle's heart. Home. It sounded good. Real good. Crawl into bed, pull the covers over her head. But how could she leave them? Would the Klan be on the warpath if she hadn't taken up with Rafe and then given in to Bourrée? It was her behavior, her bad behavior, that had caused this. She hadn't been able to stop them from driving Luther away. She wouldn't run now.

"For God's sake, Belle, this isn't your fight," Rafe shouted over the hammering.

"That's where you're wrong." Belle's voice was so low, she didn't know if he'd heard her.

He had. "What are you talking about?"

"I'm a white, Protestant woman. The Klan is sworn to protect me. I'm your only hope," she yelled. But what she thought was, If something happened to you-all, I couldn't live with the guilt.

His face changed. She's willing to sacrifice herself for us, he thought. For me. Rafe, who had tamped down his emotions until he was numb, was suddenly overcome by tenderness. She's not like Christine at all. Love, he thought, isn't just a feeling. It's what you're willing to do for the other person. He wanted to reach out and hold her in the midst of the din, but Rachel brought a washcloth and led her into the bathroom. He watched them go.

Belle caught sight of herself in the mirror. She was still dressed in pants and work boots. Droplets of blood had hardened on her cheeks and on the backs of her hands. She bent over the sink and splashed cold water in her face, while Rachel filled up the tub. Around it were stacks of shiny metal buckets.

"How's Abe holding out?" Belle asked.

"You saw him. He's all fired up." Rachel shook her head as if trying to shake off a fear too deep to name.

Belle, Rachel, and Nina filled bucket after bucket, dragging them around the house to be ready in case of fire. When that was done, they joined the men, loading guns and boarding up the windows. One thing good about owning a hardware store, you won't run out of nails, Belle thought.

Buster showed her the loopholes they'd made for their guns in the gaps between the planks. "If one of them fools comes into our yard, he'll be a sitting duck."

"Those fools," Rachel corrected him automatically.

"And if they try to burn you out?" Belle asked.

"We can't let them get close enough," Rafe said. His voice was quiet.

Rachel looked ill. Belle knew she was deathly afraid of fire. How could I have brought this on them? she thought.

The dining room was the last to be fortified. The whole family moved in to board up three long casement windows that looked out onto the garden, where big mounds of hydrangeas hunched next to the house and poisonous oleander bushes crouched in the distance. Behind them they saw lights moving up Church Street. Suddenly, they heard Flaubert barking on the screened porch. Rafe cut the lights in the dining room. For a moment he was motionless, calculating the risks. "Abe, you go and see what's happening. The rest of you, keep working."

Rafe set his flashlight on the art nouveau table and held the nails in his teeth. His right arm flew. His lean, sinewy body moved back and forth with the force of his hammer. His linen pants and shirt flowed over his body, until he looked like a picture Belle had seen in an art book. She picked up a hammer and tried to match him stroke for stroke. Their pounding took on a staccato sound as they moved together and apart. She felt the heavy nails penetrate the oak board and bite into the beautiful cypress woodwork. By the time the last window was boarded up, she was breathless. He rested his hand on her shoulder for a moment and she wondered if he'd forgiven her.

Above the rumble and clatter of cars they heard frenzied barking. It seemed to come from the front of the house. Rafe, followed by Belle, rushed into the central hall. She pressed her eye to a loophole and saw cars and trucks pulling up. The big shaggy dog was at the gate, barking, wagging his curved tail, backing up, and then barking some more as men piled out of their vehicles.

Nina came running into the hall. "Flaubert got out of the back porch! He went right through the screen." She put her hand on the door to call the dog. Rafe grabbed her arm to stop her. The dog was barking wildly.

Suddenly they heard a single shot, followed by air-wrenching whimpers. Then they heard two more shots. All whimpering ceased.

"Flaubert!" Nina screamed.

Joan of Arc came to a lousy end.

THE SOUTHERN GIRLS' GUIDE TO MEN
AND OTHER PERILS OF MODERN LIFE

Chapter 22

RAFE WRAPPED HIS ARMS around his niece and then yelled, "Take your places!" Tears streamed down Nina's face as she ran back to the kitchen. In the dining room, Buster racked the shotgun lying on the floor next to him, then he chambered a round in his backup rifle. Rafe stood in the doorway. "Now listen to me, Buster. You hold your fire until I give the order. Is that clear?"

"Unless I see somebody sneaking up on the house."

"In that case, you fire a warning shot. We want to scare them off, not kill them."

Buster nodded with excitement.

Rafe turned and went back into the long central hall. Belle saw he was focused on the fight. The shell-shock trembling she'd witnessed, when those crazy Pruetts were shooting up the forest, was gone. In its place was a grim determination to keep them all alive.

He handed her a box of shells. She and Rachel were to act as reinforcements, reloading the weapons, putting out fires if needed.

Oh, dear God, don't let us be needed. Belle had learned how to pray.

Outside, storm clouds were piling up, casting a gray radiance over the excited Klansmen, who were catching their boots in their long white skirts. A gun went off. Belle heard swearing and loud whispers.

"Hold your fire," Rafe called. "Wait to see if they come into the yard."

Belle ran to the front bedroom, relaying the order. She was worried about Abe, but he seemed calm and determined.

"Maybe they'll just light their darn cross and leave," Rachel said.

"Maybe," said Belle, heading for the kitchen to warn Nina.

When she came back into the hall, she looked through a chink in the boards next to Rafe and saw the Klansmen raising a cross between the fence and the street.

"Nice of them to wear white," Rafe said.

But there are so many of them, Belle thought. More than twenty. Suddenly, the reality of what she'd gotten herself into came at her full force. Two dozen armed men against what? One shell-shocked vet, two women, a couple of kids, and a sick man who might die from the stress of the first shot.

Buster ran into the living room. He bent over and looked through a low gap in the boards at the Klansmen milling around the cross. "We could pick 'em off right now!" His voice had all the enthusiasm of youth.

"And stand trial for murder tomorrow. Go back to the dining room!" Rafe ordered.

Belle watched the men in white kneel in front of the cross. A stray thought flashed through her mind, the kind of thought soldiers in battle report, the kind of thought that comes to us at funerals, when the minister calls for a moment of contemplation: Somebody was going to have a devil of a time scrubbing the mud off all those white skirts.

She heard the harsh voice of Brother Scaggs, the man who thought he was on speaking terms with the Almighty, call on the assembled to remember that only Christian Anglo-Saxons can maintain a just and stable society. He assured them the Good Lord was on their side. It was their duty to stand up and fight the Christ killers.

Belle stamped her foot. This was the church she'd been brought up in, the church where she'd gone to Sunday school even before the arrival of Brother Scaggs, the church where she'd first learned to pray. "How dare he use my religion to justify terrorizing law-abiding people!"

Rafe sighted Brother Scaggs through his rifle. "When men want to slaughter one another, they like to do it in the name of God. It makes them feel righteous."

"Ever wonder how it makes God feel?"

Outside, the Klansmen were singing a hymn. Belle had to remind herself, underneath those scary white robes were Titus Pruett, who pumps up bicycle tires, and D. T. Pruett, who comes over and fixes the pipes when they burst after a winter freeze, and probably that deluded Dr. Fulsom Pruett. They don't really want to kill anyone. They'd be filled with moral indignation, if someone called them murderers. They're just ordinary folks giving in to their worst inclinations.

She figured her stepfather was probably lagging somewhere in the back, taking credit for being there, but staying clear of the action. He might egg on the others, but he wouldn't want to kill anyone himself. She'd bet no one had thought this all the way through. But then, Belle reminded herself, these men don't put much stock in thinking.

Except Bourrée. Lord knows what he'll get them to do. And Pruett Walker. He'd be with them tonight, and he's already gotten away with murder once. She suspected it would be easy for him to kill again.

Belle saw a match flare, lighting up white sheets. A torch burst into flame. "They're getting ready to light the cross," Rafe said. "Tell everyone to watch the perimeter. We don't want them to plant dynamite under the house for a little extra kick."

Belle ran into the front bedroom to warn Abe. Rachel passed the message to Nina, in the kitchen, while Belle raced into the dining room to tell Buster. When she got back into the hall, the Klansmen had set the cross ablaze without an explosion.

"Look at them, lighting fires and running around in masks like savages thousands of years before civilization," Rafe said.

"Wonder how much they can see with those curtains hanging in front of their eyes," Belle said, and saw a thin smile creep across Rafe's face.

A white-robed figure stepped out from the crowd. "Abe Rubinstein! Rafe Berlin!" Belle recognized Bourrée's voice. "In your worship of the Almighty Dollar, you have conspired to cheat the true citizens of Gentry, and you have defiled a virtuous Christian lady whose honor we as Klansmen are sworn to protect."

Oh, Lord, Belle thought, he's using me as a pretext. She was engulfed by guilt.

"Think that's him?" Rafe asked. "That LeBlanc fellow?"

"I know it is." He had his rifle trained on Bourrée now. Part of her willed him to shoot and get it over with, but Rafe held his fire.

The Klansmen spread out along the picket fence, from the gate on Hope all the way to the corner. A few more took up positions on Church Street.

Abe walked purposefully into the hall, his shotgun cradled in his arms. "I want to talk to them."

"You're too sick!" Rachel said. He headed for the door. She grabbed his arm. "You can't leave me alone in this hellhole."

"Get back to your post," Rafe ordered.

"How many are there?" Abe asked.

"I've counted about twenty-five, maybe another five or so around the corner. Now return to your post." When Abe didn't move, Rafe barked at Rachel, "Pick up a gun and take his place." Abe returned to the front bedroom. Rachel followed him.

Belle saw a man approach the fence, swinging a kerosene lantern. "Rafe!" The lantern flickered, turning his robe a pale yellow.

"Dammit!" said Rafe. He raised his gun, but he was too late. The lantern was already sailing across the lawn.

It fell short of the house. The kerosene flared and smoldered in the damp grass.

"Check on Buster," Rafe said. Belle raced into the dining room.

When she got there, Buster had his shotgun sticking through the loophole. He was leaning into its sights.

Belle peered through a gap in the boards next to him and saw a couple of Klansmen wrestling a bale of hay from the back of a truck parked on Church Street. One man reeled under its weight, while the other kicked open the side gate and struck a match. The hay caught. Gray smoke spiraled out of dancing flames as the white-robed figure staggered across the side yard. Belle caught glimpses of fire moving behind oleander and hydrangea bushes. Suddenly the Klansman stumbled into the open, still carrying the flaming bale. The dry hay blazed up, bathing his billowing robe in ripples of light. He was headed for the house.

Belle knew what the burning bale could do. Once the ropes holding it together burned through, it would explode. If they let him get near enough to the house, fingers of fire would float up under the eaves, setting the roof ablaze. Worse, if he could get it under the house, the wooden floorboards would catch and the old house would go up like cellophane.

She saw Buster's shotgun shake in his sweaty hands. She grabbed the backup rifle, but before she could sight it, Buster got off a shot.

She saw the Klansman retch and then begin to howl as he fell into the fiery hay.

A victory shout rose in her throat and then died when she saw the man roll off the burning bale, flames racing up his sheets, swaddling him in fire.

Suddenly, a barrage of bullets answered Buster's blast. Shells smashed into the outside walls and cracked the boards covering the windows. A wild shot penetrated the fortifications and exploded the Tiffany vase filled with pampas grass. Belle fell to her knees. Pale puffs floated around the dim room as crash after crash rocked the house, tearing through their defenses.

Then there was silence. Were they reloading? Were they finished?

"Everyone okay?" she heard Rafe call. Answers came from all over the house.

In the dining room, Belle rose to her knees and found a big new chink in the boards. The blazing bale of hay had exploded in the middle of the yard under a crepe-myrtle tree. The Klansman had ripped off his blistering hood and robe. He was crawling on the ground, howling in pain as smoldering fingers of dried grass floated though the air, settling on his back.

Buster wailed. "I had to shoot. He was coming right up to the house! I swear, I didn't know who it was!"

But he knew who it was now.

Belle knew, too.

Buster had shot Jimmy Lee.

"Jimmy Lee, hold on," Belle yelled through a loophole.

"Aunt Belle? Is that you? Help me, for God's sake. I've been shot!"

Oh, Lord, she thought. What am I going to do now?

"You can't let me die out here!"

What in tarnation did he expect? He was trying to burn us out!

Belle was sick of men playing war. Setting down the rifle, she walked into the hall where Rafe was reloading and wrenched open the fortified front door, slamming it shut behind her before he could stop her. Jimmy Lee was still pleading in the side yard.

She walked to the front of the porch and called to Dr. Vickerson's junior associate. "Fulsom, go on and take care of Jimmy Lee, you hear?"

She looked out into the street. The brave Klansmen had no good cover. They massed around trees and behind cars. No one moved.

Suddenly Belle felt like her heroine St. Joan. If only she could find the words to move them. "I know you're out there, so go on now." Jimmy Lee's plaintive cries were becoming weaker. "Darn it, Fulsom, you're a doctor. You're sworn to save lives. Nobody's going to shoot you. You have my word. Just don't let that stupid boy die." When that didn't get them going, Belle became furious. "What are you? Men or cowards? That boy followed you. He was doing your dirty work. Are you-all just going to let him die out there in the yard? Is this what your glorious Klan is all about? Sending children to their death?" Two robed men, their shoulders hunched into their ears, lumbered into the side yard.

"And the rest of you go home. You've dealt with Abe all your lives. You-all know he's never cheated you. As for me, I'll take care of my own virtue, thank you."

In the pale light of the burning cross, she could see Jimmy Lee had his arms around the shoulders of the two robed men. They were holding him up as they made their way out of the yard. His face was twisted in pain. The boy was crying.

Flaubert's carcass blocked the gate. The white cotton robes wicked up dog blood as they swept over and around the dead animal. She couldn't see which car they put Jimmy Lee into, but she heard him groan and yelp as the door slammed.

When the car rumbled away into the gloom, she tried to think of something else to say. Sadness overcame her. "How can you-all be so cruel? What do you get out of it? Tomorrow you'll still have fields to plow and bills to pay." She saw Bourrée's fancy car, with its empty golf-bag holder. "Bourrée, you talked these boys into this. Tell them to go home. You've had your fun."

Bourrée responded by flinging words into the fiery night. They were picked up by others, until they became a kind of crazed chant. They didn't make Belle feel less than she was, but as word followed word, the Ku Kluxers who'd edged toward their cars rejoined the mob, as if those words, those puffs of air, had power. *Slut. Whore. Jew lover.* As the words crashed into one another, they saw her as something less than the flower of Southern Womanhood. Something much less.

Traitor to your race. A woman we don't have to protect. *Un-American.* A danger to the country. *Christ killer.* A danger to God himself. *Apostate.* Apostate? Whose word was that? Who even knew what that word meant?

She'd wanted to be St. Joan. What kind of foolishness was that? She knew how that story ended. As they continued to yell, she turned back toward the house. She didn't see a white-robed man step out from behind a tree. She didn't see him take aim.

"Watch out!" The front door smashed open. Rafe grabbed her, swung her around, and, shielding her with his body, pushed her into the hall.

A shot rang out.

Rafe fell to his knees.

Belle screamed and caught him. Pulling him away from the door, she slammed it shut. Rachel, Abe, Nina, and Buster raced into the room.

"Get back to your posts!" Rafe roared. "We've got to . . . we've got to . . ." He tried to sit up, but he couldn't. He crumpled over on the rug. "Don't let them storm the house. We can't let them think . . ." His voice became hoarse, not much more than a whisper. ". . . we're beaten." He was sweating, and gasping for breath. The two women unbuttoned his shirt as Abe, Nina, and Buster ran back to their posts.

Belle shone a flashlight over the long lean chest she had so recently kissed. There were no marks on it, but blood was staining the back of his shirt and pants. They turned him on his side. He bit his lips with pain. "Is it spurting?" he asked.

"No," Belle said. "Just seeping a little."

Rafe winced, but he seemed relieved. "That's good. Keep pressure on it."

Rachel ran for the alcohol and bandages.

Belle pressed on the wound and yelled through the opening in the boards. "Dr. Pruett!" Had he taken Jimmy Lee to his office or was he still out there, parading around in his white robes, smug in his pedigree? "Fulsom? Stop this craziness. We need you! A man's been hit."

The answer was blast after blast of gunfire. "Damn you, damn you-all to hell!" she yelled as Abe and Buster returned fire.

"Why, Miss Belle, I'm shocked," Rafe said, rallying. A chunk of wood from their fortifications cartwheeled through the air. Belle itched to pick up a gun herself.

Rafe must have felt the same way, because he said through his pain, "Forget about me. Keep them away from the house!" But Belle couldn't forget about him because, although the wound was in his hip, she knew he could die right there from loss of blood or, later, from blood poisoning. To hell with shooting. She bent down and softly kissed his shoulder. Rachel hurried in with a torn sheet and alcohol. They ripped the sheet to make a pressure pad, then tied it tightly around him. As they worked, they heard the clatter of a heavy truck rumbling toward them and the squeak and clang of chains.

"What the hell's going on?" Rafe wanted to know.

"Abe!" Rachel called to her husband, in the front bedroom.

He appeared in the doorway. He looked devastated. "They're bringing in reinforcements. And they didn't even bother to wear masks."

"Tell him to stay calm," Rafe whispered. "We're fortified. They're not." But she could hear his confidence leaking out.

Belle crawled to the window and looked through a low gap in the planks. The wooden cross was still burning outside the fence, although not as brightly as before. A big lumber truck filled with logs had pulled up and turned, blocking Hope Street, right in front of the house. Looking down her gun sights, she spotted men in dark work clothes and hats standing on the bed of the truck, behind the barricade of logs. A second log-laden truck backed them up. The first truck driver jumped down on the side away from the Klansmen. When the light from the cross shone on his face, Belle recognized Hugh's friend, the silent Alton Jones.

Then she saw Hugh was with him!

Alton's crew of loggers stood behind their barricade waiting for a signal. In back of them Belle spotted Darvin Rutledge walking up Hope Street. With him was Dr. Vickerson, carrying his black bag. Vince Stefano followed with a crowd of Italians.

Crippled Mike O'Malley lurched after them. Every man was armed.

The logging crew pointed long-barreled guns at the Klansmen whose only shelter was trees and cars. Their white robes stood out in the gray radiance of the cloudy night.

She heard the voice of Darvin Rutledge. "Okay, boys, you've had your fun for the evening. Time to go home."

"Stay out of this, Darvin. You interfere with the All-Seeing Eye at your peril." Belle wasn't sure who was speaking, but from the bluster in the voice she figured it was Titus Pruett.

"Don't give me that mumbo jumbo," Darvin said. "Jim, Sam, if you boys want to come to work tomorrow, you better get out of here tonight."

Belle saw two cowed figures back away from the Klan line. She heard several cars start up and drive off, but the rest of the white crew filled the street in front of the house and around the corner.

"You're a damn traitor to your race, Darvin. And so are the rest of you," a voice shouted.

Another shouted, "Alton, you and your crew belong over here! Come on, join your own people!"

Belle knew this could go either way.

She saw the Klansmen raise rifles and shotguns in the direction of the interlopers. Suddenly, the mellifluous voice of Brother Meadows reached out over the crowd. "The street's no place to settle this. Put down your guns, men. Let's march into the church together and pray to God to show us the way." The minister was speaking through a megaphone, in the shadow of logging trucks.

Bless his heart, thought Belle. The Methodist church was on the corner behind the Klansmen. A few of them turned, but they didn't seem inclined to move.

Brother Meadows began to sermonize about their duty as

Christians. He reminded them that the Prince of Peace had said, " 'Beware of false prophets, which come to you in sheep's clothing, but inwardly they are ravening wolves.' "

Nothing.

"Come, brothers, let's turn our backs on violence and march together into the house of the Lord."

"Stir your stumps, boys!" a gruff voice howled from behind the logging truck. "Make way for the preacher."

The white sea did not part.

Brother Meadows played his last card. "We'll pray for the Rubinsteins to open their hearts to Jesus."

The white sea was still.

"Oh, hell, they're not going to church. Let's shoot up their damn cars," the gruff voice yelled.

Suddenly bullets flew from under and over and around the logging truck. Tires burst. Headlights flew apart. A radiator exploded, scalding a man with boiling water. His screams filled the night air.

As soon as the volley of bullets came their way, the Klansmen hitched up their skirts and, without waiting to fire another shot, scampered down the street, abandoning their ruined cars and trucks in their frantic escape.

"Think they can run as fast as a wild turkey?" Belle recognized the voice of Jake Pruett.

"Oh, hell, I can hit a wild turkey at fifty yards," the gruff voice yelled.

"You! You're blind as a bat, you old coot."

Gunshots whizzed over the heads of the fleeing Klansmen.

It was then Belle realized Bourrée's fancy car was gone, golf-club holder and all.

The heroes crowded into the hall, but they fell silent when they saw Rafe. Dr. Vickerson, jolly doctor-good-news, pushed through them. He gave Rafe a cursory examination and announced, "He's going to be fine. That is, if you-all get out of here and let me work in peace." Belle and Rachel wanted to stay, but the doctor wouldn't hear of it. "Can't fix him up with a bunch of people looking over my shoulder. Now, I'm going to need some clean towels, rags, gauze, everything you got."

Rachel ran for the linen closet.

The doctor took some instruments out of his bag and put them into Belle's hands. "Boil these for five minutes. And I'll need some sterile water."

Belle headed for the kitchen. "Let me give you a hand," Hugh said, following her.

"How on earth did you get all these people to come out tonight?" she asked grabbing a big pot off the stove, taking it to the sink and turning on the tap.

"You shamed most of them into it," he said, picking up a box of kitchen matches. The Rubinsteins had a gas range, so there was no need for firewood. He lit the match and turned on the gas burner. "Cady knew who you'd visited. She and I went back to Dr. Vickerson and Darvin Rutledge. We told them what was about to happen and that you were already here, risking your life. I guess they felt guilty they hadn't done anything to stop those fools. They didn't want to let you or the Rubinsteins get killed. Of course, we left Brother Meadows to Miss Effie. That lady can be very persuasive."

"Don't I know it." Belle thought of all the changes Miss Effie had persuaded her to make from the wild young girl Claude had brought home. "She's an amazing lady." As the pot filled, she searched the cabinets for a strainer. "What about the Pruetts?"

A wry smile crossed Hugh's face. "Moses heard you on the phone this afternoon and talked to Alton. You know he listens all the time? He says he likes your conversations better than the picture show. All I had to do was remind him how puffed-up Cousin Titus would be if he pulled this off."

"You're going to make one heck of a son-in-law," Belle said, hefting the big pot filled with water from the sink.

He took it from her and set it on the stove. "I know."

Belle put the instruments into the strainer and placed them in the pot to boil. She watched him fill a big kettle for extra sterile water. "You think you and Cady could at least give me a grand-daughter who'll take advantage of the world we've marched and picketed and lobbied for?"

Hugh grinned as he set the kettle on the stove. "We'll work on it."

RAIN WAS FALLING when Belle passed through the dining room carrying the strainer filled with the sterile instruments be-tween two clean dish towels. Abe was handing out all the liquor he'd stockpiled before Prohibition. He gave a glass of twenty-year-old Scotch to Moses Pruett. The old man sniffed it, and made a face as if it didn't smell quite right, but he drank it all the same. "About that bill your brother-in-law's been dunning us for," Moses began.

"I figure it's been paid in full," Abe said, raising his glass. "In fact, I believe you boys have got yourselves a good-size credit."

DR. VICKERSON LOOKED UP as Belle came into the hall with the dripping instruments.

Now that all the electric lights were lit, she gasped to see how much blood had spilled onto the carpet. "Rafe?" He turned to-ward her, but his eyes didn't seem to focus.

"You're not going to get all hysterical on me, are you? I had to send Rachel and Nina out of here," Dr. Vickerson said.

"Of course not."

"You sure you're not going to faint?"

"I run a farm. I see blood all the time."

"Good, because I'm going to need your help."

But Belle had never seen this much blood. Never spilling out of the man she loved. Next to Rafe, a knot of bloody towels was in a basin.

"I've got to get in there to stop the bleeding before I can move him," Dr. Vickerson said.

Belle knelt down. The doctor poured some antiseptic onto a clean towel and showed her how to apply pressure. Rafe's pants and shirt had been cut away. Around the wound was an orange stain of iodine. When Dr. Vickerson was convinced she was applying pressure properly, he took the sterile instruments to a table where the light was good, and began setting up for surgery. Hugh brought in the kettle of sterile water.

Belle saw the pressure towel turn red. She pressed harder. She could feel him breathing. "Rafe, I'm here." She turned to the doctor. "Can he hear me?"

"I don't know."

Rain was falling. It doused the smoldering cross and extinguished all the burning tendrils of hay floating around the yard. It beat a tattoo on the porch roof, and whooshed down the drainpipes. Rafe opened his eyes and tried to focus. "Belle?"

"Don't try to talk," she said softly.

"Open the door. I want to smell the rain." Belle stretched toward the handle and managed to open it. The sweet smell of the rain wafted over them. "I had plans, you know."

Laughter erupted from the living room. The tension of the standoff was exploding into giddy hilarity. One of the heroes sat down at the piano. A raucous barrelhouse blues filled the hall.

"Dying is so hard," he whispered.

"You're not going to die!" But his blood had seeped through the towel and trickled out between her fingers.

In the living room, they were singing.

"I lost men on the battlefield, but I . . ." His breathing became labored. "I thought we'd have years. I wanted . . . Belle!" His breath shuddered.

"What?" There was no response. "What did you want? Rafe, you've got to hold on. Don't you dare die on me. Not now!"

He gripped her hand. His breathing returned to something like normal, but his voice was almost imperceptible. "I wanted to show you snow."

His hand fell open. Dr. Vickerson rushed up to them. He placed a cotton mask over Rafe's face. The mask was attached by a tube to a glass vial of ether. He clipped the vial to Belle's shirt and instructed her how to work the hand pump.

Nina came in from the living room and stopped. Her dark hair was wild around her face. She stood in the doorway, shocked. Belle looked up and said softly, "Get your parents." Nina disappeared, sobbing.

But Belle couldn't cry. The sorrow choking her, brimming up behind her eyes, would not allow the release of tears. She didn't think she'd ever be released.

She was aware of the blurred figure of Dr. Vickerson working frantically over Rafe. She heard others tiptoe in and out of the hall. Sometimes she saw knees crowding around her or heard hushed voices. She sat, dry-eyed, on the floor next to Rafe, working the bellows of the inhaler, watching his lifeblood leak out onto the Oriental carpet.

Chapter 23

THE MORNING LIGHT was pale and wan. Belle, wearing a black wool traveling suit and a lady's derby hat with its veil pinned up, jerked backward as the Panama Limited pulled out of the station. She hadn't caught the name of the town, but they were somewhere in Illinois. She was sitting in the observation car. The latest issue of *Vanity Fair* was open on her lap, but she wasn't reading. She was listening to the wheels chatter to the tracks as they traveled north. Dark silhouettes of leafless trees flashed by the windows. It had been raining off and on for hours. Her eyes were tired of watching the scenery.

Nina Rubinstein, looking very grown up in her gray suit, with her dark curls swept up on top of her head, joined her.

"It still seems strange for me to be bringing your uncle home. What did your grandparents say?"

"They were fine. They understood."

"Now tell me the true truth."

Nina rolled her eyes. "Grandma had Mama on the phone for almost half an hour right before we left. Long distance! On a weekday. So you can imagine." She squeezed Belle's hand. "It was real sweet of you to come."

Belle tucked a stray curl back behind Nina's ear. They sat together in silence as the train rocked and rumbled. The cold air rushing by outside penetrated the windows. Nina wrapped her arms around herself. Then she stood and went back to their compartment to get a shawl.

Belle turned a page and read that Rachmaninoff had been nominated for *Vanity Fair*'s 1920 Hall of Fame. She closed her eyes. Memories of the evening Rafe had played that passionate music surged through her. When she looked up, a tall, lean figure on crutches was teetering in the doorway. Dropping the magazine, Belle rushed to him. "I thought you were still asleep," Belle said, helping him lower himself into a chair on the swaying train.

"I've slept long enough." Rafe stowed his crutches next to his chair. "I want you to change your mind about going back."

"It wouldn't be right."

"A few days? See how you like Chicago."

"I'd be a *shandah*."

He exploded with laughter at her use of the Yiddish word for *shame*. "Nina teach you that?"

Belle smiled mysteriously.

"You can't take the next train back."

"I've seen three new states. I've slept overnight on a train. I've had steak and oysters in a dining car while the world flew by the window. And I've helped Nina take care of you. That's enough for now." Belle had heard about Helen's visit to the hospital in New Orleans, where Rafe had been recuperating. How she'd sat by his bedside all day, every day, for a week.

"You and your wife have things you need to work out. It would be too awkward for me to be there."

He grinned. "The conductor gave me this at the last stop," he said, handing her a telegram.

Belle read it, turned it over, and read it again. "I don't understand."

"What's there to understand? I'm free."

"But Helen came all the way down to New Orleans. What happened to your reconciliation?"

"I told her I'd fallen in love with someone else."

Belle looked up at him sharply. It was only a word, a little puff of air, but it was the first time he'd said he loved her.

"She came out of duty. The whole thing was Rachel's idea. But Helen had filed the divorce papers a long time ago. We both want to move on."

Belle shook her head. Her mouth felt dry. She looked down at the telegram again. The words jiggled in her hand, but their meaning didn't change. His divorce was final.

"You know, if you marry me, you're going to have to face all kinds of prejudice. Your country clubs won't accept you."

Belle laughed. "I've been shot at and you're worrying about country clubs? Besides, I've never been to a country club, so I don't guess I'm going to miss them."

He wound his fingers through hers and kissed her hand. "There are hotels that won't let us spend even one night. Whole towns on the North Shore have laws against our buying a house there. And if that isn't enough, you'll have to deal with my parents."

"Who said anything about marriage?"

He took back the telegram announcing his freedom, folded it, and tucked it into his breast pocket. "I did. Weren't you listening?"

Belle had dreamed of his saying those words. She'd embroidered them in her imagination, but that was when she was still a nit, before she'd taken over the running of the farm, before she knew she was capable of an independent life. "I have responsibilities. People depend on me."

"Even farmers take winter holidays. My brother, Gabe, and his wife have a big house. You can stay with them. Now that I'm free, even Miss Effie would find that perfectly respectable. Belle, I'm not going to be an invalid all my life. I'll be able to take care of you." He went on to talk about all the things they would do and see.

Belle was silent. She looked down at her hands, hardened with work. They might have been city hands once, but they weren't anymore, and they never would be again, no matter how much cream she slathered on them. She'd made a place for herself. Could she just stop and let a man take care of her? She thought about all the obligations that would entail.

What about her responsibilities to her daughter? To Miss Effie? To the farm? She'd made plans to put Claude's stallion out to stud. She'd left dozens of projects undone. *A girl shouldn't do something she's going to feel guilty about later.*

"There's your snow," Rafe said.

Belle turned around. Big, fat flakes slid across the windows, danced and whirled backward in the wake of the train. Her face lit up with delight. She let out a small whoop.

Rafe thought he'd never seen her so beautiful. "When I woke up in the hospital, I'd been dreaming of snow. I saw it on your cheeks and in your lashes." He brought their clasped hands up and stroked her cheek with the back of his fingers. "Stay with me."

Belle ticked off her duties in her head. The cotton was in. The strawberries were planted. The projects Curtis couldn't take care of could wait.

He released her hand. For a split second, she felt almost abandoned. He was looking at her, waiting for her to speak. She took a deep breath. *No sense in feeling guilty about all the little pleasures life has in store for you.* "I guess it would be a shame to come all this way and not see a little bit of Chicago."

Suddenly the train, roaring through the gray morning with soot pouring out of its smokestack, ran across a patch of sunshine. Belle knew all about smoke and fumes, she was familiar with grit and noise, but from the observation car all she saw was the glitter of the snowflakes as they swept and tumbled in their wild dance toward oblivion.

AUTHOR'S NOTE

I HAVE TRIED my best to be faithful to the "true truth" and for that I am indebted to the following experts: Samuel C. Hyde Jr., Ph.D., associate professor of history and director, Center for Southeast Louisiana Studies, Southeastern Louisiana University, whose conversations, letters, and photographs informed my view of small-town life in Louisiana in 1920. Ira Fistell shared his vast knowledge of trains and timetables. Without him, Belle might never have been able to make her escape on the Panama Limited. Jeffrey Nathan Grant, M.D., of Los Angeles patiently guided me through what a country doctor would do about a gunshot wound in 1920. James Devillier, Ph.D., county agent and faculty member at the Agricultural Center of Louisiana State University, helped me create the Cantrell farm and advised me on early-twentieth-century farming methods. Tom Davidson, amateur historian of Hammond, Louisiana, told me about brick sidewalks and special strawberry trains. James Bartlet and John Boyle of the Stutz Barecat Club enabled Rafe to roar down that country road in the middle of the night. Without Maria Schicker, a marvelous Hollywood costume designer, my characters would have had nothing to wear. Jennifer Spencer at the Historic National Woman's Party and Lamara Williams-Hackett at LSU answered my questions on suffrage. Beth A. Willinger, director of Newcomb College Center for Research on Women at Tulane University, showed me pictures of the world of women in New Orleans in 1920.

All of these experts were generous with their time and

knowledge; none asked to read the manuscript before publication and so cannot be blamed for the bad behavior of any of its characters. I take full responsibility for Belle's shocking conduct. Any mistakes in the text are all mine. For a list of some of the many books and websites that informed this novel and the real skinny on church visitations, women arrested for indecent bathing, and other historical musings, go to my website: www.LoraineDespres.com.

ACKNOWLEDGMENTS

I WANT TO THANK Claire Wachtel, a great editor, for her faith in me, her guidance, and for encouraging Belle to break all the rules. I also want to thank Michael Morrison, Lisa Gallagher, Seale Ballenger, Sean Griffin, and Debbie Stier for giving the book such a great launch, and to thank all my friends at William Morrow/HarperCollins, especially Jennifer Pooley, Sharyn Rosenblum, and Leslie Cohen for making *The Scandalous Summer of Sissy LeBlanc* and *The Southern Belle's Handbook* a success. I am forever grateful to my terrific friends in L.A. who supported and believed in me, even when I didn't, and gave parties for my first book: Bonny Dore, Gail Schenbaum, Dianne Dixon, Johnna Levine, and Felice Schulman. I am indebted to Robert Tabian, the best of agents, for his unswerving belief and encouragement. My husband, writer-producer Carleton Eastlake, read and reread the manuscript in various stages of development. His excellent notes inspired me to make the book better and better. David Despres Mulholland, my son and a brilliant writer and magazine editor in his own right, read the final draft for anything I missed and cheered me on. My thanks to Mollie Gregory for her enthusiasm and quiet encouragement, and to Dr. Gayla A. Kraetsch Hartsough and Bobbi Frank who took time out of their very busy schedules to proofread the manuscript and share their advice.

BOOKS BY LORAINE DESPRES

"Loraine Despres knows her way around a good story." —*The Tennessean*

THE SCANDALOUS SUMMER OF SISSY LEBLANC

A Novel

ISBN 0-06-050588-5 (paperback)

Set in Gentry, Louisiana circa 1956, *The Scandalous Summer of Sissy LeBlanc* is a sassy, humorous debut novel full of charming Southern fun.

"Ladies, trash those old Cosmo magazines . . . forget those tired words of advice . . , and let your imagination run wild with this captivating novel."
—*Beverly Hills Weekly*

"At once comical and serious, hilarious and thought-provoking."— *Pittsburgh Tribune*

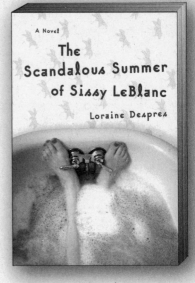

THE SOUTHERN BELLE'S HANDBOOK

Sissy LeBlanc's Rules to Live By

ISBN 0-06-054089-3 (hardcover)

Learn how to navigate life with the effortless savoir-faire of a true daughter of the South with *The Southern Belle's Handbook*.

"A humorous take on our land of cotton, good times ne'er forgotten."
—*The Tennessean*

"Pearls of wisdom."
—*New Orleans Times-Picayune*

www.lorainedespres.com